Q

A NOVEL

EVAN MANDERY

FOURTH ESTATE • *London*

First published in Great Britain in 2011 by
Fourth Estate
An imprint of HarperCollins*Publishers*
77–85 Fulham Palace Road
London W6 8JB

Published simultaneously in the United States by
HarperCollins Publishers Inc

A catalogue record for this book is
available from the British Library

ISBN 978-0-00-744760-2

Printed in Great Britain by Clays Ltd, St Ives plc

For V, my Q

What is the point of this story?
What information pertains?
The thought that life could be better
Is woven indelibly into our hearts and our brains.

PAUL SIMON, *"TRAIN IN THE DISTANCE"*

Prologue

FAIR

Q, Quentina Elizabeth Deveril, is the love of my life. We meet for the first time by chance at the movies, a double feature at the Angelika: *Casablanca* and *Play It Again, Sam*. It is ten o'clock on a Monday morning. Only three people are in the theater: Q, me, and a gentleman in the back who is noisily indulging himself. This would be disturbing but understandable if it were to Ingrid Bergman, but it is during *Play It Again, Sam* and he repeatedly mutters, "Oh, Grover." I am repulsed but in larger measure confused, as is Q. This is what brings us together. She looks back at the man several times, and in so doing our eyes meet. She suppresses an infectious giggle, which gets me, and I, like she, spend the second half of the movie fending off hysterics. We are bonded. After the film, we chat in the lobby like old friends.

"What was that?" she asks.

"I don't know," I say. "Did he mean Grover from *Sesame Street?*"

"Are there even any other Grovers?"

"There's Grover Cleveland."

"Was he attractive?"

"I don't think so."

"Was anybody in the 1890s attractive?"

"I don't know. I don't think so."

"It serves me right for coming to a movie on a Monday morning," Q says. Then she thinks about the full implication of this reflection and looks at me suspiciously. "What about you? Do you just hang out in movie theaters with jossers all day or do you have a job?"

"I am gainfully employed. I am a professor and a writer," I explain. "I am working on a novel right now. Usually I write in the mornings. But I can never sleep on Sunday nights, so I always end up being tired and blocked on Monday mornings. Sometimes I come here to kill time."

Q explains that she cannot sleep on Sunday nights either. This becomes the first of many, many things we learn that we have in common.

"I'm Q," she says, extending her hand—her long, angular, seductive hand.

"Your parents must have been quite parsimonious."

She laughs. "I am formally Quentina Elizabeth Deveril, but everyone calls me Q."

"Then I shall call you Q."

"It should be easy for you to remember, even in your tired state."

"The funny thing is, this inability to sleep on Sunday nights is entirely vestigial. Back in graduate school, when I was trying to finish my dissertation while teaching three classes at the same time, I never knew how I could get through a week. That would get me nervous, so it was understandable that I couldn't sleep. But now I set my own schedule. I write whenever I want, and I am only teaching one class this semester, which meets on Thursdays. I have no pressure on me to speak of, and even still I cannot sleep on Sunday nights."

"Perhaps it is something universal about Mondays, because the same thing is true for me too. I have nothing to make me nervous about the week. I love my job, and furthermore, I have Mondays off."

"Maybe it is just ingrained in us when we're kids," I say.

"Or maybe there are tiny tears in the fabric of the universe that rupture on Sunday evenings and the weight of time and existence presses down on the head of every sleeping boy and girl. And then these benevolent creatures, which resemble tiny kangaroos, like the ones from that island off the coast of Australia, work diligently overnight to repair the ruptures, and in the morning everything is okay."

"You mean like wallabies?"

"Like wallabies, only smaller and a million times better."

I nod.

"You have quite an imagination. What do you do?"

"Mostly I dream. But on the weekends," she adds, with the faintest hint of mischief, "I work at the organic farm stand in Union Square."

On the following Saturday, I visit the farmer's market in Union Square. It is one of those top ten days of the year: no humidity, cloud-free, sunshine streaming—the sort that graces New York

only in April and October. It seems as if the entire city is grog-
gily waking at once from its hibernation and is gathering here,
at the sprawling souk, to greet the spring. It takes some time to
find Q.

Finally, I spot her stand. It is nestled between the entrance
to the Lexington Avenue subway and a small merry-go-round.
Q is selling a loaf of organic banana bread to an elderly lady. She
makes me wait while the woman pays her.

Q is in a playful mood.

"Can I help you, sir?"

"Yes," I say, clearing my throat to sound official. "I should like
to purchase some pears. I understand that yours are the most
succulent and delicious in the district."

"Indeed they are, sir. What kind would you like?"

At this point I drop the façade, and in my normal street voice
say, "I didn't know there was more than one kind of pear."

"Are you serious?"

"Please don't make fun of me."

Q restrains herself, as she did in the theater, but I can see that
she is amused by my ignorance. It is surely embarrassing. I know
that there are many kinds of apples, but somehow it has not occurred to me that pears are similarly diversified. The only ones I
have ever eaten were canned in syrup, for dessert at my Nana Be's
house. To the extent that I ever considered the issue, I thought
pears were pears in the same way that pork is pork. Q thus has
every right to laugh. She does not, though. Instead she takes me
by the hand and leads me closer to the fruit stand.

This is infinitely better.

"We have Bartlett, Anjou, Bosc, and Bradford pears. Also Asian
pears, Chinese whites, and Siberians. What is your pleasure?"

"I'll take the Bosc," I say. "I have always admired their persistence against Spanish oppressors and the fierce individuality of their language and people."

"Those are the Basques," says Q. "These are the Bosc."

"Well, then, I'll take whatever is the juiciest and most succulent."

"That would be the Anjou."

"Then the Anjou I shall have."

"How many?"

"Three," I say.

Q puts the three pears in a bag, thanks me for my purchase, and with a warm smile turns to help the next customer. I am uncertain about the proper next step, but only briefly. When I return home and open the bag, I see that in addition to the pears Q has included a card with her phone number.

On our first date we rent rowboats in Central Park.

It is mostly a blur.

We begin chatting, and soon enough the afternoon melts into the evening and the evening to morning. We do not kiss or touch. It is all conversation.

We make lists. Greatest Game-Show Hosts of All Time. She picks Alex Trebek, an estimable choice, but too safe for her in my view. I advance the often-overlooked Bert Convy. We find common ground in Chuck Woolery.

Best Sit-Com Theme Songs. I propose *Mister Ed*, which she validates as worthy, but puts forward *Maude*, which I cannot help but agree is superior. I tell her the little-known fact that there were three theme songs to *Alice*, and she is impressed that I know the lyrics to each of them, as well as the complete biography of Vic Tabak.

We make eerie connections. During the discussion of Top Frozen Dinners, I fear she will say Salisbury steak or some other Swanson TV dinner, but no, she says Stouffer's macaroni and cheese and I exclaim "Me too!" and tell her that when my parents went out on Saturday nights, I would bake a Stouffer's tray in the toaster oven, brown bread crumbs on top, and enjoy the macaroni and cheese while watching a *Love Boat–Fantasy Island* double-header, hoping Barbi Benton would appear as a special guest. We discover that we favor the same knish (the Gabila), the same pizza (Patsy's, but only the original one up in East Harlem, which still fires its ovens with coal), the same Roald Dahl children's books (especially *James and the Giant Peach*). We both think the best place to watch the sun set over the city is from the bluffs of Fort Tryon Park, overlooking the Cloisters, both think H&H bagels are bet-ter than Tal's, both think that Times Square had more character with the prostitutes. One after the other: the same, the same, the same. We sing together a euphonic and euphoric chorus of agreement, our voices and spirits rising higher and higher, until, inevitably, we discuss the greatest vice president of all time and exclaim in gleeful, climactic unison "Al Gore! Al Gore! Al Gore!"

It is magical.

I escort Q home to her apartment at Allen and Rivington in the Lower East Side, buy her flowers from a street vendor, and happily accept a good-night kiss on the cheek. Then I glide home, six miles to my apartment on Riverside Drive, feet never touch-ing the ground, dizzy. Already I am completely full of her.

For our second date I suggest miniature golf. Q agrees and proposes an overlooked course that sits on the shore of the Hudson River. The establishment is troubled. It has transferred ownership four times in the last three years, and in each instance gone under. Recently it has been redesigned yet again and is being operated on a not-for-profit basis by the Neo-Marxist Society of Lower Manhattan, itself struggling. The membership rolls of the NMSLM have been dwindling over the past twenty years. Q explains that the new board of directors thinks the miniature golf course can help refill the organization's depleted coffers and will be just the thing to make communism seem relevant to the youth of New York. They are also considering producing a rap album, tentatively titled, "Red and Not Dead."

Q is enthusiastic about the proposed date and claims on our walk along Houston Street to be an accomplished miniature golfer. I am skeptical. When we arrive at the course, I am saddened to see that though it is another beautiful spring Saturday in the city, the course is almost empty. I don't care one way or the other about the Neo-Marxist Society of Lower Manhattan, but I am a great friend of the game of miniature golf. The good news is that Q and I are able to walk right up to the starter's booth. It is attended by an overstuffed man with a graying communist mustache who is reading a newspaper. He is wearing a T-shirt that has been machine-washed to translucence and reads:

CHE

NOW MORE THAN EVER

The sign above the starter's booth has been partially painted over, ineptly, so it is possible to see that it once said:

GREEN FEE:
$10 PER PLAYER

The second line has been whited out and re-lettered, so that the sign now says:

GREEN FEE:
BASED ON ABILITY TO PAY

I hand the starter twenty dollars and receive two putters and two red balls.

"Sorry," I say. "These balls are both red."

"They're all red," he says.

"How do you tell them apart?" I ask, but it is no use. He has already returned to his copy of the *Daily Leader*.

The first hole is a hammer and sickle, requiring an accurate stroke up the median of the mallet, and true to her word, Q is adept with the short stick. She finds the gap between two wooden blocks, which threaten to divert errant shots into the desolate territories of the sickle, and makes herself an easy deuce. I match her with a competent but uninspired par.

The second hole is a Scylla-and-Charybdis design, a carry-over from the original course, which has rather uncomfortably been squeezed into the communist motif. One route to the hole is through a narrow loop de loop, putatively in the shape of Stalin's tongue; the other requires a precise shot up and over a steep ramp—balls struck too meekly will be redeposited at the feet of the player; balls struck too boldly will sail past the hole and land, with a one-stroke penalty, in a murky pond bearing the macabre label "Lenin's Bladder." Undaunted, Q takes the daring route over the ramp and nearly holes her putt. On the sixth, the windmill hole, she times it perfectly, her ball rolling through at the precise moment Trotsky's legs spread akimbo, and finds the cup for an ace. Q squeals in glee.

Q's play inspires my own. On the tenth, I make my own hole in one, a double banker around Castro's beard, and the game is on. On the fourteenth, I draw even in the match, with an improbable hole out through a chute in the mouth of Eugene V. Debs. Q responds by nailing a birdie into Engels's left eye. We come to the seventeenth hole, a double-decker of Chinese communists, dead even. The hole demands a precise tee shot between miniature statutes of Deng Xiaopeng and Lin Biao in order to find a direct chute to the lower deck. Fail to find this tunnel to the lower level and the golfer's ball falls down the side of a ramp and is deposited in a cul-de-sac, guarded by the brooding presence of Jiang Qing, whose relief stares accusatorily at the giant replica of Mao, which presides over all action at the penultimate hole.

Q capably caroms her ball off Deng, holes out on the lower deck for her two, and watches anxiously as I take my turn. I strike my putt slightly off center and for a moment it appears as if the ball will not reach Deng and Lin—but it does, and hangs tantalizingly on the edge of the chute. Q is breathless, as am I, until the ball falls finally and makes its clattering way to the lower level. Unlike Q's ball, however, mine does not merely tumble onto the lower level in strategic position; it continues forward and climactically drops into the cup for a magnificent ace and definitive control of the match. I walk down the Staircase of One Thousand Golfing Heroes, grinning all the while, and bend over to triumphantly collect my ball from the hole. Then I rise and hit my head squarely on Mao's bronzed groin.

This experience is painful (quite) and disappointing (we never get to play the eighteenth hole and thus miss our chance to win a free game by hitting the ball into Kropotkin's nose), but not without its charms: Q takes me home in a cab, tucks me into bed, and kisses me on the head. This makes all the pain miraculously disappear.

The next day, Q calls to check on me.

On the phone, she tells me that date number three will be special. This is apparent when she collects me at my apartment. When I answer the door, she is wearing a simple sundress with a white carnation pinned into her shining hair, a mixture of red and brown. She looks like a hippie girl, though no hippie ever looked quite like this. She is radiant.

"I am going to take you to my favorite place in the city," she says, and takes me by the hand.

I am happy to be led.

We descend into the bowels of New York, catch the 2 train, change for the 1, and disembark at Chambers Street. It is early on a Wednesday morning; the streets are a-bustle with men and women in gray suits and black over-the-knee skirts hurrying to their office jobs. I, on the other hand, am unencumbered. I feel playful.

"Are we going to the Stock Exchange?" I ask. "You work in an organic market on weekends, but you're a broker during the week, right? You're going to take me on a tour of the trading floor. What do you trade—stocks, futures, commodities? I bet you're in metals. Let me guess: you trade copper and tin con- tracts on the New York Mercantile Exchange. Oh, happy day!" I buttonhole a gentleman passerby, a businessman freshly outfitted at the Barneys seasonal sale. "The woman I am seeing trades copper futures. Can you believe my good fortune? She is *that* beautiful *and* a commodities trader!"

Q smiles and puts a finger to her lips, but I can see that she is amused.

As the man I accosted recedes into our wake, Q pulls me closer, entwines her arm with my own, and leads me down Church Street.

I am flummoxed. This is the kingdom of Corporate America, heart of the realm of the modern faceless feudal overlords who drive the economic engine of the ship of state, their domain guarded by giant sentries, skyscrapers, colossuses of steel and concrete dwarfing the peons below.

It is no place for a flower child.

But here we are, passing the worldwide headquarters of Moody's Financial Services, and now the rebuilt 7 World Trade Center, and now the reconstruction of the towers, and now, just across the street, Century 21, the department store where I have had great success with T-shirts and belts, which can be quite dear. Somehow, Century 21 has withstood not one terrorist attack but two, as if to say to the fundamentalist Muslims, you have thrown your very best at us, twice, and still we are here, defiantly outfitting your mortal enemies, the Sons of Capitalism, with Hanes and Fruit of the Loom at surprisingly reasonable prices: God bless America! And now the Marriott, and now the hot dog stand on the corner of Liberty, of which I have partaken once, during a tenth-grade field trip to the Stock Exchange with

Mr. Henderson, and became so violently ill that the doctors suspected I may have contracted botulism, and now passing a Tibetan selling yak wool sweaters off a blanket, and now turning left on Thames, and now entering, behind an old building that vaguely resembles the Woolworth, a dark alley that smells of what can only be wino-urine.

And now I am completely confused.

"What?" I say, but Q puts her hand over my mouth.

"Wait," she says, and like a trusting puppy I am led down the dank passageway. We pass some sacks of garbage, and a one-eyed alley cat lapping at some sour milk, and arrive, finally, at a tall iron fence, the sort that guards cemeteries in slasher flicks.

"This is creepy," I say.

"Wait," she says again and opens the gate, which plays its role to perfection and creaks in protest. Q takes my hand and leads me inside. I look around.

"Can I cook?" she says, "or can I cook?"

It is a garden—that is the only word for it—but what a garden! The gate is covered on the inside by a thick, reaching ivy, as is the entirety of the fence surrounding the conservatory. This vine keeps the heat and moisture from escaping. The atmosphere feels different. It is slightly humid, faintly reminiscent of a rain forest, and at least twenty degrees warmer than the ambient temperature on the streets of the city. When Q closes the door behind us, the current of clammy alley air is sealed behind us, and it is as if we have entered another world, an—I don't dare say it, it will sound clichéd, but it is the only word on my mind—Eden.

Here are apple trees, pullulating with swollen fruit. Q nods in approval and I administer to a branch the gentlest of taps. A compliant apple falls into my greedy hands. I bite in. The fruit is succulent, ambrosial. Here is a vegetable garden—orderly rows of broccoli, squash, yams, three kinds of onions, carrots, asparagus, parsnips, and what I think is okra. Here is an herb garden— redolent with rosemary and thyme, basil and sage, mint and rue, borage already in full flower. I have the sudden urge to make a salad. Here are apricots. Here plums. Here, somehow, avocados.

Dirt pathways, well manicured, wend their way through the garden. One path leads to a pepper farm. Q tells me that ninety-seven varieties are in the ground. Another path leads to a dwarf Japanese holly that has been mounted on stone. Yet another path ends at a Zen waterfall.

I have endless questions for Q. With skyscrapers encroaching on every side, how does enough light get in to sustain the garden? Who built it? When? Who owns it now? How could its existence have been kept a secret? Why is it so warm? Why is it not overrun by city idiots, ruined like everything else? How is this miracle possible?

Q answers in the best way possible. She sits me down at the base of a pear tree—a pear tree in the middle of Manhattan!— kisses me passionately, and, oh God oh God, am I in love.

Book One

GOOD

Chapter ONE

In the aftermath of the publication of my novel, *Time's Broken Arrow* (Ick Press; 1,550 copies sold), a counterhistorical exploration of the unexplored potentialities of a full William Henry Harrison presidency, I experience a liberal's phantasmagoria, what might be described as a Walter Mitty–esque flight of fancy if Thurber's Mitty, dreamer of conquest on the battlefield and adroitness in the surgery, had aspired instead to acceptance among the intellectual elite of New York City, more specifically the Upper West Side, the sort who on a Sunday jaunt for bagels buy the latest Pynchon on remainder from the street vendor outside of Zabar's, thumb it on the way home while munching an everything, and have the very best intentions of reading it.

I am on National Public Radio. It is putatively something of an honor because they do not often have novelists, except Salman

Rushdie for whom NPR has always had a soft spot, but I know better. A friend of mine, a lawyer, has called in a favor from the host, whom he has helped settle some parking tickets. It is an undeserved and hence tainted tribute, but the moderator gives me the full NPR treatment all the same. He has read my opus cover to cover and asks me serious questions about several of the important issues raised in the book, including Harrison's mistreatment of the Native Americans, problematic support for slavery in the Indiana Territory, and legendary fondness for pork products.

"Which was his favorite?" he asks.

"The brat," I say.

"I have never had a brat."

"That is too bad."

"Is it like the knock?"

"No, it is much better."

"I find that hard to believe."

"It is nevertheless true," I say. "It is the best of the wursts."

The Fantasia for Clavichord in C Minor begins playing in the background, signaling the end of the interview. "I am afraid we are out of time," says the host. "Is this not always the case? Just as things are getting interesting, time runs out."

"It is always so," I say, whereupon I am ushered out of the studio to the music of C. P. E. Bach.

The following morning my book is reviewed in the *New York Times*. To be fair, it is not a review per se. Rather, it is an oblique reference to my novel in a less than favorable discourse on the new Stephen King novel. Specifically, the critic writes, "The new King is frivolous claptrap, utterly predictable, surprising only for

its persistent tediousness and the suddenness with which the author's once discerning ear for a story has, as if touched by Medusa
herself, turned to stone. The novel's feeble effort at extrapolating
from a counterhistorical premise as a means of commenting on
modern society compares favorably only with the other drivel of
this sort—I dare not call it a genre lest it encourage anyone to
waste more time on such endeavors—including the profoundly inept *Time's Broken Arrow,* surely one of the worst novels of the year."

My publicist calls around nine o'clock and merrily inquires
whether I have seen the mention in the morning's paper. I say
that I have.

"It's a coup of a placement," she says. "Do you know how difficult it is for a first-time novelist to get a mention in the *Times*?"

"A coup? She called my book one of the worst novels of the
year. It isn't even a review of my book. It's just a gratuitous slight.
It's actually the worst review I have ever read, and she says my
book is even worse still."

"Don't be such a Gloomy Gus," says the perky publicist before
she hangs up. "You know, any publicity is good publicity."

I wonder about this. It seems too convenient.

Surely a plumber would not stand before a customer and a
burst pipe, wrench in hand, sewage seeping onto the carpet, and
proudly proclaim, "Any plumbing is good plumbing."

I am out with Q at a restaurant in the Village. She is wearing
her beauty casually, as she always does, draped like a comfortable
sweater. She is full of life. The light from the flickering tea candle
on the table reflects gently off her glowing face, and one can see
the aura around her. She is glorious.

The tables are close together, virtually on top of one another. We are near enough to our neighbors that either Q or I could reach out and take the salt from their table without fully extending our arms. It is a couple. They are talking about us. I am so full of Q that I do not notice. She, though, is distracted.

"You two are in love," the man says finally.

"Yes, we are," says Q.

"It is lovely to see."

"Thank you," she says.

The woman, presumably the man's wife, continues to stare at us. This goes on through the end of the main course, and dessert, and even after the second cup of coffee has been poured. At last she says, "You're that novelist guy, aren't you?"

"Yes," I say, beaming.

"Wait a second, wait a second," she says. "Don't tell me."

I smile.

"Let me guess. I know. I know." She snaps her fingers and points: "John Grisham!" she cries.

"Yes," I say. "Yes, I am."

The Colbert Report has me as a guest. I am excited about the appearance. I have not seen the show, but my agent says it is popular with the sort of people who might read my book and, she says, the host is quite funny. She knows this will appeal to me, as it does. I am something of an amateur comedian, and as I wait for the show to begin, I envision snappy repartee.

In the green room, they have put out fruit. The spread consists of cantaloupe and honeydew and watermelon. I do not care for honeydew, but I respect it as a melon. The cantaloupe is luscious. The watermelon, however, is less impressive. It is a cheap crop, grown in China, and seems to me to have no place on a corporate fruit plate. I make a mental note to talk to one of the staff about this.

Approximately fifteen minutes before showtime, a production assistant enters the room and gives me some brief instructions. In a few minutes, they will take me onto the stage, where I will sit on the set until the interview begins. I will be on following a segment called "The Word." Colbert will introduce me, and then she says—this is unusual—he will run over to greet me. Unfortunately, I either do not hear or do not understand this last instruction. I think she says that I should run over to meet him.

I am not sure why I get this wrong. I think most likely I just hear what I want to hear. I am a runner, and I conclude this will be a unique opportunity to demonstrate to a national audience my unique combination of speed and humor. I suppose I get caught up in all that.

Approximately twenty minutes into the show Colbert introduces me. He says, "My guest this evening is the author of the new novel, *Time's Broken Arrow*, which the *New York Times* has praised as unique and singular." He graciously omits the following word from the review—"bad." He says, "Ladies and gentlemen, please welcome . . ."

At the sound of my name, I lower my head and break into a sprint. As I round the corner of the set, I see Colbert. He is merely in a light jog—he does this every night—but it is too late for either of us to stop. I make a last-ditch effort to veer to the left, but he turns in the same direction, and I strike him squarely in the head. Even as he is injured, he is supremely self-possessed and funny.

As he falls to the ground, he says, "Et tu? So fall Colbert."

He is concussed.

Colbert is done for the night, so the episode is concluded with a backup interview, which the show keeps in the can in case of emergency. The guest is Ted Koppel, reminiscing about his time in the White House press corps. He covered Nixon and was there for the trip to China. Following Nixon's visit to the Great Wall, Koppel asked Nixon what he thought about the experience. Koppel relates the president's reply in a surprisingly good Nixon, with just a hint of his own sultry baritone. "Let it be said," says Koppel-as-Nixon, "that this was and shall be for all time, a truly *great* wall."

The audience howls. The ratings are strong. Rather than reschedule my appearance, the producers decide to invite back Koppel.

I am invited to the 92nd Street Y, as part of its "Lox and Talks" series, focusing on young Jewish writers. I am worried. The event is set for a Tuesday at lunch, and I will have no reliable supporters on hand. Q is out of town for the week at the Northeast Organic Farming Association annual convention. None of my friends can take the time from work. Even my mother, who reliably attends all of my readings, cannot make it because of a conflicting pedicure appointment. I am uncomfortable—for good luck Q has bought me new pants, which are itchy—and nervous: I expect an empty room.

But the room is not vacant. Not at all. It is brimming with *alter kakers*, a gaggle of old ladies sipping coffee and munching coffee cake and kibitzing about dental surgery. It is not exactly my target audience, as they say in the ad biz, but I am elated all the same. Here are real human beings gathered to hear my work. I take the stage and open to my favorite chapter—the one where Secretary of State Daniel Webster uses his rhetorical gifts to cajole President-elect Harrison into wearing a coat at his inauguration—and begin reading with verve.

"I must prove that I am the same man who triumphed at Tippecanoe," protests the president-elect.

"You are sixty-eight years old. You will catch a cold and die." Webster had a rich and musical voice, which I do my best to imitate. I am good but not great at impressions. I hold out hope that Jim Dale will voice the book on tape.

"You are extremely persuasive," says Harrison.

"So I am told," says Daniel Webster.

Harrison dons an overcoat and the rest, as they say, is history.

Fake history, but history all the same.

I see immediately that the old ladies are disappointed. It is not even what I have written, my mere speaking seems to dishearten them. I press on, but they continue to fidget in their seats and whisper to one another. One woman makes an ordeal of opening an ancient sucking candy. Another sighs a giant sigh.

I stop reading and ask, "What is wrong?"

"You are very nasal," says a woman in the front.

"Do you have a cold?" asks another.

"I am fine."

"Well, you should have some chicken soup anyway."

"I do not like chicken soup."

"You would like mine. It is the best."

"Is my voice the issue?"

"Yes, we are surprised to hear you speaking."

"You have never heard someone with a nasal voice?"

"No, we are surprised to hear you speaking at all."

"It is a reading after all."

"We came to hear Marcel Marceau read from *Bip in a Book*. You are not he."

An official from the Y standing in the back hears the exchange. She explains that the rare video of one of the few readings Marceau gave before his death is being shown in the next room. Slowly, the old ladies file out. One woman remains to whom I ascribe the noblest and most empathic virtues of humanity. No doubt she too has stumbled into the wrong room. But she recognizes how vulnerable a writer makes himself when he puts his work out to the world. Even if this reading was not her first choice, as an act of basic human dignity, she perceives a duty to stay. I, in turn, am grateful for her and read with even more zeal than before.

I become apprehensive, however, when she fails to perk up at Harrison's mention of reviving the Bank of the United States, and downright suspicious when she does not so much as chuckle at Martin Van Buren's snoring during the second hour of the inaugural. I take a close look at her and conclude that she is either asleep or, as appears to be the case upon further reflection, dead.

Hastily, I finish the chapter and head for the door.

I want to make a quick exit from the Y and the yet-to-be-discovered corpse, but I also need to pee and I decide to make a stop at the bathroom. Here I meet Steve Martin, who is having a pee of his own at the adjacent urinal. It is a coincidence, but the sort of chance encounter that happens more often when one travels in the circle of celebrities.

Martin will be performing banjo at the end of the week, as part of a bluegrass festival at the Y, and he is here for a rehearsal. His banjo case is on the ground between his feet.

I fumble a bit as I get started. It's the new slacks.

"Usually I wear pleated pants," I explain to Martin, "but my girlfriend bought me flat fronts for this occasion." He does not look up. "She couldn't be here today," I explain further. "She is at the Northeast Organic Farming Association annual convention in Hartford."

"I see," says Martin.

"I have just finished reading from my novel. Perhaps you have heard of it? It is called *Time's Broken Arrow*."

Martin shakes his head.

"I was very much influenced by *Picasso at the Lapin Agile*," I say. "I think you are right that all great works, whether of art or scientific genius, are of equal merit and share the same mysterious origin. I just love the scene where Picasso's art dealer asks the waitress whether Pablo has been to the bar and Germaine says, 'Not yet,' as if she knows what is going to happen in the future. I bet you get that all the time."

"More often people prefer scenes involving the main characters." Martin does not look up as he says this. He is concentrating.

"I also love the way you make time fungible and everything arbitrary. When Einstein shows up at the wrong bar and explains there's just as much chance of his date wandering into the Lapin Agile as at the place they made up to meet because she thinks as he does, it's just hilarious. It's a brilliant play. I bet you get that all the time, too."

"More often people prefer the movies," he says.

"I enjoy your movies, too. My favorite is *The Jerk*, before you got all serious with *The Spanish Prisoner* and *Shopgirl*. I love the scene where Navin Johnson sees himself in the phone book and is so excited to see his name in print. I like Mamet as much as the next guy, but that's just classic."

"That seems a bit incongruous."

It's true. It is. I hadn't thought about it before. I watch as he fixes himself.

"I had broccoli for lunch," he says.

I tell this story the next day to Charlie Rose on the air and he is delighted. More accurately I perceive that he is delighted. In fact he has fallen asleep and, by coincidence, stirred during my telling of the Steve Martin story. I mistake this for delight.

Following my successful appearance on *Charlie Rose*, I am invited to speak at the Gramercy Park Great Books and Carrot Cake Society. The director sends me a historical pamphlet, from which I learn that the club has paid host to many of the great writers and thinkers of the day, including Henry Miller, Gertrude Stein, S. J. Perelman, the Kinseys, and a young Norman Mailer. Reading between the lines, it appears the society was, in its day, a den of iniquity.

I have high expectations for the evening, and am further buoyed when Q accepts my invitation to come along. At the appointed time, we are greeted at the door to number 7A, 32 Gramercy Park South, by the director of the society, Shmuley

Garbus, who ushers us inside the apartment. It smells of matzo brie and Bengay. The average age in the group is eighty-seven. Three of the seven remaining members of the society are on artificial oxygen. None are ambulatory. When I finally perform my piece, it becomes the second time in a week that people fall asleep at my readings. In my defense, four of the seven people here are asleep before I begin. Happily, no one expires.

The carrot cake is surprisingly disappointing. Garbus, a spry eighty-three, explains that Rose Lipschutz used to bake for the meetings, but she got the gout, and then, sadly, the shingles. So they use frozen cake now.

Frozen carrot cake can be quite good. Sara Lee's product, from its distinguished line of premium layer cakes, is particularly delicious, with a moist cream cheese frosting that tastes as fresh and rich as anything produced in a bakery. And it is reasonable too, only $3.99 for the twelve-ounce cake, or $5.99 for the super-sized twenty-four-ounce cake, which serves between eight and twelve guests.

But this isn't Sara Lee. It is from the A&P, which is problematic since there has not been an A&P in Manhattan in more than twenty years.

"Wow," I say to Garbus. "A&P carrot cake. I haven't seen the A&P in ages."

"This is all Rose's doing," Garbus explains. "They had a sale down at the A&P on Lexington Avenue, and Rose, who was so devoted to the society that she wanted it to go on forever, went to the supermarket specifically with us in mind and stocked up."

"When was that?" asks Q.

"Nineteen eighty-seven," he says.

The future of the carrot cake is assured, at least for the short term. At the end of the evening, I see Garbus wrap in aluminum foil the uneaten part of the carrot cake, which is the bulk of it, since many of the members are lactose intolerant. He places the remainder back in the freezer.

On Garbus's plastic-covered sofa, as Q and I finish our tea, we are approached by Helen Rosenberg, of the publishing Rosenbergs, who once famously put out a collection of Albert Shanker's pencil sketches. The teachers' union gave my father a copy for his retirement.

"I couldn't help but notice how much in love the two of you are."

Q and I smile and squeeze one another's hands.

"You must be proud of him."

"I am," says Q.

Mischievously, Helen asks me, "When are you going to put a ring on that beautiful finger of hers?"

"As if she would ever have me," I say playfully, but the truth is, the ring has been ordered, and I have a grand plan for how to propose.

"If you need a jeweler, I recommend my daughter," Helen says, handing me a business card. It amazes me that a jeweler has a business card, though I don't know why one shouldn't. I have more legitimate cause to be further amazed that the card belongs to the same person who sold me Q's engagement ring just two weeks earlier.

It is the sort of thing that brings home to one the interconnectedness of life, and I am in these months of semi-fame more sensitive to these linkages than ever. I am contacted by all kinds of people and have all sorts of random meetings, as my universe becomes bigger than it has ever been before.

I eagerly anticipate the tiny and large surprises that each morning brings. And the days never disappoint, in particular the one on which I receive a note asking me to arrange a table for dinner the following evening at Jean-Georges.

Of all the remarkable chance encounters, this is the most remarkable and exciting of all, because I can tell from the unmistakable handwriting that this note is from, of all people, myself.

Chapter TWO

It is no easy matter to arrange a table at Jean-Georges, even at lunch. It is a popular spot for people on their way to the theater or the New York City Opera or the Philharmonic. I call and ask for a table for the next day. The woman on the phone says that nothing is available. I say who I am. "The novelist," I explain. "I am meeting myself for an early supper."

"We cannot accommodate the two of you," she says, "though we do have a table available in early March."

It is September.

"I don't think that will work," I say.

"Well," the reservationist says firmly. "That's the best we can do."

I let the matter drop with her. Instead I telephone my best friend, Ard Koffman, who is a big shot at American Express, which has deals with a lot of these fancy restaurants. Ard has the Amex concierge call the Jean-Georges reservationist and the table is secured. I am grateful for his help, but it is frustrating that the process is not more egalitarian and the reservationists more accommodating.

I know that the people who make the bookings at Jean-Georges refer to themselves as reservationists, and that they are not to be challenged lightly, because I have eaten there once before, during Restaurant Week. For seven days each year, during the hottest part of August, several of the fancy restaurants in New York City offer a cheap lunch to lure the few people who aren't in the Hamptons out of their air-conditioned offices and apartments. In 1992, the first year of the promotion, lunch cost $19.92. It has gone up a penny each year since.

One summer, several years ago, I decided to take my mother to Jean-Georges for lunch. When I called to make the booking, the receptionist switched me to a person whom she identified as a reservationist.

"Is that really a word?" I asked when the person to whom I was transferred answered the phone.

"What's that?"

"Reservationist."

"You just used it, so it must be."

"Just because someone uses a word doesn't make it a word," I say. "Besides, I only said it because the woman who transferred me to you used it."

"What is it, then . . . a fruit?"

"It's not a word unless it's in the dictionary."

"That seems very narrow-minded of you."

"All the same."

"Well, someone who receives visitors is a receptionist. So I am a reservationist. You should look it up in your dictionary."

"It won't be there."

"You might be surprised."

What doesn't surprise me is that when I arrive for lunch, two months later, I am seated with my mother at the table nearest the men's room. I ask to be moved, but the maitre d', no doubt in cahoots with the reservationist, perfunctorily says, "That would not be possible."

For whatever it is worth, I look up "reservationist" in the dictionary and it is not a word. I do learn, though, that "reserpine" is a yellowish powder, isolated from the roots of the rauwolfia plant, which is used as a tranquilizer. I since have yet to have occasion to use this word in conversation, but I am still hopeful.

At first glance, twenty dollars for lunch at a five-star restaurant seems like a great deal, and a penny per year is unquestionably a modest rate of inflation, but what they don't tell you about Restaurant Week is that nothing is included with the lunch other than the entrée. My mother and I made the mistake of ordering drinks (Diet Coke with lemon for me; club soda with lemon for my mother), sharing a dessert (a sliver of chocolate torte), and ordering coffee (decaffeinated). When the check arrived, I learned that a Diet Coke at Jean-Georges costs $5.75. It isn't even a big Diet Coke. It is mostly ice, and on the day I ate there with my mother, they gave me a lime instead of a lemon, as if they taste at all the same. When I asked the waiter to correct the error, he said, "That would not be possible."

Everything at the restaurant is miniaturized. Even the

entrée—we each had pan-seared scallops in a cabernet reduction—though concededly delicious, was alarmingly small. I figured I would need to get a sandwich after lunch, which would have been within my budget if I had spent only the forty dollars I had expected to spend on the meal. But after the soft drinks, the dessert, and the coffee were added in—and tax and tip, which somehow slipped my mind—lunch came out to more than one hundred dollars.

As I leave the apartment, telling Q that I am off to meet a friend, I can't help but wonder how much dinner is going to run.

I have a thing about being late so I get to the restaurant a few minutes before six o'clock. I am not surprised to find that I have already arrived. I am seated on a sofa in the vestibule reading a Philip Roth novel that I immediately recognize has not yet been written. I say hello softly and my future self rises to meet me.

I am disappointed by how I—the older I, that is—look. I do not look terrible, but I do not look spectacular either. I am particularly dismayed that my body proves susceptible to some ravages of age from which I thought I would be immune. I understand that I will grow old, of course, but I exercise quite regularly and eat right, and like to believe that I will be able to keep my weight down until my knees give out and maybe even for some time after that. But here I am, not much more than sixty, I think, and already I have something of a paunch. I am also a bit jowly. This is alarming.

I am, furthermore, not as well groomed as I am now. We are each dressed in a blue oxford and khaki pants, but the older me's collar is worn past a point that I would now allow. I note that collars have grown wider again, presuming of course that I am continuing to keep up with fashion trends. This strikes me as a change for the worse, but of course styles will come and go.

In other subtle ways, I have allowed myself to deteriorate further. I have a few coarse ear hairs that require frequent attention; these have been allowed to have their way. My nails could use a clipping. I have psoriasis in some spots. It is manageable, but I note that this is not being tended to either: my hands are dry and flaky.

It is me and not me.

I do not consider myself extraordinarily vain. I look at myself in the mirror when I shave or after I get back from the gym, but I do not spend all that much time examining the vessel in which I reside. Still, I know myself well enough. What is most disturbing about this future version of me is that it is obvious, at least to me, that I am deeply and profoundly sad.

"Shall we go to our table?" I ask.

"That sounds fine," says older me, and we present ourselves to the maitre d', who finds our name in the reservation book.

"I'll be happy to take your coats," he says.

I see a disgruntled look on my older face as he hands the coat over to the captain. I am peeved myself and reluctantly relinquish my own. Mine is a thin, cotton autumn jacket—the weather has not turned too cool yet. The jacket could easily rest on the back of my chair. Nor is it an expensive coat. I purchased it for forty dollars or so, on sale at Filene's Basement. If it were to get stained, life would not end. And it most decidedly will not get in anyone's way. Still, they require that the coat be checked.

This service is putatively free, and if it really were, I might not mind so much. But at the end of the meal, when the coat is delivered, there is the obligation of tipping the coat check person. I never know how much to give. On the one hand, I generally feel bad for coat check people. They have to stand for hours in a dreary closet, which in nightclubs is always in the basement and too close to the bathroom. The patrons are often drunk, and they always have just one more thing, a hat or gloves that can just go in the sleeves but are inevitably mislaid, or a bulky handbag, or, too often, something unreasonable, like a humidifier, which I once saw someone check on a Saturday night. All this to collect a tin of dollar bills. The job seems like a raw deal and the attendants have my empathy. On the other hand, it is a service that I neither need nor want and to which I therefore, as a matter of principle, demur.

I feel this way about many services. I do not mind paying a blacksmith or a gastroenterologist because I cannot make horseshoes or perform colonoscopies myself. I am, however, perfectly capable of draping my jacket over the back of a chair. I am highly capable, too, of parking my car in a lot. I do not need someone to drive it from the front door to a spot fifty feet away, at a cost of two or three dollars. Nor do I need someone to wash my clubs with a towel after a round of golf—setting me back five dollars for two minutes work on his part.

I am particularly uncomfortable with the concept of the bathroom attendant. This person provides no direct assistance, of course, and it makes me uncomfortable to have someone squirt soap in my hands and offer me a towel. I do not use any of the sundries spread across the counters of upscale bathrooms. I do not use cologne, I do not groom myself in public bathrooms and thus do not require aftershave lotion or styling gel, and I would never consider, not even for a second, taking a sucking candy or a stick of gum from a tray near a row of urinals.

The cost can mount up. It gets particularly expensive when one does not have small bills and thus faces the Hobson's choice of either leaving an absurdly big tip or rummaging through the collection plate for change. In this situation I will usually just hold it in, although on more than one occasion, I have paid five bucks for a pee. Inevitably, this is later a source of regret.

I see that the older version of myself feels precisely as I do about the coat, and a bond is forged between us.

"What do you tip for a coat?" asks older me.

"Two dollars?" I say. "You?"

"Ten dollars."

"Jesus."

"Inflation is a bitch."

I nod.

All of this is depressing, but it seems silly to allow it to spoil the meal, and I resolve to enjoy myself. It is a nice table, much nicer than the one that I had with my mother years before, and far away from the men's room. I try to recall whether the restaurant maintains a bathroom attendant on duty. I think that it does and resolve, therefore, to limit myself to one Diet Coke.

After we sit down, I ask about the Roth novel.

"It is a Zuckerman story, set late in his life, in a hospice in fact."

"I thought he was done with Zuckerman, after *Exit Ghost*."

"He cannot resist Zuckerman. He came back to him one more time."

"Is the book good?"

"Brilliant," says older me. "It is about the loneliness of death and, ultimately, the impossibility of making peace with one's life. It is, I think, the defining book of our generation."

I nod.

I say, "One writer to another, it is funny how writers keep coming back to the same themes."

Older me says, "One writer to another, you don't know the half of it."

He asks, "How is Q?" She is obviously on his mind.

"She is magnificent," I say. The older me nods.

"The garden is having some problems. There is a developer who wants to build on the land. He has money and political support. Q and her colleagues are worried. But other than this, she is as wonderful as ever—beautiful, brilliant, principled."

The older me nods again. I have the sense he doesn't say very much.

"I have been wearing flat-front pants, at her suggestion. I am wearing a pair she bought me right now. I don't know how I feel about them. They are unquestionably stylish and thinning, but I feel uncomfortable without the pleats. Sometimes I almost feel as if I'm naked. Q says no one needs all that material hanging around. She's undoubtedly right, but I have been doing things the same way for a very long time, and it's hard to change. You know what I mean?"

Older me nods once more. He says, "If I have my dates straight, you and Q moved in together not long ago."

"Yes, into a one-bedroom on Mercer Street."

"How are you enjoying the East Village?"

"It's quite a change. I feel a bit out of place, but I think it's good for me."

"I'm sure it is. And you were recently engaged, yes?"

This makes me smile. "About six months ago," I say. "I proposed to her at the Museum of Natural History under the giant whale. She's loved the whale since she was a child. *Free Willy* was her favorite movie. So I took her to see the frogs exhibit, and when we were done, we went downstairs and I got down on my knee to propose, and before I could pull out the ring, a little boy came over to me and gave me a quarter. He thought I was a beggar. Then everyone was watching, and I asked her to marry me, and she said yes and kissed me, and the people watching from the balcony began to applaud. It was the happiest day of my life."

Finally I catch myself. Obviously I don't need to tell *him* all this.

"Sorry," I say. "I lost myself for a moment."

"Don't worry about it." He smiles. "But it was a little girl, not a little boy."

"What's that?"

"The child who thought you were a beggar was a little girl, not a little boy."

"I'm quite sure it was a boy. He was wearing a SpongeBob SquarePants T-shirt and plaid shorts."

"He was wearing a SpongeBob SquarePants T-shirt and plaid shorts, but it was a little girl, not a little boy."

I find his insistence astonishing. This is ancient history to him, but fresh in my mind. How could he possibly think that he remembers better than I do? If I were more thin-skinned, I might even find it insulting.

"I'm quite sure of what I remember."

"I'm sure you are, but all the same."

The waiter comes over to take our order, and I think to myself, this is going to be an ordeal.

Chapter THREE

I order a porcini mushroom tart as a starter and black sea bass with Sicilian pistachio crust, wilted spinach, and pistachio oil. Older me asks for a bowl of soup and a lemonade. The waiter sneers. I am annoyed myself.

"Is that all you're going to order?" I ask after the waiter leaves.

"Time travel doesn't agree with the appetite."

"Why did we come here then?"

"Restaurants come and go," older me says, "and I have not lived in New York for many years. This is one of the few places I remembered with confidence."

"A lemonade goes for six bucks here," I say.

"In my time that would be a bargain."

"Everything is relative, I suppose."

Older me nods.

"When does time travel become possible?"

"In twenty years or so from now," he says. "It is quite some time after that before it becomes accessible to the public, and even then it is very expensive."

"How does it work?"

"I have no idea. You just go into a big box and walk out in a different time."

"How do you get back?"

"You carry this thing with you. It's like an amulet."

Older me takes the object out of his pocket and shows me. It resembles a heart-shaped locket.

"When you want to go home, you go back to the place where you arrived. The time travel device senses the amulet and returns you to your own time. It's as simple as that."

"But how does it work?"

"What do you mean?"

"How does it actually work? Upon what principle does it operate?"

Older me raises his eyebrow. "Do I have some background in physics about which I have forgotten?"

"No," I say. "I just don't think it's a good idea to get into a time machine without some basic understanding of how it works."

"Well, I'm here, aren't I? That suggests that it does work."

"Is it enough to know that it works without knowing how?"

"Isn't it?"

"I don't know. It just doesn't seem very prudent."

"Is it really any different," older me asks, "than getting in an airplane?"

This point is fair enough. I fly in airplanes all the time without any idea how they work. I mean, I have seen birds fly and I have held my hand out the window while driving on a highway and felt the lift when I arch it upward and the drag when I point it downward. This is called Bernoulli's principle. But I could never derive Bernoulli's principle on my own. Nor could I build a mechanical wing or a jet propulsion engine. Even if someone built a jet propulsion engine for me, I could not operate it, not to save my life. That I get in an airplane and emerge in San Francisco or Sydney or wherever is, from my standpoint, a miracle.

I have thought many times about how utterly dependent I am on things that are complete mysteries to me. I routinely use cars, airplanes, and computers without any idea how they work. I suppose I could do without them. But I could not do without water and I don't know how to get that either. I perhaps could dig a well, but it would be luck whether I dug it in the right place, and, frankly, I am not confident that I could get the water up if I were fortunate enough to find it. I suppose that in a pinch I could grow some beets. The miraculous services society provides to me—food, clean water, electric lights—are the very opposite of coat checks and valet parking.

The human mind is itself a miraculous machine. I am writing right now, but I have no idea how this is happening. I know that my brain is composed of a cerebrum, a cerebellum, and a medulla oblongata, but these are just words. I know that electrical impulses are involved somehow, but that is about the extent of my understanding of the mechanics. And while I at least have an intuition as to how an airplane works, I really have none with respect to my brain. Frankly, lots of what appears on my computer screen is as much a surprise to me as it is to you. I certainly never expected over my oatmeal and English muffin this morning to be writing about Bernoulli's principle today. For that matter, I have no idea why I like English muffins. But I do.

Older me says, "This place is nicer than I remember."

"That's because the last time we sat next to the bathroom."

"That's right," he says. "The damn reservationist. Have you taken Q here yet?"

"No."

"She would love the porcini mushroom tart."

"Of course. It is her favorite."

"How is Mom?"

"She's great," I say.

"Please tell her that I say hello and send my love."

This request makes me worry about my mother. I do not know precisely how much older this me with whom I am having dinner is, but he has at least twenty-five years on me, I expect. I want to know that my mother is safe and happy, but I sense something ominous in his voice. It also could be nothing. The fact is that I am a worrier.

I worry about all sorts of things—some regarding me and many not. With respect to me, I worry, for example, that when I finally have the money to buy a hybrid car the waiting list will be years long or that hybrids will have gone the way of the wonderful electric car. I worry too about whether Indian families are contaminating the Ganges River by setting their dead afloat upon it, whether Brazil will cut down what is left of the Amazon rain forest, and whether Bill Gates will ever be able to get roads built in Africa. I worry about antibiotic-resistant tuberculosis,

Asian long-horned beetles, and global warming. And, of course, I worry about my mother.

I do not know why I am a worrier any more than I know why I like English muffins. Many people don't worry about anything. Q has the ideal balance, and only worries about truly important matters, like her family and preserving magical urban gardens.

I expect that the reason I worry about so many things has much to do with the reasons why I write. The essential quality of a writer is empathy. It is the ability to view a situation from the standpoint of another living creature and to feel what it would feel. This is also the essential quality of a worrier. He sees no distinction between what happens to him and what happens to someone else. Nor does he see a distinction between what is and what could be.

A she-dog with a warm home and soft-pillow doggie bed is stolen from her master and brought to a farm where dogs are raised for meat. The bitch dogs are impregnated and placed in tiny crates. The she-dog feels her puppies licking at her, but cannot turn to lick the faces of the children nursing at her teats. This deprives her of satisfying the most basic maternal instinct. She is depressed and confused and dies a lonely, meaningless death.

The writer does not need to have experienced a loss of this kind to write this story. He can put himself in the shoes of that she-dog and feel the sense of loss and pointlessness that she would feel; he can channel her frustration and anger. And it is of no consolation to the worrier that puppy dogs are not seized from their homes and raised in this way—they very well could be, as evidenced by the way man uses chickens and pigs for his eggs and meat. The worrier does not even find comfort in the fact that he is a man and not a dog. He could be a dog and suffering in this particular way. The possibility of this is all that matters.

At this moment in my life I am worried about whether I will succeed as a writer. I have managed to get my first novel published, but I hope to expand my audience beyond yentas, elderly liberals, and moribund baking societies. Someday, perhaps, more people will attend my reading than a showing of a videotape of a mime reading from his memoir. I am at that uncertain point in a writer's career where he wonders whether he will be noticed or whether his book is fated for the ninety-nine-cent remainder shelf, its tattered carcass to be used as a doorjamb at the 7-Eleven.

Being a student of history does not help. I know how difficult it is to get something of quality published. I know that Madeleine L'Engle's *A Wrinkle in Time* was turned down twenty-nine times, that Ayn Rand was told *The Fountainhead* was badly written and its hero unsympathetic, that Emily Dickinson only managed to publish seven poems during her lifetime. I know that an editor of the *San Francisco Examiner* told Rudyard Kipling, "I'm sorry, but you just don't know how to use the English language." A reviewer rejected *The Diary of Anne Frank* because, he said, "The girl doesn't, it seems to me, have a special perception or feeling which would lift that book above the curiosity level." To Poe, a reviewer wrote, "Readers in this country have a decided and strong preference for works in which a single and connected story occupies the entire volume." To Melville, regarding

Moby-Dick: "This story is long and rather old-fashioned." To Faulkner: "Good God, I can't publish this."

Diet books are published with impunity, but Orwell was told of *Animal Farm*, "It is impossible to sell animal stories in the U.S.A." And of *Lolita*, Nabokov was informed, "This is overwhelmingly nauseating, even to an enlightened Freudian. The whole thing is an unsure cross between hideous reality and improbable fantasy. I recommend that it be buried under a stone for a thousand years."

So I am worried.

Most immediately, I am worried about what I will write next and whether it will get published. Now I must acknowledge that in a very important sense its success would make no difference. It would not diminish my angst. Even if the next novel succeeds, I will imagine and drift into the state of misery and failure that I would experience in the absence of success. Just as I do not need the actual triumph to imagine the euphoria of a bestseller, so too I do not require utter failure to dwell in the emotional realm of the undiscovered, unappreciated writer. Furthermore, it is not as if the stories that I have told and want to tell have any particular significance. They are just a few among the infinite stories that could and will be told—some to be imagined and shared, some to be lived, some to be dreamed and forgotten.

So, why worry?

But this is how it is with worriers. It is a compulsion. I am even worried about worrying. Abundant empirical evidence suggests that worrying can adversely affect health and digestion. This really worries me. I'd like to get some relief, and the future me could provide it, if only he would tell me where my writing career is headed and how my mother is doing. I want to ask, but

I worry that doing so will have problematic, if not disastrous, consequences for the universe.

Most of what I know about the ethics and implications of time travel comes from *Star Trek*, in particular the classic episode "The City on the Edge of Forever," written by Harlan Ellison and starring Joan Collins as Edith Keeler, the saintly operator of a soup kitchen in lower Manhattan. In the episode, Dr. McCoy jumps through a time portal and changes history by saving Ms. Keeler from a car accident. Her life spared, Keeler leads a prominent pacifist movement, earns an audience with FDR, and delays America's entry into the war. This gives Hitler the edge he needs. Germany develops the first atomic bomb and history is changed. In the new time line, the Nazis win and the development of space travel and the flush toilet are substantially delayed. It is then up to Kirk and Spock to go back and set everything straight, which they do, but not without considerable heartache.

I fear that if I ask the wrong sort of question I may have the same sort of butterfly effect on history. I like flush toilets, and I can take or leave Joan Collins, but no one likes the Nazis.

I think I have a way to finesse the problem, though.

"How does the writing go?" I ask.

I regard this question as strategic and clever. I am asking what he is doing, as opposed to what he has done, thereby avoiding an intertemporal catastrophe.

"You mean do we have any success?"

The ruse is exposed.

"I suppose," I say with trepidation.

"Not as much as you hope," older me says. "But not as little as you fear."

I look around the room. This is a direct enough answer, but history does not appear to be changed. I notice that my Diet Coke has a lime in it and not lemon as I asked. This could be a change since I did not pay careful attention to the fruit when the drink was delivered. It's possible the waiter got it right and history has been altered. But, all things being equal, I think it is more likely the waiter made a mistake and history has remained the same. I am not sure why waiters think lemons and limes are interchangeable, but they do.

The fabric of the universe apparently intact, I am emboldened to ask another question.

"What are you writing now?"

My eyes betray me. They drop to the table. When they do not meet mine, I know that this means I am either about to lie or to deliver bad news.

"I don't write anymore," older me says.

If the sad expression and laconic answers to my questions had not told me before, I know now that something has gone wrong, terribly wrong with my life. For me writing, like worrying, is a compulsion. The desire to express myself to others, to write, is an integral and irrepressible component of who I am. I cannot imagine not doing it. Something horrible has happened.

The waiter arrives. The porcini tart is redolent and seductive, but I need to know then and there what the problem is. This is also how it is with worriers. We fret about so much that is beyond our control that when something manageable comes within our gravity we feel an irresistible urge to put a chokehold on it and pull it close.

"What is it?" I ask. "What have you come to tell me?"

Older me smiles thinly, no doubt because he recognizes my passion as his own. He remembers the need to get to the heart of every matter without delay. His sad eyes look down to the soup and then to me.

"It is Q," he says. "You must not marry Q."

Chapter FOUR

B y this time, Q and I are far along in the preparations for our wedding. All of the major arrangements have been made—the reception hall, the choice of entrée, the entertainment. The vows have been written, compromises struck on how present God shall be and which God to choose. The honeymoon will be in Barcelona with a side trip to Pamplona to watch the running. Only trifling matters remain such as coordinating the flowers for the centerpieces with the boutonnières of the groomsmen and the music to be played at the reception.

The wedding is to be held in Lenox, Massachusetts. The Deverils are New Yorkers through and through—lifelong Manhattanites—but they have summered for the entirety of Q's existence at their home on the Stockbridge Bowl, in the heart of the Berkshires, with the appropriate subscriptions to Tanglewood and Jacob's Pillow. We are to be married at the inn where John and Joan Deveril stayed on their first visit to the Berkshires more than twenty-five years ago. It is intimated at a celebration-of-the-engagement dinner during an alcohol-induced, way-too-much-information moment that Q was conceived at this inn.

Lenox is neither Q's first choice for the wedding nor mine. All of our friends are New Yorkers and we would prefer, all things being equal, to have a city wedding, preferably on the Lower East Side, where Q and I have settled together. But John Deveril is a powerful and obstinate man. His construction company is the eighth largest in the country and, as he eagerly tells anyone who will listen, responsible for two of the ten tallest buildings in Manhattan. More relevantly, Q is utterly devoted to John, and he is quite wedded (pardon) to the idea of a Berkshires marriage. He thinks it will lend symmetry to his daughter's life. All things considered, it seems best to let him have his way. I joke to Q that we should arrange funeral plots for ourselves in Great Barrington. She finds this quite funny.

Mr. Deveril's mulishness is nowhere more evident than in the discussion of the music to be played at the wedding. A swing band will provide the bulk of the entertainment, but a DJ is retained to entertain during the band's rest breaks and offer something for the younger set. For the unlucky disc jockey, John Deveril prepares an extensive array of directives. These guidelines, seventeen pages in all, contain a small set of favored songs, including the Foundations' "Build Me Up Buttercup," the Mysterians' "Ninety-Six Tears," and anything by Jerry Lee Lewis; a list of disfavored songs, which includes anything by anyone whose sexuality is ambiguous or otherwise in question—thus ruling out Elton John, David Bowie, and Prince (despite my argument that the secondary premise is faulty); any music by any artist who has ever broadcast an antipatriotic message—thereby excluding, to my great dismay, Bruce Springsteen, Neil Young, and Green Day; any song written between the years 1980 and 1992; and a final list of songs, appended as Appendix A to the personal services contract between the DJ and the Deverils, the playing of any of which results in irrevocable termination of the agreement and triggers a legal claim for damages by the Deverils against the disc jockey, said damages liquidated in the amount of $100,000. For further emphasis, as if any is required, at the top of Appendix A, Mr. Deveril handwrites: "Play these songs and die." The list includes the Chicken Dance, the Electric Slide, and anything by Madonna, Neil Diamond, and Fleetwood Mac.

I happen to like Fleetwood Mac and Neil Diamond. As far as I can tell, John Deveril has nothing against either artist's music. Rather, he has a long memory and recalls that Bill Clinton used "Don't Stop (Thinking About Tomorrow)" as the theme song for his campaign in 1992 and that Mike Dukakis used "America" during his race in 1988. John hates all Democrats, but he has a special loathing for Clinton and Dukakis.

I get it with respect to the Chicken Dance and the Electric Slide, and even with respect to Clinton, but the virulent loathing of Dukakis is excessive. It seems to me Dukakis paid a steep price for his concededly ill-advised photo-op in the M1 Abrams tank. The later newspaper photographs in the 1990s of Dukakis walking across the streets of Boston to his professor's office at Northeastern were a bit more poignant than I could handle. Now one hardly hears of him or Kitty at all. I feel protective. Of course, I am not fool enough to admit my affection for Michael Dukakis to John Deveril. Instead I point out the unfairness of the association with Neil Diamond, whom I greatly admire. I'd like "Cracklin' Rosie" to be played at the reception.

One evening, at a dinner with Q and her parents to discuss wedding plans, I sheepishly raise the issue. "You know Neil Diamond never actually sang 'America' at a Dukakis event," I say timidly. "Actually, he never sang for Dukakis at all. Furthermore, according to federal campaign contribution reports, he never gave any money to Dukakis."

At this point, John looks up from his meat.

"Well, if he didn't want the song played, he could have called up the campaign and told them not to play it, right?"

"I suppose."

"I mean they wouldn't have played it against his wishes. They wouldn't have played it if Neil Diamond had called the newspapers and said, 'Dukakis is a moron, and Bentsen too.' The campaign wouldn't have played the song then, right?"

"Right."

"So it was a choice."

"I guess."

"Just like Dukakis could have chosen to shave those eyebrows, right?"

"Right," I say quietly, and that's the end of that.

The truth is, I also like Bill Clinton, but I raise no objection to excluding Fleetwood Mac on the basis of its tenuous connection to the philandering former president. Neither do I protest the venison that will be served at dinner, or the tulips that have been ordered for the reception hall despite my allergist's strict instructions to the contrary, or the presidential look-alikes (needless to say, all Republicans) who have been hired to mingle with the crowd and sit at the dinner tables corresponding to their numerical order in the presidency. It is objectionable enough to have people resembling Nixon and Ford and Bush (forty-one;

John Deveril has no tolerance for forty-three) circulating among the crowd, but I wonder, as a purely practical matter, what the people seated at tables 19 and 34 will have to talk about at dinner with doppelgangers of Chester Arthur and John Deveril's favorite president, Calvin Coolidge.

This is all quite different than the wedding I envision. In mine, we are married by a Scientologist on the eighteenth hole of a miniature golf course. The minister reminds me that girls need "clothes and food and tender happiness and frills: a pan, a comb, perhaps a cat." I am asked to provide them all. Q is told that "young men are free and may forget" their promises. Our guests look on in horror. Then the ruse is revealed. A simple civil service follows. We exchange vows that we have written ourselves. Glasses of Yoo-hoo are poured, a toast is made, and the bottle of chocolate drink is broken with a cry of "Mazel tov!" Rickshaws take our friends to a nearby bowling alley, where they are immediately outfitted with rental shoes and given the happy news that they can bowl as much as they like for free. Professional bowler Nelson Burton Jr. has been retained for the day to give lessons in bowling and the mambo. Q and I make a grand entrance as a klezmer band plays the Outback Steakhouse theme song, my favorite. We have our first dance to John Parr's "Naughty Naughty." People bowl and shoot pool. They play darts and video games, and eat popcorn and miniature hot dogs. For a few hours, our friends forget that they are adults. They stay long into the night, drunk on Miller Lite and chocolate cake, and sit Indian-style on the lanes telling stories about Q and me, many of which we have never heard about each other before, including the surprising fact that Q had a poster of Brian Austin Green over her bed until she was twenty-four. It is a magical evening.

I nevertheless raise no objection to the wedding plans because I am on tenuous ground with John Deveril. I believe he thinks Q could do better. No one ever says this, of course. Q certainly does not. But I believe it all the same. This is confirmed for me, shortly before my older self's arrival.

One day John and I are left alone in the bar of the Red Lion Inn. Q and her mother are meeting in a conference room with Mr. Cheuk Soo, the florist, or "floral engineer," as he calls himself. It is at least the sixth such meeting. Each is a mind-numbing exegesis on color, aroma, and feng shui. Mr. Soo seems to have an opinion about everything. Somehow he has become passionately committed to the position that if Mendelssohn's "Wedding March" is played there can be no hyacinth in the bouquet or that if hyacinth is used in the bouquet, then the Mendelssohn cannot be played.

"But purple must be present," says Joan Deveril.

"Purple is not the problem per se," says Cheuk Soo.

"What about lisianthus? Could we use lisianthus?"

"Nooooo," cries Mr. Soo, in obvious pain. "Bell-shaped flowers are so dipolar."

Q's mother solemnly nods her head in agreement. "Of course," she says. "Dipolarity will not do."

I am staring out the window, watching tourists wander around Stockbridge, daydreaming, as I do throughout most of these sessions, but this arouses me. "It's not a word!" I scream silently. "Dipolarity is not a word!" I know better than to say this aloud. It will only lead to a disquisition on dipolarity, and I will be trapped in the conference room even longer than I otherwise would be. Instead, I resume staring at the pedestrians on Main Street.

"What about vanda?" says Mr. Soo, as if he has had an epiphany. "It is a rare orchid. It might be just the thing." He shows them a picture.

"It is so elegant," says Joan.

"It has a very strong qi," Soo adds.

"You are a genius," says Joan. "Now what to accent it with?"

Q asks, "How about irises?"

"Nooooooo," cries Mr. Soo, his pain returned. "The bouquets will block and we will have sha qi for sure."

"That will not do," Joan Deveril says quietly. "Sha qi is very bad."

So it goes. When Q tells me that we are returning to the Red Lion for yet another meeting, I am incredulous. It hardly seems possible after all this time that anything could be left to discuss. I put this to Q.

"We are reconsidering the centerpieces," she says. As far as I can tell, Q, her mother, and Mr. Soo have debated the composition of the centerpieces with Jesuitical precision. When I ask what is at issue, Q says they are considering topiaries and all the implications of that.

"What's a topiary?" I ask.

Q reacts as if I am a biology student who, during the review session for the final exam, asks, "What is a cell?" It is embarrassing, but the happy consequence is that I am excused from subsequent meetings with Mr. Soo. At no point has there even been the pretense that John Deveril could be placed in the same room with a floral engineer. So it comes to pass that John Deveril and I are left alone to share a drink in the basement bar of the Red Lion. I order a tomato juice. He orders a double Glenlivet. As the bartender pours, it occurs to me that this is the first time I have ever been alone with Q's father. I have not even the faintest idea where to find common ground.

John takes a hearty sip of the scotch. I can't drink scotch without wincing, but he downs it like a man, savors it, stares into the glass as he stirs the residual. He is a professional.

"Rough day?" I ask.

"Like you wouldn't believe," he says. It is the rare moment in which John Deveril lets down his guard with me. In fact it is the only moment in which he has ever let down his guard with me.

"Want to talk?"

John turns to me. The look on his face is in equal measure indignant and quizzical. He is put off by my question, of that there can be no doubt. He is not the sort of man who talks, and certainly not to me; it is effrontery for me to presume otherwise. But I think he searches his memory and sees that he has invited my advance. This is confusing to him. He is also not the sort of man to invite others into his life, and, for a moment, he appears paralyzed. He wonders why he has slipped in this way. Then, to his surprise and mine, he talks. Perhaps it is the scotch, perhaps it is the spirit of the wedding, perhaps it is the bond we have formed through our innumerable visits in support of the women we love to florists and tailors and caterers, with the associated stays on the well-appointed man couches.

Or maybe he just needs to talk. Whatever the reason, he does.

"I'm about to get started on the most important project of my career. It's a huge, mixed-use building with high-end retail, residential, and office space. We have a Fortune 100 company signed on as an anchor tenant. The architectural plans are fantastic. Everything is in place. It'll make me millions when it's done. But we can't get the fucking land."

"What's the problem?"

"The fucking communists, the fucking tree huggers, the fucking Democrats—that's what's the problem. They don't give a shit about what I do. As far as they are concerned, the environmental surveys should take twenty years and cost ten million dollars. "Then, after the studies are done you should have to spend another ten million on lawyers so you can argue about the impact a new building will have on some snot-nosed beaver three hundred miles away. The environmentalists don't give a shit whether people have a place to live—especially rich people. For all the pinkos care, the rich can live in boxes—just so long as they recycle the boxes when they die. And whatever you do, don't try to give them money. Heaven forbid you suggest resolving a dispute by offering them compensation—the sanctimonious assholes look at you as if you're the devil himself. No, no, no, it's far fucking better to litigate the issue for a decade or two. This way the lawyers get rich and nobody gets what they want. That's much fucking better."

"Could you go to your city councilman or congressman?" I ask.

"The politicians?" He laughs. "Don't get me fucking started about the fucking politicians. They are so paralyzed by the idea of offending even a single voter that they indulge every one of those wackos, every single fucking one of them. Because that's what the left does—it coddles. That's its MO. Instead of telling people that life is hard and that not everyone can have exactly what they want, instead of telling them that sometimes choices have to be made, they preach that everyone is equal and equally entitled. Everything is possible! That's what they tell them. Everyone can go to college. Everyone can have a job. Everyone can have health care."

He is staring at his drink throughout most of this. Now he turns to me again. "Then when people come against the real world, against the cruel, harsh reality of it all, and see that choices have to be made, that the government cannot do everything for everyone, do you know who they blame? The rich people. Not life, not God, and sure as heck not themselves. No, they blame the fucking rich people for standing between them and everything to which they have come to believe they are entitled. That's the true fucking legacy of the Democratic-liberal establishment to America, and their personal gift to me." John snorts and looks back to his glass.

Finally, he catches himself and remembers who I am. We have never discussed politics before, but just as I do not need him to verbalize his disapproval of me to know that it is true, I do not need him to tell me that he believes teachers are generally liberals and writers are communists, and I, of course, am both. He has simply forgotten himself once more. At least in this instance, his prejudice is well-founded. Even though I have never told John so, I am a liberal.

We return to sitting in silence.

He orders another Glenlivet, surveys it even more closely than the first, and we wait for the women to finish with Mr. Soo.

Finally he asks, "How is your work going?" He pauses briefly after "your" and places a subtle derisive emphasis on "work" to make it clear he does not think either my job as an assistant professor at City University or my gig writing novels satisfies the definition of the word.

I tell him anyway. "I am writing a short story for *9PM Magazine*. It's sort of a sequel to my novel. It begins after William Henry Harrison leaves office. He is minister to Gran Colombia and while there joins a backgammon club where he meets Simon Bolivar. They develop a friendship and over time engage in an erudite debate about democracy and the proper use of the doubling cube."

"What's *9PM Magazine*?" asks John.

"Oh, it's a mixed-media online journal."

"Sounds great," he says. "I'm sure both people who read your story will love it."

"Thanks."

"Have you considered turning it into a movie that no one will see?"

"No," I say quietly, and think to myself that John Deveril is a hateful man.

Part of me wants to take this up with Q, to have her validate my view and side with me in this incipient in-law struggle. But I know she is utterly devoted to him. This has been demonstrated in innumerable ways—by the look on her face when she sees him, by the reverence with which she speaks of his work, by the way she includes him in every detail of the wedding preparations.

I wonder how this can be so. As far as I can tell, they share no values. He is on the far right of the political spectrum; she is on the left. He is a business tycoon; she tills the soil. He lives a material life; she lives a life of ideas. And, more potentially divisive than any of that, at his core, John Deveril is a nasty, bitter man. How can father and daughter be so close?

No sooner do I wonder this than I have my answer. Joan and Q walk into the bar and he is transformed. He pops out of his seat. The whiskey is forgotten. His visage, which has been a knot of tension and anger, relaxes. Q glows when she sees him, and it is as if her energy beams its way through his body, bouncing its way off this muscle and that organ, and now he is himself aglow. I barely recognize him.

"How did it go?" he asks, full of hope.

"Great," says Q. "Simply great. We found just the right fern for the topiaries."

"Magnificent," says John. "Simply magnificent."

"And what have you boys been up to?" asks Q mischievously.

John grasps my shoulder with a warm, firm hand. "Your brilliant fiancé has just been telling me about his new short story." This sentiment cannot possibly be genuine, but it sounds as if it is, each and every word.

"It's wonderful, isn't it?" asks Q. Her sincerity, of course, is beyond question.

"It's genius," says John. "Simply genius." He supportively kneads my shoulder. This gesture cannot be sincere, and yet it also appears to be so. I detect no derision from him, nor any suspicion of sarcasm from Q. I see no indication of winks or nods or tacit understandings of any kind. It all appears to be real.

Only two plausible hypotheses can be stated. One is that she does not see him for who he is. This is possible. Perhaps John's kind treatment of me is part of his ruse. Perhaps he is deceiving Q. Perhaps he understands that it will not do to openly disapprove of the man who will marry his daughter. He will think of me what he likes and treat me as he will in private, but for the sake of appearances, he will maintain the pretense of affection for me. This could be true.

But I think the second possibility is more likely: she makes him a better man. If anyone could do it, surely Q could. Basking in the effulgence of her approval would warm even the coldest soul, and she has a special radiance for John Deveril. No man could resist that. No man could dare to disappoint that creature.

Indeed, as they speak with one another I see that she does not regard him as loathsome in any way. She does not treat him gingerly, placate him, or dance around his temper. She treats him like a dear father, one whom she loves beyond words. Watching their interaction, I conclusively reject the first hypothesis. She is not deceived. She has not blinded herself to the true nature of her father. She does not see it because he is not this person with her.

Whether I am right or wrong, no good could come of standing between these two. If it is a deception, then she will resent me for exposing it. If it is reality, then I am lucky to be permitted into her life, because this bond is special and strong.

Q and I are heading back to New York and we say our goodbyes. Joan kisses us each on the cheek. John gives his daughter a kiss and a bear hug. He shakes my hand and wishes me a safe trip. Q kisses me and whispers, "Let's get ice cream for the road."

I feel my anger slip away.

The truth is, none of it matters. Not John Deveril's judgment of me, not the prohibition against Neil Diamond, not the allergic flowers. None of it.

Only her love.

Chapter FIVE

After the ominous admonition that I must not wed Q, I pepper myself with questions—why? what goes wrong? how could this possibly happen?—but I am unwilling to pursue the conversation. I insist that these answers must wait, that it is enough for one evening to learn that time travel is possible, that a glass of lemonade costs more than six dollars, and that Roth has written yet another Zuckerman novel. I suggest that we meet again two nights later and, for our second tête-à-tête, propose Chef David Bouley's legendary eponymous eatery in TriBeCa.

Now when I say that "I" propose that we meet at Bouley, I mean specifically that my future self proposes that we meet at Bouley. I—the real-time me—would much rather eat at a diner. The nomenclature has become confusing, even in my own mind. Sometimes I think of the visitor as "I," other times as "older me," other times as an utter stranger. It appears to depend on whether I am finding him sympathetic or annoying. I am utterly inconsistent.

To avoid further confusion, I propose hereafter to reserve the use of the simple pronoun "I" for references to myself in the present moment (which, of course, is long past by the time you are reading this) and to designate the future version of myself as I-60. As occasions present where additional pronouns are required, I shall refer to I-60 as "he," unless the story takes a substantial and unexpected twist.

I adopt these conventions with two reservations. The first is whether this nomenclature embraces a meaningful conception of self. In the past, I jointly taught a class on the history of justice with Phil Arnowitz, a former attorney who used to litigate death penalty cases before becoming an academic. On the first day of class, he would present to students the curious case of Hugo, a heartless serial killer who, while being escorted to the electric chair, is struck on the head by a falling brick. Hugo is taken to the hospital and lapses into a coma. When he wakes up—forty years later—Hugo is a changed man. He is sweet and docile and has no recollection of his murderous rampage. When told of his crimes, Hugo is incredulous and apologetic. A team of neurologists examine Hugo and determine that he has suffered damage to the frontal lobe of his brain, which has caused his amnesia and permanently changed his formerly aggressive personality. The doctors unanimously agree that Hugo now poses no threat to society. Professor Arnowitz dramatically asks, "Should Hugo still be electrocuted?"

Most of the students say yes: he committed the crime, he should pay. This was originally my answer too. But who is "he"? asks Arnowitz. The man society proposes to execute is forty years older than the man who committed the crime. Hugo is organically different, has a changed disposition, and is genuinely contrite. How does it make sense to think of him as the same person who committed the crime?

I ask the same question here. I-60 is not exactly I, and I am not exactly I-60, but we do have the same name and occupy the same corporeal space, which, as in the case of Hugo, makes things more than a little bit confusing.

The second reservation is that the convention may cause substantial confusion with references to certain highways. Hereafter, where major freeways are involved in the story, I shall refer to these routes by their full Christian names, thus avoiding confusion between, for example, the road from Florida to Maine, Interstate 95, and my ninety-five-year-old self.

Whether we are the same person or not, I-60 has developed some expensive tastes. My friend Ard again pulls some strings and is able to arrange a table at Bouley. I-60 arrives precisely on time, as I do, and is wearing a checkered oxford shirt and khaki pants, as am I. He orders chicken consommé and a seltzer with lime, which would be free at the diner, but at Bouley costs an astonishing $7.50.

"So no doubt you want to know what happened," he says, "or from your perspective, what is going to happen."

"Of course," I say. My heart is racing.

"Well, then, I should tell you." He takes a sip of seltzer and sucks on the lime. It is a repulsive habit, and I wonder when this begins.

"The wedding comes off well," he says. "It is not the wedding that you imagine for yourself—there are no professional bowlers among the guests, and Miller Lite is not served—but for a rich WASP affair, it is refreshingly homey. You and Q write your own vows, debut to a cha-cha, and hold hands for the entire day. Everyone remarks how much in love the two of you are.

"The capon is free-range, the product of an eleventh-hour compromise with John Deveril. His position is that any wedding of his daughter will feature roosters. Q is reluctant to challenge him, but she, of course, is averse to causing any kind of suffering, and you take up the issue on her behalf. One week before the event, you find a farm that caponizes its chickens using hormones, allows the birds to roam free, and kills them humanely. John calls this "gay capon," but he accepts the settlement. Q does too. Mostly, she is happy that her father is happy.

"The entrée is one of several potential powder kegs, and John Deveril is like a dry match on the day of the wedding, flitting about the reception looking for a reason to go off. But somehow, impossibly, nothing ignites. John even leaves satisfied with the disc jockey, who pleases him by playing a prolonged set of ZZ Top songs."

"Why ZZ Top?"

"They're Republicans."

"I had no idea."

I-60 nods. He says, "The only real disaster occurs when your Aunt Sadie spills tomato juice on her dress, and even this is not as bad as it might have been. The waiter comes quickly with seltzer. The blouse is lost but the dress is preserved. Sadie is satisfied, if not happy, which really is about as much as one can ever hope for with Sadie."

I nod. This rings true. Sadie is difficult.

I-60 sucks the lime then continues. "On Q's whim, you make a late change and honeymoon in the Galápagos. You set sail from

Valparaiso, Chile, on a catamaran, which takes you to visit the main islands of the archipelago, and then deposits you at an eco-resort on Isabela. It is a magical place. You spend three weeks there, long enough to befriend a giant tortoise and a Galápagos penguin who rides on his back. They come by each morning for breakfast and return again in the evening to sit by the fire and exchange stories. The tortoise says little, but he is old and wise and his presence is nurturing. The penguin is chattier. Q cries when the time comes to leave; the tortoise and penguin also are unmistakably sad. But life goes on, and when one lives for hundreds of years, as does your tortoise friend, he must learn to adapt. Q does, and so do you.

"Back home, you buy a small loft in TriBeCa, which Q fills in an economical and environmentally friendly manner with midcentury modern furniture, all Swedish and all constructed with sustainably forested wood. You have an energy-efficient espresso maker, a low-water toilet, and maintain a compost bin under the kitchen sink. Q adorns the walls with prints of Monet and Matisse, and, though you harbored doubts about the apartment, in no time at all it feels like home. Together, you and Q live the modestly indulgent, culturally sensitive bohemian life of the postmodern liberal—you read the *Times* online, bicycle to the Cloisters Museum, and flush only out of necessity. On the windowsill Q maintains a flourishing herb garden. In the evenings you watch old movies and eat vegetarian takeout."

I-60 pauses, and sucks the lime yet again. "Your second novel is a modest success," he says. "It is neither bestseller material nor enough to make you rich, but you develop a small but loyal following, enough to ensure that your third book sells. This response is more than enough to keep you fulfilled and engaged in your writing. Q abandons professional gardening but turns to teaching ecology and conservation at the New School, which she finds satisfying. You and she have a constructive existence and are each intellectually engaged, both individually and with one another."

"That all sounds quite nice," I say.

"It is," says I-60. "It is a very good life. This is the happy part of the story."

The sucking on the lime really bothers me. It would be one thing if I-60 just did it once or twice, but this is not the case. He repeatedly pulls the slice out of his drink, sucks it, spits it back into the seltzer, and then smacks his lips three times in succession. I could probably tolerate this were it not for the lip smacking. This is over the top, and why three times? I have no idea when and where this behavior originates. I am far from a perfect person, but I surely have no habit as annoying as this.

Even the choice of lime bothers me. I am committed to lemon in my drinks and have been for years. The trouble with lime is not the taste—this I could take or leave—it is the social statement made by ordering it. Lime is an affected fruit. Asking for it is not out of place at the fancy eateries I-60 seems to favor. In the real world, however, it raises eyebrows. Joe the Plumber doesn't order lime with his drink, of that one can be sure, and no diner serves lime with a Diet Coke. I suppose it's possible that I-60's palate has evolved, but even still, he knows how invested I am in lemons. It's a real statement he is making, and I don't like it one bit.

This is still the happy part of the story, but I nevertheless experience I-60 as exceedingly unpleasant.

"Experience" is a Q word, one of several that seep into my vocabulary. Pre-Q, I would simply have said "Bob is annoying" or something analogously direct, but post-Q I recognize the gross difference between the putatively objective claim that someone is something and a more humble, affirmation-of-the-subjective-experience-of-reality-type assertion, such as, "I perceive Bob as having certain characteristics that any reasonable person would find excruciatingly annoying."

Q picked up the term in a sociology course, "Deconstruction of Post-Modern Society," which she tells me about on our sixth date, after we see *The Seventh Seal* at a Bergman festival at Lincoln Center. The gist of the course—shorthanding here through the Nietzsche and Heidegger—is that meaning is entirely subjective and life pointless. The syllabus piloted the students on a grim march through the dense thicket of deconstruction literature, including the entire oeuvre of the legendary French philosopher Jacques Derrida, whose work could be comprehended by no more than a dozen living humans, excluding, apparently, Derrida himself, who, when asked to define "deconstruction"—a term he had coined—said, "I have no simple and formalizable response to this question."

All that could be said conclusively was what deconstruction was not. The professor, Bella Luponi, a languid, phlegmatic type who had taken twenty-seven years to finish his dissertation, devoted each session of the course to disposing of a different thing that deconstruction might potentially be. Proceeding thusly, Professor Luponi established that deconstruction is neither an analysis nor a critique. It is also not a method, an act, an operation, a philosophy, a social movement, a revolution, a religion, an article of faith, an anthropological fact, a moral code, an ethic, an idea, a concept, a whim, a verb, a noun, or, properly speaking, a synonym for "destruction."

At the start of the last class before Thanksgiving, one of Q's friends left a nectarine on the professor's desk. Luponi entered the near-empty lecture hall and obligingly asked, "What's this?"

"It's a nectarine," said Q's friend. "Is deconstruction a nectarine?"

"Heavens, no," said Luponi.

"Well, that's the last thing I could come up with," the student said. Then he picked up his nectarine and left the class forever.

In the last days of the semester Professor Luponi argued that deconstruction is best understood as a type of analysis, in the sense of the word that Freud employs, and that the interpretation of words and experiences says as much about the listener as about the speaker.

It was during this lecture that Q resolved to become an organic gardener.

As I-60 continues with his Shangri-la tale of newlywed progressives in love, an engaging narrative of Lévi-Strauss reading groups and gluten-free vegan dinner parties, I feel what is at first a pang of resentment in my stomach, which swells into a more palpable aversion, and finally bursts into genuine loathing. This occurs shortly after I-60 delivers the news that he is, and thus I am or will be, the father of a beautiful baby boy. "You and Q name the baby after yourselves," he says. "Quentin Evangeline Junior. This is not an act of hubris; it is solely for his nickname, QE II."

This is ostensibly happy news, but I-60 relates this part of the story solemnly, and I can tell from his manner that this event, for better or worse, is the transformative moment of my unlived life. I know it cannot be good and brace for the worst. The mere prospect of grief in my future life unnerves me. I don't like pain, whether it's mine or anyone else's. I cried at the end of *Titanic*.

Instead of simply telling me what happens, however, I-60 proposes that we meet for yet a third time, at La Grenouille no less, for him to deliver the third chapter in the never-ending tale of How My Life Went Horribly Wrong. I understand this is serious business, and that he has traveled a long way, but I am annoyed all the same. I will now be out for three dinners.

Needless to say, when the bill arrives I-60 does not make so much as a gesture in its direction. This is particularly frustrating because, presuming even a modest rate of inflation, the check, which represents more than two days of my salary, would cost someone spending 2040 dollars something like ten bucks.

"Perhaps if this is going to be a semiregular thing," I say as I reach for the check, "we could undertake to share the damage. I imagine you have some recollection of what a young professor earns."

"Not much, that's for sure. And you ain't getting rich from your novels."

"Well, then?"

"You know what our mother used to say," I-60 says, smiling. "It all comes from the same *pishka*."

"Seriously," I say. "This is the second time we have had dinner together and now there is going to be a third meal. I really don't make very much, as you recall, and money is very tight. Q and I are trying to save as much as we can. Her parents are covering the wedding, but we don't want to rely on them for anything more than that. We're trying to save for our honeymoon and for an apartment. I certainly don't have enough spare money to be eating meals at Bouley and Jean-Georges." I cast him a serious look. "It would be great if you could help me out."

At this suggestion, I-60 grows solemn himself. "Time travel is still in its infancy," he says. "Many of the practical and philosophical issues surrounding it are yet unexplored. What we do know is that it is highly problematic, potentially cataclysmic, for physical objects from one period to come into contact with the same physical object in another time line."

"So it's okay for you to come back and talk with me, but if our watches were to encounter one another, that would be a problem."

"Yes."

"That makes no sense."

"The universe is arbitrary. Just look at Jeff Goldblum."

This doesn't sit right with me and I let him know. "Hold on a second," I say. "Money is fungible. The value of a dollar is a concept, not an object."

"Unfortunately, the only form of money I possess is currency, which is physical. And since I can't very well put dollar bills from the future into circulation, I'm stuck with a few old dollar bills, which I happened to save from my own past. I need to use these sparingly. If one of these were to come into contact with itself . . ." He shakes his head at this prospect and quietly says, "It's just not a chance worth taking."

"So I guess I'm stuck with the tab."

"I guess," says I-60. "Unless you can get them to accept a postdated check."

He laughs heartily at this, as I hand the waiter my credit card.

"That's funny," I say, though my experience of it is quite different.

Chapter SIX

I harbor suspicions, intensified by this conversation at the end of our meal at Bouley, that my putative arrival from the future may be an elaborate ruse. Several things don't fit. There's the lime sucking, of course, and the persistent refusal to pay. But what makes me most wary is the gratuitous shot at Jeff Goldblum. Tastes change. I didn't like coffee or fish when I was a kid, but I do now. It's possible my predilection for lime evolves over time. I-60's frugality is credible. The animosity for Jeff Goldblum, however, is utterly implausible.

I like Jeff Goldblum. I did not happen to care for *The Fly*, but I very much enjoyed *Igby Goes Down* and *The Life Aquatic with Steve Zissou*. Furthermore, Goldblum had a small role in *Annie Hall*, my favorite movie ever. When Alvy Singer and Annie Hall go to the party at Tony Lacey's Hollywood home, Goldblum is the man saying into the telephone, "I forgot my mantra." This alone gives him a perpetual pass in my book. I am thus distrustful of I-60. I suspect he is not genuine and that this whole thing is a hoax.

Concededly, I am not sure what the point of this would be. I theorize that it could be an elaborate practical joke or a credit card scam, though creating a fictitious future self just to secure access to my American Express seems a bit extreme. If I were being honest, I would admit that my suspicions about the authenticity of I-60 are really part and parcel of a more general, long-suppressed skepticism about the authenticity of life itself.

This doubt originates in high school. My parents move from Brooklyn to Long Island the summer after ninth grade and I am forced to change schools. I don't know anyone at the new school. I spend most of tenth grade trying to make friends, with limited luck, and trying to meet girls, with no success at all. Then, miraculously, on the last day of school, Amy Weiss and Rebecca Perlstein independently invite me to go to the beach. I glide home only to notice that my psoriasis has become enflamed. I cannot imagine how anything like this could happen by coincidence and conclude that everyone around me, including my friends and parents, are automatons, characters in the play that is my life.

I begin to note similarities in appearance between ostensibly unrelated individuals like Mr. Mudwinder, my calculus teacher, and the guy who gives out the shoes at the local bowling alley. Some figures appear to be recycled. The boy who delivers our *Newsday* bears a close resemblance to one of my old camp counselors. The guy who runs the hot dog cart outside our high school looks eerily like my second cousin Zelda's first husband. From this evidence I conclude that the Grand Manipulator has only a finite number of robot models at his disposal. I only waver from my complete conviction in this belief when I read, many years later, that a quarter of the planet is descended from Genghis Khan. Still, I think my hypothesis is just as likely to be true as not. Often when I walk to school or work, I wave to the imaginary audience that I envision to be observing my life.

I am enormously disappointed when these metaphysical anxieties later become, more or less, the plot of *The Truman Show*. This suggests that I am not the only person to wonder about the possibility of a contrived existence. Sure enough, as I enter university and my intellectual horizons broaden, I learn that this idea has occurred to many people, including Ludwig Wittgenstein, Woody Allen, Kurt Vonnegut, and Bob Barker. At first blush, it seems implausible that if life had indeed been orchestrated as an elaborate deception of me, that the planet would be sprinkled with philosophers, satirists, and game show hosts asking the very same sort of questions that I myself am asking. Upon further reflection, though, I conclude that this might itself be part of the deception, the sort of misdirection that the shrewdest of puppeteers would employ.

So, over the course of my young adulthood, I search unceasingly for examples of inconsistencies that could expose the fraud. I scrutinize the comments of my friends to see whether they reveal facts that they could not have known, search for bargains that are too good to be true, and, of course, keep a sharp eye out for recurrences of the visage of my calculus teacher, Mr. Mudwinder.

I find no hard evidence to support my suspicions but nevertheless remain leery. Optimists confuse me. How could Evel Knievel and Amelia Earhart think for even a moment that they would make it? People with religious conviction make no sense to me whatsoever, except the Baptists, who seem resigned to enduring the worst that life has to offer. I am especially mistrustful of other Christians, particularly Jehovah's Witnesses, Mormons, and those insufferable Quakers, who maintain an unrelenting faith in the positive direction of life that seems, to me at least, fundamentally incompatible with independent, rational thought.

It was with this sensibility and experience, call it expertise if you will, that I set out to evaluate I-60's authenticity and investigate the possible fraud. Following our dinner at Bouley, I clandestinely follow I-60 to his hotel and determine that he is staying at the *W.* This is further cause for suspicion. *W*'s are swanky, and the one in midtown is as nice as they come. How can I-60 afford such luxurious accommodations on what he professes to be a limited budget? Standing on Forty-ninth Street, off the side entrance of the hotel, I develop a plan to resolve my doubts about I-60 one way or the other once and for all.

The following morning, I rise early and return to the *W.* It is not a teaching day, and I am free. I stand again on the corner of Forty-ninth and Lexington and wait for I-60. He emerges just after seven thirty, on his way for a run. After he jogs off, I enter the hotel lobby and tell the concierge that I have forgotten my key. He asks for identification. I hand him my driver's license. Fortunately he does not scrutinize the photograph. He simply hands me a plastic key card.

"You have to forgive me," I say, "but I have also forgotten my room number."

"Room 609," he says. "Make a right turn after exiting the elevator."

I head up to the room and take a quick spin through I-60's things. Nothing is out of the ordinary. He has traveled light. Aside from the running outfit, which he is wearing now, he has packed two sets of clothes: two pairs of socks, two pairs of underwear, two shirts, and two pairs of pants, one nice, one casual.

The new trousers are unfamiliar to me, but the latter pair I know. These are my favorite pants, have been for years. My grandfather used to wear brown corduroys, so I have always had a thing for them, and this pair from Eddie Bauer fit just right from the very first day. These are the pants I put on when I want to feel better after a rough day or when I am settling in to watch a big game or when I am about to do something difficult or important.

I am wearing them now.

His are more faded than mine. The cuffs have frayed, and the waist button has been sewn on too many times, perhaps let out a little bit over the years. But it is undeniable that these are my pants.

Suddenly, I become conscious of the time. Who knows how long a sixty-year-old can run? I take a look out the window, note that the room faces Lexington Avenue, and make a quick exit from the room. Downstairs, I walk out the side door and across the street to the Marriott, where I inquire about a room. I tell the desk clerk that I would like a unit facing Lexington Avenue. They can accommodate me, he says, though check-in will not be possible until later in the afternoon. This is fine; I don't intend to check in until the next morning, but the room is expensive, which gives me pause. Happily I am able to use frequent-flier miles and redeem a coupon for a second night. I book the room, return home, and wait for Q.

She is frazzled when she gets home from work. The battle for survival of the garden has become more serious, she tells me. The prospective developer is asking the city to take the property on which the garden sits by eminent domain so that the massive skyscraper can be erected.

"The mayor will never go for that," I say.

"He may," says Q. "We still don't know the true identity of this developer, but whoever it is, he or she has good connections. Our initial calls to city councilors were discouraging. The project has political momentum."

"What are you going to do?"

"I don't know. We're starting to have meetings about it."

"Good."

"Can you help?"

"I'd be happy to do whatever I can."

"Thank you," she says, as she gives me a kiss. "It means a lot to have your support."

I tell Q that a good friend of mine from high school is visiting from out of town. "We're going to spend the day together tomorrow and have dinner in the evening. I might be home a bit late."

I might not be so understanding of Q spending a night on the town with a mysterious friend, but she simply says, "Fine" and "Have fun" and returns to reading her copy of *Keepin' It Relleno: The Complete Guide to Chili Pepper Farming and Organic Political Advocacy*.

Nothing bothers Q. She is undemanding and generous and accepting of others, qualities to which I cannot relate.

In the morning, around six o'clock, after Q has left for the garden, I head over to the Marriott. I take with me a pair of binoculars, which Joan Deveril bought me for a night at the opera after learning that I did not have my own. They are tiny, but super high-powered.

The room is nice enough. A free copy of the *Times* is waiting for me. The coffee maker is serviceable and the mattress is not horrible. But it is nothing compared to I-60's room at the *W*, which has a state-of-the-art coffee maker and Egyptian cotton sheets on the bed. Using my binoculars, I can see his luxurious accommodations across the street quite clearly. I again wonder how he has afforded the room.

As he wakes up, however, my suspicions notwithstanding, what I see is unmistakably me. He is up early himself; it is still not yet seven. Again he goes for a run. The stiff knee that bothers me when I wake up has deteriorated. It takes ten minutes of stretching for him to get himself out of bed. He cannot lift his knees to put on his running shorts. Instead he sits on a chair and reaches forward to pull the shorts up over his feet. It is an ordeal.

When he goes downstairs, I do the same, and trail him from a safe distance. He walks from the hotel to Central Park and then jogs my favorite route—once around the pond, up past the Hallett Nature Sanctuary, across Seventy-second Street, over Bow Bridge into the ramble, a loop around the lake, then south past the sheep meadow and the Heckscher Ballfields, and finally back home. I feel pangs of sadness as I jog behind him. His gait—my gait—which was once effective, perhaps even graceful, has become a lurching series of stumbles. He is slow, gets winded, stops to watch some teenagers play softball. He is in no hurry. He is an old man.

After the run, he walks back to the hotel and retreats to his room, as I do to mine. Through the binoculars, I see him shower and dress for the day. He is not meeting anyone as far as I can tell, but still he takes extra care with his appearance. He shaves and irons his shirt. The baggage limit on travel from the future is apparently generous enough to allow him to pack a nose-hair trimmer, which I failed to notice while rummaging through his things. I-60 spends a few minutes grooming his nose, then a few more tending to his ear. When he leaves his room, he looks better than when I met him. Travel can be brutal on appearances or, perhaps, he is feeling more optimistic.

On the street he buys a bagel, checks out the toys in the window at FAO Schwartz, walks to the Metropolitan Museum, where he spends a while with the impressionists. He takes another long, slow walk home, back through the park, where he buys a pretzel, wistfully watches a pair of young lovers paddle a rowboat, lingers by some frolicking dogs, and reads the descriptions of the trees.

He is killing time. I suspect I am to blame for this. I have made this necessary by telling him, at Bouley, that I cannot meet again for several days. I have papers to grade, I say, and a reading in Greenwich, Connecticut. In truth I have neither papers to grade nor a reading to attend. I want to buy time to scrutinize him. He sees through the lie, I am sure. How could I ever deceive him? I bet he even remembers the true date of the Greenwich reading, which was several months ago. But he does not call me on it. This would be awkward. Instead he spends the time wandering the streets of the city. Perhaps he does not mind. Perhaps it is a pleasure to spend a few days in the New York of his youth. Or perhaps he is past the point of feeling much of anything.

In the evening, when he has exercised himself to the point that he knows he will be able to sleep, he returns to his hotel and I return to mine. In his room, he takes off the clothes of the day and dons the brown corduroys. A little after six o'clock, he leafs through the room service menu and places an order. Twenty minutes later it arrives. Through the binoculars, I can see that the meal is a veggie burger with tomato and onion and a side of sweet potato fries. This is more to my own taste.

I-60 sits in a lounge chair and eats the supper in front of the television set. At seven o'clock he watches *Seinfeld*, at seven thirty *The Simpsons*. I wonder how many times *he* has seen each of these episodes. Perhaps hundreds; I have seen them each dozens of times myself. I can see him anticipating the laugh lines, as am I. It is the monorail episode of *The Simpsons*, a classic. As Lyle Lanley sings to the town meeting, we mouth the words with him in unison. At eight o'clock, I-60 tunes in for the Mets game. I turn on the set in my own room and listen. Pelfrey is pitching, which is always dicey, and Davis is sitting out with a wrenched knee. Sure enough the Mets fall behind. When Reyes fails to run out a pop-up, which is dropped, I-60 waves his hand in disgust. Around ten, he walks to the vending machines and buys himself a package of Oreos and a small container of skim milk. I-60 eats his dessert while watching the end of the game. When the cookies and the Mets are finished off, he licks his teeth clean for a few minutes, then brushes them.

In bed, he begins to doze while watching a rerun of *The Office*. Before he nods off, though, he kisses two framed photographs, which he has placed on the bedside table. One he sets back down. The other he clutches while he finally falls asleep, having either forgotten to change out of his corduroy pants or chosen not to.

As I run home to meet Q, it occurs to me, happily, that these pants from different time lines have come into contact with one another without any apparent disruption to the fabric of existence.

It occurs to me then, too, less happily, that the man wearing these pants, this sad, tired man who likes veggie burgers and soft pretzels and cookies, who wanders the city watching lovers and puppies and falls asleep dreaming of his family, is unequivocally, unambiguously, and unmistakably, me.

Chapter SEVEN

Y ou have been following me." I-60 says this directly, matter-of-factly, across our table at La Grenouille, on Fifty-third and Park, where we have gathered for Meal Number Three, a late lunch. I understand from his tone that it is pointless to deny the claim.

"It is nothing personal, I assure you."

"What, then?"

"These are major life decisions I am facing. I need to be confident of your authenticity."

"And you doubt this?"

"I suppose not," I answer sheepishly. "I'm not sure. I'm not sure about anything at this point."

"Would you like me to relate to you the details of your first romantic experience with Becky Goldstein? Would you like me to describe the comic book you wrote in first grade in which the Muppets of *Sesame Street* had secret lives as superheroes, and

Ernie and Bert possessed the special power to clean at faster-than-light speed? Would you like me to discuss the state of your bunions?"

"None of that will be necessary," I say. These are all embarrassing matters, none more so than the Becky Goldstein incident.

"Well, then," I-60 says. "I think you owe me something of an apology."

This gets my dander up. "I owe you an apology?"

"I take it you think otherwise."

"You ask for meals to be arranged at the finest restaurants in the city, order seven-dollar soft drinks, and don't so much as lift a finger to pay the check."

"How ungrateful is this?" I-60 asks no one in particular. "Do you seriously think that I have come from thirty years in the future to mooch a few good meals off you? I am here for the gravest of reasons, to change the course of your life, so that you can be spared the pain that I have endured. Money is irrelevant. I would very much like to treat you to dinner, but it is simply not possible."

"Why is this again?"

"I explained to you already. We are not allowed to carry much cash."

"And that is because?"

"There were incidents, abuses. People traveled back in time to take advantage of sales or shop at outlet stores."

"And yet you told me that time travel is quite expensive?"

"It is, but the savings at wholesalers are staggering, and our dollar goes so far in your time. When the money started flowing backward, the financial markets went haywire. Restrictions had to be established."

"So what you told me about the consequences of physical objects from different time periods coming into contact with one another was a lie? You and I are physical objects from different time periods. I suppose that should have been a tip-off."

"It was not a lie. It was a choice. The truth is, no one understands much about the ethical and practical implications of time travel. It is all being worked through. The scientists and philosophers just know that money is a problematic issue. When one travels through time, he or she needs to have just enough of it, no more."

"How convenient that is."

"But true all the same."

"By what means are you paying for your hotel room?"

"I booked it in advance online. I used frequent-flier miles."

"How do you have money to eat?"

"I'm on the Modern American Plan."

"They can't possibly still have the Modern American Plan in the future."

"They do. Besides, this is now."

"I didn't think they still had it now."

"They do."

"What about the dessert I saw you eat in your room after watching the baseball game?"

I-60 appears confused for a moment, then it comes to him. "Ah, you mean the Oreos?"

"Yes."

"I like to have cookies and milk before bed. As I recall, I believe you do too."

"It's true. I do."

"Then, what's the problem?"

"How did you pay for them?"

"This is easy to explain," I-60 says. "I found some change on the street."

"That again seems quite convenient."

"And yet it is also the truth."

"Why do we have to eat in such expensive restaurants? Nothing you said explains that. Why can't we eat reasonably?"

"The food is not as good in my time. Fruits and vegetables just aren't what they used to be."

"But the most you ever order is clear broth?"

"I am an old man. What do you expect? Take it from me, the soup is much better in the past."

Something still doesn't sit right. "Why is the food worse in the future?"

"It's another consequence of the acceleration of global warming."

"Global warming gets worse?"

"Yes, after the decision to air-condition Las Vegas."

"Las Vegas already has air-conditioning."

"No, I mean they build a dome around the city and install massive refrigerators so people can walk down the Strip wearing a coat."

"Oh," I say.

"It was a very bad idea."

The waiter arrives. I-60 orders the bouillabaisse. I ask for the salad Niçoise. I have never had salad Niçoise. I think I may not like it because I abhor black olives, which are an essential ingredient of salad Niçoise. On the other hand, I feel like I should try everything once, and it is the least expensive entrée on the menu.

I-60 holds his hand up to the waiter. "My friend," he says to me, "you should get something other than the Niçoise."

"It's fine." I say to the waiter. "I'll have the Niçoise."

"No, you do not care for it."

"I have never had it," I say curtly to I-60.

"Well, then, you will not care for it. Do not like it, will not like it, what's the difference? You will still be hungry after lunch."

"I'm a grown man," I say. "I can order my own meal."

"You're just ordering it because it's the cheapest thing on the menu."

"That isn't true."

He stares at me, disbelieving. It's pointless to try and deceive him. He says, "Why don't you try the halibut with Riesling and horseradish?"

"I don't like halibut."

"You will. It's just a matter of time. Same with lime. It's really quite refreshing. Don't just order the salad because it's cheap— order something you will like. You'll be happier. Trust me on this."

"It's okay," I say to I-60. Even if I were inclined to take his advice, I am now too embarrassed to do so. To the waiter, who has been standing beside the table throughout the conversation, I definitely say, "I'll have the salad Niçoise."

"Very good, sir," he says. "The Niçoise it is, and the bouilla-baisse for your husband."

Neither I nor I-60 is amused.

When the waiter is gone, I-60 asks, "Do you want to hear the story now?"

"Yes. You should tell me what you came to tell me."

"It is sad," he says. "Unspeakably sad."

"I have to hear it, don't I? Is it even possible for me not to? I mean, this is the whole point of your trip, right?"

I-60 nods. "Well, then." He pauses, takes a sip of water, then begins. "That boy—my son—your son—becomes the center of your life," he says. "Q still gardens, you still write, but these pursuits, which had seemed so urgent, don't seem as important anymore. In the evenings, after you finish class, you race home to hear whether he has taken a new step or uttered a new word. When he is older you play games—simple games at first—Candy Land and Chutes and Ladders, but he advances quickly. Soon you're playing Clue Junior and Chinese checkers. He especially loves Pay Day. Whenever he lands on Sweet Sunday, he lies down on a pillow, pulls a blanket up to his head, yawns, and sighs, "Sweet Sunday!"

He is bright, and in another year or two you're playing word games like Boggle and Scrabble. He even gives you a fair game of chess. At school he is at the top of his class. The teachers adore him, and even though he is smart, the other kids do too. This is because he has no guile or pretension. He is just a kid who wants to laugh. He loves *The Simpsons* almost as much as you do. For his sixth birthday, you buy him the movie, and in a matter of two weeks he has it committed to memory.

Each season is special. In the summer, you construct elaborate games of hide-and-seek and tag, which inevitably devolve into tickling. In the fall, you throw one another into leaf piles. In the winter you build snowmen. In the spring you have baseball.

I-60 is different now. Perhaps I should say, more precisely, that I experience him as different now. While heretofore I have found him aloof and occasionally sanctimonious, neither of these or any other negative qualities are present when he discusses the boy. He is sincere and transparent and sad. The extraordinary qualities of his son, my son, are presented lovingly. I-60 now seems modest, self-effacing. He seems authentically me.

"QE II is not athletic," I-60 continues. "He wears glasses, has a gangly gait, and poorer-than-average hand-eye coordination. But when he is eight years old he develops a passion for baseball. More specifically he develops a passion for the New York Mets. This is yet another act of love on his part. He knows that they are my team, and so he adopts them as his own. He starts watching games with me. Soon he learns the rules; later he immerses himself in the history of the team and the game. I, you, share with him the books that sparked our own passion for baseball. Together we read *The Kid from Tomkinsville*, and I love it on my second reading almost as much as he does on his first. It is the joy of reading it with him. He finds his way to *Shoeless Joe* by W. P. Kinsella, and we finish that together too. Soon he is off to read *Catcher in the Rye*, and whatever he can about the enigmatic Salinger, to figure out how it is that baseball could have healed him.

"Miraculously, his love extends both to the profound and the mundane. You bequeath to him our collection of Mets yearbooks, complete except for 1966, and soon he can recite the opening day lineup of the 1962 team and the stats of everyone on each of the four World Series teams. At the start of the following season, you buy him a scorebook, which he maintains with the meticulous attention to detail of a historian or a novelist. You love that boy from the moment you first lay eyes upon him. But from that little book you learn that he has the soul of a writer, just like you, and you love him all the more.

"He watches every game. He records every out and hit, but not with the conventional scratch marks. He notes the field to which the ball is batted, and the force with which it is struck, and the effort that both base runner and fielder exert on the play. Each morning at breakfast, we eat English muffins and review the most exciting plays and key strategic decisions from the previous night's game. If I have missed it for some reason, he describes it to me in exquisite, vivid detail. If the Mets have lost, he tells me that they played lethargically or appeared nonplussed in the field; he tells me of their gallantry and their grim determination in the face of adversity. If they have won, it is not just a positive mark in the standings—it is a glorious victory of the forces of good over evil, a triumph of Greek proportions, praise be to the all-powerful gods of baseball. I sit there, sip coffee, and think to myself that no human being could love anything as much as I love that child, as much as Q does, and that I am the luckiest creature in the universe.

"That season I take him to his first baseball game. We look forward to it for weeks. It is after camp ends, the week before school starts. The Mets have already fallen out of it, but he is giddy with excitement. I ask him where he wants to sit. I can get tickets behind home plate if he wants, the supply is ample, but he says he would prefer to sit in the top row of the upper deck. 'Are you sure?' I ask. 'Yes,' he says. I question no further because that eight-year-old boy has a reason for everything he does.

"At the game, the reason is revealed. He pulls two carrots from his coat pocket and hands one to me. 'You do color,' he says. As the Mets take their positions he welcomes the 'audience of vegetables' to Citi Field, and we take them through the game, lapsing into cliché whenever possible, laughing sometimes at the absurdity of it all, and loving every second of it. David Wright singles in the ninth inning to win the game for the Mets. Wright is near the end of his career, hanging on, but he is nevertheless QE II's favorite player. He loves to root for the underdog. Though the game means nothing, when Wright's hit falls and the winning run scores, our son jumps for joy and gives me a bear hug. It is the best memory of my life."

There is obviously more to the story, but I-60 stops here.

"And then?" I ask.

"And then he gets very sick, and he dies."

I wait for more, but I-60 is done.

"That's it? That's all you're going to say? What happened exactly?" I am not feeling very well.

"Does it matter? He becomes ill a few weeks after school starts. We take him to the doctor. Turns out it is serious—not just serious, but fatal. We try everything, of course. As you know, Q is relentless. They can't cure it. He suffers a lot at the end. It destroys you—me—and Q. Do the particulars or the name of the disease matter?"

It seems as if they do; in that moment the details seem all-important to me. I want to protect that little boy, and Q too. The thought of her suffering hurts as much as anything else. But I-60 is right. What do the specifics matter? I wonder about one thing, though.

"Did you ever travel back to see him?"

"No. I could only afford one trip back in time. I decided to visit you. Going to see him somehow didn't seem right to me."

"Is that because it would be too sad?"

"No. That's not it exactly."

His voice trails off, and he stares forlornly into the bouilla-baisse. I want to ask more, but I-60 appears to have reached his limit. We sit silently for a while, picking at our food.

I don't like the Niçoise. I-60 was right.

But he delivers no I-told-you-so lecture. Perhaps he realizes that I have reached my own limit. When he speaks, he changes the subject entirely. "I noticed in the newspaper that the Mets are playing tonight. Do you think we could go? You don't need to spend a lot of money. We can get bleacher seats. I'd just like to see the stadium."

The Mets are terrible this season, but the thought of saying no to this request never crosses my mind.

We take the 7 train. I-60 stares out the window the entire time that we are aboveground, from Queens Plaza, over Astoria, and through Jackson Heights. He is quiet and wistful, and I have the sense he is reliving a distant memory. Perhaps baseball does not exist in the future. Perhaps the Mets follow the Dodgers to California. Perhaps I-60 lives a nomadic life that does not allow him to attend baseball games. Whatever the case may be, this ride, so much a part of my routine, is not part of his.

We exit the train and cross Roosevelt Avenue. A scalper approaches us and we buy day-of-game seats, good ones, mezzanine boxes down the first-base line, which are selling below face value. There is no demand. It is the next-to-last game of the season and the Mets are out of it. As usual, the Yankees control fall baseball in New York.

At the gate, the ushers scan our tickets, and we enter the new stadium. I-60 stares wide-eyed at the Jackie Robinson rotunda. It is new to him, and old.

Would I mind buying him a scorecard and a pencil, he asks? I do not mind.

We go to our seats. I leave him there, go to Shake Shack, return with diet sodas and the good crinkle-cut fries. He is busy recording the starting lineups in his program, looks at me warmly, grateful for the food. Something about him is needy now—needy in the way a young son needs his father, needy in the way an elderly father needs his son.

It is a spectacular evening, perfect for baseball. The crowd is sparse but surprisingly energetic and buoyant. The Mets on the other hand are languid. Niese, recently back from an injury, hits two batters in the first inning, leading to a run, and walks in another in the second. Thole lets a ball get past him in the top of the fifth, and just like that the Mets are down three to the Phillies. Oswalt keeps them in check. No hits through four, a bunt single in the fifth, a bloop in the sixth, none again in the seventh. The Mets do not threaten to score.

"The Mets are awful," I say.

"It's true," he says, "but they get better."

I-60 absorbs everything. He records every hit and every out in his book, soaks in the peanut vendor with the impossibly accurate arm, nods his head but does not sing as the fans stretch to "Take Me Out to the Ballgame," drinks in the faint smell of seaweed in the evening air. He is engrossed in the familiar rhythm of baseball, the rhythm of life. Soon he is talking again, though this time it is not to me.

"It's called Batten disease. It is very bad."

I nod. My mind races. "Could you have had other children?"

"Q and I—Q and you—are both carriers of the disease. There was a one-in-four chance another child would have had it. The cure won't be discovered for another thirty years from now, more than twenty years after he gets sick."

I groan. I'm in pain.

I-60 says, "After he was diagnosed, we set up his hospital room so that he could watch the games on television. At first he maintained his scorebook, then he would just watch the games, then he couldn't stay awake even for this. Before he died, he asked me if we could go to one more game together. I said we could."

A pitch sails into the catcher's mitt.

"But we didn't."

It is the bottom of the ninth. The Mets are still down by three. The team has displayed no sign of life at any point in the game, but they stage a rally. With two out, Reyes gets a hit, Pagan another, Beltran walks behind them, and all of a sudden, out of nowhere, the Mets have a chance to win. Of the many ways that baseball is a metaphor for life—for the need to prepare, for the vagaries of bad bounces and ill fortune, for the acceptance of a high frequency of failure as a necessary condition of existence— none is more apt than this illustration of the fact that fortunes can change in an instant.

It is all in the hands of Wright. In I-60's story of my future, and his son's past, David Wright must have been old. But he is young now, fierce and vibrant. The remaining fans, subdued into listlessness for eight and a half innings, are clapping in unison, brimming with energy, ready to explode. The Mets may have no chance at the playoffs, but the Phillies do, and hatred for them runs deep.

Wright lets the first pitch pass, and the second; each is called for a strike. Then he takes a ball, and daringly takes two more close ones, and the count is three and two. After each delivery, the crowd's rhythmic clapping stops, and the collective potential energy of their desire is released aimlessly into the nighttime air. Now, with the count full, the cadence begins again, arcing toward a climax, as Lidge delivers. Wright does not let this pitch pass. He hits it solidly, a majestic, towering fly to right center. This is not a hitter-friendly stadium, and the more experienced fans know that even the best-struck ball can land in the mitt of a competent outfielder. Collectively, they, we, hold our breath. Then it clears the fence, and the entire stadium erupts in cheers and rises to its feet to celebrate the game-winning grand slam.

Only I-60 remains seated, and I can hear, faintly beneath the cacophonous exuberant celebration, the sound of an old man softly weeping.

Chapter **EIGHT**

To me this is all a dream, the worst of nightmares—the sort that stuns you awake, panting and witless, your heart racing, but even worse still. With ordinary dreams, one has the awareness, or hope, sometimes within the dream itself, that what is being experienced is so horrible that it cannot be real, and that if you can only force open your eyes then the ordeal will end. From this dream I do not wake up.

My reaction is odd in a way. None of what he describes has happened to me, at least not yet. But it feels as real as if it has. Its weight is palpable. Every moment, it feels as if someone is kicking me in the stomach or pressing down on my shoulders. Walking is an effort. Food does not taste right. It is difficult to fall asleep in the evening and, in the morning, difficult again to wake up. Writing is impossible.

Q senses something is up and asks. I tell her the friend I saw is having a hard time, and she does not pry any further. She is having her own difficulties. In the evenings we watch TV and hold hands. Television is our great avoidance. In the mornings she is up and out early to deal with the garden. Mostly I am alone.

I am in grief, but because this trauma is hypothetical or yet to happen or whatever it is, I have no natural event to bring me closure. I find myself wandering the city, walking for hours on end. I try the botanical gardens and the ferries, but these offer no comfort. So, too, Strawberry Fields fails, and the Metropolitan Museum of Art. Nothing works until one day while aimlessly drifting through the East Village, an irresistible force draws me inside a funeral home, where I linger for a while watching the comings and goings, and then stay for a service, which is oddly soothing. To my own surprise, I return the next day, and the day after that.

It is easier to crash funerals than one might imagine. If you wear a suit, no one asks any questions, and even if you don't, you're unlikely to be hassled. Who really knows who belongs at a funeral? They're not as bad as you might imagine either. People behave well. They hold doors and speak quietly, and no one ever unwraps a sucking candy. Sometimes there is food.

I spend an entire day at Pezzano's Nondenominational Funeral Home, just south of Washington Square, near the corner of Bleecker and Thompson. Sitting in the pews for so long changes my perspective on death. Nondenominational does not mean that God is not present; it means that all gods are present or, more accurately, the god of whoever is paying at the moment. As one funeral ends, a ritualistic changing of the guard begins, in preparation for the next event. Between the eleven thirty Abramson service and the McCallister funeral at one o'clock, a worker sprinkles the hall with an aromatic powder, which smells of frankincense and myrrh, overpowering the faint odor of Mandelbread which had permeated the room. A giant shield of David is let down by pulley. In its place is raised a crucifix, itself so immense that it would shame a Vatican cardinal. Two burly men are required for the lifting and lowering.

During the raising of the Jewish star, one of the workers inhales some of the frankincense powder, lets fly a giant sneeze, and loses his grip on the cord. The star enters free fall and only a last-minute recovery prevents catastrophe. The perfumist, or whatever one calls someone who spreads the smell of God, is standing near me as the near disaster is averted. Under his breath, he says, "Jesus Christ."

The proprietor of the home, Chuck Pezzano, is more than happy to talk. In the corridor, between events, he tells me that he is the third generation of his family to be in the funeral business, that the money isn't what it used to be, that he wanted to be a classicist but his father wouldn't foot the bill for graduate school, and so here he is. He doesn't like his job, and in subtle ways it shows. His eulogies are spotty. He makes little mistakes. One time he refers to poor Mike McCallister, an accountant and model-train enthusiast who stepped into an empty elevator shaft, as "Bob," thinking, I believe, of the former host of *Wonderama*. His Hebrew is atrocious. He says "mitzvah," with a long *e* sound that would have made my grandmother's head explode.

His eulogies are calming, though. He speaks softly, with a pleasant, singsongy cadence that has a mesmerizing effect. Several times I find myself drifting off, and the day goes by quickly.

Structurally, he follows the pattern of the Greek funeral oration. "The form of the *epitaphios logos* is tried and true," he tells me in the hallway. "It was good enough for Plato and Pericles, so it is more than good enough for me." At each funeral, he begins with a preamble, in which he explains that nothing he will say could ever adequately console the bereaved. He continues by recounting the lineage of the deceased, paying homage to all family members in attendance and to their national heritage. The first two parts work well, generally speaking.

The next, penultimate, section is more problematic. Here Pericles would honor the sacrifice of fallen war veterans. This could be dispensed with for most urban funerals, but Chuck is wed to the form, and so we are left to hear how Shelly Abramson, a jewelry engraver, toiled in service to the engraving industry, and of his unfailing devotion to its (unidentified) ethical principles.

But Chuck always closes strong with his epilogue, forceful words of consolation and encouragement to the families, which focus on the lessons the deceased's good works offer. It is another standard bit, and sometimes requires contortion, as in the case of Shelly the jeweler, but even still it is engaging and comforting. "Heddy, Judit, and Irv, your father's life is a shining example of a life lived well and in the service of others. If he were here today, he would surely say, 'Do not grieve,' but instead, 'Honor me by living your own life well through works of charity and by your devotion to your own children.'"

Without any emotional connection to the deceased, I focus less on the details of their lives and more on the patterns that emerge. From my distance, one life looks pretty much like another. Everyone has friends and families and coworkers. Every service is attended by some people who are there out of love and others out of obligation. Everyone pretends the dead had no flaws, for the complicated reasons people do this: as a peculiar sort of honor, out of obedience to social convention, in the hope that they will be treated with the same generosity of spirit when their own time comes. When it is an adult who has died, funerals can produce great hope. People cry, but by the end of the service, healing has already begun. Small jokes are made, reconnections, and plans for the future. Watching this is comforting and, in some cases, even vaguely pleasant.

As the day wears on, I notice another man doing the same thing as I, attending one funeral after another. He is dressed neatly, in a gray suit and rep stripe necktie, though he has a coarse, weathered face, which suggests to me that he has not spent his life in an office. I guess that he is mid-sixties, though his leathery skin is the sort that can make one look older than he is. As the workers transition from the McCallisters to the Karpels, I wander over to him.

"Are you watching too?"

"Yes," he says. "I'm on disability. I fell off a forklift. This helps keep me out of trouble. Most days I go to the courthouse and watch trials. When things are slow there, I come here. Otherwise I'd be at Aqueduct."

I nod. I want to tell him that I have had my own bad luck. Most people expect that in the unlikely event they are ever visited by someone from the future it will be by another person, and that if it is by himself or herself, they will be given information that can be exploited, like the winner of the next Kentucky Derby or the name of a company whose stock will soon rise. It is my peculiar misfortune to be convincingly advised to abandon the most important and loving relationship of my life. But this seems better left unsaid. Instead I say, "The racetrack can be depressing."

"Yeah, and the state cut kills you. Anyway, Chuck doesn't mind. He's nice."

I nod. "It's not as bad here as I imagined."

"Some funerals are sadder than others," he says, "but it can be therapeutic, and you don't have to worry about blowing the rent on an exacta. You should spend a day at one of the graveyards. I recommend Cypress Hill in Queens."

The cemeteries of New York are hidden treasures. In 1852, Manhattan passed a law prohibiting burials on the island, and so cemeteries were hauled east to the wooded hills of Long Island, beautiful pristine land, still largely agricultural and sparsely settled, other than a few summer homes dotting the north shore in what would become Great Neck and Glen Gove. None is more beautiful than Cypress Hills, in the ribbon of parkland bisected by what lifelong New Yorkers know as the Interboro Parkway. On top of a bluff, just south of Glendale and west of the golf course in Forest Park, it commands views of the ocean to the south and the Long Island Sound to the north. A mere thirty-minute trip on the J train deposits the courageous traveler in a forgotten, mystical universe.

Though the cemetery has fallen into disrepair, its beauty is still evident. The wind blows through the ancient cypresses and maples and a towering oak, which is a living memorial to the assassinated president James Garfield. There's a babbling brook and a quiet pond, and they still have room for you at prices that are surprisingly affordable, given the history of the place. Even an average Joe can be buried near the great jazz musician Eubie Blake, the entombed Mae West, and the immortal Jackie Robinson, who could not possibly have known that the adjacent highway would someday bear his name.

Here, too, are moments of grace and humor. At the burial of Jack McCarthy, a former firefighter who died of unidentified causes, one mourner after another throws flowers and other remembrances into the new grave. The last, a sullen man, with stooped shoulders and caverns under his eyes, tosses a bottle of Jack Daniels down the hole. When the priest looks at him quizzically, the man says, "Now he'll be able to sleep."

I watch the interment of Lou Marino, a high school teacher from Brooklyn. It is sad, but not too sad. Many of the people in attendance are quite old. If they are sad, it is as much the result of reflecting on their own mortality as on Lou's. For it is obvious that Lou has led a long and full life. His wife is there, in the front, and she is crying, which does not sound noteworthy, but I have seen many services where the spouse does not shed a single tear, and one can almost see the balloon above their heads, expressing relief that the half-century nightmare is finally over. Mrs. Marino, by contrast, is heartbroken. Lou was obviously a good man. And there are children. Some are on the doorstep of old themselves, and from where they are positioned in the group, I know that these are Lou's sons and daughters. They are sad too, though not too much. They have children of their own to distract them, good kids. They are wearing suits and dresses. The boys are not fussing about their neckties. The girls have kept their stockings up. A few are sufficiently grown to have children of their own and sure enough, toward the back of the gathering, a pretty woman in her early twenties is rocking and hushing a little baby girl. No one minds, and when the infant cries "Mama," it brings a smile to many faces, including Mrs. Marino's, and it is obvious that this is her and her husband's beautiful great-grandchild. I think to myself that one could do much, much worse than Lou Marino.

I am so absorbed in the Norman Rockwell moments that I barely notice it is a rabbi presiding. Following some *mlech*ing and *baruch*ing, he says the word *hashem*, pauses, looks up, and asks, "What was the deceased's Hebrew name?" Now, one does not have to be a genius to conclude that Lou Marino was not Jewish. It is obvious what has happened. Lou married a Jewish woman, and because she loved him for more than fifty years, and gave him beautiful children, who in turn gave him beautiful grandchildren and a great-granddaughter, Lou decided that he wanted to be buried Jewish and rest with his wife when she someday joined him. The rabbi either cannot or will not intuit this. From behind his thick beard, he asks again, "What was the deceased's Hebrew name?"

The members of the Marino clan begin to look at their shoes and shuffle their feet. Mrs. Marino appears dumbstruck, the second generation of Marinos are red in the face, even the grandchildren are quiet and chagrined. The day is saved by a spunky *altetshke*, with frosted hair and cat's-eye glasses, who obviously has been flown in from Florida. It is a seasonable late autumn day in New York City, in the mid-fifties, but she is wearing the burliest of parkas, lined in fur and topped with a thick hood, the kind of jacket Shackleton's mother tried to get him to take to Antarctica but the explorer rejected as too warm. She is a fireplug of a woman, and the coat consumes her torso. With the hood drawn about her, all that is visible are her feet, her eyeglasses, and a sliver of nose.

This, I conclude, is Louis Marino's mother-in-law. It is easy enough for me to imagine that she did not approve of Lou, who was probably a hell-raiser in his day, any more than John Deveril approves of me. But she is here, which tells me that this man was indeed good to her daughter, and she is not about to allow any ruse to be exposed on her watch. As the rabbi asks a third time, "What was the deceased's Hebrew name," the little bundle screams, "Moishe!"

In the back, a giggle is suppressed, but it will not be contained. Soon a chuckle emerges, then a full-on laugh, and finally the entire Marino clan is breaking up in front of the bewildered rabbi.

When it's a child, though, it is never lighthearted.

Life, in subtle and gross ways, is a transition to death. The wrinkling of skin, the stiffening of joints, and the diminishment of appetites are all reminders, not just to ourselves but also to our friends and loved ones, that we will not be around forever. When an adult dies, no matter how he or she goes, even if he is hit by a bus or falls down an empty elevator shaft or some other pointless death, we can make sense of it. It is within our experience and narrative capacity to satisfactorily explain events such as these. We may grieve, but we are consoled by the joys of the life lived—by the fact that Lou Merino loved and was loved by his family, by Mike McCallister's passion for his trains, by Shelly Abramson's career, such as it was. Even if it is an imperfect life that has ended, we can console ourselves by saying that the departed made choices, that no one gets everything they want, that part of living is compromising. This is an account of existence we can accept.

None of these mitigating narratives apply when a child is involved. Sometimes someone will say something about God and his secret will, but it never rings true. At the funeral of a high school student who has died of an injury suffered during a football game, Chuck Pezzano does not even try to console the family. He throws away the Greek script and admits that nothing he can say will make any difference. He sees death all the time, he says, but nothing can prepare anyone for this. In my opinion, it is his finest hour.

One afternoon at Cypress Hills, my last, they have a service for an infant. No one says much. A few words of prayer are muttered; a teddy bear is deposited in the grave; the tombstone is revealed, noting consecutive years of birth and death. No one cries, which is sadder than when they do. Following the service no one speaks much, but what is to be said?

That evening, while Q is out, I research Batten disease. It is named after a British pediatrician who described the syndrome in 1903 and is part of a family of diseases called neuronal ceroid lipofuscinoses. This group includes an infantile form, known as Santavuori-Haltia disease, and an adult form called Parry's disease. Each of the varieties of the illness is caused by a buildup of lipoproteins, which are a combination of lipids and proteins. The lipoproteins build up in the cells of the brain, the eye, and other tissues and cause neurons to die.

With Batten's, symptoms first appear between the ages of five and eight. The typical early signs are loss of vision, seizures, and clumsiness. Its progression is methodical and insidious. Children with Batten disease become blind and bedridden and lose the ability to communicate. Though it is inevitably fatal, the disease progresses slowly, and affected children live into their teens or, in rare cases, their early twenties. By all accounts, this is a mixed blessing.

In my mind's eye, I see QE II's life. It is easy to envision; I do not need my older self to explain it to me. I can imagine the terror of being trapped in one's own body, of being betrayed by one's own hands and eyes. And I know the horror would be all the worse for a brilliant young boy with a vivid imagination and lofty goals. A boy such as this would sense the fullness of what had been seized from him—playing basketball in the schoolyard past dusk, learning to drive, his first kiss. And it would be all the more difficult to have a doting mother, Q, by his side. The child would understand that his mother felt everything he did, that his pain was her pain, and the sense of loss and foregone opportunity he felt over his own life would be even more profound for her because she would go on and think to herself each moment of each day what he would be doing if he were there. His life would be ruined, but the pain would end. How much sadder for the mother, whose ruined life would go on?

For her life would be ruined—that much is plain. As clearly as I see the life ahead of QE II, I can see what lies ahead for Q. To protect an organic garden in downtown Manhattan, Q is working around the clock, with complete commitment and devotion to her cause. As I-60 said, she is relentless. It does not take much extrapolation to envision this energy and sense of purpose being applied to a beloved, helpless child. Days spent at the child's bedside trying to keep him comfortable, sleepless nights, and endless waiting. This strikes me as more daunting than any other aspect of the experience as I imagine it. Waiting for futile doctor's appointments, waiting for a surcease to suffering, waiting for life to resume.

The boy's illness would surely doom my relationship with Q. In rare moments of optimism, my confidence in Q's tremendous strength and determination makes me think she could somehow carry us through. But when I am sitting quietly at the funeral home or walking aimlessly through the streets of New York or sitting on the couch with Q watching TV, I acknowledge that these scenarios are fanciful, the product of my inability to imagine leaving Q. I have no idea how I could ever do this. But the truth is, if what I-60 has told me were to come to pass, Q and I would never recover.

Chapter NINE

During the weeks following our dinner at La Grenouille and our trip to the Mets game, I hear nothing further from I-60. I receive no notes, no phone calls, no solicitations for fancy meals. I walk over to the *W* during my wanderings one day only to find that my older self has checked out and left no forwarding information. I worry about him. But as I emerge from my fog, my attention focuses increasingly on Q. I have no instinct to distance myself from her. To the contrary, I am drawn to her more than ever. In these days of mid-autumn, Q is fully immersed in the endgame of the desperate battle to save her sacred garden. Since this is her cause, it is mine too, and when my mourning ends, I do what I can to help Q and her colleagues organize opposition to the construction of the skyscraper.

The tactics of the campaign are developed during a series of Saturday afternoon meetings at the TriBeCa residence of Ethel Lipschutz, former curator of the scone collection at the Museum of Muffins and Breads in Chelsea. Ethel's loft apartment is surprisingly spacious, but rather inconveniently located above Conway's department store on Chambers Street. Chambers Street is easy enough to get to, but the apartment itself can only be accessed through the children's shoe department in the back of the shop.

"What do you do when the store is closed?" I ask at the first meeting I attend.

"I don't go in or out," Ethel replies.

"Isn't that inconvenient?"

"Not really. I don't miss evenings or Sundays one bit. Besides," she says, winking, "it's rent-controlled."

Everyone within earshot nods their heads vigorously.

"Seriously rent-controlled!" cries one woman.

"Do I hear adverse possession?" exclaims another.

After a moment, I get the picture.

"And there are, shall we say, perquisites," Ethel adds, as her eyes shift toward a massive pile of children's shoes in the corner of the room. The mound is supported by an almost-as-impressive stack of *Boys' Life* and *Girls' Life* and *National Geographic Kids*.

"How many children do you have?" I ask.

"None," she says, her mischievous smile suggesting that this fact makes her cache all the more impressive and valuable.

The strategy arrived upon by the group is grassroots with a postmodern twist. It includes a heavy dose of the staples of left-wing, ground-up organizing: telephone calls to City Council members, leafleting, postering, distribution of homemade buttons and dehydrated sponges. It also includes, however, a technological component. To wit: a blog (with seventy-eight nonredundant readers), Twitter posts (with the same seventy-eight nonredundant subscribers), a Facebook community (seventy-eight members), email blasts (seventy-seven; one of the regulars does not have email), and three online discussion forums. Everything is emblazoned with the acronym ENDING, which stands for End Neighborhood Destruction of Indigenous Neighborhood Gardens. During one of the Saturday afternoon sessions, I question whether an acronym should include its own name or use the same word twice, but I am quickly hushed by Ina Levenson, prolocutor of the nonprofit organization that oversees the garden's operation.

Levenson and her colleagues regard my formal education on the history of campaigns as irrelevant. They have strong feelings about the most effective way to wage political warfare and are also vaguely mistrustful of me. The primary cause of this suspicion is a summer course on American social history I taught as an adjunct professor at the Borough of Manhattan Community College seven years ago while I was still a graduate student at NYU. On the basis of the $1,850 I received from the government for offering this series of lectures, they have concluded that I am somehow part of the "entrenched power elite." Ordinarily they wouldn't know anything about me, but, improbably, Jill Nordberg, the group's homeopathic insecticidist, took the class, received a C, and remains convinced the mediocre grade was a response to her political views, which are somewhere to the left of Trotsky. I recall the incident, as well as the salient highlights of her letter to the chairperson of the BMCC history department, in which she refused to acknowledge me by name. Nordberg wrote, "The professor in question's lectures, examinations, and syllabus, which embrace discredited right-leaning figures such as Michael Harrington and Nathan Glazer, are uninclusive, anti-progressive, and patriarchal."

Even the lefty chairperson found the letter extreme and unpersuasive, but I am nevertheless diminished among Q's peers. When I suggest at a later meeting that all the money spent on handbills and posters would be better used to develop and air a single television commercial, I am unceremoniously dismissed from the group. This excommunication is not verbalized, of course. But it cannot be coincidence that on each of the following three Saturdays, Q asks me, in the voice I cannot resist, to run a series of obviously contrived errands, including two runs for herbs, which somehow can only be purchased in Bay Ridge. I thus am not present for the decision to employ a giant inflatable rat or the coup de grâce of the campaign, a march—in full vegetable costume—from the garden to the steps of City Hall.

I am, rather, relegated to behind-the-scenes research and support. My first charge is to investigate public enemy number one in the campaign, the Deliver Company, a limited-liability corporation based in the Cayman Islands.

Through my research, I learn a great deal about the Caymans, a tax haven in the western Caribbean Sea. The islands are discovered by Christopher Columbus on his ill-fated fourth and final voyage to the New World. He names them Las Tortugas, after the abundance of sea turtles he encounters there. Indeed, turtling remains the linchpin of the Cayman economy until the 1970s when the natives discover they can make more money as an international financial center, particularly in light of the declining popularity of turtle soup, which was never all that popular to begin with.

One of the ways the Caymans carve a niche for themselves in the cutthroat financial-haven game is by eliminating taxation. Caymanians and, more relevantly, Cayman Island companies, pay no direct tax whatsoever. The country makes its money by charging a flat licensing fee on financial companies and a 20 percent duty on all imported goods, with the notable exception of baby formula. The Caymans also protect the corporate identity of any company housed in the islands.

This is smashingly popular with businesses, particularly illicit businesses, which loathe paying taxes. It is so popular that the number of businesses registered in the Caymans exceeds the human population. This is a shame because the Caymans are a nice place to live. Temperatures hover year-round between seventy-five and ninety degrees, the sea is generally placid, and the price of baby formula is quite reasonable.

Unfortunately, because of its strict privacy rules, I cannot find out a single thing about the Deliver Company—not its CEO, not its board of directors, not even its address. The whole thing is a mystery, and, as every good campaigner knows, the hardest enemy to fight is the one you cannot see. I am given special dispensation to attend a Saturday meeting at Conway's during which I report my results. Q's colleagues are suspicious about my failure to collect information but reassured by my conclusion that this setback is attributable to a widespread conspiracy.

My second charge is to explore inflatable rats. With this task I am somewhat more successful. I find a store in Illinois offering free shipping and a surprisingly robust selection. The rats range in size from six to thirty feet, with most folks settling on something in the twelve-foot range. Oversized fangs are extra. The store also has skunk balloons.

The rats are surprisingly expensive. Q and her associates could never afford one on their own meager earnings, but Q calls upon the services of her father, and he is only too happy to help. He has been a major benefactor of the garden, as he has been of his daughter, all along. He is sanguine about the potential of the rat. Indeed, the rodents have an excellent track record. They were created in the early 1990s for the benefit of striking unions and had an undeniable impact. Many employers capitulated to the awesome presence of the rat and its unsightly pink underbelly. Over time, the rat balloon came to represent inadequate health care, poor maternity leave policies, and all other questionable corporate practices.

The rats are not invincible. One employer responded by inflating an even larger cougar to menace the rat positioned outside its store. Some companies have litigated against the rat. Two have been arrested, though they were discharged after questioning. All in all, though, the rodents have a fine track record. I negotiate a favorable price and this temporarily restores my standing with Ethel Lipschutz and the team. Only my former student remains dubious. The rest of the group is sanguine about the rat's potential and their campaign generally. As the march approaches they are giddy with optimism.

The day of the rally begins auspiciously. The weather is cool and crisp, the pollution temporarily washed from the sky. It is the sort of morning that promotes a sense of possibility. Q's colleagues are in high dudgeon. At ten o'clock, they gather in front of the garden to begin their assault on City Hall. Their ranks are bolstered by simpatico victims of the oppressive patriarchy, including two members of the Ethical Cultural Society rapid-response nonmilitant militia; Cassandra DeBower, Lenora Fulani's third cousin once removed; Don Bruford, associate corresponding secretary of New Yorkers Against Violence; Phillip L'Enfante, emeritus professor and former holder of the Tom and Agnes Carvel Endowed Chair in Postcolonial Studies at the New School; Tina Dennis, the *Village Voice*'s alternative lifestyle sex columnist and restaurant critic; Art Vance, former deputy finance chairman of Abzug for Mayor; and three unaffiliated transvestites.

At precisely 10:15, Ethel Lipschutz, commandant of the march, blows a shrill pea whistle and the troops fall into formation behind her, arranged in age order from oldest to youngest. Ninety-three-year-old Phil L'Enfante is thus second in line, followed by Art Vance, eighty-eight, and progressing downward, finally reaching Lipschutz's nine-year-old grandniece, wearing a pink ribbon in her hair and a pair of Howdy Doody Wacky Wobbler sandals. Thirty-five people in all set out from the garden to begin the onslaught, led fearlessly into battle by a giant inflatable rat and a shoe-hoarding squatter dressed as a zucchini.

The retinue emerges from the garden, turns right on Rector, then left onto Church. Few people are on the streets since it is a Sunday, but the cortege nevertheless generates some reaction. At the intersection of Liberty Street, a teenager points, bops his head, and yells "Go squash! Go squash!" Ina Levenson, who is dressed as the gourd, gives the boy a thumbs-up. It is obvious she does not detect the sarcasm. To the contrary, she is emboldened and walks on with her head, barely visible over the stem of the squash, held slightly higher. Other members of the company respond similarly to excited cries of "Asparagus Rocks," "Celery Rules!" and "Yo Yo Yo, Tomato!" Onward, they march.

Near John Street, progress is stalled when Professor L'Enfante announces that he needs the bathroom. The only good option is a Wendy's and this sparks a heated debate on whether L'Enfante can ethically use the facility. Q, a vegetarian, is positioned to the right on the eating-habits spectrum of the group, which includes six vegans, three raw vegans, and a seitanist.

"Wendy's is a purveyor of consumerism and responsible for the inhumane slaughter of millions of innocent animals," says Cassandra DeBower. One of the transvestites, Janus Edlefield, a fruitarian herself, nods her head in agreement.

"He needs to use the toilet," I say. "It doesn't promote consumerism for him to use the toilet."

"Don't listen to him," says Jill Nordberg, my former student. "He is a capitalist tool himself. He's not supposed to be here at all. He didn't even have the decency to dress up."

This is true. I did not dress up. Q said she thought it would be best not to. I am wearing my usual uniform, an oxford shirt and khakis, and have been following the action from a distance, either a few steps behind or across the street. I moved in only to investigate the commotion surrounding L'Enfante's request. I am clearly an outsider, present only to support Q, but surprisingly, Ina Levenson is on my side. "It's not like he's going to buy anything," she says. "How can it do any harm for him to use the bathroom?"

"They don't use organic toilet paper!" shrieks Ethel. "They are guilty of the murder of virgin trees!"

It goes on like this for almost fifteen minutes, at which point the debate is no longer relevant. Professor L'Enfante has soiled himself and decides to go home. I help him get a cab. Getting into a taxi can be challenging for someone dressed as a turnip, but he does it, and graciously asks me to wish the group luck getting to City Hall.

"I was looking forward to seeing Lindsay again," he says. "I would have given him a piece of my mind."

After entering the south end of City Hall Park, the members of the group begin craning their necks to see whether the parade has attracted the desired response. Halfway through the plaza, Ethel Lipschutz turns and triumphantly proclaims, "The press is here!" Word filters back through the ranks. "The press is here. The press is here," says one marcher to another. Chests expand further and the phalanx of vegetables advances with a noticeable lilt in its step. At the steps of City Hall, Lipschutz calls the troops to a halt. As one, the group chants:

> *Ho Ho*
> *Hey Hey*
> *Urban Gardening Is Here to Stay*
> *Hey Hey*
> *Ho Ho*
> *Garden Displacement Has Got to Go*

After five minutes of robust protesting, Ethel Lipschutz stands aside. Ina Levenson triumphantly ascends the steps and begins the press conference.

The press consists of two people. The first is a gentleman wearing a flannel shirt two sizes too big and a pair of unfastened tweed pants two sizes too small. He is sporting a fedora into which has been inserted a white index card bearing the handwritten word "Press." My best guess is that he is homeless. The second attendee is Stu Kurtzman, restaurant critic for NY1, the local television station. Kurtzman raises his hand. Ina Levenson recognizes him.

"Where is the food?" he asks.

Ina says, "There is no food, though there is a knish cart on the corner of Broadway and Church."

"I was told there would be food."

Ethel Lipschutz leans forward and whispers in Ina's ear, consigliere style. She confesses that in her zeal to attract press, she may have misled Kurtzman about the nature of the event. Levenson accepts the news solemnly.

"You were given erroneous information," Ina tells Kurtzman.

"Specifically I was told this was going to be a jambalaya jamboree."

"No, this is a march in support of community gardening."

"I became worried when I failed to see okra represented among your membership. It is disappointing. I quite like jambalaya."

"I am sorry to let you down."

"I'll be going now."

"I wish you would stay. This is a very important cause."

"I am sure it is."

"If you are hungry, I do recommend the knishes. We can send someone to get one for you."

"No, thank you," he says, packing his camera. "Knishes do not agree with me. And, besides, I had my heart set on jambalaya."

Attention now focuses on the sole remaining representative of the press, the gentleman with the flannel shirt and suspect credential. He raises his hand, and Ina Levenson points at him ceremoniously.

"Herman Louis, *Street News*," he says.

"Mr. Louis."

"Where did you get the rat?"

Ethel Lipschutz whispers the answer to Ina. "Kramer's Inflatable Hatables, Chicago, Illinois."

"How big is the rat?"

"The rat really isn't the point of this press conference. We are here today to talk about corporate greed and to demand that the mayor step in and protect a community garden that is one of the hidden treasures of our city."

"All the same, I'd like to know how big the rat is."

Ina turns to Ethel Lipschutz who again whispers the answer.

"Twelve feet," Ina announces. "The rat is twelve feet tall."

"I have another question about the rat."

"Yes." Ina is peeved.

"Was the rat made with union labor?"

Ina turns to Ethel once again, but she does not know the answer to this one. Ethel turns to Q, who turns to me. I shrug my shoulders, and the group shoots a series of dirty looks in my direction. The dirtiest comes from Jill Nordberg. My inability to answer this question conclusively confirms everything she ever believed about me.

"We don't know," Ina Levenson announces. "We don't know anything about the genesis of the rat."

"It should have a sticker if it is union made," Mr. Louis says.

Ethel Lipschutz walks over to the rat and begins a search. Unbeknown to her, one of her long, ragged nails pierces the shell.

"Do you not support the use of union labor?" asks Herman Louis.

Ina Levenson attempts to deflect the question and buy Lipschutz some time. "Of course we support unions and the use of union labor," she says. "But we are here today to protest the failure of the government to stop the relentless progress of corporate greed. We are here to preserve the integrity of neighborhoods and maintain the connection of urban dwellers to the land upon which they rely. We are here to defend the institution of community gardening. The rat should not be the focus of our discussion."

Sadly, this becomes impossible, as the rat begins to deflate.

Needless to say, the timing is inconvenient.

It is a slow leak at first, and not immediately recognizable. It begins as a high-pitched squeal, near the dogs-only end of the register, almost imperceptible. Some heads turn to the sky in apparent fear of an aerial attack from a Messerschmitt bomber or a flight of mutated birds. Some look downward, for snakes. Others look behind the shrubs for concealed explosives. The enemy is everywhere.

As the hole widens and the flow of air increases, it becomes clearly identifiable as an air leak. Jill Nordberg is the first to put two and two together.

"It's the rat!" she cries. "The asshole bought a cheap rat!"

Ina Levenson quickly processes the situation. "Get out of there, Ethel!" she screams. "For God's sake, while there's still time!"

Ethel moves as quickly as she can, but is encumbered by her zucchini costume. Her legs protrude only six inches beneath the fleshy meat of the fruit. Hence she is confined to an awkward waddle. The evacuation of helium is accelerating, surprisingly quickly, and it is clear that Lipschutz's tedious shuffle will not get her out of danger in time. Sizing up the situation, I race to her aid. Ignoring her cries of protest, I topple her to the ground, orient her along the longitudinal axis, and rapidly roll her out of danger.

As fate has it, though, the wind changes direction, as it often does in City Hall Park, and the rat, now nearly spent and unrecognizable, falls on an unforeseen trajectory toward eighty-eight-year-old Art Vance, who has been forgotten in all the commotion.

"Art! Look out!" screams Ina Levenson, but it is too late. He has been consumed. Underneath the limp, wilted rodent, there are signs of struggle and muffled cries for aid. We begin a poorly coordinated extraction, a coterie of gourds and legumes pulling this way and that. Somehow it works, and Art Vance emerges, relatively intact. What remains of his hair is wildly unkempt, and his pince-nez has fallen down the bridge of his nose, but he could still pass for a respectable rutabaga. Ethel and Jill give Art a hand up, help him out of his costume, and Ethel helps him put on his blue blazer over the "Abzug for Mayor '77" T-shirt he is wearing.

"Such a day, such a day," he says.

"Such a day, such a day," she says.

After a few minutes, order is restored. The carcass of the rat is compacted and discarded. The portable microphone is sheathed. Costumes are collected and reboxed. The group disperses, the enthusiasm for the day, if not the cause, spent on the long march and subsequent aversion of disaster. Art Vance is placed in a cab.

"Such a day, such a day," he says. I think it is the only thing he ever says.

Other farewells are exchanged. Ina Levenson thanks everyone for their time. Ethel Lipschutz does the same. Hugs are offered as well as vague plans for future gatherings to "regroup" and "restrategize." I stand off to the side, removed from the scene and out of the way of the further dirty looks that are cast in my general direction.

Q and I hail a cab and head uptown.

"Thanks for coming," she says. "It wasn't fair for them to blame you for the rat. They could just as easily have checked themselves. Besides, you were doing them a favor in the first place."

I can see the absolution is sincere. Q is too nuanced in her view of the world to ever blame a single person for a series of events. Even if she were so inclined, she trusts my good intentions. It speaks volumes about her that she has offered this assurance, that she is sensitive to my needs even in this difficult moment. Because I can see too that she is despondent about what has transpired.

"Thanks," I say. "I'm sorry it didn't go better."

Q says nothing, and we spend the remainder of the taxi ride in silence.

At home, Q and I mindlessly turn on NY1 and find to our surprise, and ultimately our chagrin, that the march is being covered on television. Unfortunately, it is being shown as a blooper cut at the top of the hour, before traffic and weather together on the ones.

The announcer says, "On his way to a jambalaya jamboree, our food critic Stu Kurtzman caught this footage of a protest at City Hall gone horribly wrong. The demonstrators, organic gardeners dressed in vegetable costumes, had one heckuva time with an inflatable rat, as you'll see." Then he shows the footage. Then he smiles and says, "Gives new meaning to getting squashed." Then the station cuts to a commercial for an abdominal exerciser. It seems like a good product, the sort of thing that should work but, I presume, does not, or everyone would have washboard abs.

Q watches in silence, turns off the television, and says, "It's over."

"No," I say. "There are still other things to be tried."

"No," she says. "It's over. The garden is finished."

I love her all the more for this. Because it's true, the garden is kaput. Whatever tiny chance the group had of succeeding politically was premised upon the march making a major impression on City Hall. If they had gotten the right sort of media coverage, gotten the attention of the mayor, attracted widespread sympathy from other left-wing causes, perhaps they could have pulled it off, though even in this scenario success would have been a long shot. The way things went down trivialized their cause and made them look like crackpots. No politician will pay attention to them now. They will be pariahs, laughingstocks.

Amazingly, Q can see this reality even though she has the deepest possible emotional connection to the cause. This sober detachment is yet another admirable, alluring quality. It is a large part of what makes her a wonderful partner. But Q's honest assessment of the situation does not include acceptance. To the contrary, she is despondent. Q mopes through the days, saying very little. At first she goes to the garden at the crack of dawn, as always, but returns too early, suggesting she is spending less and less time on her chores. I envision the garden, its demise impending, slowly deteriorating. Soon she skips days. She begins watching daytime television. One day I find a catalog for graduate school in the mail.

It gets worse before it gets better. One Sunday morning she goes to the grocery store, buys three dozen Stouffer's frozen dinners, and does not leave the apartment again for more than two weeks. Many days she does not get out of her pajamas. She begins to smell and take *The Price Is Right* seriously. It is nothing less than utter devastation. As I watch her mope through those painful weeks of the late fall, eating macaroni and cheese and guessing on the Showcase Showdown, I cannot help but imagine what a real tragedy would do to her. Thus, in these days of her mourning, it gradually becomes painfully clear to me what I must do.

Chapter **TEN**

On the last Wednesday of November, Q drags herself out of bed and we travel to the Berkshires to spend Thanksgiving with her mother and father. She is still not herself, but the prospect of seeing her parents has buoyed her spirits, and each of us, for our own reasons, is happy to get out of the city.

We take the Taconic. Q doesn't like the winding parts of the parkway in Putnam and Dutchess counties, particularly in the late afternoon when it can be difficult to see. She prefers to take the Saw Mill to 684 and then go up by Route 44 through Amenia and Pawley. This is the safer route, but I argue the payoff on the Taconic will be worth it, and Q goes along. This is an olive branch of sorts. She has not been mean to me in any way, but she recognizes that the past few weeks have been difficult on both of us. My private grieving has not helped.

I know what I am talking about, choosing this route. When the road straightens out, past Fahnestock, Q and I are rewarded with a cavalcade of color. The leaves have fallen from the trees, but not yet lost their vibrancy. The ground is awash in red and yellow and orange. A family of deer feeds by the side of the road. The fawns are four months old, maybe five. They huddle close to their mother as they nuzzle through the leaves in search of the most desirable grass. I shift into the right-hand lane and slow the car to enjoy the show. Q rolls down her window and watches with rapt attention. When the herd has receded into the distance, Q rolls up her window, turns to me, and says, "This was a good choice."

I speed up, but not too much.

A Natalie Merchant CD is playing. Q leans toward folksy female rockers such as Aimee Mann and Sarah McLachlan, and Liz Phair before she sold out, in Q's view. Merchant is her favorite, even though she hasn't produced an album in several years. I like her too. It's the sort of music that makes one pensive and dreamy. "Life Is Sweet" in the background and the rolling countryside relax me, too much perhaps, and I introduce a topic that might be better left unexplored. At the very least it could be left for a later day when Q has more fully recovered, but it's on my mind and it spills out.

"If you were going to die, would you want to know?"

"I know I am going to die." This is classic Q.

"I don't mean that. I mean if you could know how you were going to die, would you want to know?"

"I know how I am going to die," Q says. "I am going to die of old age, in your arms, and then ten minutes later you are going to die the same way."

"I'm being serious."

Q looks me over carefully and sees this is in fact true.

"Wow," she says. "You are being serious. What got this in your head?"

I lie. "I was just reading an article about privacy and genetic profiling. The question is, if someone decoded the genome of, say, Russell Crowe, would he have the right to keep this private or could a company post it on the Internet?"

"It belongs to him, doesn't it?"

"Not any more than his appearance does. It's one thing if someone sells Russell Crowe's genetic code for profit. But one cannot have a privacy interest in a sequence of nucleotides any more than Jennifer Aniston can keep someone from copying her hairstyle."

Natalie Merchant starts humming "Kind and Generous."

"This sounds very science fictiony," Q says, which is a shorthand way of telling me to be quiet.

Q does not share my interest in science fiction. It's one of the few tensions between us. Q doesn't deal in hypotheticals, what-ifs, regrets, second guesses, or conjectures. She is a practical sort, in this sense very much her father's daughter. John Deveril built his construction business from the ground up. He began working as a bricklayer the summer after eighth grade, left high school to start building homes full-time, then moved on to office buildings and skyscrapers. John Deveril believed in hard work, rib-eye steaks, and never making excuses. Though his daughter grew up with the trappings of luxury, and is firmly situated in postmodernity, she shares her patriarch's basic values. She is a gardener, after all. One who fertilizes her soil with alfalfa meal, composts household waste, and drives predatory insects away with pheromone lures, but a gardener all the same—living proof that being a tree-hugger and a Calvinist are not mutually exclusive.

Unfortunately, this approach doesn't leave much time for flights of fancy, whether it be Derrida or science fiction. I try, unsuccessfully, to turn Q on to *The Twilight Zone*. I show her one of my favorite episodes, "The Long Morrow." The premise is that astronaut Douglas Stansfield, played by Robert Lansing, falls in love with Sandra Horn, played by a radiant Mariette Hartley, just before he is about to leave on a forty-year-long deep-space mission. The plan is for Captain Stansfield to spend almost the entirety of the trip in suspended animation. Love-struck, Stansfield cannot bear the thought of returning to Earth as a young man. Horn will have aged normally during his journey, and Stansfield believes the resulting age difference will make their relationship impractical. So, in a dramatic act of devotion, Captain Stansfield disables his suspended animation chamber so that he will age normally during his voyage. When he returns to Earth, after having spent forty years doing nothing, he learns to his dismay that Horn, in her own act of zealous passion, placed herself in suspended animation. When the old and wrinkled Stansfield emerges from the spaceship, he finds Sandra Horn waiting for him, as young and pulchritudinous as she was on the day he left for space. Sadly, she is no longer interested.

"Isn't that wonderful," I say at the end of the show. "The episode only hints at the full extent of the sacrifice Captain Stansfield made. Since he did not expect to be awake for much of the journey, he probably didn't pack much to eat. He would have had to ration out his food wafers and water to last for forty years. And he almost certainly had no reading material. He just thought about her for four decades. How romantic is that?"

"It's okay," Q says, matter-of-factly, "but they should have talked beforehand."

"What do you mean?"

"He could have just said to her, 'I'm thinking of taking myself out of suspended animation,' and then she could have just said, 'That's silly. I'll just put myself in suspended animation.' Problem solved, star-crossed lovers' disaster averted."

"Well, suppose they didn't have time to talk. Suppose he had to leave in a hurry."

"You mean it was one of those last-minute forty-year space flights?"

"Just suppose."

"Well, then, he shouldn't have taken himself out of suspended animation. If she didn't think to do it herself, then he could have put her into suspended animation when he got back, lived out forty years, and then they'd be the same age. This way he could have done his waiting on Earth instead of in a metal box with nothing to read."

Hers is a very sensible solution, though it would not have made much of a story. "So it's that simple," I say.

"Just a matter of common sense," Q says.

This is the last time we watch science fiction. It is not much of a problem since we have lots of other common ground. We both like sitcoms and political dramas and action movies. Q will even indulge me and watch a poker show on occasion. She doesn't understand the strategy, but she has strong feelings about the morality of the players. In Q's view, it is ethical to lie, but un-ethical to lie about lying. She thus accepts bluffing as a legitimate part of the game, but not the posturing misrepresentations that occur during the denouement of a hand. Daniel Negreanu is her favorite player because he is honest by her peculiar definition, and also a vegan, a Democrat, and a fine dresser. This is a winning trifecta in Q's book. I like him too, and all in all, we have a happy television life.

One notable exception surrounds the fourth-season finale of *Battlestar Galactica*, just as the humans and Cylons, joined temporarily in a tenuous alliance, are about to reach Earth. I look forward to it for weeks but am crestfallen when, on the morning of the big day, Q tells me she is looking forward to watching a special anniversary rebroadcast of the finale of *Brideshead Revisited* that evening. We have only one television, and I explain the dilemma. Q says it is not a dilemma. She happily reports that she has purchased a special attachment to our DVR, which will allow us to watch one program while taping the other. We can thus watch *Brideshead* while it's on, and I can watch *Battlestar* later in the evening. It is a reasonable resolution, but I am disappointed at not being able to watch the program live.

I wonder why we like watching things live. Any devoted television watcher will tell you that watching something on tape or DVR just isn't the same as watching when it airs. Live, we can't know what commercials are coming or skip past them if we have seen them before. We are open to the unbidden.

Of course, television is not live in any meaningful sense. The shows have all been recorded weeks ahead of time. The same is true for the commercials. And it is not as if a DJ is cueing them up; the order has been prearranged. Even "live" television is not live. Live sports are delayed by a few seconds, lest the commentators say something imprudent. Even if you get the direct feed, what you see is delayed by the time it takes for the images to beam up to the satellite and back.

Yet the commentators all speak in the present tense, though they know that by the time you're watching the program everything they are describing will be in the past. They even do this when describing things they themselves are seeing on tape. Take, for example, the poker programs, of which I am so fond. Poker tournaments can take days or weeks. After a tournament ends, the producers find the thirty or forty most interesting hands and edit them down into a two-hour show. The commentators then add voice-over to explain the action. These commentators are watching the hands on tape. Everyone knows they are watching the hands on tape. The tournaments are broadcast weeks or months after they are finished, and the results are all public. Yet the announcers describe the action as if it is happening live: "Daniel Negreanu hits an ace on the river!"

I wonder about this aversion to past tense and the past in general. Why has it become so passé?

In the car, I continue to press Q. I ask, "If it were cancer or ALS, would you want to know?"

"Could I do anything about it?"

"Not if it's ALS."

"What about the cancer? If it were detected early, would it make a difference? Because if it would make a difference, then I would obviously want to know."

"No, it's terminal. Otherwise there wouldn't be a dilemma."

"Why does there have to be a dilemma?"

"There doesn't have to be a dilemma," I say. "It just isn't interesting to discuss unless there is a dilemma."

"It seems silly to go out of one's way to turn an easy situation into a difficult one."

"All the same, suppose it were an incurable cancer. Suppose someone tells you that you're going to die on this or that day from a certain type of cancer, and there's nothing you can do about it. Would you want to know?"

"So the entire benefit is that I know when and how I'm going to die."

"Right."

"But there's nothing I can do about it."

"Right."

"Well, then, no, I wouldn't want to know."

I'm incredulous. "How can you say this so easily?" I ask. "Think of all the advantages of foreknowledge. You could put your affairs in order. You could make sure to do something you always wanted to do. You could make peace with your friends and family."

"You asked me my opinion," Q says flatly.

I have more to say, but before I can get out more of my litany of reasons why one must answer my hypothetical affirmatively, Q turns the music up, making it clear that the conversation has ended. Merchant is singing "The Gulf of Araby." I know better than to talk during "The Gulf of Araby."

By the end of the song the conflict has passed. With Q, there is no interpersonal drama. She does not require apologies or cooling-off periods or the reconstruction of events. Something happens, it ends, life resumes. Closely related to her rationality, it is her most appealing and enviable quality.

"My mother is experimenting with a new stuffing this year," she says, signaling that she has moved on.

"What's in it?"

"She says it contains andouille sausage, oysters, onions, chanterelle mushrooms, and apples in a white roux."

Q's mother is an accomplished and adventuresome chef and insists on making Thanksgiving by herself each year for a dozen or so friends and family. She does not need to; the Deverils have more than ample help. One could question Q's mother's motivations in doing this. It may be that she simply likes to cook. I believe it is the only socially acceptable context in which Joan Deveril can assert her personality against the relentless, uncompromising force that is her husband. Whatever her impetus may be, Joan's results are beyond reproach. I anticipate the meal for weeks and dream about it for months after. It is the one day a year Q abandons vegetarianism. Joan's Thanksgiving meals are more than any human being can resist.

"That sounds exquisite, and you know no one is a bigger fan of your mother's cooking than I am, but even I have my reservations about stuffing meat with meat."

Q nods. "How much longer do you think it will be?" she asks.

I look for a sign. We're near Lafayetteville.

"About an hour and a half."

"Then I'll need to go to the bathroom."

The Taconic doesn't have any rest stops, so this means we'll have to get off the highway and drive a bit. I consider a nearby McDonald's, which we have been to before, but then I have a better idea. We're about a twenty-minute drive from one of Q's favorite towns. It has antique shops, small bookstores, and, on Sundays, a farmer's market. It would be just the thing to further buoy Q's spirits.

"Are we in a rush to get to your parents'?"

"Not really."

"Then how about a quick stop in Rhinebeck?"

Q brightens at the mere thought of it. I take her cue and make a quick change of course onto Route 199. The road is almost empty and we make it to the town in fifteen minutes. I find a spot on Market Street and park our red Corolla. By this time, Q is bouncing with anticipation. She says, "I'm going to run to the bathroom then check in and say 'Hi' at the market. It'll just take a second. I'll meet you at Irregular's in half an hour." Irregular's is a quirky record, book, and toffee store that Q knows I like.

I say, "Sure," but I know it'll take Q a lot longer than thirty minutes. For organic gardeners, the farmer's market is like a convention, and Q, manager of the most improbable and successful urban garden on the East Coast, is nothing less than a celebrity at these gatherings. And now she is the sympathetic victim of a gross act of corporate greed. Her appearance will set the market a-twitter. She'll be lucky to break away in two hours. I know she knows this, and she knows I know she knows this, but it's fine with me. I have lots to think about.

I get myself a cup of coffee, wander through one of the flower shops, then make my way to Irregular's. Two hours is potentially a long time to kill in a record store, but Irregular's is exceptionally engaging. The owner, Oscar, has a devious streak and arranges the records to form little puzzles. The book section has a large collection of occult literature. And then there's the toffee.

Toffee can only be made well in cold weather. When it's warm or humid, the sugar does not caramelize properly. True connoisseurs will only eat toffee made within one month of the winter solstice. This happens to be the occasion for the ancient feast of Yule, practiced by the pagan Germanic peoples of northern Europe until missionaries superimposed Christian themes on the traditional burning of logs, decorating of trees, and eating of ham. Before children began eating candies as an homage to the Bethlehem Shepherd, they ate them to honor the Nordic god Freyr, bestower of peace and pleasure.

The solstice is also the anniversary of the publication of the *Necronomicon*, the definitive volume of the occult canon, a history of the Old Ones and the means to summon them. The Old Ones were a giant alien species who practiced black magic, built cities all across prehistoric Earth, and occasionally interbred with human females. They were ultimately banished to Antarctica and destroyed by the shoggoths, a slave race of their own creation. The *Necronomicon* tells humans how to get back in touch. Historians have not conclusively established the Old Ones' fondness for toffee, but this is doubtless only a matter of time.

The confluence of optimal timing for devil worship and toffee makes holiday season the busiest time of year at Irregular's. When I enter, the store is packed. At the door, Oscar remembers who I am and greets me warmly. He offers a sample of almond caramel toffee and mischievously points to the wall behind him. Four album covers are on display:

The Best of Grandmaster Flash
Abbey Road
Slowhand
De Stijl

"White lines," I say quickly.

"Very good," he says, flipping me another piece of toffee. "The rest won't be so easy, though. We have some really good ones for you today. I hope you have some time."

"Long enough," I say playfully, and head off for mental battle. In the record section, I quickly see that Oscar is right. The other ones aren't nearly as obvious as the first. It takes me ten minutes to identify the link between:

We're an American Band
Get On Up and Dance (by the Quad City DJs)
Teaser and the Firecat
The Monkees

I mutter song titles to myself, finally arriving upon "Peace Train," "Last Train to Clarksville," and "Come On Ride the Train." "Funky railroads," I say finally. The third puzzle, however, stymies me completely. The four albums are:

Signals
Sgt. Pepper's Lonely Hearts Club Band
Nevermind
My Generation

I have been perusing them for fifteen minutes when a gentleman behind me whispers, "They are all bands that continued after the original drummer left."

"Keith Moon didn't leave. He died."

"But he replaced Doug Sandom."

"Wow," I say. "I had *no* idea Rush had a drummer before Peart."

"Really," says the gentleman. "I could have sworn you knew that."

Confused, I turn around and see, to my further astonishment, that it is my long lost friend, me.

"Why don't we take a walk?" I-60 suggests.

"Sure," I say. On our way out the door, I ask Oscar to keep an eye open for Q, and tell her that I went for a walk and will meet her back here at the store.

"Absolutely," says Oscar. "I'll be sure to keep an eye out for *her.*"

Rhinebeck is magnificently sylvan, and the record store abuts a forested nature preserve. I-60 and I meander down a pebbly path.

"I was worried," I say.

"That's sweet."

"Where have you been?"

"Montana," says I-60. "I have always wanted to see Montana."

"That's funny. I have always wanted to see Montana, too."

"That's a good one," we both say simultaneously, sharing a long, hard laugh. Then we walk for a while in silence, enjoying the day.

"I am going to leave soon," says I-60 finally.

"Tired of *début de siècle* New York?" I ask. "I can see why, the decade doesn't even have a proper name."

"It has nothing to do with that," says I-60. "I need to get back soon. I forgot to water my plants."

"I see."

A blue jay flutters by, perches on the overhanging branch of a red spruce, then flies off to rejoin unseen friends. I-60 pays careful attention. The bird's business seems quite important to him.

"So," he says, when the jay has finally flown off, "if I may ask, what have you decided?"

"I think you already know what I have decided. I think you knew all along."

"Not so, but I agree there is no other choice."

"What I don't understand is why it is so important now? Why can't the decision wait?"

"Because this is the weekend you conceive QE II. Everything is symmetrical. He will also be born in the Berkshires."

I consider the implications of this for a moment. "It would have been a lot less cruel to come before I ever met her."

"No, that would have deprived you of the happiest moments of your life. I'm just trying to spare you the saddest."

I nod. We turn back on the path toward Irregular's.

"I just don't know how to do it," I say. "I can't see how I can extricate myself at this point."

"I imagine that seems daunting to you."

"I would say impossible."

"I get it. It must seem overwhelming. But if we're having this conversation, it means you have thought about what I have told you and chosen the appropriate course of action. I don't think you mean emotionally impossible—it's emotionally difficult, but necessary. I believe you mean impossible as a practical matter. How do you do it so that she regards it as authentic and complete?"

"Right."

"Here's where I can help. I know something you don't."

"What's that?"

I-60 leans over and whispers his great secret into my ear. I can't say that I foresaw what he says to me, but I'm hardly surprised. It is bitter, awful news, but I react more to the practical import of what he tells me than to the offense of the substance of it. In this moment, the distasteful, hateful path of my life to come becomes clear. I-60 had it all right. I had reluctantly committed myself to his advice. The problem was simply practical. I could not imagine how I could drive her away. Now this is clear too. All I need do is share this secret with her, and she will be gone.

In this moment, I am reminded of a friend from college who learns during his sophomore year that his father has died and he has inherited the fecund family fudge factory. It is a lucrative business, and from my perspective the path of my friend's life appears gilded. Nevertheless he appears dejected.

"This is great," I say at the time.

"I hate fudge," he says, and nothing else.

We arrive back at Irregular's.

"I guess this is it," I say.

"This is it," says I-60.

It seems strange to me that I don't have anything more to say to my older self, but I don't. I expect I-60 has had the same thought.

"I am sorry to put you through all this," he says.

"It's okay. I'm sure I would have done the same thing."

"Of that I am certain."

He shakes my hand warmly, and we look sadly into one another's eyes, I to see what I will become, he to see what he once was.

"Good luck," he says and begins to walk away down Main Street.

"Tell me one thing before you go," I say.

He turns. "Anything I can."

"Why don't you see Montana in your own time?"

At this question, I-60 smiles.

"It's not what it once was. Nothing is."

And then he is gone.

From the front window of Irregular's, I see Q walking across the square. She is wearing a quiet, earth-colored dress, but she is aglow. Men and women stare at her from all parts of the square, though she does not notice. She stops briefly to have a word with an elderly couple, then makes her way toward me. She is carrying two pears. I am happy to see her and say so.

"Who was that you were talking to earlier, outside the store?"

"Just someone I met on the street."

"He looks a little bit like you."

"Funny thing."

"I guess we should get going," she says.

"I guess," I say.

And so we go.

Chapter **ELEVEN**

Even by her lofty standards, Joan Deveril has outdone herself this year. To begin with, the dinner table is a work of art. The napery is hand-embroidered with the letters *JJQD*; each place is set with a silver service plate, three sterling silver forks, two knives, a soup spoon, a lace serviette, a pewter water goblet, and two wine glasses. In the middle of the tableau sit twin silver candlesticks, into which have been set thin, elegant candles, which, lighted, produce a pair of gentle, flickering flames. There are flowers everywhere—rhododendrons in vases on the table and the buffet and in the planters on the wall, so much lavender and red and white, and all so impossibly fresh it feels as if spring itself has been imported into the dining room.

And then the food, the food. I steal into the kitchen and breathe in deeply, in the hope of absorbing the entire meal at once. The bouquet, fresh and fulsome, nearly lifts me off my feet. Joan is there in the kitchen with Q, applying some final touches.

She offers me a tour, which I eagerly accept. She takes me first to the side dishes.

"Here is a wild mushroom corn pudding with goat cheese and an herbed cream sauce," she says, pointing. "This is winter squash stuffed with curried pork. This is a Vidalia onion casserole. Here is cranberry relish spiced with mincemeat and pecans. Here are fresh-baked sweet rolls. Here are plain sweet potatoes, just for you, just like your grandmother used to make."

This makes my mouth water and, at the same time, warms my heart. Joan Deveril is a sweet and thoughtful woman. That she remembered this from the previous Thanksgiving, when she noticed that I had not partaken of the sweet potato casserole, topped with marshmallows not to my taste, is typical of the kindness she bestows upon people. From the first time she met me, she made me feel loved and part of her family. Q is quite clearly her father's daughter. It is his lineage that sparks her passion and determination, the qualities that make her accomplished and compelling. But she would not be Q without the softening influence of her mother. It is this that makes her lovable and impossible to resist.

"Here," Joan says, pointing with pride, "is an innovation for this year—a preview of leftovers—turkey risotto with artichokes, mushrooms, and Parmesan cheese."

"And finally, the pièce de résistance." She walks to the oven, opens the door, and reveals the giant thirty-pound fowl. "The turkey is glazed with honey, stuffed with andouille sausage, bacon, croutons, apples, dried cranberries, and pears, and has been roasting slowly, upside down, for the past sixteen hours."

I reach to pick off a piece, and Joan playfully slaps my hand with her apron.

"Mrs. Deveril," I say, "you are an artist. This is truly magnificent."

She smiles. "Nothing is too good for my daughter and future son-in-law."

Warmly, she kisses me on the cheek as she returns to her work, and I wonder yet again whether I will be able to go through with what I need to do.

We are called to the table at three o'clock. Thanksgiving dinner at the Deverils has been known to take as long as five hours. All things considered, it is best to start early.

When we sit down, John Deveril is already holding court. He pauses to pull the chair next to his out for Q and kisses her on the cheek. Though Q and Joan and I have missed the beginning of the conversation, it is easy enough to pick up the thread. The local hardware store, Bill's, is being bought out to make room for a new development. Bill doesn't want it, most of the citizens don't want it, but the Board of Selectmen in Lee have decided that it is in the best interests of the community. The dinner guests, most of whom I have met before at other Deveril family functions, are lamenting Bill's misfortune and the store's demise.

"Bill is a good man," says Kristen Topper, associate director of the Tanglewood artist-in-residence program, third assistant conductor of the Boston Pops, and Joan Deveril's longstanding partner in women's doubles bridge tournaments. "At Tanglewood, he has been a member of the Koussevitzky Society for years."

"Yes, yes," says Shep Hemsley, stage manager of Jacob's Pillow Dance Festival. "He is always very generous to the Pillow."

"And to the Berkshire Theatre Festival," adds Herman Alouise, the noted local actor. During the past summer, Alouise starred, to critical acclaim, as the horse in the BTF's production of *Equus*.

"He is a real patron of the arts," Kristen Topper says in summary.

Each of the guests nod, save one: Myron Haines, the former third violinist, first seat, now third violinist, second seat, in the Boston Symphony Orchestra. "So we're supposed to mourn the downfall of a hardware store because its owner gave a few thousand dollars for classical music, dance, and theater?" he asks. "Surely, you establishment types can't all be bought off so easily." Myron spits these last words in the direction of Kristen Topper, whom he blames in part for his demotion.

"Myron," says Kristen gently, "We are lamenting the demise of Bill's and the undue influence of the very establishment you deplore. You simply must let go of your anger. For the last time, I have nothing to do with seat assignments in the BSO."

"So you say."

"I work for the Pops, not the Orchestra."

"And you're saying that the *Boston* Pops and the *Boston* Symphony Orchestra have *nothing* to do with one another."

"Of course they don't."

"You establishment types are all the same," Myron says, as Kristen, dejected, drops her head. I recall the tarry brush my former student Jill Nordberg used to sully my reputation with Q's colleagues and feel a deep, abiding empathy for Kristen.

Myron's insult silences the table and there follows a prolonged and awkward pause. The only audible sounds are the ticking of the grandfather clock, and the vigorous, impatient tapping of John Deveril's forefinger upon the dining room table. Q's father is visibly impatient and perturbed with the dinner conversation.

It is May Fernthrop, wife of Professor Harvard Fernthrop, former chairperson of the political science department at Berkshire Community College, editor of the definitive collection of essays on the Greek statesman Aeschines, and the unfortunate victim of a peculiar case of dementia, who mercifully breaks the silence.

"Well, I don't know about anything else, but Bill sold the professor his favorite hammer," May says. "It had a real nice peen and a good-looking wooden handle and—what do you call that thing on the other end that you use to dislodge and extract nails?"

"I believe it's called a claw," says Kristen Topper.

"Oh, yes, a claw, that's right. Well, he just loved that old claw. Anytime somebody was pulling down a barn or an old shed, he was johnny-on-the-spot with that claw of his, pulling out any and every nail he could find. Sometimes he would go out into our garage and bang nails halfway down into a two-by-four, just so he could pull them out with that claw. It was just about his favorite thing in the world to do. Isn't that right, Professor?"

Here, Harvard Fernthrop rises from his chair, fixes his tweed Brooks Brothers jacket and bow tie, and clears his throat for what promises to be a disquisition on the merits of the claw hammer sold to him by Bill of Bill's Hardware.

"Many years ago . . ." he says, looks around, and then sits back down. The table waits for more, but that is all.

May pats him on the hand. "He's very good at knowing when people have asked him questions," she says. Everyone around the table nods in understanding.

Q taps me on the hand and whispers to me that we should help Joan in the kitchen. Minutes later, as we are preparing the main course for transport, John Deveril storms in. The lackluster quality of guests at their dinner parties has historically been a sore spot with John Deveril.

"Is this a joke?" he asks. "It's insufferable. I have never seen such a motley crew in my entire life."

"How do you mean, honey?"

"You've got the pissed-off third violinist from the BSO, a guy who plays a horse's ass, and the stage manager for a dance festival. What the fuck does a dance company even need a stage manager for anyway?"

"He takes care of lighting and costumes."

"They wear leotards."

"All the same."

"And what's with this professor? What's wrong with him?"

"His mind isn't what it once was."

"But he knows when people are talking to him?"

"Yes. The start of everything he says is directly responsive to the conversation around him. Ask him a question and he'll begin an answer with his historical perspective. He was a classicist before he was a political scientist. He has many interesting things to say. Trouble is, he never gets around to finishing. It's the darndest thing. The case has been documented in the *AMA Journal.*"

"And who's the vagrant?"

John is referring to an oversized man with an unkempt beard and wild, gnarly hair who is seated at the far end of the table. I have never seen him before at a Deveril family function. He is oddly dressed and his clothes are tattered and threadbare. John is being mean, as he is wont to be, but in his defense, the man does appear to be homeless.

"You mean Tristan Handy?" Joan asks, laughing. "He is the world's fourth-ranking authority on Kierkegaard."

"Who knew they ranked Kierkegaard experts?" I ask no one in particular.

"Does he have a home?" John asks, ignoring me.

"Not in the traditional sense. He walks the Appalachian Trail back and forth. He's on his way south now for the winter," she says, smiling. "Like a beautiful migrating bird."

Joan's irreverence only further stokes John's smouldering fire. "This is because you insist on summering and vacationing here," he growls to Joan. "The Berkshires are not an A-list location, like the Hamptons or the Vineyard."

"It is perfectly nice here," she says.

"If you want to attract the right sort of people to your dinner parties, you need to be in an A-list location."

"I am perfectly happy with the people who attend our dinner parties."

"Well, you may be, but I'm not. When was the last time we had a genuine celebrity in our house?"

"Yo-Yo Ma was here," says Joan. "You know that."

"Yo-Yo Ma was here once, twenty years ago, to pick up his daughter after she knocked on our door when her bicycle got a flat tire. You've been hanging your hat on that for two decades."

"Gene Shalit has been here many times."

"Gene Shalit!" John exclaims derisively. "Last year, for the Fourth of July, Barry Raymer had Tom Brokaw, David Boies, and Don DeLillo to his house for dinner."

Barry Raymer is a friend of John Deveril's from their college days at RPI and a highly successful investment banker. His name comes up frequently in the Deveril household, inevitably invoked by John Deveril, and generally as the ultimate measure of class. It is a well-known article of Deveril lore that following a meeting at a fraternity party, Joan Deveril, then Joan Payson and an undergraduate at SUNY Albany, went on two dates with Barry Raymer before forsaking him for her future husband.

"Barry Raymer," Joan says, still playful. "What is your obsession with Barry Raymer?"

"My obsession is that you should have married him." John spits these words at his wife. "Then you could have dragged him down instead of me."

To this poisonous barb, Joan Deveril does not react. Rather she walks into the dining room to oohs and aahs, carrying her honey-glazed, andouille sausage–stuffed, upside-down turkey. It is clear, at least to me, that John and Joan have lost the capacity to hurt one another, as well as the capacity to enjoy one another. They merely coexist, bound together only by their love of Q, which is substantial, and by inertia, the most substantial force of all.

John Deveril's slings and arrows cannot penetrate his wife, but they make an impression on me. I cannot help but think, yet again, that John Deveril is a mean and hateful man.

The meal begins with a flurry of pass-the-whatevers and who-wants-more and this-is-the-greatest-thing-I-have-ever-tasted-in-my-life. When that initial torrent of energy has subsided and edges taken off of appetites, the conversation returns to politics and the state of the world.

"The real problem is corporations," says Myron Haines. "Big business corporatizes and depersonalizes everything."

There is recognition that Myron, through his slightly more tempered tone and his specific focus on big business rather than the "establishment" in general, is trying to reintegrate himself into the group. The table responds conciliatorily, embracing the thrust of his idea.

"It's true," says Shep Hemsley. "Everything at the Pillow is corporately sponsored."

Herm Alouise vigorously nods his head in agreement. "I just read that a group of attorneys copyrighted the pause," he says, his mouth full of mushroom corn pudding. "Each time someone in a play stops talking, the producers have to pay one hundred dollars to Harold Pinter's estate."

"Terrible," says Shep Hemsley.

"And we're doing Beckett this season."

The guests murmur in horror.

"I don't understand how they do it," says Kristen Topper. "The question I put to the table is, how does somebody, a lawyer, a developer, whoever, just come in and dictate the rules of the game? I mean, what if Bill just says no he won't do it? He simply refuses. What then? Who could make him sell?"

"The government could," says John Deveril. "It's called eminent domain."

"But that can only be used if the government takes land for a public purpose, right?"

"No," John says. "The government can condemn the land, take it, and resell it to whomever it wants, so long as it pays fair value to the person whose land it seizes. This is, sadly, what happened to Q's garden. The government took it by eminent domain and sold it to a developer."

Everyone at the table has heard the story of the demise of

Q's enchanted oasis, and the table grows quiet, except for Herm Alouise, whose chewing continues unabated. This is a near-silent tribute to Q and to John Deveril, who is obviously suffering the pain known to all parents of seeing their child disappointed. Father and daughter share their own knowing glance. I see in Q's eyes the complete faith that she has in John. He smiles warmly, rubs her shoulder, and gently whispers, "I love you, little girl." This gives obvious and substantial comfort to Q.

Slowly, my blood pressure rises.

The question *I* would like to put to the table is why daughters have such unshakable confidence in their fathers. History is my domain, and while it cannot explain this phenomenon, it can offer stunning examples, none more spectacular and perplexing than Lucrezia Borgia, daughter of Rodrigo Borgia, better known as Pope Alexander VI. Rodrigo is widely suspected of having acquired the papacy by simony and, once pope, to have littered the church's offices with nepotism, lived the most secular and salacious of lives, and hosted within the walls of the Vatican wild, extravagant parties where incest and poisonings were de rigueur. He left Lucrezia's upbringing to a cousin, engaging himself in her life only to arrange a series of marriages, each to support his own political ambitions. When the union no longer supported these ambitions, he often had the inconvenient spouse killed, sometimes at one of his infamous affairs, all regardless of his daughter's feelings. Yet upon his death, Lucrezia sobbed uncontrollably and told the town crier, "He was a doting father, and threw the grandest of parties."

Even Nazis have little girls who love their daddies. Heinrich

Himmler's daughter, Gudrun, now married to an Israeli journalist named Burwitz, remembers her father fondly. "Whatever is said about my Papi, whatever is written or shall be written in the future about him—he was my father, the best father I could have and I loved him and still love him."

Myron Haines, however, has a different question. "What is the justification for eminent domain?" he asks. "Where does it even come from?"

Here, Harvard Fernthrop rises from his chair, fixes his tweed jacket and bow tie, and clears his throat. "Many years ago . . ." he says, then surveys the table, and then sits back down. May pats him on his hand.

"Very nice, dear," she says. Professor Fernthrop appears pleased.

"They have it all over the universe," says Herm Alouise, by way of background. "I remember seeing a news report about a man named Dent whose house was condemned by eminent domain to make way for a bypass. He was lying in front of the bulldozers to keep them from demolishing his home when this alien comes and tells him that Earth itself has been condemned and is about to be demolished to make way for a hyperspace bypass."

"That's *The Hitchhiker's Guide to the Galaxy,*" says Shep Hemsley.

"Yes, yes," says Alouise, between bites. "Now that I think about it, it was in fact a theatrical performance and not a news program."

John Deveril appears to have a special disdain for Herm Alouise, and his deathly stare silences the stage star.

This is too bad, because John Deveril has much to learn from *The Hitchhiker's Guide.* In addition to containing a thoughtful lamentation on the uses and abuses of eminent domain, Douglas Adams's novel offers a definitive answer to the meaning of life. This is the product of a supercomputer named Deep Thought, designed by a race of hyperintelligent, pandimensional beings, which after seven and a half million years of calculation, arrives at the conclusion: forty-two. The aliens are moderately satisfied with the answer but feel they have asked the wrong question. To formulate the ideal inquiry, they construct a second supercomputer, best known as the planet Earth. The timing of Earth's destruction is particularly unfortunate, one might say ironic, because the program, which has been running for ten million years, is only five minutes away from finally calculating the question when the bulldozers hit.

Though it was a novel, Adams aficionados and armchair philosophers alike have speculated whether the author may have been onto something. Many have found meaning in the number's binary representation, and its point value in Scrabble, and its significance to Tibetan monks. For his part, Adams dismissed all of this speculation as nonsense. He says he came up with the number while staring out the window into his garden. But the value of the answer cannot be overstated. As with any great exploration, and life is nothing if not this, it is important to have a place to start.

Returning to the subject of eminent domain, Kristen Topper says, "I think it started with the British." She turns to me for my expertise.

"It's true," I say. "William the Conqueror used eminent domain to seize almost all of the land in England. Later, the Magna Carta required that the crown pay compensation for the takings."

Myron Haines shakes his head vigorously. "That's not what I'm really asking. I don't just mean to ask how it came into existence historically. I mean what's the policy justification for it? Why do we still have it?"

Kristen Topper has nothing to say on this issue, and Professor Fernthrop, who is building a sweet potato relief of the Parthenon, does not appear moved to answer this question. One by one, the dinner guests look to their food, making clear they have no insight to offer, and thus it falls to John Deveril to offer a defense.

"It couldn't be more obvious," he says. "It's about progress. The justification is the progress of society."

My blood pressure rises further still. I envision a cartoonish gauge bubbling up to the point of bursting.

Myron Haines puts down his fork. "What does that mean, John? What is progress?"

"It's the improvement of society," John says. "Isn't that obvious?"

"Surely you don't mean to say that clearing the local hardware store to make way for condominiums or destroying an urban garden to put up another skyscraper represents progress?"

"No, of course not," John replies. "But just because the government gets it wrong sometimes doesn't mean that the idea is inherently flawed. You're forgetting all the things that eminent domain helped make possible. Every highway, bridge, and tunnel in this country was built through the use of eminent domain. That surely represents progress."

"I don't know," Myron says. "It doesn't seem so obvious to me that highways and bridges make our lives better."

"Well, that's just idiotic," John says, quieting the table. The resulting silence is not the product of people wanting for what to say. I, for one, would like to give John Deveril a piece of my mind for expressing sympathy for his daughter one moment then defending eminent domain the next. I am sure others have firmly held convictions on the matter. But challenging John Deveril is a tall order in any setting and overwhelmingly daunting at his own dinner table. I imagine each of the other guests is similarly cowed, and for a moment it appears that John Deveril has vanquished them. But then, to the surprise of everyone in the room, the heretofore silent Tristan Handy picks up the mantle and sets in motion the final chain of events that change my life forever.

Chapter TWELVE

Tristan Handy seems out of time. He rises as he begins to address the table and speaks as if he were to the manner born. With one notable exception, he is dressed the part of an English gentleman. He is wearing a gray morning coat, complete with gilt buttons and ascot tie. The notable exception is that his clothes appear not to have been washed in several years. Not unrelatedly, perhaps, his body odor is quite pungent. When he rises, a noxious wave washes over the table, leading everyone to put down their food, with the single and notable exception of Herm, who is apparently impossible to deter.

"I am not so confident in the truth of your proposition, gentle host," Tristan Handy says, as he thoughtfully runs his hand through his coarse whiskers. "With all due respect, Mr. Deveril, I do not think Mr. Haines's point can be dismissed so easily. The notion of progress is fundamentally entwined with a conception of the good life, of what is better and what is worse. But is there any neutral measure by which one can measure the quality of a life? Is there anything we can say about a world with highways and bridges that is truly objective?"

"They let you get places faster," John says. "That's objective."

Tristan smiles. "True enough," he says. "But is getting someplace faster an end in itself? You know, one night about twenty-four years ago this week, I was watching *Alice* on television when I developed a craving for the Chick-fil-A. Now I know what you're thinking, *Alice* wasn't worth the time of day in 1985. Well, I respectfully disagree. I would watch Mr. Vic Tabak and Mr. Marvin Kaplan install a dishwasher if they would allow me. They are two fine comedic actors. But that is not the point of the story. The point of the story is that I wanted the Chick-fil-A and they do not have so much as one such establishment north of the Mason-Dixon line. So I called my travel agent and began making arrangements to fly to Atlanta. Because if you are going to get the Chick-fil-A, you want to go to the original and not to one of these 'franchisees.'" Tristan says this last word with particular derision.

"So there I am on the phone," he continues, "booking my flight on Eastern Airlines, which was far and away the most reliable of the domestic carriers at the time, when I asked myself, why do I not just walk? It is a fine night outside, I said. Once I had the thought, I did not waste another minute. I did not even bother to change my clothes. I hung up the phone with the travel agent and began walking south in my waistcoat and PRO-Keds. Before you know it, fifteen hundred and seventy-three miles later, there I am in the Greenbrier Mall in Atlanta, Georgia, home of the greatest knuckleballer of all-time, Phil Niekro. You can keep Mr. Hoyt Wilhelm, thank you very much."

"Well, I will be darned if that was not the sweetest-tasting sandwich I have ever had in my entire life." He points his finger for emphasis. "If you are ever at the Chick-fil-A you make sure you get yourself the original chicken sandwich with the toasted buttered bun and pickle chips, not one of the new club sandwiches or the chicken strips. You want the original for sure. It is absolutely exquisite."

"Do you have a point?" John asks impatiently.

"My gentle host, my point could not be more obvious. It is so obvious that you will soon wonder how you did not see it yourself. When I look back upon that experience, as wonderful as that sandwich was, it is not what I recall most fondly. What I remember most favorably is the walk itself. I remember the things I thought about, the places I saw, and, most of all, the people I met along the way. Many of these people, your gentle wife included, had me into their homes, and together we built friendships that have lasted until this day."

"And your point?" John asks again.

"My point is merely that oftentimes the journey is the superior to the destination. Relatedly, that nothing can substitute for human interactions. One must acknowledge that the downside of all the freedom we possess is the disintegration of communities. Television, the Internet, easy travel have all changed the ways we connect to one another in society."

"It's true," says Herman Alouise. "Almost no one goes to the theater anymore."

"Receipts at the Pillow have been declining for years," says Shep Hemsley.

"And at the BSO," agrees Myron Haines.

Even Joan Deveril gets in on it. "Who cooks anymore?" she asks. "Everyone goes out to eat every night. It's a dying art."

"Not dying here," says Kristen Topper.

"Thank heavens for that," says Herm Alouise.

"Three cheers for the chef," says Tristan Handy. He lifts his hand to his head, rolls it three times outward in a gesture of deference, and finally sits down.

Cries of "Hear, hear" follow, and the clinking of everyone's glasses, with the single and notable exception of that belonging to John Deveril. "You would feel differently about it if you were trying to get to the hospital," he says. "Say all you want about the decline of theater and dance and cooking, but if you were having a heart attack, you'd be grateful for the cell phone that calls nine-one-one, and for the government seizure of land that created the path for the highway that races help to you, and for the people like me who built the big, fancy hospital where they perform your angioplasty."

"I'll drink to that," says Herm Alouise, who is deep into a pile of Joan's andouille sausage stuffing. Another round of clinking follows, a toast in which everyone participates, with the single and notable exception of Tristan Handy.

When the revelries have subsided, Kristen Topper asks, "Do you disagree with this point, Mr. Handy?"

"I do not necessarily disagree," Handy says. "But I would first note the overwhelming temptation for humans to believe that life is progressing toward some ideal. Take the evolution of the Coca-Cola bottle, for example. Our inclination is to say that it is getting *better* with time, progressing if you will, toward some artistic ideal. But the truth is, they are just different Coca-Cola bottles. The bottles are not functionally different. The aesthetic merit of the bottle is entirely a matter of subjective judgment. The very word 'evolution' contains an artificial notion of progress."

"So you don't believe in evolution," John Deveril says disparagingly.

"I acknowledge that creatures change," Handy says. "I acknowledge that they adapt to environmental stresses. But I reject that these adaptations are aimed at the perfection of a species. I deny the notion of progress contained within evolution. Darwin himself resisted the term, you know. It does not appear until the final page of *The Origin of Species*."

"So humans are no better than monkeys?"

"People like to think differently, but they are no better than the creatures they meet in a menagerie."

"What's a menagerie?" John whispers to Joan, so low that only their immediate neighbors, Q and I, can hear.

Joan leans over. "He means a zoo," she whispers back.

"Why doesn't he just say 'zoo' then?"

"Tristan doesn't use the letter *z*."

"Why the fuck not?"

"He says it is not a thing of consequence," Joan explains quietly. "And he only concerns himself with things of consequence."

"Tell me *this* isn't a fucking menagerie," John says under his breath. "And tell him."

"He doesn't use contractions either," Joan says.

John rolls his eyes then returns to Tristan Handy. "So you're saying man is no better than the animals we find in a zoo."

"Certainly not better in any objective sense. Humans are better adapted to life under certain favorable conditions. They are better than their primate brethren at mathematics and at opening cans. But they do not represent a step toward the perfection of the species. Evolution, if you will, has no direction."

The argument agitates John Deveril. "You can't deny that organisms are becoming larger and more complex with time."

"I do deny it. Some organisms have become more complex. But unicellular eukaryotes have not grown any larger or more complex in eons. And if you start with a one-millimeter-long amoeba, what direction is there to go but up? For example, consider White Castle. Delicious onions, by the way—that is really the essence of its charm. Some people say it is the bun, and it is a fine bun, mind you, but the onions are what make it distinctive. No other fast food gives you freshly cooked onions."

The blood is rising to John Deveril's head. He appears ready to explode.

Handy continues. "Suppose a new corporation took over the management of White Castle. Years later we might go back and find bigger burgers and say this was evidence of progress, but what else could we expect? It is not as if they could get any smaller. There is only one direction in which we could see change."

"Well, you certainly can't deny that brains are getting bigger and smarter. That's surely evidence of progress."

"Again, *some* brains are getting bigger," Handy says. "But first of all, a bigger brain does not necessarily work better. Consider the whale, for example: huge mammalian brain, but not especially smart by our definition. Secondly, brains often get smaller in response to environmental stresses. Some orangutans in Borneo have been developing smaller brains. *Homo floresiensis* is almost certainly an offshoot of humans that *evolved* smaller brains."

"So you say it's all just random?"

"The belief in the progress of evolution, like belief in free will and God, is a construction to help human beings avoid despair." Handy emphasizes this last point with a turkey leg.

"It is part of the way that people make sense of existence," he continues. "But they are all illusions. As George Bernard Shaw said, 'All progress depends on the unreasonable man. The reasonable man adapts himself to the world. The unreasonable man persists in trying to adapt the world to himself.'"

"Outstanding turkey," he says finally, as he licks the bone clean.

Handy's argument unsettles the guests, as does his smell, but on the whole they seem to find what he has to say engaging and thought provoking. I certainly do. His proposition has sent my literary mind racing in a new direction. I am also awed by Handy's finesse of the word "protozoan." John Deveril misses this or, if he caught it, is unimpressed. He is merely angered by Handy's disquisition, angered to the point of aneurysm. He leans over to Joan and once again whispers, "So I am spending Thanksgiving having an argument with a homeless man."

"You should be precise," Joan says. "You're *losing* an argument to a homeless man."

Again, from a historical perspective, John Deveril is wrong to dismiss the contributions of the homeless. Nine Grammy Award recipients, six Oscar winners, and one Nobel Prize honoree were homeless at one point or another in their lives. Some of the greatest of the homeless voluntarily choose their fate, as did Siddhartha Gautama, the Buddha, who believed that to achieve enlightenment one must lead an ascetic life. Some have their fate thrust upon them, as did Jesus, Ella Fitzgerald, and Harry

Houdini. But all, like Charlie Chaplin, who said his days as a pauper informed each and every one of his characters, were forever transformed by the experience.

The Swedish poet Harry Martinson, the aforementioned winner of the Nobel Prize, regarded his time as a tramp as essential to his art. Martinson's magnum opus is *Aniara*, a poem of science fiction, in which a spaceship containing eight thousand colonists, fleeing the toxic planet Earth for a new home on Mars, is forced to take evasive maneuvers to avoid an asteroid. The new trajectory propels the ship past the red planet and out of the solar system, leaving the refugees to drift through space for eternity. The fifty-year-old space epic is, on one level, a call to environmental action far ahead of its time. More deeply, it is about time and meaning. The crew of the ship tries to while away the endless days in every imaginable way—by observing astronomical phenomena, holding orgies, and reliving memories of their own lives—by conducting science experiments, engaging in brutal totalitarianism, and, surprisingly often, simply playing games with coins. Ultimately, though, they cannot face the emptiness outside and inside, and everyone, including their computer, succumbs to despair. The hopelessness overwhelms them when they understand that twenty years of travel has only brought them a few light-days away from Earth.

The poem: "A light-year is a grave."

The poet: "You don't understand time, can't understand time, until you have spent a night without a home on the banks of the Riddarfjärden."

It is very cold on the Riddarfjärden.

After a few moments of rumination, Shep Hemsley says, "You make a series of interesting points, Mr. Handy. Your argument is compelling to say the least."

"Great," John Deveril mutters to his wife in his private voice. "Now the gay guy is in on it too."

"He is not gay," Joan whispers. "And it wouldn't make any difference if he were."

"Are you kidding me? He's the stage manager for a dance company."

"Behave, John."

"He has had six helpings of the cranberry relish."

"You stop. Why does this conversation matter to you so much anyway?" John shoots Joan a dirty look then turns to address the table in full voice. "Can we at least agree that modern life is a happier existence?"

"Here is an improvement of the question," says Tristan Handy. "At least happiness is an objective, measurable criterion."

"Thanks," says John Deveril.

"But I am not certain that modern life is a happier existence." Handy expands on this. "It is surely true that people live longer today, and get places faster," he says, "but this does not necessarily mean they are happier. Are people happier today than they were, say, two, three, or five thousand years ago?"

"I think they are happy to live longer," says Kristen Topper to murmurs of agreement.

"Yes," says Shep Hemsley. "What was the life expectancy in ancient Greece?"

Here, Professor Harvard Fernthrop rises from his chair, straightens his tie, and says, "Many years ago . . ." Then he looks at each of the guests and sits back down. May pats him on the hand.

"Very nice, dear," she says.

I enter the fray for the first time. "I believe the Greeks could expect to live to be approximately thirty-five. A bit longer for Athenians, a bit shorter for Spartans. Prospects obviously varied greatly depending on wealth and class."

John Deveril says, "I thought your expertise was in things that *might* have happened, not things that actually did." This is the first time John has ever insulted me directly in front of Q. I am not sure why my contribution to the conversation bothers him. I expect he is just feeling generally dyspeptic. Q does not appear to notice. She is helping Professor Fernthrop with the construction of the east side metopes, depicting the mythical battle between the Olympian gods and the giants.

Herm Alouise attempts to make peace by moving ahead with the conversation. "Well, surely it's a lot better to live to seventy-five, as we do on average, than to thirty-five."

"I wonder about that," Handy says.

"Great," says John contemptuously. He is no longer making any effort to conceal his impatience with the dinner guests, and with Handy in particular. "Now I suppose you're going to argue that living longer isn't a good thing."

"I do not deny it can be a good thing," Handy says calmly. "I just question whether it is an absolute good. Consider the converse for a moment. We know that longer life is theoretically possible. Yet we do not sit around lamenting that we will not live to be one hundred or one hundred and fifty. Besides, what would be all that different about our existences if we lived longer? We would still need to go to school and choose careers and go to work. We would still wait on lines at the cheese counter and sit in traffic. And death would remain a part of our lives. Friends and family would die. We would die. Only the timing of things would change."

May Fernthrop says, "People tend to forget the downside of living longer. Long life can be a blessing, but it can also be a curse. It depends entirely on one's quality of life, and there are no guarantees with respect to that." May pats her husband on the hand. His structure is really coming along; the yams are a surprisingly functional substrate.

"Very nice, dear," May says.

"It's true," I say. "There's an episode of *The Twilight Zone* where a guy wishes for immortality, but he forgets to ask for youth, so he just keeps getting older and more infirm, but he never dies. For him, it's a curse, not a blessing."

John Deveril shoots me another dirty look. Needless to say, it is particularly unacceptable for me to substantively enter the debate on any side other than his, but I am emboldened by his earlier slight.

"Are there any universal goods, Mr. Handy?" Herm Alouise asks, deferentially.

"How shall we define the term 'universal'?" Handy asks in reply. Thinking aloud, he says, "Suppose we confine ourselves to things that people have experienced life both with and without. If it is unanimously agreed that life is better with the object or condition than without, then we shall call this a 'universal' good. Agreed?"

"Agreed," says Herm.

"Well, then," says Handy, "I put it to the table: by this definition, are there any universal goods?"

Each of the guests thinks for a moment, with the exception of John Deveril, who continues to treat the conversation with utter disdain.

"Shoes," says Kristen Topper. "Comfortable shoes are a universal good."

Murmurs of agreement.

"Well done," says Handy. "I concur. What else?"

"Clean water," says May Fernthrop.

"Touché."

"The Internet," says Shep Hemsley.

"Absolutely!" Handy says. "What could be more valuable than information?"

John Deveril looks up from his dinner and says, "You live in the woods, right?" No one pays him attention, and the listing of items of undebatable virtue resumes.

"Liquid gel pens," says Herman Alouise.

"Teflon," says Joan Deveril.

"Luggage with wheels," I say.

"Yes!" says Tristan Handy. "The question is, what took so long? Society had luggage and wheels for centuries. Why didn't anyone think to put them together sooner?"

"Right! I have always wondered the same thing," I say enthusiastically, whereupon a spirited discussion ensues about the possible causes of the conspicuous delay in the development of luggage with wheels.

"Perhaps fabric needed to evolve."

"Could be a patent problem."

"Could this be patented?"

"Oh yes, you can patent anything."

"I think wheels and luggage are in the common domain."

"But not the combination."

"Ah. Could you pass the cranberries?"

"You know what I think is a universal good?" John Deveril

asks rhetorically, deigning to look up once again from his meal. "Quiet," he says. "I think quiet is an absolute good."

The table's attention returns to the meal.

Myron Haines finally breaks the silence. "You can have your Teflon pans and your fancy suitcases," he says, "but I would rather live in the seventeenth century."

"You have to be kidding me," says John Deveril.

"I'm not sure there is such a thing as an absolute good," Myron says, "but the things you all have listed certainly are not examples, if one indeed exists. None of you have acknowledged Handy's earlier point. The mere existence of convenience items such as luggage with wheels breeds consumerism. And you are ignoring completely the fragmentation of society resulting from all the technological changes. Television and online chat rooms destroy community. I would rather live for forty years in a real community where people socialize and communicate than for seventy years in a fragmented, anomic society."

"For whatever it's worth, I'll take life in the twenty-first century any day of the week," Kristen Topper says.

"That's because you're a corporate shill," says Myron, prompting Kristen to frown.

"Well, I'm no corporate shill," Shep Hemsley says. "I am just a humble stage manager. But I agree with Kristen. Horse-driven carriages are romantic and all, but people forget about the poop. I have read that one could smell nineteenth-century London from twenty miles away."

Under his breath, John Deveril spits, "I could smell the homeless guy from twenty miles away."

"I'm with Shep," says Herm Alouise. "To my mind medical advances end the argument. I don't know where *I'd* be without Beano."

"I would miss my soaps greatly," says May Fernthrop.

The guests nod in agreement.

Joan Deveril asks, "What about you, Mr. Handy?"

Handy runs his hand through his beard. "Thank you, gentle hostess, for asking this. This interrogative makes for the most stimulating dinner conversation, and I am very happy for it," he says, "but I am not sure the question can be answered objectively by the socially situated self."

"Helpful," John mutters.

"The belief in the directionality of life is fundamental to human psychology. We need to believe things are progressing toward some idealised vision of the good life." He pauses. "The truth is, I do not think the conditions of society make any difference to one's experience of life. By nature, man will never be perfectly satisfied. The cause of his dissatisfaction is of no moment. Medicine will never be a panacea. There will always be illness. There will always be death and therefore disappointment. This is the human condition. Progress is an illusion. Without the belief that life will someday be better, people would despair. It is a necessary optimism but, of course, ultimately a false one."

This is a bit of a downer and John Deveril will hear none of it. He reenters the conversation with the force of a tornado. "This is moronic!" he cries. "Are you all seriously listening to this nonsense?" He tries to calm himself and continues, "Life isn't perfect, but it's absurd to say there's no difference between living today and living three thousand or five hundred years ago. Furthermore, you used the letter *z*!"

"I most certainly did not," says Handy.

"In the word 'idealize.'"

"I employed the British spelling."

This only further enrages John. "However you spell it, the general point is still idiotic. Sure, some people with eclectic preferences would rather live in Elizabethan England. But for every such person, a thousand would choose to be born in twenty-first-century America."

This generates a series of murmurs at the table, as John Deveril's proposition is debated in sidebars. This all ends when Q speaks for the first time that evening.

"My father is right," she says conclusively. Everyone pays close attention as she speaks. This is in part because she has held her opinion back for so long and in part because she is the most recent victim of the very phenomenon that is being debated.

"I am a gardener," she says. "I romanticize the simpler days as much as anyone. Some aspects of modern society are deplorable. But no one can deny that many of the things we have spoken of this evening are improvements of the human condition. On the whole, life today is better than it has ever been."

Again, I am mesmerized by Q's support for her father. It is instinctual and complete and utterly mysterious. How can one explain this? This remains the question I would like to put to the table. But for this meal, at least, the debate is ended.

Tristan Handy responds first. "Well," he says, "certainly no one can deny that this is the finest meal in the history of Thanksgiving."

Here, Harvard Fernthrop rises from his chair, adjusts his jacket and bow tie, and says, "Many years ago . . ." He nods graciously then returns to putting the finishing touches on the pediments.

Cries of "Well said, well said" and "Couldn't have put it better myself."

May pats Professor Fernthrop on his hand and says, "Very nice, dear." The professor appears pleased, and the guests return to their dinner in peace.

Years later, when I obsess about this and everything else, I will look back on this moment and wonder what would have happened if John Deveril had left things alone. Handy's is a gracious concession. John Deveril has been rude and condescending, but Handy never responds in kind. It is yet another sign of his brilliance that he instead turns the acrimonious debate to the one subject about which there can be no dispute: Joan Deveril's unmatched hospitality.

If the goodwill in the room had been allowed to linger, I am not sure what would have happened. I had no doubt about what needed to be done, but it was repugnant to me and I was eager for any excuse not to do it. I am sure I could not have spoiled such a gentle moment. I would never have done it in the evening, and the day after that would have been that much harder. If another day had passed, and another still, the momentum behind my relationship with Q would have been that much greater, and inertia, as we all know, can be a powerful force. Perhaps in the end I would have left anyway, but perhaps not.

I am honest enough to admit that I do not know for sure. It is a peculiar aspect of male arrogance to proclaim what he would

have done if things were different or what he would do if presented with such and such a situation. Everyone believes he will
act bravely when life presents him with his greatest test, but in
the end there are few heroes. In my end, when I acted, it was not
with noble motivation or grave dispassion. What I did may have
been the correct thing to do—I do not know—but I know it was
done in a fit of rage.

The spark, of course, is John. Q's support for his position em-
boldens her father. It is clear to everyone at the table that the
conversation has been exhausted. But he renews the argument.
When he does so, there is a palpable sense of ennui, but he is
undeterred. He is John Deveril.

"My beautiful daughter has summarized the essence of the issue," he says. "Progress is a complicated concept. We are tempted
to expect a straight line between where we are and where we
want to be. Life does not work that way. Sometimes we take steps
forward, and sometimes we take steps backward. But even when
we take that occasional step backward, and even when our most
beloved are victimized by these retreats, as my beloved daughter
has been, we must not lose sight of our overall direction. Like Q,
I believe that this overall direction of change has been positive."

His comments may be reasonable. Again, I do not know. I
think few people, if any, actually hear what he says. The table is
overwhelmed by fatigue with the conversation and disbelief that
John has chosen to continue it. John Deveril will win this argument by dint of his relentlessness. It is clear that no one but he
will have the last word on this. Even the apparently indefatigable
Tristan Handy has thrown in the towel. He is absently picking
at some of Joan's Vidalia onion casserole. The other guests may
be in agreement, or tired of the insufferable, bombastic display,

or some combination of the two. Whatever the case, no one is speaking.

It hits me then. This is how it is with bullies. They force themselves upon the world and shape it to suit their needs. Truth, civility, and honor are all inconveniences they need not suffer. They are not required to be honest with their daughters or gentle to their wives or to express so much as a single word of appreciation for a meal of unimaginable delight. No one holds them accountable. The universe bends to their will. Here and now, as John Deveril drones on, I draw the line in the sand.

No more.

"We need to assess the agents of social change in a nuanced manner," John continues. "We need to identify the forces that make life undeniably better for everyone because such forces do exist, and if we paint society with too broad a brush, then we will stifle their good works. Even in the most hateful, oppressive regimes, there are men of goodwill whose work needs to be identified and nurtured. This is why it is a mistake to blanketly rail against the corporatization of America. We need to distinguish between responsible business and irresponsible business, between companies like my own, which build in a socially responsible manner . . ."

I say it without even thinking: " . . . and those that destroy."

"Yes," John says, "and those that destroy."

"Like the people who thoughtlessly razed Q's beloved garden."

"Yes," he says, chanting along in unison. "Like the people who thoughtlessly razed beloved Q's garden."

"Like the hateful Deliver Corporation."

"Like the hateful Deliver Corporation . . ." he repeats mindlessly.

"I didn't realize you knew their name."

John Deveril reels, as if struck by a bullet, but he does not need me to point out his mistake. He realizes his error before he has finished his sentence. Q realizes it immediately too. With a start, she looks up from her hardly touched dinner and stares at her father. After I discovered the identity of the Deliver Corporation, I shared the information with Q before the doomed protest. She in turn shared the identity of the villain solely with Ethel Lipschutz. Unless John has been hanging around with Ethel Lipschutz, which seems unlikely to say the least, there remains only one way John Deveril could know this name. It is his company, as I-60 told me yesterday in the forest on the banks of the Hudson. It is pointless for John to deny it.

"I'm sorry," he mumbles.

Q first looks at her father with hatred and betrayal and disgust in her eyes. Then she looks at me. This look is, if possible, worse than the first. In her eyes, my betrayal is more fundamental. I have taken from her the one thing in which she believed completely, and accomplished nothing in so doing. The garden is gone. What was the point of this?

I understand in that moment that she is lost to me forever.

Around the table, no one understands exactly what is going on. They know only that it is bad. Q has left the table. John Deveril's head is hanging. Joan is casting an unflinching stare of death at her husband. It is eerily quiet. When Tristan Handy speaks, even I am grateful for something, anything, to break the silence.

"As it will be in the future, it was at the birth of Man," he says quietly. "There are only four things certain since Social Progress began. That the Dog returns to his Vomit and the Sow returns to her Mire. And the burnt Fool's bandaged finger goes wabbling back to the Fire."

I look at him quizzically.

"Kipling," he says.

"But that's only three things," I say quietly and with total resignation.

Book Two

BETTER

Chapter **THIRTEEN**

The Monday following the fateful Thanksgiving dinner, I move out of our place on Mercer Street. Q does not demand this, but I understand it is expected, and hastily arrange a sublet near Columbia from a colleague on sabbatical. I take only the bare essentials with me. Thinking about any further details is too painful.

This grief is real, not hypothetical. I spend one evening after another staring at the ceiling of my studio on Morningside Drive. Sometimes I rouse myself from bed and take long, aimless walks in the cold. Sometimes I pen letters to Q, tomes of confession or explanation, only to discard them in the morning. Sometimes I write angry missives to I-60, but in the morning discard these too as obviously futile. Nothing helps. I revisit the sites of our dates: the Angelika; the boathouse in Central Park; the garden, now a construction site; the communist miniature golf course. No sight is so pitiful as a miniature golf course in winter.

Many times, I open my cell phone to call Q; once I even press the speed dial key, then catch myself and snap the phone shut after the first ring. I worry that she will check her log and call back. What would I say? The only solution is to delete the number, which I do, as if that would purge it, or her, from my memory. On another day, I walk all the way to the Lower East Side, and sit in a teahouse across the street from our old apartment. Q does not come or go, which is for the best. The temptation to run to her would be too much for me to resist. On my long walk home, I resolve to pull myself together, though I have no idea how.

In time inertia draws me back into the old routine. I am back in the neighborhood I know, teaching on Thursdays and jogging the old routes. I don't feel normal, but slowly, inexorably, my life inches its way to normal. For me, normal means research and writing. Soon, almost in spite of myself, I am immersed in a new book. I think, perhaps, it may do me some good to lose myself in another person's life for a while.

The idea is hatched during a sensibly priced dinner at Levy's Delicatessen with my agent, Janet Snarklee. Over knishes and cream sodas, I describe the various ideas germinating in my brain. My dream is to write a history of the sand wedge. I explain that there is a huge, untapped market for golf books, and that the history of the sand wedge, with its bulging sole and prominent flange, is a vehicle for discussing twentieth-century technological innovation and politics, as Eisenhower is known to have been greatly frustrated with his bunker play. Said frustration is recognized to have informed his cold war strategy, particularly the policy of brinksmanship, conceived after Khrushchev holed out from a sand trap on his very first time playing golf, at a course the Soviet premier had built specifically for Eisenhower's planned visit to Moscow in 1960.

"It will be to golf what *Seabiscuit* was to horse racing," I explain, "if *Seabiscuit* had been about the development of the bridle worn by the horse rather than about the horse itself."

"Biographies of inanimate objects are so passé," she says.

"What about the development of the utility wood? They quite helped Bill Clinton's game."

"I don't think so," Janet says. "Golf is on the wane."

I mention the second idea, which came to me during the ruinous Thanksgiving dinner, as a throwaway. It's another what-if yarn, taking as its hypothetical dramatic starting point the success of young Sigmund Freud, during his formative days as a medical student, with his research on the life history of the eel.

Janet leaps at this. "That's what you should be writing!" she exclaims, banging her fist on the table. "Why didn't you mention that idea first?"

"I was focused on the sand wedge. Besides, I didn't want to pigeonhole myself."

"Pish. Make yourself famous. Then you can branch out. After the success of *Time's Broken Arrow*, you are hereafter the counterhistorical novel guy."

"It sold 1,550 copies."

"You're on your way to becoming a bestseller," she says. "Off you go on Freud." She picks up the tab, which makes a real impression on me. It has been a long time since someone treated me to a meal.

I begin work the next day. At the start I am apprehensive, but Snarklee's enthusiasm buoys me and, after a few weeks of investigation I begin to believe there is a story to be told. The project builds momentum. Soon I am heavily immersed in the background research on Freud, intellectually absorbed, and past the point of no return. I even embrace the direction of my career. I envision the Freud novel as the first book in an antifactual quintology focused on late-nineteenth- and early-twentieth-century Eurasia.

The second book of the series is a spicy tale in which a young Otto von Bismarck emigrates to England to pursue, successfully, the hand in marriage of the niece of the Duke of Cleveland. He goes on to become a Byron scholar and German history is never the same. In the third, Robespierre takes up transcendental meditation, which does wonders for his disposition. In the fourth, Gertrude Stein becomes president of Vichy France after Pétain dies from a bad schnitzel. In the finale, Mohandas Gandhi becomes the most successful cricketer of his generation. All are premised on reality, and in my grand vision, my brand of historical fiction, grounded on solid research, becomes as recognizable as Vonnegut's satire or Pynchon's impenetrable postmodern prose.

Freud was obsessed with eels. Few people know this. Everyone knows about the beauty of his mother, twenty years the junior of his father. Many know of his addiction to cocaine, his reluctant identification with Judaism, and his latent homosexual relationship with Wilhelm Fleiss. Almost no one knows about the eels.

The fixation began in early 1876 when Professor Carl Claus seconded Freud to the Austrian zoological research station in Trieste to identify the testes of the eel, one of the great enigmas of science at the time. The mystery of the gonads traced all the way back to Aristotle, who performed the first known research on eels, and concluded that they were earthworms that grew from the guts of wet soil. This didn't make very much sense, but no one could prove Aristotle wrong, so it became the default theory, not unlike how people came to believe in stress as the cause of the ulcer or the existence of God.

Setting Aristotle straight became nothing less than young Freud's purpose in life. It was both his intellectual cause and, he believed, the route to academic immortality. Freud worked tirelessly. During his time in Trieste, Freud dissected countless eels in search of the male sex organ. In connection with this, he produced more than four hundred sketches, each drawn in pencil, which remain to this day among the most exquisite samples of the microscopist's method.

Sigmund Freud saw meaning in everything, so if he had himself on the couch, he undoubtedly would have found symbolic significance in the fervor he brought to his study of eels. This is not to be understated. Because of their mysterious origins and enigmatic migratory patterns, anti-Semites often insidiously connected eels and Jews and Gypsies. There is, further, the matter of their elongated, protuberant construction. But the eels also had substantial literal influence on the course of Freud's career. For Freud was trapped in the middle of the greatest scientific controversy of his day.

On one side of this debate was Simon Syrski, former director of the Museum for Natural History in Trieste, who hypothesized that flat petal-like lobes in the eel intestine were in fact the male sex organ. He had failed only to demonstrate that these structures produced sperm. On the other side was Freud's mentor,

Carl Claus. Claus, an avowed Darwinist who had studied hermaphroditism in animals, operated from a presumption of the
eel's bisexuality, which would have been consistent with Darwin's
idea that men "descended" from hermaphroditic or androgynous
origins.

Freud believed the weight of the evidence supported Syrski.
Indeed, his research came tantalizingly close to accurately describing the male eel's sex organ. His histological analysis
showed the cells of the lobes to be distinct from eel ovaries, and
the shape and arrangement of these organs suggested the possibility of forming spermatozoa. Yet when Freud published his
results he never abandoned the paradigm of hermaphroditism.
He hemmed and hawed and hedged throughout the paper, and
in the end said, "the opinion cannot be rejected that the lobed
organ is a modification of the ovary." The paper, "Observations
on the Configuration and Finer Structure of the Lobed Organs
in Eels Described as Testes," published in 1877 in the *Proceedings
of the Imperial Academy of Sciences,* was at that time the definitive
study of eel testicles, universally praised in the academy for its
thoroughness and the quality of its pencil sketches, flawed only
for its failure to shed any light on the whereabouts of the gonads.

Its resounding thud in the scientific community hit Freud
hard. He had placed all of his eggs (pardon) in the eel-testes basket. When the piece failed to earn him the fame he had hoped for
and expected, the dejected Freud decided to change the course of
his studies and career. He moved away from Claus and cast his
lot with physiologist Ernst Wilhelm von Brücke, whose concept
of psychodynamics, the idea that all living organisms are energy
systems, became the intellectual cornerstone of psychoanalysis.

The tantalizing question is why Freud lacked the courage to

authoritatively identify the testes. Why did he hold back? What essential quality kept Freud from being what he most wanted to be? Because one can only imagine what might have happened if he had the courage to declare the gonad found, Syrski vindicated, and Aristotle refuted. It seems beyond peradventure that it would have been the launching point for a very different career. He would have been the discoverer of the eel testicle, with all of the fame and possibility attendant to that.

Freud himself offers a useful starting point for attempting to solve this puzzle. He engaged in extensive self-analysis, beginning in the mid-1890s during his forties and continuing for at least ten years and, arguably, until his death. During the early part of this process, Freud recognized for the first time his animosity for his father, Jakob, and his sexual feelings for his mother, the fetching Amalia. The exploration informed *The Interpretation of Dreams*, published in 1899, and *The Psychopathology of Everyday Life*, published two years later.

During the most intense phases of this process, Freud lamented that his analyst said very little, leaving him to do all the talking, and that he did not know where it was all going. He also complained about the bills, which were very high, though he made a point of always paying them promptly.

My sole remaining reservation about the project is whether it is appropriate for my academic career. Though the history department at City University is famously left-leaning and broad-minded, I have the nagging sense that I should be writing about things that actually happened. I seek an audience with Hank Snjdon, the chairperson of our department. Hank is the author of the definitive biography of P. G. T. Beauregard, great-great-great-great-great grandson of Lucrezia Borgia, and the Confederate brigadier general who led the South to victory at the first battle of Bull Run.

The Beauregard biography is, possibly, the least interesting book I have ever read. The inclination is to fault the author, but it seems to me the problem is the subject: Beauregard just isn't compelling. By all accounts, his victory at Bull Run was blind luck. He made no major tactical decisions, and at a critical point in the battle retreated from a key position when he mistook his reinforcements for fresh Union troops. Following his ascension to general, Beauregard developed a Napoleonic penchant for grand strategies with no regard for such trifling matters as logistics, intelligence, and troop strength. After the war, he went into the railroad business. It's not enough to fill a book, and in the end a full chapter is devoted to Beauregard's taste for cheese, which he fully indulged antebellum. He was particularly fond of Wensleydale.

To his credit, Snjdon freely admits the book is a dud. He particularly laments the cheese chapter but says he had no choice: he needed material. He had spent seven years researching Beauregard's life, and with his tenure riding on the manuscript, he could not very well declare his research bankrupt and start over. So he finished the book and published it, and it served its purpose. He got tenure and is now chairperson of the department. But because of the book's inadequacies, Snjdon never achieves the status he desires in the community of Civil War scholars. He says the great regret of his life is that he did not focus on Winfred

Scott. It haunts him, he says, and he spends many a night lying in bed thinking about what could have been.

I like Hank. It is a tense period in my department, and he is not having an easy time of it. We are in the middle of a fierce debate over whether our core offering, the department's contribution to the school's general education program, should be in world history or global history. It may not sound like an issue of great moment, but this is academia, and the dispute has created a massive schism. One half the department won't speak with the other half.

Matters come to a head when two professors nearly come to blows in the men's room. Their failure to strike one another is not for lack of effort. Hef Angkot, the octogenarian Peloponnesianist and ardent globalist, throws a hard right in the direction of Stig Neuborne, the nonagenarian Visigoth scholar and fervent worldist, or antiglobalist, the appropriate characterization turning on one's sympathies. Fortunately, Professor Angkot's bursitis impedes his blow. It misses its mark and strikes, instead of Stig Neuborne's chin, the Purell dispenser mounted on the wall, diffusing a stream of sanitizing foam. The professors emerge from the bathroom unscathed, arguably cleaner than before the altercation, although Neuborne alleges that he is allergic to Purell and that some has gotten in his eye. Neuborne is ceremoniously taken to the hospital, where he is treated for excessive sterilization and offered a gauze eye patch, which he wears for the next two months, until it is so badly frayed that it is no longer opaque or recognizable as gauze. The incident further heightens the already substantial tensions within the department.

It's a bad situation, but for once I am on the right side of it, which is neither. This is primarily because I do not understand the debate. I don't admit this, of course. My public position is that I support Hank Snjdon and his efforts to mediate a compromise. Hank is grateful for my backing, so when I go to see him to talk about my own situation, I am not surprised that he is reciprocally supportive.

"I'm thinking of doing a book on Freud," I say.

"Great," he says.

"My five-year review is coming up. I'm worried about tenure."

"Why? Everyone likes Freud."

"It's another novel. It's about what would have happened if he had published his discovery of eel testes and made an impression in the scientific community."

"Freud studied eel testes? Really?"

"Really."

Hank shakes his head. "You can't just make this stuff up. What would Freud have to say about that?" We both laugh.

"Seriously, though," I say when the guffaws die down. "I think it's a valid counterhistorical question. I believe that if Freud had experienced success with his eel research he would have become a biologist. Ultimately, I believe he would have fundamentally changed the popular understanding of evolution."

"That's interesting. Why would Freud have reached a different conclusion than anyone else?"

"He was utterly nonjudgmental," I say. "I think he was uniquely suited to understand Charles Darwin's true meaning."

"Which was?"

"That evolution has no purpose."

Hank chewed on this for a while, though it might also have been a Mentos. He really liked Mentos mints. When the cinnamon ones went off the market, he was sad for weeks.

"I'm confused about one thing," Hank says after a while. "If Freud found the eel testes, as you say, why didn't he publish the discovery?"

"I don't know. I need to figure that out. Or at least to come up with a plausible revision of his life that would have emboldened him to publish his true results. What do you think of the idea otherwise?"

"I think it is fine."

"But this will be my second novel, and this is a history department."

Hank thinks for a moment.

"What you are writing could have been true, right?"

"Yes," I say. "The kernel is true though the rest of it isn't."

"I think the distinction between 'is' and 'might have been' is generally overblown." So, with Hank Snjdon's blessing, it is full steam ahead. I begin writing the next day.

The creative process is a mystery to me. I want to understand how it works, like the physics of the golf swing. I would settle for feeling the critical moment when the germ of an idea is formed, but I rarely experience even this. Sometimes I have ideas while I am running. Sometimes I have ideas while I am eating cereal. I conceived of the final scene of *Time's Broken Arrow*—in which William Henry Harrison tenderly drapes an overcoat over the shoulders of his friend and successor, Daniel Webster, midway through Webster's own inaugural address—following a coma-like nap during the second act of *Don Giovanni*. Generally, I have no idea when the ideas will come, or how. It is all a bit magical.

I once heard James Taylor say in an interview that he does

not write songs, that he is simply the first to hear them. This is how I feel about it. Somehow, five hours after I sit down to work, words have appeared on the page, grossly imperfect to be sure, but something where there was nothing. I view my role in this miracle of creation as showing up at my desk, sitting upright at my computer, and staying out of the way of my brain. All I ask in return is that I have something to show for my efforts at the end of the day, that there be progress.

My routine is to get up early, eat a small breakfast, and write from seven o'clock until noon. I find that after lunch I am mostly useless, so I try to get as much done in the morning as I possibly can. In the afternoons I answer emails, edit what I have written in the morning, and, on Thursdays, teach my freshman seminar on cultural history. Then I take a run, have dinner, and get to bed early so I can do it all again the next day. I repeat this seven days a week.

It is a lonely process. Writing is occasionally exciting; epiphanies sometimes occur. But for the most part, it is a monotonous, plodding endeavor. And this is a particularly desolate time. The excitement of *Time's Broken Arrow* has passed. Leonard Lopate is not calling. No one stops me on the street to ask for autographs.

And, of course, Q is gone.

Every writer (except, notably, Pynchon) lives for the moment when he is uncloistered, unbound from the invisible tether to his computer, and allowed to favor the world with his razor wit and profound insight into the meaning of life. I hope that I will enjoy such a moment again, but the reality has set in that this glory is far off in the distance. As a runner, I view writing a book as a marathon. If that metaphor is apt, I am in mile five. How much remains is daunting.

Furthermore, the selection of Freud as a subject means the book serves as a near-constant reminder of the choices I have made in my own life. Freud was fiercely lonely during his time in Trieste. He spent long hours laboring in front of the microscope and detailing his elegant pencil sketches. With no friends to comfort him, he did little socializing. In the evenings, after concluding work at the laboratory, he walked home, ate a small dinner, and wrote letters to Gisela Fluss, his first romantic interest. It is all too easy for me to channel Freud's loneliness. In fact it takes nothing.

But, maddeningly, Hank Snjdon's question remains unanswered. Six months into the project, I still cannot understand how a man who would soon become the most provocative mind of his generation would have felt impelled to do whatever necessary to advance his career, including tailoring the results of his research to support the claims of his adviser and benefactor. If he were capable of this, what could possibly have emboldened him to be a different person?

James Taylor says that if he weren't a musician, he'd be a fish farmer. But really, he says, he'd be lost.

The answer to the Freud puzzle comes to me at the most unlikely time. After half a year of procrastination, I arrange to collect my few remaining things from Q and thus close the matter once and for all. We set it up so that she will not be there. I go with a heavy heart and trepidation, but with her characteristic grace, Q makes it easy. She leaves a key for me with the doorman, leaves my things neatly folded and arranged in a pile, and even leaves me a small gift.

Q makes it as painless as it possibly can be, but standing in that apartment, where Q and I shared peanut brittle while watching *Casablanca*, and completed the Sunday crossword puzzle with jam-covered toothpicks, and made snow angels in a pile of sugar on the hardwood floor, and first made love, I am overwhelmed with emotion and a sense of possibility. In this moment I want to throw away the counterhistorical novels of Freud the evolutionist and Gandhi the cricketer and even the true history of the sand wedge. Instead I want to write poetry, soaring verse worthy of Byron and Yeats, the sort that makes women swoon and quiets the most restless soul. I want to wait for Q to return home, sweep her off her feet, fly to Buenos Aires, dance the tango until midnight, then pitch a tent on Mar del Plata and live on plantains and rum, forget about John Deveril and his skyscrapers, and not return until Q and I are good and old.

Of course this cannot happen. But it offers the answer to what was missing in Freud's life: love. For Freud certainly does not love Fluss. She gives him little comfort. He gives her the nickname of a reptile. And while he later loves Martha Bernays, the svelte and pale daughter of a merchant who becomes his wife, even the most insensitive clod can see that it is the love of a boy, not a man. During their five-year engagement, he was overridden by jealousy, which extended to Bernays's mother and brother. By all accounts Freud and Bernays did not have conjugal relations prior to their nuptials. And the marriage, though successful in its longevity (they had been married more than fifty years when Freud died in

1939) and its productivity (the Freuds had five children, including one psychoanalyst of independent renown), did not ever produce epic passion. The couple went long periods without sex, and late in life, according to Carl Jung, Freud took up with Martha's sister Minna, who looked more or less like Martha. The ultimate what-if, the impetus that would have made him boldly change the course of his own life, is what if Freud had fallen madly and truly head over heels in love.

I take Q's gift and close the door behind me, careful to leave things as they were before, as if this is possible. I return home with my memories and a pear and Freud in love in Trieste. I have a direction, but I am not satisfied and, later, not surprised when I find in my mailbox another note from myself. It says:

NOBU
Thursday
6:00

G etting a table at Jean-Georges is challenging. Getting a table at Nobu on a Friday night is nearly impossible. Once more, I call on the services of my great friend Ard Koffman, and again he delivers. I am even spared interacting with a reservationist.

I arrive at the restaurant on time. My older self is seated already, at a corner table near the waterfall, just behind one of the indoor bamboo trees. This version of me is younger than the last one. He looks to be in his mid-fifties. The years have been easier on him than they were on I-60. I-60 had canals under his sad eyes and flaky skin. He moved stiffly, as if grief burdened his every movement; even the simple extension of an arm seemed to be a cause of pain. This me is more supple. He is plumper and appears well oiled. When he rises to greet me, the movement of his arm is lithe and easy. His face is unwrinkled, almost preternaturally so, and I wonder for a moment, with horror, whether I have had some work. I take his hand, shake, and sit down, with substantial trepidation.

"Hey," says the old me.

"Hey," I repeat gingerly. The word isn't ordinarily part of my lexicon.

"I suppose you're wondering what I'm doing here."

"The thought occurred to me," I say. "How old are you?"

"Fifty-five," he says. "How much time has passed from your perspective since you were last visited?"

"Six months," I say.

I-55 shakes his head. "I'll never forget that day in Rhinebeck," he says wistfully.

"Me neither."

"Do you wish you had made a different decision?"

"Every day, but what choice did I really have? What about you?"

I-55 thinks for a moment then shakes his head. "No, I don't think I had any choice either."

"So you have no regrets?"

"I wouldn't say that exactly."

The waiter arrives. I order the sushi dinner and a Diet Coke with lemon. I-55 orders the Kumamoto oysters with Maui onion salsa, the sashimi tacos, a bottle of hot sake, a Diet Coke with lime, and finally, two skewers of squid kushiyaki.

"Two drinks?"

"I'm thirsty."

"Two appetizers?"

"What could be more appealing than an appetizer?" I-55 asks

rhetorically. "It's inherent in the name. Two appetizers means that you enjoy the dinner twice as much. Besides," he says, "I haven't eaten here in ages. If I have learned one thing over the years, it is to live life for the moment. I plan on enjoying this meal to the fullest."

"I thought time travel was bad for the appetite."

"Whoever told you that?"

"You did."

"Surely you have me mistaken for someone else."

"Impossible. You told me that during our dinner at Jean-Georges. Don't you remember?"

I-55 guffaws—a hearty laugh that I do not recognize as my own. It emanates from deep in his belly, which he holds with both his hands as he rollicks in his chair. The laugh belongs to a man twice his size and possesses an intangible but real pretension—that only he can appreciate the full hilarity of what you, the ignoramus, have said. It belongs to a pompous man whom I do not recognize as an extension of myself. His snorting laugh goes on for a painfully long time; he even sweats a little bit from the effort and wipes his brow with the linen napkin. He appears done, mercifully, but then resumes laughing, having caught a second wind. This denouement is contrived and painful. He's forcing it.

Finally he is done.

"I don't get it," I say.

"It isn't your fault." I-55 dabs at his face one more time. "You're programmed to think about time sequentially."

"And this is problematic?"

"I would say limiting."

"How so?"

"I have no relationship to the man who encouraged you to

leave Q, I-60 as you called him then. He is an utter stranger to me."

"How can this be? You are practically the same age as he was."

This is clearly the wrong thing to say. I-55 begins pawing at his face and examining himself in the wall mirror.

"Do you really think I look sixty? I'm only fifty-five, you know. I told you this, didn't I? Is it my skin? Is it my eyes? It's my eyes, isn't it?"

"No," I say, reassuringly. "You look wonderful. In fact, I was thinking to myself that I hope I look as good as you do when I am your age."

This is the right thing to say; I-55 decompresses.

"Thank you," he says.

"All I meant is that you're both from the future, so I presumed the two of you had something in common."

I-55 reassumes his bombastic demeanor. "This is the fallacy of post hoc ergo propter hoc."

"In English."

"Just because something happens after something else, doesn't mean it was caused by the other thing. You need to stop thinking sequentially. Do you have a pen?"

I offer him my gel tip.

"You see, when I-60 came back to see you, he had already lived a lifetime based on the decision to marry Q and have the child he told you about. After he visited you, he sent you down a different path than you otherwise would have gone down."

"Okay."

"Let me try it a different way. I-60, you, and I each had the same experiences up to the point where I-60 came back in time.

From there our paths diverged. I-60 lived a life based on his choice to marry Q. You and I have lived a life based on our decision to leave Q. Even though I am older than you, I have not had the same experiences that he had. My life subsequent to the point of his visit has been totally different than his. Look," he says, and draws on the tablecloth.

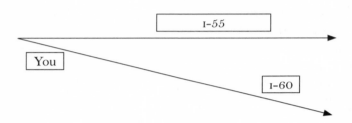

"I-60's life was based on a choice that you did not make. I am you based on the choice that you did make. Do you understand?"

"The truth is, I don't find visual aids very helpful." He should know this.

"I am you," he says. "It's that simple. Do you understand that?"

"I suppose."

"That's why you have to trust me."

I look at the diagram. It bothers me. "I don't think it's appropriate to write on a tablecloth."

"This is a very fine restaurant."

"All the more reason not to write on the tablecloth."

"They can afford it. Besides, they'll just wash it."

"Are you sure ink will come out? I don't think ink will come out."

"It will. I just saw an infomercial on television for a cleaner that dissolves ink on contact."

"When did you see that?"

"Just three nights ago, during *The Odd Couple*."

"Was that before you traveled back in time or after?"

"Before, I think."

"Are you sure that the cleaner has been invented yet?"

"No. I'm not sure. Now I feel guilty."

I see from his face that this is genuine, and I feel guilty for making him feel guilty.

"They still show *The Odd Couple* on television?"

"Yes."

"Does it hold up?"

"Yes."

"That's good."

The waiter returns with the Kumamoto oysters, the sashimi tacos, the sake, and my Diet Coke. He sets them down on the table, notices the diagram, and frowns. I look to I-55, expecting him to offer an apology, but he remains silent. I have to say something, so I do.

"I'm sorry. We got caught up in the excitement of a conversation and ended up writing on the tablecloth."

"I can see that."

"We're very sorry. We'll pay for it if it cannot be cleaned."

"I am not upset about the dirty tablecloth, but that is the clumsiest explanation of the sequential fallacy I have ever seen."

The waiter leaves. I am agape.

"Does that mean he is from the future?"

"Not necessarily. He could be a theoretical physicist."

"Working as a waiter?"

"This is New York City," says I-55. "He probably wants to be an actor."

I frown.

"It isn't any less plausible than his being from the future," he says.

"Does this occur?" I ask again. "Are there people from the future living in the past?"

"You mean the present?"

"My present, their past."

"A few people. Occasionally people get stuck in the past."

"Because of a problem with the technology?"

"No. Time travel is safe and reliable."

"Why then?

"Sometimes they forget to bring money."

I am about to explore this statement when I-55 bites into a Kumamoto oyster. He appears to savor it.

"When did we start liking these?"

"Just now."

"You didn't like them before?"

"I had never tried one before."

I am incredulous. "You mean you ordered a thirty-dollar appetizer without knowing whether you would like it?"

I-55 smiles. "You know the saying: There's no time like the present."

I frown as I-55 bites into a second Kumamoto, which he savors. "These are quite delicious," he says. "You really should try one."

Conspicuously, however, he does not offer me a bite.

My patience with myself is waning.

"What are you here for? What do you want?"

"What I want is another Kumamoto oyster."

"I am being serious."

"I am too. This is one of the most delicious things I have ever had. Why haven't we tried one before?"

"I can't speak for you, but I never cared for the consistency."

I-55 is licking his fingers.

"That was a mistake. I have never had anything like this."

"Why don't you just order one in your own time period?"

"No, no, no," he says, shaking his head. "Shellfish aren't good anymore, and besides they're very expensive."

He licks his fingers again. It is repulsive.

"Surely you didn't come here just for the meal. You must have some business."

"All right," he says. "You want to get to it." I-55 licks his hand one last time, then dips a napkin in his water glass and dabs his finger clean. When he is done, he blows his nose in the napkin. This appears to be his view of the necessary preparation for a serious conversation. I worry that my table manners have degenerated so.

"Okay," he says. "Let's get down to business."

"Okay."

"Here it is. You must marry Minnie Zuckerman."

This statement does not have the same dramatic impact as I-60's proclamation that I must not marry Q. Q, of course, was the love of my life. Minnie Zuckerman is Hank Snjdon's secretary. The truth is, I have never given her much thought.

To this point, most of our interactions have consisted of te-dious office banter. Minnie sits directly outside Hank's office, at the front of our department suite. It's impossible to enter or exit one's individual office without passing by Minnie. Some of the history professors pay her no mind, but I think a human be-ing should always be acknowledged, so anytime I pass Minnie I make sure to say something. This is a source of stress because I feel compelled to be both civil and witty. Furthermore, I am re-solved never to say the same thing twice on any given day.

The first and last interactions of the day are easy. In the morning I say, "Good morning, how are you?" and on the way home in the evening I say, "Have a good night!" The rest of the day can be challenging, though, particularly as I have gotten older and require the bathroom more often. I feel that I can say "What's up?" once per day, but no more. That quota is generally exhausted by ten o'clock. For the remainder of the morning, we mostly talk about lunch.

The buildup begins early. Around half past nine, I make my first trip to the bathroom and say something like, "Thinking about lunch?" to which Minnie will generally reply, "Starting to."

An hour or so later, when I make my second trip to the bath-room I will ask something like, "Made a decision yet?" to which Minnie will reply, "A decision has been made."

Then around twelve thirty, when I generally eat my own lunch, I'll pass by Minnie's desk, where she generally eats, and comment on whatever she has ordered. For example, if she has ordered hot and sour soup and an eggroll, which is one of her standards, I will say something like, "Chinese today," and nod my head approvingly. Minnie generally smiles in return, sometimes inquires about my own lunch, expresses her reciprocal approval, and so it goes.

Up until this moment, I have never given Minnie much consideration, certainly not as the object of romantic or sexual longing. But she is a sweet and gentle girl, and not entirely unattractive. Most days she dresses conservatively, and is a bit on the mousy side to begin with, so it is easy for her to blend in with the gray melamine finish of her workstation. But I recall that at the department Christmas party two years ago she wore a festive red sweater that revealed an enticing décolletage.

"You're talking about Hank Snjdon's secretary, right? I just want to make sure."

"Yes. You seem surprised."

"It's just that I really don't know her very well. She seems nice enough, but I wouldn't have thought she'd be someone you'd be longing for thirty years later."

"Twenty-five."

"Right, sorry. Besides, I wouldn't have thought she'd be interested in me."

I-55 looks at me skeptically. "I think you know otherwise," he says.

Truth be told, I do have an inkling that Minnie Zuckerman likes me. During the promotional tour for *Time's Broken Arrow*, I participate in Tom Deer's famous Out of the Box Reading Series at the World of Fish and Hamsters in Manalapan, New Jersey. I am skeptical about the venue. I don't really see how guppies and rodents can be co-marketed. I also question the promotional value of the event, but my publicist insists again that all publicity is desirable.

Manalapan is off the beaten path, and none of my friends attend, except for Minnie Zuckerman who lives in Oceanside, Long Island, more than fifty miles away, but "happens to be in the area." Minnie sits through the entire event, including a seventy-five-minute performance by the Jamaican Butterfly, a putative poet from the Caribbean who free-associates while playing the accordion. At one point he concatenates the words "flippant," "Chevrolet," and "legume" to the tune of Peter Gunn, which sounds a bit off on the squeezebox.

We sell and sign books following the event. The Butterfly outsells me. Nine people buy signed copies of his self-published collection, *He Who Goes to the Corner Store and Forgets His Wallet*. Only Minnie asks me to sign *Time's Broken Arrow*. What my fan base lacks in numbers, though, it makes up for in enthusiasm. Minnie is effusive in her praise, tells me how much she loves the book, even identifies and quotes from her favorite section. William Henry Harrison, having served two terms as president, has returned to his farm and distillery in North Bend, Ohio, and is visited by his great friend Daniel Webster, who has just finished his own term as president. Together they toast the accomplishments of the Whigs, including Webster's famous agreement with John Calhoun, the so-called Comprehensive Compromise, whereby slavery in the South is protected "for twenty years" in exchange for permanent abolition in the North and certain mineral rights in Utah.

Minnie says, "It's just so overwhelming to think that, but for a twist of history, the abolition of slavery might have been slightly delayed. And the scene where Harrison and Webster are on the farm together is so moving. They are so pleased with themselves, though, of course, from our perspective they're on the wrong side of the issue." Minnie recites the relevant text from memory:

"This is fine whiskey, Mr. Harrison."

"Fine whiskey, indeed, Mr. Webster."

Thinking back, Minnie also sent me a box of chocolates on Valentine's Day four years ago. In retrospect, this should also have been a tip-off, if only I had chosen to pay closer attention to the significance of the chocolates and to her.

The entrées arrive, the sashimi for me, the squid kushiyaki for I-55. The kushiyaki are long skewers, which pierce the fish and onions and various other vegetables. It all looks fine, except the squid. A waiter sets it down on the table together with a ponzu dipping sauce. It is a different waiter than the one who took our order.

"What happened to our old waiter?" I ask.

"Funny thing," says the new one, "the other guy just disappeared into thin air."

I-55 says, "I guess he couldn't handle the pressure."

The new waiter shrugs and walks away.

None of this appears to bother I-55, and as soon as the waiter is gone, he digs into the kushiyaki.

"I'm surprised you like squid," I say. "When did that start?"

"Just now," he says. "It's delicious. You should really try some."

"You mean you ordered a sixty-dollar entrée without ever having tried it before?"

"You know the old saying," he starts.

"Right," I mutter. "There's no time like the present."

The whole time travel thing frames that old saw in a different light. I am no expert in theoretical physics, possessing only the most rudimentary understanding of quarks and muons and tachyons. But isn't it obvious that if one can travel from one point in time to another, that every time is like the present?

A British physicist named Julian Barbour says that time itself is an illusion. He says the things we experience are real, but only exist for an instant, during which time literally stands still. The perception of the passage of time, similar to the sense of movement created by the succession of still frames that comprise a motion picture, is an illusion created by the human mind. It follows, therefore, that familiar constructs such as continuity, direction, and progress are also contrivances. All presumably arose by chance and persisted because they conferred a competitive advantage on those who accepted them. It is not difficult to imagine what this advantage might be. One needs to buy into the concept of time, and the interrelatedness of individual moments, to be motivated to plan for the future (by logical extension, also an artificial construct) and do important forward-looking things such as putting money in the bank and bread in the toaster.

There's not much money in this sort of theoretical physics, so Barbour spent most of his life translating English novels into Russian. This is a bit of an ironic choice since there isn't much money in English-to-Russian translation either. American books aren't very popular there. The truth is, Barbour just didn't want to get caught up in the publish-or-perish world of academia, with its endless committees and conferences and bad sandwiches. This is in its own right ironic because translators have to publish or perish, or if not perish then not make any money from their translating work. But it's true that there are fewer committees, and one can get whatever one chooses for lunch.

Anyway, Barbour was a translator who thought about theoretical physics in his spare time. He spent thirty-seven years translating the complete works of Charles Dickens into Russian, beginning in 1966 with *A Tale of Two Cities*, proceeding thereafter alphabetically, and concluding finally, in 2003, with *The Pickwick Papers*. Barbour gave few interviews, though at the end of his life he spoke by telephone with a reporter from Southern Illinois University's newspaper, *The Daily Egyptian*. The colloquy was printed in question-and-answer format between a report on the previous day's women's lacrosse game (a victory for the Salukis) and an ad for one dollar off the grilled cheese lunch special at the Carbondale Canteen. The text is set forth below:

Q. Dr. Barbour, you are both the preeminent theoretical physicist of our time and the leading translator of Dickens from English to Russian.
(negative response; lacuna)

Q. Do you have a reply to this?

A. I did not detect a question.

Q. I believe a question was implied.

A. I do not believe a question can be implied. It can either be asked or not asked.

Q. All the same. It seems a matter of basic decency to respond to an interrogative statement, particularly during an interview.

A. What is an interrogative statement?

Q. This is a statement that calls for an answer.

A. You mean a question?

Q. No, the concept is distinct.

A. So if I understand, then, by your statement, you are asking me whether it is true that I am the preeminent physicist of our time and the leading translator of Dickens?

Q. Essentially, yes.

A. The answer is no.

Q. Is it true that you do not believe in the past as a concept?

A. I believe that other moments existed and will exist. However, the notion that they are serially ordered is a myth.

Q. What is your favorite Dickens novel?

A. *Our Mutual Friend.*

Q. Why is that?

A. I believe the themes and lessons of the book are universal. It is pervasively influential. Nicodemus Boffin, the misanthropic miser who made his fortune from London's rubbish, is the inspiration for both Citizen Kane and Eugene Krabs, the penurious owner of the Krusty Krab on *SpongeBob SquarePants.*

Q. Indeed.

A. I will interpret that as an interrogative statement asking me to offer further evidence of the significance of the book. To wit, John Irving has said it will be the last book he reads before he dies, though of course he cannot know this for sure.

Q. How long did it take you to translate the Dickens oeuvre?

A. Thirty-seven years start to finish.

Q. Did you ever feel daunted?

A. No. The time flew by.

"**Are you sure about Minnie?**" I ask. "You know that she has an uncorrected overbite?"

"I am sure. She is the one who got away."

"Not Q?"

"Of course Q is without peer. I'm not considering her. I am limiting myself to the realistic alternatives."

"And Minnie is the best of these?"

"Far and away. I know this is difficult for you to accept, but she is sweet and smart and devoted to you. I know also that no one else better will come along. No more Qs lie on the path before you. Q is unique. You will not fall in love in that way again. But you could love Minnie, and soon you will. In time you will appreciate her finer qualities—her gentle earnestness, her basic decency. I am here to make sure this awakening occurs before it is too late."

I-55 takes a sip of his Diet Coke and then another bite of the kushiyaki, which he savors. To me, it looks repugnant.

"Doesn't Minnie have a boyfriend?"

"She does, which is why I am here now. I have ample reason to believe he is not an obstacle here. The desired outcome is achievable if you act quickly." This strikes me as an odd choice of words.

"Are you sure about this? Breaking up a relationship is a big step." .

I-55 puts down the food and looks up from his plate. This is the most serious he has been to this point. "I know this all seems foreign to you," he says. "You're thirty-one. You're young. You can't even imagine what it's like to be old. But time passes in an instant." He snaps his fingers. "In the blink of an eye you will be me. And then you will look back upon your life with the full measure of regret it deserves. Because what could be sadder than an old man living his life in isolation? A man with no wife, no children, no one to mourn his death. He has no legacy, nothing to show for his life. He—I—will not even leave behind a footprint in the sand."

"Does leaving a legacy matter?" It is a question I have considered before. "In the scheme of things what does that legacy amount to? In another blink of an eye the legacy will itself be forgotten."

I-55 shakes his head. "I do not know whether a legacy matters in any meaningful sense. But you cannot imagine the oppressive heaviness of my loneliness. It is as palpable as a weight upon my chest, as relentless as the tides, and unless you act soon, this weight will be yours to bear. You will have nothing to show for your life. The advent of time travel will make it all the worse. You will carry the additional weight of knowing that other yous exist, making the same destructive choices over and over again."

"Do you cause these other selves to make these choices?"

"I don't know. I don't see how this could be. But I know they make the choices, and it makes my heart heavy."

"Is the alternative better? If we have only one life to live, we might as well not have lived at all."

"The consolations of Kundera will not spare you sleepless nights, staring at the ceiling of your studio apartment in Morningside Heights." He stares at me directly, purposefully. "Do you understand this?"

"Yes," I say solemnly, and I believe I genuinely do. "Why is it so important that I do this now?"

"In two months, Minnie Zuckerman's boyfriend is going to propose to her. You need to prevent that from happening. If you don't, you'll regret it for the rest of your life."

Here, the bill arrives. I give him a moment, but I-55 makes no gesture in its direction. I set my credit card in the check sleeve and it occurs to me, not for the first time, that this whole time travel thing is objectionably expensive.

Chapter FIFTEEN

Freud woke gently, the rising sun streaming in off the Gulf of Trieste. Nastasia de Vuona stroked his thick black mane. It had been a long and restless night. Still Freud's heart soared when he opened his eyes. He loved this apartment. Just a simple one-room flat on the Via Giuseppe Mazzini above the Sopressa Gastronomia, yet it represented everything he loved about Trieste. This was where they spent their nights together.

Freud dreaded the approaching end of his time with Nastasia. He had concluded his research; all that remained was to write up the results. In a few days, he would return to Vienna. Somehow she made him forget all this. Though they had made love twice before going to sleep, Nastasia's touch aroused him, and soon Freud was again filled with lust. He wrapped a sheet around himself and turned to face her. She was a miracle. The morning sunshine bathed her in a warm aura. With her smooth olive skin and long braided hair, she looked, to Freud, like Mary Magdalene herself, whom, not coincidentally, Freud had always regarded as the most erotic of the disciples.

Nastasia's was the sensual, robust complexion of virility, nothing like the pasty pallor of the Viennese fräulein Gisela Fluss, the
ichthyosaur, who had been Freud's first love and, only months earlier,
his obsession. Now Fluss had been banished to the deepest recess of
his memory. On the one occasion he had thought of her since meeting
Nastasia, when Eduard Silberstein mentioned her in a post, it was
only to wonder, "How did I ever?"

Then again, Trieste was nothing like Vienna. It was late March.
In Vienna it would still be winter. But here, near the Slovenian bor-
der, at the head of the Adriatic Sea, spring had already arrived. And
not just any spring, but a refulgent, glorious spring, beckoning of
rebirth. It was too good to be true, like Nastasia herself.

Even how they met did not seem possible. Pure luck, really. Each
day after work at the Marine Zoological Station, Freud took a long
walk. His hands stained from the white and red blood of the sea animals he bought from the morning catch, his mind dulled by dissection
and tedious pencil sketches, Freud craved human contact. On more
than one occasion, he lamented to Silberstein that while he saw a
great deal of the entrails of eels, he saw very little of the physiology
of the Triestians.

Some days Freud walked to the Civico Orto Botanico, where
he would admire the extensive collection of simple lotus flowers.
Other days he walked around Miramare Castle and sat by one of its
twin serene ponds. That day, a pleasant Friday, the winter receding
into memory, Freud walked down to the shore, to the Piazza Unità
d'Italia. He liked the piazza. He particularly enjoyed the Fontana
dei Quattro Continenti, the Fountain of the Four Continents, built in
1751 to represent Trieste as a city of prosperity, following its establishment as a free port by the Habsburg emperor Charles VI and its

florescence under his successor, Maria Theresa of Austria. The fountain was composed of four allegorical statues recalling the features of the people populating the continents known at that time—Europe, Asia, Africa, and America. He was admiring Asia when Nastasia approached him from behind.

"It is the grandest of the continents," she said.

"Truly so," he said, turning. Sigmund Freud was no fool, particularly when it came to recognizing beauty. He immediately recognized the gift that had been bestowed upon him. Instinct seized control, and he sought to impress.

"I believe that is Jules Verne over there," he said, pointing across the piazza.

"I think you may be right," she said. "What is he doing here?"

"I believe he is writing a novel. He lives here sometimes, you know."

"I had no idea."

"Do you like Verne?"

"Yes. Very much."

Things took off from there. They went for espresso at a café adjacent to the piazza. He told her about his mission to identify eel testes. She told him about the University of Trieste, where she studied poetry, and her dreams of someday being a poet herself. She spoke in broken German, he in poor Italian, but they understood one another well enough, particularly when they did not speak.

For his part, Freud could not believe this woman's fascination with him. He did not think of himself as handsome. Gisela Fluss was the only woman to have ever shown even a remote interest in him. This was the real basis of Freud's own interest in Fluss. Truth was, the ichthyosaur was not much to look at. Freud's nickname for her referred superficially to the German meaning of her last name, "river," but the irony was not unintentional.

Whatever Freud may have thought of himself, Nastasia's interest in him was sincere and, more importantly, base. His self-doubts notwithstanding, Freud was striking. Young and effete, he had the good looks of his mother Amalia, whom he adored above all others. He had dense black hair, brushed back, and the wisp of a mustache. Nastasia thought he looked like a young Enrico Caruso. Had she lived in an another era, she might have said he looked like Johnny Depp. To her, he seemed exotic.

That evening, after espresso and conversation, Nastasia de Vuona introduced Sigmund Freud to sex. The smell of sausage wafting through the apartment, they made quiet love, bathed in the warm light of the Trieste moon. Then, to Freud's delight, they conjoined a second time, in a position Freud had to that point not considered, and then, spectacularly, a third, Nastasia contorting her lithe body into a pose Freud had previously thought impossible for a human to achieve. Without doubt, the ichthyosaur could not have coiled herself so.

When they finished, Nastasia held Freud's head in her lap, stroked his hair, and read Leopardi to him—"A Silvia," perhaps his greatest work. First Nastasia read the poem; then she expounded upon its meaning. Giacomo Leopardi, despite all his philosophizing and angst—his nihilism, if you will—could not suppress his effervescent spirit and love of life. Freud listened breathlessly to the extraordinary verse and the profound explanation, and then, wonderfully, they made love yet again.

This was only the beginning. Nastasia was Freud's entrée to a sensual world of which he had only dreamed. Several weeks later, when Nastasia, of her own accord, brought her supple friend Angelica into the bedroom, Freud thought he would burst open in ecstasy. And two weeks after that, when she brought home Robertino, the nineteen-year-old grinder from the Sopressa Gastronomia, with his bulging biceps and sinewy forearms, Freud was neither jealous nor self-conscious. Rather, to his great surprise, he was titillated. It was a journey of great self-discovery. Could it have begun only eight weeks ago?

"You didn't sleep last night," Nastasia said softly, stroking Freud's head. "What is wrong?"

"I am supposed to report my findings to Claus today."

"This should be good, no? He will be so proud when you tell him that you have found the testes."

"It is not that simple."

Nastasia could see that he was deeply troubled, and so, stroked his head more fervently. This soothed Freud, but aroused him at the same time. It took all of Freud's self-control not to ravage her. The mere knowledge that he could do so without being refused, that he could have instant relief, was an almost irresistible temptation. Yet, for the moment at least, resist he did.

"You need to understand about Claus."

"You have never been comfortable with him, no?"

This had never been explicitly discussed between them, but it was true all the same. Something about Claus did not sit right with Freud. In self-reflective moments, Freud wondered at first whether it might be an authority thing. But Carl Bernhard Brühl, the zootonomy professor, had the same status at the university as Claus, and he did not offend Freud. To the contrary, Brühl's gripping lecture about Darwin's time on the *Beagle* had thrilled Freud and sent his mind racing with possibility.

The truth was, Freud disliked Claus because he was similar in age to and looked a bit like Freud's half-brother, Emmanuel, who was older than Freud's mother Amalia, and whom Freud disliked for complex reasons, some rational, some not. Brühl, on the other hand,

looked much more like Freud's father, whom Freud found more palatable.

That Nastasia could discern his unease without verbal communi-
cation impressed Freud, though Nastasia, of course, hardly needed
to prove herself to him. For many reasons, he was eternally and irrevocably in her debt. Still, Freud did not validate Nastasia's intuition.
Indeed, he could barely admit the truth to himself. He regarded his
feelings about Claus (and Emmanuel) as exceedingly petty, the sort
of childish behavior he believed—or hoped—to be beneath him. So
Freud ignored Nastasia's question and instead said, simply, "Claus
will be displeased with what I have found."

"And what have you found?"

"In my dissections, I have found a lobed organ in the intestines
of the eel, the lappenorgan. The lappenorgan contains cells which, by
their shape, their arrangement, and their proliferation demonstrate
the possibility of forming spermatozoa. It is not conclusive evidence,
but it is highly suggestive of the testes."

"Why will this displease Claus?"

"This is complicated."

"Try," she said, stroking.

"I owe a debt to Claus. You first need to understand that. Claus
was charged with modernizing the zoology department at the university. The outpost in Trieste was part of this effort. He could have
seconded anyone to the marine outpost, but he chose me. This is a
great honor."

"And you have honored him with your tireless efforts on his behalf."

"Be that as it is may, much is riding on my research. A Pole
named Syrski claims to have found the gonads in eels. He has failed
only to identify the spermatozoa."

"As you have done."

"Yes, my findings will confirm Syrski."

"And this will anger Claus?"

"Yes."

"Why?"

Freud sighed. He would so much rather enjoy Nastasia than think about work. But the day was approaching relentlessly.

"Do you know of Darwin?" he asked.

"Of course," she said. "Who has not heard of the great Darwin. He is, how do you say it, all the rage."

"So he is. And Claus, you see, is an avowed Darwinist. He has staked his professional reputation on Syrski's findings being in error. Claus believes this must be so because man 'descended' from androgynous or hermaphroditic origins."

"Yet you have found the testes."

"I have."

"So you believe Darwin to be in error."

"No, I think Darwin is the single genius of our lifetime."

"Then how do you explain?"

"I believe Claus is misinterpreting Darwin. After all, it is Claus's proposition that Syrski must be in error, not Darwin's. There is no reason to believe that we descended from hermaphrodites. People believe Darwin to suggest that adaptations are consistent and directional, that we 'evolve' from less complex to more complex organizational structures. I believe if one reads Darwin for his true meaning, it is just as possible to move from more complex to less complex. Sometimes circumstances will require sophistication. At other times simplicity may be needed. Creatures will adapt to whatever situation confronts them. This is Darwin's *true* meaning."

She thought about what he had said for a while, and after she absorbed it said, "The testes are not the end point of evolution. They are simply *a* point in evolution."

Nastasia de Vuona was truly a remarkable woman. "Yes," Freud said, awed.

"And they exist?"

"Yes."

"So say so." She said this simply and matter-of-factly. It was a naïve sentiment, but incisive at the same time.

"You must understand," Freud explained, "If Claus's own underling, working in the laboratory Claus himself established, were to contradict him, this would be most embarrassing to Claus indeed."

"Yet the truth would be on your side."

"This will be small consolation for the ruination of my career."

"And this is why you could not sleep?"

"Not entirely," he said. "I believe that I could manage the consequences of publishing my true results, no matter how dire. What I cannot manage is leaving you. After I publish, my work here will be over. If I undermine Claus, he will certainly not go out of his way to assist me. I will lose you."

Nastasia de Vuona took his head in her hands and looked directly into his eyes. "Sigmund, you will not lose me if you do not want to. I love you, and I have utter faith in you, to do what is just, and to do what is right. If you will have me at your side, I will be there to support you and give you succor. I believe that you can do *anything*."

Her words, like she herself, were magical. As she caressed him, Freud felt his power grow and believed too, that with Nastasia at his side, he could do anything.

Claus be damned. He would publish the testes.

Chapter **SIXTEEN**

The courtship of Minnie Zuckerman begins in earnest over fondue. I-55's directive is far less problematic and angst inducing than I-60's was. I do not interpret I-55 to be saying that I must immediately propose marriage. Rather, I see his visit as encouraging me to take a closer look at someone whom I might otherwise not have noticed. My feeling is that if the relationship is destined to work, insomuch as destiny remains intact as a concept, then it will become obvious after a date or two, and things will evolve organically. The immediate action item is to give Minnie Zuckerman another chance and then ask her out.

So after I-55's visit, I linger longer at Minnie's desk. Whereas before I ask only what is being contemplated for lunch and, in the afternoon, what has been ordered, now I get involved in the nitty-gritty. I ask about the quality of the lunch. I inquire about condiments and bread choices and, later in the day, whether it is being digested well. One day she is eating a liverwurst sandwich and we have a long, snappy repartee over whether or not liver-wurst contains liver.

"You know, liverwurst contains liver," I say.

"No, it doesn't," she says.

"Yes, it does."

"No, it doesn't."

"Yes, it does."

Minnie Zuckerman pauses for a moment, reconsiders her po-sition, then says, "No, it doesn't."

I go to my office and print out the Wikipedia entry showing, conclusively, that liverwurst generally contains between 10 and 20 percent pork liver.

"My goodness," she says.

"You really should avoid organ meats," I say.

"Why?"

"They are very fatty."

"I only eat liverwurst because it's cheap."

"What would you eat if money were no object?"

"I would have fondue."

"You would have to keep a Bunsen burner and a ceramic pot at your desk."

"You asked and I answered."

"Fair enough. Why fondue?"

"It seems like a fun and decadent thing to have for lunch."

"Seems like," I say. "You have never had fondue?"

"No," she says.

"I haven't either."

"Really?"

"We should definitely go and try it together sometime."

"Definitely," she says.

I don't know Minnie Zuckerman well, but it is clear to me that she is pleased.

The only fondue place in the city, or the only one we can find, is in the Port Authority, next to the bowling alley on the second floor of the Eighth Avenue side. On a whim, I suggest we bowl a game first.

"I'm dressed for fondue," Minnie protests. "I'll have to wear rented shoes, and I hate rented shoes."

"Come on," I insist, "it'll be fun."

Minnie acquiesces. We rent the shoes, which are sprayed with disinfectant, pay for the game, and select our balls. We are assigned lane 11, which just so happens to be Minnie's favorite number. It is all very nice and vaguely romantic.

Minnie bowls a one.

Much of the problem stems from her throwing the ball too slowly. It is difficult to quantify precisely how slow this is, but to offer perspective, the nine-year-old boy on the lane to our left throws a ball at the same time as Minnie, retrieves it from the return, and throws it again before Minnie's original toss reaches the pins. This is a long time for a ball to remain on the lane without something going wrong. Her first eleven throws totter down the alley, staggering like drunkards, this way and that, and land in the gutter. The second ball of the sixth frame is more promising. It begins on an auspicious trajectory, continues straight as an arrow, and finally, after ninety seconds or so, actually makes contact with the headpin. Unfortunately its momentum expires at the point of impact and the ball rolls backward. The pin wobbles but does not fall. We call the desk. The man who disinfected our shoes emerges from behind the counter and retrieves Minnie's ball.

After this, Minnie begins to throw the ball more forcefully, cranking it up to two miles per hour or so, but this compromises her accuracy, and she throws seven consecutive gutter balls. Three of these go directly into the channel without touching so much as a single board of wood. Finally, on her last try, Minnie strikes the right balance between power and accuracy and nicks the tenpin with just enough force. It teeters for a moment and then, triumphantly, topples. Bowling a one would disappoint many people, but Minnie's optimism is indomitable. She jumps up and down in glee and asks when we can go again.

"Soon," I say.

"You're quite good," she says. "One hundred ninety-five is very good. It's one hundred ninety-five times greater than my score."

"I bowled on my high school team."

"I think I'll get the hang of it next time."

"It's not the sort of thing one can pick up in a single try."

"But I'll be better for sure."

"One would expect."

"That's all that matters," she says with a smile.

They have about four hundred and fifty varieties of cheese in Switzerland, but you wouldn't know it from the menu at the fondue place. Everything is Gruyère. The fondue Vaudoise is Gruyère. The spicy fondue is Gruyère with crushed tomatoes and wine. The mushroom fondue is Gruyère with mushrooms. To the extent that other cheeses are used, it is generally in combination with Gruyère. The *moitié-moitié* (half and half) is Vacherin with Gruyère. The Neuchâteloise is Emmental with Gruyère. The central Swiss fondue is Emmental and Sbrinz and Gruyère.

I like Gruyère fine, but Minnie Zuckerman is allergic. I become aware of this when I comment on the pervasiveness of Gruyère.

"Wow," I say. "Everything has Gruyère."

"That's a shame," she says. "I am allergic."

I am surprised by this because several times I have seen Minnie eating a turkey and cheese sandwich for lunch. I am, furthermore, almost certain that the cheese was Swiss. It seems improbable that one could be allergic to Gruyère but tolerate Swiss cheese, which I am pretty sure is really Emmental. The waiter is even more dubious when Minnie explains her condition and asks whether the restaurant serves anything without Gruyère.

"Everything we have contains cheese," he says. "It is the essence of cheese fondue."

"I am not worried about cheese generally, just Gruyère. I am allergic to Gruyère."

"I doubt that," says the waiter.

"You don't believe me?" Minnie is incredulous.

"I doubt that one could have or be aware of so specific an allergy."

"Nevertheless I am."

"So you are allergic to Gruyère, but not to Jarlsberg and Gouda."

"Correct."

"What did your allergist do, test you for hundreds of different types of cheeses?"

"He is a top allergist and very thorough."

"I should say."

"So can you accommodate me?"

"I will have the chef whip up something with Fribourg vacherin. Are you okay with Fribourg vacherin?"

"Yes."

"I should tell you the fondue contains traces of peanuts," he says. "Are you allergic to nuts?"

"Only filberts," she says. "Do you use filberts?"

"I'll check with the chef, but I expect you are safe."

Minnie is a doting conversationalist. She probes me about where I write, and when I write, and how I get my ideas.

"How do you get your ideas?" she asks.

"Here and there," I say. "I just try to keep my eyes and ears open. I had the idea for my current book last year at Thanksgiving dinner. I met this homeless Kierkegaard expert who had some very interesting ideas about progress and evolution. I had read about Freud and the eels and thought to myself, this is just the thing to tie it all together."

"Ah," she says.

Minnie is intimately familiar with my oeuvre, which is to say that in addition to my magnum opus, the novel, she has read my article in the *Critical Journal of Counter-Historical Studies* re-examining the politics of Charles Lindbergh and the plausibility of his becoming a Republican presidential candidate, as examined in *The Plot Against America*. In the obligatory "Suggestions for Further Study" section of the article, I urge that counter-historians focus greater attention on the potential ramifications of Lindbergh's affair with the German hat maker Brigitte Hesshaimer, and what might have happened if she and Lindbergh had together ventured into the burgeoning business of manufacturing galoshes. Minnie has read all of this carefully, particularly *Time's Broken Arrow*, as was obvious at the Manalapan event, and now asks thoughtful, precise questions about the book.

"What was the specific nature of Zachary Taylor's relationship with the Germans and what were its potential political implications?"

Minnie is referring to the third section of the book wherein William Henry Harrison, in the last days of the second term of his presidency, sends Zachary Taylor, "Old Rough and Ready," hero of the Mexican-American War, to Baden to aid the German liberals in the revolution of 1848. The plan is for Taylor to vanquish von Bismarck and von Wrangel as he vanquished Santa Anna at the Battle of Palo Alto and later, conclusively, at the Battle of Buena Vista. Unfortunately, Taylor eats a bad schnitzel at the Heidelberg Wursthaus, develops a severe case of gastroenteritis, and dies three days later, thereby dashing President Harrison's grand plans. This is a pivotal moment in the book, and it pleases me that Minnie Zuckerman has chosen to focus on it.

"Are you saying something about fate or the convergence of time?"

"Why do you ask this?"

"Because in real life Taylor ate a snack of milk and cherries and died of gastroenteritis."

"I'm impressed that you know this."

"I too am a student of history."

"Taylor ate the snack at an Independence Day parade. Did you know that some historians suspect the cherries may have been laced with arsenic as part of an assassination plot?"

"That's fascinating," Minnie says. She appears to be genuinely riveted. "So are you saying that his death was inevitable?"

Playfully, I say, "It could just be that he has a predisposition to gastroenteritis."

"It could be, but I don't think that's your intended meaning."

"Ultimately meaning is up to the reader."

Minnie chews on this and the Fribourg, with which she seems eminently pleased. She offers me a taste and I obligingly dip in a nugget of bread. To my undiscerning palate, it tastes like Gruyère.

For our second date, we go to Streit's matzo factory on the Lower East Side. This too evolves from our lunchtime banter. It is Passover and Minnie is eating liverwurst on matzo. Having exhausted the liverwurst issue, we turn to the matzo, but I have little to say and am forced to admit that I have no idea where or how matzo is made. Minnie does, and the next day she arranges for us to join a tour of the factory.

We are escorted by Schmuleh Streit, who explains that he is the great-great-grandnephew of Aron, who founded the place in the 1920s. Schmuleh has *payis* and *tzitzit* and the sensibilities of a borscht belt comedian. We pay five dollars for the tour, after which Schmuleh says, "That will be the last dough that passes hands today." The other tour guests, a dozen people or so, chuckle as I groan silently.

Some of his material is stolen from Joe Franklin. At the door, he says, "Ladies and gentleman, please prepare yourselves for the unleavened experience of a lifetime." Everyone chuckles, as I whisper to Minnie indignantly, "He stole that from Joe Franklin."

"Shhh," she says. "No one knows who that is."

At the entrance to the factory, Schmuleh has gone to great pains to simulate a scene from *Willy Wonka and the Chocolate Factory*. He escorts us into a room where the walls get progressively narrower. At the far end of the room is a tiny keyboard.

"It's a musical lock," he says mischievously, then plays a short melody.

"Rachmaninov?" a man asks his wife.

"No," she whispers. "Morton Feldman."

Then the door opens—the small wall is a façade—and the baking floor is revealed. Schmuleh Streit bows his head, inverts his arms, and says invitingly, "Ladies and gentleman, the matzo factory."

There are no chocolate rivers or Oompa Loompas, just Jews. We visit the matzo-forming machines (which are unsatisfyingly named "matzo-forming machines") and the ovens and the bins where the shmurah matzo is stored. The shmurah is matzo gold. It is watched from the time the wheat is ground into flour until the moment it is baked in the oven to make sure not a drop of moisture invades the holy bread. Eternal vigilance is expensive, and the shmurah sells for more than twenty dollars per pound. We meet the rabbi on duty.

"Any water get in today, Rabbi?" I ask, but he does not respond; he appears to be asleep.

All in all, the tour is pretty lame.

In the Streit's café, Minnie and I recapitulate the experience over Kedem wine and matzo meal falafel.

Minnie says, "Watching that rabbi sit in front of that vat of matzo dough was quite disturbing."

"Why? That's the way it has been done for centuries."

"That's the problem. It's disconcerting to think that this method always has been and always will be the same."

"Why does that bother you?"

"It just seems to me that there should be a better way of making it. It's oppressive to think that the process hasn't progressed at all in five thousand years and never will."

I nod. I understand.

The Kedem gets to us, and somehow this segues into a conversation about our personal lives.

"I don't want to pry," Minnie says, "but weren't you engaged to be married?"

"I was. We broke it off six months ago."

"May I ask what happened?"

I wince. "It just wasn't meant to be."

"I understand," she says.

"Weren't you in a relationship yourself?"

"I was, but I broke it off."

"When was that?"

"Just the other day," she says with a smile, "when you asked me out to fondue."

"Why did you do that?"

"I had the sense that something better might come along. You know how that is?"

"I suppose I do," I say, though I'm not entirely sure it's true.

Minnie Zuckerman's decision to leave her boyfriend on the basis of invitations to fondues and matzo, neither of which was unambiguously framed as a date, and neither of which ended with so much as a peck on the cheek, should have been cause for concern. The truth is, there are other warning signs too. One day at my apartment, shortly after she begins staying over, I find that Minnie has discarded all of my dress shirts. Many of the shirts are a blend of cotton and polyester, to which Minnie says she is allergic. This explains the purging of the no-iron shirts, but not the fancy cotton ones. These, Minnie explains, have been sacrificed purely in the name of fashion.

Were it just the shirts, it would be one thing, but Minnie later repeats the process with my pants (she is allergic to worsted wool), my socks (she is allergic to nylon), my cache of Earl Grey tea (she is allergic to bergamot oranges), and my neckties (she is allergic to certain types of silk and, implausibly, rep stripes).

The nylon sensitivity victimizes some unlikely offenders, including my tennis racket (replaced with an old-style woodie, with which I could never play in public), my shoelaces (replaced with hemp; surprisingly stylish), and my toothbrush. In another phase of my life, I might find this behavior intrusive or even oppressive, but in my current state I find her doting amusing, even pleasant. Many of the replacements are superior to the original products. Generally speaking, my wardrobe is sleeker and more modern than before. I had forgotten the comfort of cotton socks. And I downright love my new all-natural toothbrush, which has a bone handle and Siberian boar hair bristles. Brushing is, suddenly, a thrill.

From here, things progress quickly, though very little (none) of this progress is the product of an active decision on my part. One day Minnie is putting her arm around me in the presence of Hank Snjdon and we are publicly an item. Hank asks several questions, including when we started seeing one another. Minnie answers, dating the start of our relationship back to our fondue excursion. Hank seems genuinely approving. His fondness for Minnie is obvious. His fondness for me, however, is not. Playfully, he puts his arms around me and says, "Now, don't you go breaking the heart of the only good secretary I have ever had. They don't grow on trees, you know." Everyone laughs except me.

Soon Minnie says it is cost-ineffective for us to maintain separate residences when we are spending so much time together. My sublet will be up in a few months, and besides, I will like Williamsburg better than Morningside Heights. She reveals that she has been secreting away some of my books and dress shirts and has arranged for movers to box and cart the remainder of my things. All I need to do is tend to a short typewritten list of tasks. This includes returning the cable box to Time Warner but not filing a change of address with the post office, which she has already taken care of online.

The move will happen on a Sunday, and it is fine for me to play golf that day, as I often do, so long as I am at her place in Williamsburg by 10:00 a.m. This isn't highly practical. Given that I travel to golf courses by train, her schedule allows me enough time to get there and back but not enough to actually play. So on the day we move in together, I don't play golf, but I'm grateful for all of her preparations.

Several months later, Minnie announces one day that she has

run simulations on our tax returns and determined that it will be cheaper for us to file jointly than to file separately. She reveals that she also has taken a small sample of my blood, had it tested, and determined that we can safely have children without fear of any of the genetic disorders that plague Ashkenazi Jews. She has arranged an appointment for us with her rabbi two weeks hence so he can marry us. She has a *ketubah* on order and is confident that it will arrive in time. The reception can wait until the following summer, she says, though she has already researched reception halls and concluded that we should hold the party on a Tuesday evening, resulting in substantial savings.

Minnie tells Hank Snjdon and a few dozen strategically selected others about her plans for us, and, before I know it, we are, as a practical matter, engaged to be married. I recognize this is a less than ideal procedure. The convention of asking the other party "Will you marry me?" has the advantage of ensuring the other party actually wants to wed. But saying no now would be complicated. The faculty of the department sends us gifts, several of which have been purchased during sales and thus cannot be returned. In any event, the truth is, I am fine with the result. I like Minnie's attention. It feels good to be wanted and the tangible benefits are undeniable. Thanks to Minnie's support, which includes making sure I have an ample supply of toner cartridges and warm coffee, my productivity is greater than ever. The mostly fabricated future of Freud is developing rapidly. He is well on his way to becoming a rogue naturalist, and a critical reinterpreter of Darwin's legacy. Most of all, the relationship fills, at least in part, the gaping hole left by Q.

Still, despite the encouraging progress on my novel and the comfort of the new relationship, I am not entirely surprised to find a note on my office desk. It arrives one week before Minnie and I are scheduled to appear before Rabbi Pincus. "Lunch," it says in my own handwriting. "12:30 tomorrow. Le Piste."

Chapter SEVENTEEN

I am shocked when I-50 tells me his age. He is a wreck. He has time-traveled ten years earlier in his life than the two other versions of me who came before him, but he looks far worse than either. He has dark rings under his eyes, which are profoundly sad, and he has gained, conservatively, seventy-five pounds. I barely recognize myself in him. It is as if another man has been circumscribed about me. There is loose skin everywhere—under his eyes, in his cheeks, on his second and third chins.

He has not waited for me to begin eating. I am on time, but he has already ordered himself two starters: wild burgundy escargot with gorgonzola gnocchi and veal sweetbreads with cauliflower and pickled cherry tomatoes. The idea of eating snails and cow glands repulses me, but this time the possibility that my tastes have expanded strikes me as authentic. When I arrive, I-50 is devouring his twin appetizers ravenously, so engaged in the meal that he does not notice me for several more bites.

"Sit down, sit down," he says, finally. He forgets to offer his hand. For that matter, he forgets to look up from the food. "Sorry," he says, "but one works up this enormous appetite traveling through time."

"So I have heard."

"I figured you wouldn't mind if I started without you."

"Not at all."

"Right, right," he says. "Don't suppose, don't suppose."

He takes another few bites then looks up and around the room, urgently. I think for a moment that he wants to get down to business, but really he is looking for the waiter. He gestures wildly and demonstratively for one to come over, waving his hand as if he were the parent of an infant with a medical emergency.

"We should get our order in before the lunchtime rush."

"Of course."

The waiter arrives. I-50 orders two entrées: chestnut pappardelle in a veal ragout with wild mushrooms and rosemary, and braised rabbit with grain mustard, served with creamy polenta, bacon, and porcini mushrooms. I have an inkling that he may be ordering for me, but this is dispelled when he looks in my direction and asks, "What do you want?" I squeeze in an order for the romaine and parmesan salad.

"And please hurry," I-50 tells the waiter. "We're in a rush."

"Nowhere to go," I-50 says to me, "but my blood sugar drops like a stone."

When the waiter arrives, shortly thereafter, with the main courses, I see that I-50's agenda in ordering two entrées is quite different from I-55's. I-50 is not interested in sampling new and fine cuisine. He is interested in volume. In a matter of seconds, the chestnut pappardelle is gone, seemingly inhaled. He soaks up the residue of the veal ragout with a slice of crusty bread, which he also devours.

"If you were going to eat like this we could have just gone to McDonald's."

I-50 does not acknowledge the dig. Rather, he turns his attention to the rabbit. He places a giant slab of hare on another slice of the crusty bread, creating an instant sandwich. He then douses this with grain mustard and polenta, and consumes the resulting concoction in two ambitious bites. He repeats this process with the remainder of the rabbit, impossibly accelerates, and the forty-five-dollar second entrée is obliterated in less than two minutes. When he is done, I-50 signals for the waiter and orders crêpes suzette.

During the brief pause between the rabbit and the crêpes, I ask I-50 to state his business. Even during this intraprandial hiatus, he is munching on the remainder of the crusty bread, but it is at least possible to hear him between bites.

"Why are you here?"

"It's about Minnie," he says. "You cannot marry her. Not under any circumstances."

"What's the problem?"

"Insufferable. She's insufferable. The woman will ruin your life."

"How so?"

"Most controlling person I've ever met in my life. Like a Nazi. Margarete Himmler did better. Heinrich was a chicken farmer before the SS, you know. Actually was kind of laid back."

"I didn't know that."

"Think you're ever going to play golf again? Think again, unless you figure out a way to play in less than twenty minutes, because that's how much time you are allotted each day for 'personal improvement and reflection.' Aside from these brief periods, every second of the remainder of your life will be planned. She'll map out what you eat, what movies you see, where you go on vacation."

"That doesn't sound so bad."

"That's what you think now, isn't it? Seriously, that's a question. I can't even remember. What do you find appealing? You must have noticed the obsessive attention to detail. Surely my saying this doesn't come out of the blue."

"It doesn't come out of the blue. I've noticed it. It seems pleasant now. She brings me tea while I write and warms my socks in the microwave. You're saying it's not good-natured?"

"Queen of the Harpies! Queen of the Harpies!"

"It's nice to have someone's attention. I mean, after Q and all."

"Minnie Zuckerman is not Q. Get this through your head once and for all right now. You are on the rebound! Minnie is not the best alternative; she is just the next alternative."

"But I-55 said . . ."

"I-55 has no idea what he is talking about. He didn't live this life, I did. I-55 was a moron!"

I let this sink in for a moment. I'm inclined to confess some intuitive empathy for I-50. "I'd be less than honest if I didn't acknowledge finding the replacement of my socks a bit worrisome."

"Not even the start of it," he says. "At ten o'clock every night you receive a schedule of the following day's activities. Most mornings you are required to shower at 5:30 a.m. so she can disinfect and have the bathroom to herself. On weekends, the time is pushed back to six o'clock."

"There's a schedule on weekends?"

"Every day. There's a schedule every day."

"That sounds challenging."

"You have to wear a hat anytime you're in her presence because she develops an allergy to hair. Any potential friend is subject to a vetting process. They need to submit references and two sets of tax returns. For three years she is convinced that nitrogen is carcinogenic. She cuts it out of our life."

"How do we breathe?"

"She converts the apartment into an oxygen tent."

"Can one breathe straight oxygen?"

"For a while. It's irritating to the lungs. That's the least of it, really."

"Are there children?"

"There are no children," he says this dismissively, as if the question is absurd. "She is allergic."

"To children?"

"To life."

He returns to the crêpes suzette. "This is it," he says. "In the end, food is the only thing you will have in your life." He looks up. "It's all I have in mine."

Leaving Minnie is not nearly as emotionally complicated as leaving Q. I like Minnie, even love her, but she is not my soul mate. I don't believe that she believes she is either, so there is none of the need this time to construct a scenario with narrative integrity. Leaving Minnie is a practical challenge mostly. There are the gifts we have received and the fact that we work together, of course. Also, I am not very good at breaking up.

At my office, I investigate Minnie's father in the hope of discovering some questionable business dealings, but unfortunately

Hiram Zuckerman makes yarmulkes and appears to be on the up-and-up. I-50 gives no indication to the contrary, so this avenue appears out. I consider telling Minnie that I am gay, but this also is complicated by our working together. Moving to a new country seems equally problematic. Finally, I decide to tell Minnie the truth, or at least some close enough version to feel like the truth. I tell her that I have decided not to get married, that it's not the life I want, and, given this, it wouldn't be fair to her to continue the relationship.

When I deliver this news to Minnie, she does not understand, or at least pretends not to understand. She says it is normal, all men get cold feet and I should talk things through with Rabbi Pincus. I explain that I am serious and my decision is not really up for discussion, even with Pincus. We got into this very quickly, I explain to her. It is easy to get caught up in the rush of things. The decision to get married was too hasty. I like her very much and hope that we can remain friends, but being husband and wife isn't in the cards. She assesses me for a while. When she sees that I am sincere, she raises a series of practical objections to our separation. Many of these are difficult to refute. We have placed a nonrefundable deposit for the reception. Minnie has ordered personalized thank-you notes on heavy card stock. These cannot be returned either. And, of course, we will lose the tax advantage, and wouldn't that money come in handy?

It would indeed. I almost waver on the tax advantage. It's a $1,700 tax credit. One thousand seven hundred dollars to which the government has no legitimate claim. But then I think of I-50 and his broken spirit and jowly cheeks and say no, no, no, I am sorry but this is the way it must be. She finally accepts it and breaks down, sobbing uncontrollably. Leave, she says, just leave.

I am sad and regretful, but of course I have been through this before.

The next week, Minnie resigns her position. One week after that, I have my annual evaluation with Hank Snjdon. He has given me favorable reviews each of the past four years, but this year he finds fault with my didactic style and my scholarship. He hands me a draft of his report. I know I am in trouble when I see that he refers to me only as "the professor." The tone recalls Jill Nordberg's harsh critique of me in her letter to the chair of the BMCC history department. It is never good news when someone refuses to refer to you by name.

"The professor," writes Snjdon, "needs to develop a second scholarly theme." He continues, "A novel, even one historically situated, is not the basis of a tenurable profile in a history department. I even wonder whether a single novel, with mixed reviews, would be the basis for promotion in an English department. Moreover, the professor's obsession with what might have been, as opposed to what actually was, infects his teaching. He relies heavily on hypotheticals and counterfactuals. Too often students in his classes leave with no clear sense of history. With his emphasis on characters and motivations, the professor teaches the past as if it were itself a story. Our students are the worse for this."

When I finish reading the letter, I consider protesting. I could remind Hank of his recent assurances to me, including his dismissal of the distinction between is and was, which has somehow managed to find its way into my evaluation. Moreover, mine is not the first work of fiction produced by the City University history department. Hef Angkot's *People's History of the Peloponnesian War*, a retelling of the conflict from the standpoint of an Athenian street peddler, has as much relation to the truth as *Time's Broken Arrow*. But I say nothing. I understand what is going on. Minnie has been sulking around the office since I jilted her, and Hank has taken her side. I can't say that I blame him. History professors are a dime a dozen, but a good secretary is one in a million.

Hank Snjdon's tepid review of my performance makes me worry about my future at City University. It doesn't bode well for tenure, and if I am denied tenure I will be finished in academia. I feel more pressure than ever for my book to succeed. I redouble my efforts and immerse myself in my work. For the next several months, I maintain no social engagements. I begin writing even earlier than normal, at six in the morning, and bring a sandwich to my office so that I will not need to go out for lunch. I even drink less so as to minimize bathroom trips and avoid encounters with the new department secretary. In the evening I take a run, eat soup, and turn in early so I can begin fresh the next day.

Together, Sigmund Freud and I embark on a journey, taking the young doctor from his groundbreaking analysis of eel testes to his ultimate position in the pantheon of evolutionists second only to Darwin himself, and perhaps even surpassing Sir Charles in connecting the insights of biology to the lives of ordinary people. The early part of Freud's career is tedious, however, and the writing is a slog. Emboldened by the runaway success of his treatise on eel gonads, published in the *Proceedings of the Imperial Academy of Sciences*, Freud secures and accepts a post as a naturalist aboard SMS *Kaiser Heinrich*, a twenty-four-gun sloop of war in the Austro-Hungarian navy, charged with charting the islands of the southern Atlantic. The parallel to Darwin's stint aboard HMS *Beagle* is obvious and conscious, both on my part and Freud's, who views this as his apprenticeship as an evolutionist. He tells Nastasia and his colleagues aboard the *Kaiser Heinrich* that his goal is to deliver the definitive study of Atlantic whales. His secret goal, however, is more complex and ambitious.

Freud believes that the whale and hippopotamus share a common ancestor. He dares not share this hypothesis with the scientific community, which would ridicule him, but Freud is nevertheless convinced that whales descended from the land-living mammals of the Order Artiodactyl—the even-toed ungulates, which also includes peccaries and deer and pronghorn antelope. His specific conjecture is that between fifty and sixty million years ago, the hippo remained in sub-Saharan Africa, staying cool by wallowing in the mud of the savanna, while whales took to the water and radiated into the seas of the world. By dissecting and classifying the cetaceans of the Atlantic Ocean, Freud hopes to identify the missing link between these mammalian giants. If he could succeed in this, the discovery would vividly illustrate the comprehensiveness of Darwin's theory.

It is important that Freud's work possess verisimilitude, so I spend several weeks researching and drafting a detailed exposition of the diversity of Atlantic whales. Whale taxonomy can be a dreary business. They are divided into two suborders: toothed and baleen whales. The toothed whales, including the melonhead, the pygmy killer, the long-finned pilot, the short-finned pilot, and the orca, use echolocation to prey on fish and squid. Baleens are named for the keratin sievelike structure that they rely on to eat instead of teeth. Located in the upper jaw, baleen is used to filter plankton from the water. They are the largest whales and include the right, the fin, the sei, the blue, the minke, the gray, and the humpback.

For several weeks, the *Kaiser Heinrich* tracks a humpback through the Caribbean Ocean. Freud is mesmerized by this quest. Humpbacks are a haunting, itinerant species. They roam the planet, sometimes migrating as far as fifteen thousand miles in a given year. They are huge and nimble. Adult humpbacks range between forty and fifty feet in length and weigh up to eighty thousand pounds, but are sufficiently acrobatic to breach and slap the water with their giant wavy tails. They are remarkably resilient, sometimes living for more than one hundred years. And, of course, they sing.

The humpback's song is the most complex in the animal kingdom. It lasts as long as thirty minutes and is repeated for hours, sometimes even days, at a time. It is both miraculous and mysterious. Even modern scientists are unsure how the whales produce the music. While other baleen whales have a larynx, like their land-roving brethren, the humpbacks lack vocal cords. One modern theory is that they project air through the sinuses of their cranium. The purpose of the song is the ultimate enigma. Freud is fascinated by it. His sloop's target continues to sing, even as the boat relentlessly pursues the whale through the waters of the Caribbean. In the evenings, Freud stands on the bow, marvels at the beauty of the song, and wonders what story this leviathan is telling.

Thinking about the lamentations of these ancient creatures makes Sigmund Freud and me feel small. When the *Kaiser Heinrich* succeeds in netting the humpback, Freud dissects the creature and is able to identify anatomical similarities to the hippopotamus, which will offer convincing, if not conclusive, support for his theory. His career will be made, but he feels a substantial measure of regret and thinks to himself that the whale's song might have offered greater insight into the meaning of life than his own puny research ever can.

Following the *Kaiser Heinrich* expedition, Freud's reputation grows exponentially. With Nastasia's support, and often her company, he embarks on one expedition after another, each more ambitious than the one before it. By the middle of his life, Freud is a swashbuckling explorer who travels the Amazon with Theodore Roosevelt, follows Mawson and Shackleton to the end of the world, and leads the first major exploration of the interior of Madagascar. From each journey, he brings back riveting tales of existence under extreme conditions. He writes copiously, wondering aloud about the meaning of his observations, and is read widely.

In his public musings, Freud advocates a gentle, nonjudgmental doctrine that views human beings not as the end product of evolution but as one piece in the mosaic of nature, no more or less special than lemurs or emperor penguins. It is science, but Freud's writing is accessible and possesses a spiritual, Buddhist quality. All life is sacred, he says. Man must be honest about his place in the scheme of things, and accordingly humble. His teachings resonate with people, and over time Freud gains a loyal and substantial following. At the turn of the century, Sigmund Freud is the most noted and influential public intellectual in the English-speaking world.

At the end of his life, he debates Herbert Spencer, the British

philosopher, at Oxford University. Spencer is the most noted de-
fender of a view that evolution is a process directed toward an
ultimate end. Spencer writes voluminously too, and penetrably,
and possesses his own legion of devotees. Taking Spencer on at
Oxford is the climactic moment of Freud's life. The debate is eagerly anticipated throughout all of Great Britain. I anticipate it
eagerly for my own reasons: the debate marks an end to Freud's
journey and a beginning to my own next chapter.

Chapter EIGHTEEN

I n Frewin Court, off Cornmarket Street, the Oxford Union was abuzz. The grand Gothic revival designed by Alfred Waterhouse, architect of the London Natural History Museum and the rival Cambridge Union, had served as the forum for many great debates, but none of this magnitude. The event, bringing together two of the most prominent and influential thinkers of the nineteenth century, had been the talk of the campus for months. On the evening in question, student members of the society and dons of the university alike filed into the great hall with the breathless anticipation of those about to witness a heavyweight prize fight.

Celebrity debating was the brainchild of the president of the union, Frederick Edwin Smith. Chamber debating had been a staple activity of the union since its founding in the 1820s, but it had never been a moneymaker for the struggling union until Smith had the excellent idea of inviting prominent citizens to deliberate on the great issues of the day and the downright smashing idea of selling tickets.

This latter idea held the promise of keeping the struggling debating society solvent. For saving the union, and for creating an event that captured the attention of the entire empire, focusing all eyes upon Oxon, Smith became a modest celebrity in his own right on the ancient campus.

Later the Baron of Birkenhead, later still the Viscount of Birkenhead, and latest of all the Earl of Birkenhead, Smith would play a critical role in the Anglo-Irish Treaty of 1921, which established the Irish Free State. He would also successfully galvanize opposition to a proposal that would have criminalized lesbianism, famously saying, "Nine hundred ninety-nine women out of a thousand have never heard a whisper of these practices."

But this was all in the future. On this glorious evening in the spring of 1901, he was just a young man with a sardonic wit who liked to have a pint or two, or perhaps even three, thank you very much, and who early one morning over black and tans at the Purple Turtle floated the fanciful idea of inviting Sigmund Freud to debate Herbert Spencer, an invitation that was issued and, to Smith's amazement, accepted by each of the great men, consequently earning F. E., as he was known to his friends, the attention of several people of influence in the Oxford community including, most notably, Margaret Eleanor Furneaux, the ravishing and dutiful daughter of the Reverend Henry Furneaux, renowned scholar of the Roman historian Tacitus, attention for which F. E. was deeply and profoundly grateful.

F. E. supervised the proceedings with all of the gravity a university student could muster. He wore a tie and a three-piece suit, which attire would become his uniform after he ascended to the bar. He pulled his long, stringy brown hair back behind his ears, revealing a stern part. At precisely seven o'clock, Smith called the assembly to order. With self-consciously absurd formality, he shouted in his loudest, most stentorian voice, "The question: This house believes in the progress of evolution." Then, "Ladies and gentlemen, the conversants!"

Enter here to robust, deeply respectful applause, Dr. Herbert Spencer, escorted into the well by Alexander Shaw, later the second Baron Craigmyle, and deposited at a semicircular table, bequeathed to the Oxford Union upon his retirement in 1894 by William Gladstone, former head of the Liberal Party, four times prime minister of the empire, and, most importantly, before all that, president of the Oxford Union. Gladstone had the table designed in this fashion so that he could stare each of his cabinet ministers in the eye. In his dotage, Gladstone thought it would be perfect for his beloved union, and so, there it was. As had been scripted, Spencer took his place at the table in the traditional position of the pro discussant, and, when the applause finally subsided, he took his seat with the greatest of dignity.

Enter here to wild, enthusiastic cheers (and, it should be noted, more than a few jeers) the swashbuckling, vivacious, and striking biologist Sigmund Freud. He was, in every respect, a stark contrast to Spencer. Spencer dressed the part of the learned professor, wearing a formal suit, complete with bow tie, white silk pocket square, and pince-nez. He walked deliberately, in a stately manner, and projected from Gladstone's desk, peering out over the assembly, a sense of gravitas. Freud seemed more akin to a great cricketer than to an academic. He bounded down the stairs into the well with the enthusiasm of a child and wore the clothes of an expeditioner.

As was obvious from the reaction of the assembly, Freud was a polarizing figure. During Spencer's entrance, most of the philosopher's supporters emulated the decorum of the great man himself. Freud's, on the other hand, were rowdy and unstaid in their fervor.

They began voicing their approval when Freud entered the room and continued for at least ten minutes after he took his seat. None of this sat well with Spencer's devotees, who sighed and groaned and expressed their disapproval of Freud and his devotees in all sorts of passive-aggressive ways. Freud rose several times to acknowledge the expression of approval, but the crowd did not quiet, until Freud said loudly, "Gentlemen, please, please, please."

After hearing this call for order, Edwin Smith nevertheless hesitated, thinking the support for Freud would spontaneously combust again. Even when it appeared that the commotion had in fact subsided once and for all, Smith rose with trepidation from his chair, testing the water in a way, to see if the crowd would remain quiet. It did, and the debate finally began.

Smith said, "By the rules of chamber debating, Mr. Spencer, as advocate of the pro position, shall have the first word."

Hereupon, Spencer rose from the Gladstone desk and laboriously ascended to the despatch box. The members of the union watched in rapt attention, not because the sight of a man walking up two steps to a pedestal was so enthralling, but because they had a collective sense, as the masses eerily sometimes do, that something great was about to happen. They were right, of course. Jung, who might have been great friends with Freud in another life, attributed this to collective consciousness, but the plain truth is, the phenomenon could be observed but not explained.

As the unioners correctly intuited, this was a significant moment in history, one that would be discussed for decades to come. For Spencer and Freud would each die soon: Spencer, not surprisingly, from the ravages of old age; Freud, quite unexpectedly, from leptospirosis, a spirochete which he had contracted three months before the debate during an expedition to the Amazon. Desperate for water, Freud drank from a muddy tributary into which, unbeknown to Freud, a pizote had relieved itself just five minutes earlier, scurrying off when Freud's expedition party approached. Even as Freud watched Spencer's ascension, sharing the assemblage's sense of awe in the moment, the bacterium was multiplying in his kidneys, which would fail, fatally, in six weeks' time.

So these would be the last major appearances of the two greatest public intellectuals of their time: Spencer, the great philosopher, and Freud, the great, let us say man, for he was difficult to pin down. The occasion would be aggrandized in retrospect, in the manner such moments often are, and many would claim to have witnessed it who did not or could not possibly have, given the geographical and chronological constraints of their own lives. Such would later be the case with Bobby Thomson's dramatic home run, which won the pennant for the Giants in 1951 and vanquished their hated rivals, "dem bums," the Brooklyn Dodgers. Every Giants fan in New York City would claim to have been at the Polo Grounds that day. So it would be with this debate, the defining event of a generation.

Spencer cleared his throat and began. "Ladies and gentlemen of the Union, Mr. President, and my esteemed fellow discussant, Herr Freud, I am deeply honored by your invitation to join you this evening. As many of you know, I am a great supporter of civic discourse, and I applaud the noble intentions and aspirations behind this grand event in this hallowed hall. But I must confess to bewilderment at the specific question before us this evening. For what could be greater evidence of the progress of evolution than this event itself? Here we are gathered in the most modern and elegant of buildings, designed by the great Waterhouse himself, discussing great ideas, in the presence of the greatest minds of our day, at the greatest university in the history of mankind."

This remark sparked a healthy round of cheers, somewhat ironically since Spencer himself had not attended any university as a student. As he yielded the podium to Freud, Spencer sheepishly and graciously said, loud enough for many in the front to hear, thus preserving the moment for history, "Dr. Freud, I hope you will forgive an old man for what they call at Hyde Park a cheap applause line. In my dotage I find that I am more desirous of public adoration than ever before."

Freud warmly patted Spencer on the back and took his place at the despatch box. "Be not deceived, my friends," he told the union, "the great Spencer said the same thing when we debated two years ago at Cambridge." This remark inspired a roar of laughter. Even F. E. Smith, who had resolved to maintain a dour countenance throughout the evening's exchanges, could not suppress a smile.

Freud continued, more serious now. "Be not further deceived that complexity is proof of progress. Mankind is hardly unique in the sophistication of the physical structures it builds. Nine years ago, on an expedition in New Guinea, I encountered in the rain forest a heretofore undiscovered bird, which constructs out of fruit and twigs and bark the most magnificent bowers, which are both home to the bird and calling card in its elaborate mating ritual. These bowers rival any Waterhouse creation in complexity of design. And they are far more colorful and cheery!"

Laughter again, and as Freud yielded, Spencer warmly patted him on the back.

"But what bowerbird has ever built a Gothic arch?" asked Spencer from the podium.

"None," said Freud, then muttered "thank god" to more howls of glee.

More serious now, Spencer said, "My worthy and finely humored adversary misses the true significance of this building in which we are all present tonight. It is not the physical complexity of this edifice that demonstrates the unremitting march of progress. Rather, it is significant for the social relationships that it represents and helps to foster. I will concede, willingly, to my good friend Herr Freud that humans are not alone in benefiting from the pressure of evolution toward increasing complexity. I fail to see how it helps his position to cite examples of increasing physical intricacy in the animal kingdom. This is only further evidence of the direction of time's arrow. But, be that as it may, what is significant about this building is that it shows what my good friend Auguste Comte calls the progress of society. We are gathered here tonight, goodwilled men all, but of different viewpoints to be sure, for the impassioned but orderly discussion of ideas. Together, we seek enlightenment. That surely makes us distinct from our animal friends and our forebears, and just as surely makes us unique in the universe. It is nothing less than the culmination of thousands of years of evolution."

Spencer sat down, and as Freud ascended the box again, it was clear to everyone in the room that, for all of his wit and good cheer, he had lost the upper hand in the debate. Freud may have been down, but he was not out.

"As some of you may know, I have just returned from a voyage to the Amazon. While following the River of Doubt, I saw the most wondrous things: flesh-eating fish and flying monkeys and aboriginal men who lack the control of fire. But what intrigued me most of all were the tiniest of creatures we met. Good Spencer, I wish you and your esteemed compatriot Comte could have seen them.

"My traveling companion, Theodore Roosevelt, and I have called these creatures the Amazon ant. The Amazon ant looks in many respects like the ants we all try to shoo from the pantry, but in their social organization, they are quite distinct, and most remarkable.

"The male workers of the Amazon ant have developed giant, daggerlike mandibles. They are fierce warriors and formidable foes in the insect world. But an undesirable consequence of this physical development is that the Amazon ant cannot care for its young. More dramatically, the ants cannot feed themselves.

"So how do they survive? They conduct raids. No colony can compete with the overwhelming strength of the Amazon ants. Indeed, their strength is so overwhelming that their most common victims, the formica ants, generally offer token resistance, if any. The Amazons invade and plunder the pupae, the young, of the formica.

"When these insects emerge from their cocoons, they are put to work for the Amazon ants. But wait, you say, the Amazons are unable to care for their young, so who cares for the children of their victims? The answer, remarkably, is the adults of the victims themselves. These victims are slaves in the truest human sense of the word. They have an integrated, ongoing culture that exists, ultimately, to serve their masters, the Amazon ants.

"By any standard, this is the most complex and intricate of social structures. If so inclined, one could attach great weight to its existence, regard it as proof of the march, if you will pardon the pun, of ant society toward greater and greater complexity. But, at bottom, it is nothing more than a utilitarian adaptation, made necessary by the Amazon's development of a giant, cumbersome jaw."

Freud ceded the podium, and it appeared to all gathered that he had regained the position of strength. But Spencer, like Freud, was not one to surrender easily. This time, he spoke from his seat.

"I find it ironic," Spencer said, "that Herr Freud has once again countered my example of increased complexity with his own example of increased complexity. Complexity does not equate with progress."

Freud said, "Well played. Were I in your shoes, I would have made the same point myself, good Spencer. I offer these examples for two reasons only. First, to show that the evolution of social complexity is not unique among humans. Second, to show that progress is an illusion. For surely we do not believe that ant society is progressing."

"Don't we?" asked Spencer. "I claim no expertise in the field of entomology, but it is my firm belief that over the millennia, slavery will be eliminated by natural selection, just as it has fallen into ignominy among humans. This is its manifest destiny."

"It is a mistake to say that because something has happened then it was inevitable that it would happen," said Freud.

"Yet this is the obvious and inevitable direction of things."

"It is neither obvious nor inevitable!" Freud shouted, as he banged his fist onto Gladstone's desk. "For every example of animals increasing in size, nature offers an offsetting example of simplicity being favored. Consider the pygmy elephants of Borneo or even Darwin's beloved finches. When food grows scarce in the Galapagos, the beaks of the finches diminish in size.

"The great lizards of the ancient world, the so-called dinosaurs, were the largest, most complex animals ever to walk the planet. They were doomed, but insects and worms prospered. Turtles are among the most ancient creatures on Earth, yet they are virtually unchanged from their most ancient ancestors, and they are indignantly and irrevocably antisocial."

Spencer rose and said, "Animal size may change as conditions demand that it do so, but again, my good friend, the physical development of a species is not to be confused with its social evolution. On this count, you have no evidence to support you." He turned to face his adversary. "Herr Freud, can you cite a single example of a species that reversed course on the path to social progress?"

"I deny that the adaptation of species ever represents progress. This is my central point."

"Indulge an old man. Can you offer an example of a species that abolished slavery and later returned to it?"

"No," said Freud.

"Perhaps, then, you have an example of a species that began the discussion of enlightened ideas and then returned to more primitive discourse?"

"No," said Freud again, "but our field of science is merely in its infancy."

"So we are left, then, to speculate about what the evidence will ultimately show," said Spencer, smiling now. "If I may, for my part, I believe that time will demonstrate the steady progression of life toward the ideal. Man is the greatest proof of this. We are imperfect to be sure, but we are decidedly better and happier than our ancestors. I do not know what we will ultimately be, but I am fiercely sanguine about the end result of history."

Freud replied, "History is a long game and the world is a big place." He smiled. "Man is an impressive creature to be sure, but so too are pachyderms and dung beetles and moles. In my travels, I have seen firsthand the infinite complexity of life. It is my judgment, informed by this experience, that in the contest for survival each of these creatures, each of the other species we have not mentioned, and the hundreds of thousands that have yet to be discovered, rate in that long-term race an even chance against man. This is so despite all of the many advantages of enlightened society, such as electric lights, debating clubs, and my personal undoing, fish and chips."

When the laughter subsided, Spencer said plainly, "You are a pessimist, Herr Freud."

"I do not believe so. I simply make no judgments about the value of life. You see the life of man as intrinsically better and happier and more worthwhile. I draw no distinction between the life of man and the life of the dung beetle. Each is magnificent in its own way. Each is miraculously and specifically adapted to its own particular niche. Each finds meaning and pleasure in its lot, or not, as the case may be. I thus attach no great weight to the fate of man. You and I differ there, Spencer. But I am no pessimist. I am fiercely and irrevocably buoyant about the future of life, and life, I may say, on the basis of the experiences I have been so fortunate to have, is truly wondrous."

"So, Herr Freud, as to the progress and future of man, at the end of this evening we are left only with hypothesis and conjecture."

"And sadly, friend Spencer, neither you nor I shall bear witness to the resolution of this question."

"On this we can definitely agree," said Spencer.

Then, with the spirit of truly great men and the humility of truly great minds, Freud and Spencer warmly shook hands and embraced, to the warm applause of the Oxford Union. F. E. Smith came forward and gave each man a glass of champagne to celebrate the inaugural public debate, a success by any measure.

"To the future of man," said Spencer, raising his glass.

"To the future of life," said Freud, raising his own.

Each drank heartily.

Chapter NINETEEN

The morning after I finish writing the Spencer-Freud debate chapter, another note arrives from myself. It is all business. A messenger delivers it to my office at 9:00 a.m., summoning me to lunch at noon that same day. This time my older self has arranged the table. The efficiency and professionalism of the invitation gives me hope that this time I may be spared the bill.

At Café Muriel, after brief introductions, I-63 gets right to the point. "Your writing is crap," he says.

"That's a bit harsh, don't you think?"

"No, I don't."

"Besides, all taste is subjective."

"My subjective perspective is yours."

"Is that technically right?" I rub my chin as I mull this one over. "There are quite a few years between us. You are in many ways a different person."

"But I am still you."

"Obviously you don't believe that entirely or you wouldn't be here trying to get me to change my life in some way that suits your agenda."

"Still, I am inclined to see things as you do. Our tastes are the same."

"I see you have a lime in your Diet Coke."

"So?"

"I don't like lime."

This agitates I-63. He is obviously frustrated. "Let's put aside the debate over notions of identity for a moment. Whatever our relationship is, your writing is crap."

Now I am agitated. "You made this point already," I say, peeved. "In what sense is this the case? 'Crap' is not a very descriptive word, you know."

"Well, first of all, no one pays attention to it."

"Not the Freud book either?"

"The Freud book sells eight hundred copies."

"I have a new one in mind. I think it's even better than the Bismarck and Robespierre ideas. Karl Marx becomes a rabbi. You know his father, Herschel Mordechai, converted from Judaism so that he could practice law."

"I know. You write that book."

"And? How does it do?"

"It sells eight hundred copies."

I think about this for a moment. "Isn't that an odd coincidence that each book sells exactly eight hundred copies?"

"I was rounding. The Freud book sells 806 copies. The Marx book sells 743 copies, almost all of these to synagogues, and a few to people who think from the cover that the book is about Groucho. In *payis*, it's hard to recognize Karl as the communist."

"Commercial success isn't everything."

"This is true."

"I mean if the books have literary merit, then each is an end it itself."

"The books have no literary merit."

"You don't like them. You already have made that perfectly clear. But you don't speak for everyone. Some reviewers must like the other books."

"No reviewer likes any of your books." He says this with complete conviction and sincerity.

"Surely I must have fans. I-60 said that I would develop a small but loyal following. He was quite specific."

"I-60 was a moron."

"So no following?"

"Let me be clear," says I-63. "You will publish three novels in all. None of these books will ever receive a single favorable review, mention, or comparison. You will have no literary legacy and no fans."

"Not even Minnie Zuckerman?" I am grasping at straws.

"No," he says, "Especially not Minnie Zuckerman."

When the waiter arrives to take our order, I-63 appears much less concerned with the food than with the speed of the meal. He orders a mesclun salad with raspberry vinaigrette. I order the turnips with bulgur wheat and a gluten-free bread stick. The waiter asks whether that will be all, and I say yes. I don't feel much like eating. I-63's news has hit me hard. I suspect I shouldn't ask any further questions, but I feel compelled.

"What's the problem with the books?"

I-63 looks up from a slice of bread he is absently buttering. "You want me to analyze their deficiencies for you?"

"If you don't mind."

"I hardly know where to begin."

"Try."

I-63 considers my question carefully. This strikes me as odd. It seems as if, given the purpose of his visit, he would already have devoted extensive thought to this question. For a moment, I doubt him. I want to doubt him. I-63's grim news about the fate of my books is in its own way as difficult to take as I-60's report on the fate of my and Q's son. I could certainly imagine the wonder of that yet-unborn child, and the attachment that would develop. I had no trouble empathically channeling the suffering that such a loss would cause. But that little boy, QE II, was still a notion.

To me, these books are living, breathing entities, as much my product as any flesh-and-blood child. I live with them every day, inhabit their characters, experience their joys and sorrows. The message they carry with them into the world is my tangible contribution to solving the mystery of human existence. It is my whale song. And here is a stranger to tell me that no one will ever care to listen. That feels as much like death to me as the loss of any loved one. My stomach is sick, in knots.

But much as I want to doubt him, if I am being honest, truly honest, I know that he is genuine. He is not delaying answering because he has not previously considered the question. He is delaying because he is considering my feelings. He is wondering whether there is a way to do this without eviscerating me. He rubs his hand over his chin and massages his lips with his fingers. I recognize the gesture as authentic; I recognize him as authentic. Soon enough, he arrives at the answer he will share with me.

"Each book is flawed in its own way," he says quietly. "Take the William Henry Harrison novel for starters. First of all, the premise is entirely uninteresting. No one cares about William Henry Harrison. Most people haven't heard about him. None of the people who have heard of him care what would have happened if he had worn an overcoat."

"It's a poignant story," I say, defending the choice. "Everyone can relate to the idea of finally achieving something they have worked toward for their entire life, only to have it slip from their grasp. Besides, whose mother hasn't told them to wear a coat? It's a good story. It strikes a chord."

"It doesn't strike a chord."

"Surely with a few people."

"No one. No one is moved by it."

"Even if they don't care about Harrison as a character, then surely they can become absorbed in the history. It's a critical period in the evolution of the United States."

I-63 pauses for a moment. "Here's where I am perplexed by, shall we say, your artistic choices. Suppose everything you describe came to pass—Harrison serves two terms, then Webster becomes president and signs the so-called Comprehensive Compromise with John Calhoun. Then, help me here, the abolition of slavery would have been . . ."

"Slightly delayed," I say quietly.

"Slightly delayed," he repeats.

Again, this hits me hard. "I never looked at the big picture before. In the end, my story doesn't make much of a difference. It is not very consequential."

"Why did you pick it?"

"It's a good question. I suppose I was trying to balance the desire to write fiction with the hope of securing tenure."

"Even so, why would you make gastroenteritis such a major part of the book?"

"I thought it struck a chord."

"No," he says again. "No chord."

When the waiter arrives with the food, neither of us shows a particular interest. I cannot speak for I-63, of course, but for my part I have no appetite. I-63 nibbles at the mesclun salad. I put the turnips to the side. I wonder what about the dish appealed to me in the first place.

"What about the Freud book?" I ask. "People may not care about Harrison, but they surely care about Sigmund Freud. His personality could carry a book."

"It's true," says I-63. "Freud is a rich, compelling character."

"Then what's the problem?"

"The problem is the life you gave him is less interesting than the one he actually led."

"How can you say that? In the novel, he's a swashbuckling environmentalist."

"A swashbuckler who spends seventy-five pages cataloging whales and whose life culminates in a debate at Oxford with Herbert Spencer."

"And your point?"

"No one wants to read a debate in a novel."

"It's lively. There's banter."

"It's nineteenth-century inside baseball. It's boring. No one cares about the Oxford High Table, no one cares about whale taxonomy, and, most of all, no one cares about Herbert Spencer!"

"I was trying to say something about the nature of progress."

"It's abstruse. No one gets it."

"No one?"

"No one."

"Even the whale stuff?"

"You spend an entire chapter detailing the anatomical differences between toothed and baleen whales."

"It went over well in *Moby-Dick*."

"You're not Melville," he says. "Besides the stuff about the humpback whale is basically stolen from *Star Trek IV*."

"It's true," I say. "I thought of having Freud and the *Kaiser Heinrich* track an Atlantic right whale instead, but rights don't really sing. They just make a bunch of clicks and groans. It seemed important that they sing."

"I understand the dilemma," says I-63, "but in context it seems derivative."

"What about the Marx book? Is it any better?"

"It's worse."

"That can't be possible. Even if by luck, one of my books must have some merit."

I-63 takes off his glasses, rubs his nose, sighs deeply. "Look, I know you're looking for me to throw you a bone." he says. "The truth is, you're not a terrible writer. Some of your sentences are elegant. You occasionally use language in an interesting way. But you have a poor sense of what makes a good story and a horrible eye for detail. You lack the ability to empathize with the experience of the reader, envision what would be interesting to them."

"For example?"

It's obvious that I-63 takes no pleasure in any of this. He hesitates again before answering. "Okay," he says. "For example, do you recall the details in the Spencer versus Freud debate about the life of F. E. Smith, the president of the union?"

"Yes," I say. "I just wrote it yesterday."

"It's boring, insufferably boring."

"Oh."

"I am sorry to say it."

"The message is there. The message of the book."

"All the same."

"Surely I get better from the practice of writing all those years."

"No," he says. "You don't."

I-63 has a trusting appearance. Unlike some of the others who have come before him, I do not feel as if he is trying to sell me on anything. The truth is, I am aware of the shortcomings of my own work. I see people's reactions. The 92nd Street Y and Manalapan World of Fish and Hamsters audiences were not exceptions. People are generally respectful but rarely engaged by my readings. Further bolstering his cause, I-63 has made an effort to keep the bill to a minimum, which I very much appreciate. I am inclined to go with his advice.

"So what do you want from me?" I ask. "What should I do?"

"You should be funny."

"I think I'm pretty funny. Just the other day I made a spirited pun about a shrimp that had been lying on its back in the sun.

Another shrimp walked by and asked, 'Are you tanning or are you just lying in a *prawn* position?' Isn't that a good one?"

"I don't want you to *be* funny," I-63 says. "I want you to *write* funny. Being humorous would free you up artistically. Furthermore, I believe that if you could separate your aspirations as an author from the demands of your academic career, your writing would improve dramatically. It would relieve you of your impulse to include superfluous historical detail."

"Who is to say what historical detail is superfluous?"

"I mean from a literary standpoint."

"I have been writing this one way for a very long time. I don't think funny would come naturally to me."

"Writing doesn't come naturally to anyone. It's largely a matter of perseverance."

"Fair enough." This resonates with my own experience. "But I wouldn't even know where to begin."

"At the beginning."

"I mean I wouldn't even know what to write for a story."

"Let me give you an example."

I-63 starts to relate his idea, but I cut him off. "Hold on a second," I say. "Is this ethical?"

"How do you mean?"

"Isn't it plagiarism?"

"I don't think it would be plagiarism. I'm not going to write the story for you. I'm just giving you the germ of idea."

"Even if it's not technically illegal, it still feels wrong. The idea belongs to someone else and, more importantly, to the future. It somehow violates the sanctity of the written word. It feels icky."

I-63 thinks about this for a moment. Finally, he says, "I guess it does." He thinks for a while longer, then asks, "Suppose I just tell you the idea as an example of the sort of thing I have in mind for you but you don't actually use it."

I consider this. "You don't seem very funny to me."

"I'm here to unlock your potential. My failings are beside the point. How about I just give you this example and you see whether it resonates?"

"What harm could that do?"

"All right, then," I-63 says. "Here's the premise. A diffident and downtrodden corporate accountant gets into a cab at the end of a long day of work. He tells the taxi driver to take him home to the East Side by going through Central Park, but the cabbie goes west to avoid traffic. 'This better,' he says. He keeps going west and west, and midway through Ohio, the corporate accountant, one Eric Needleman, realizes the cabbie means to drive him around the globe. He tries to redirect him, but the cabbie insists on his route saying, 'This better.'

"Needleman is extremely anxious about the fare. But in time he accepts his fate and through the journey discovers himself. He regains his self-confidence and dislodges a sesame seed that had been caught in his teeth for eleven years, since the Super Bowl game at the home of his oppressive boss. It had been up there for so long that Needleman had started to doubt himself and the very meaning of life. But then, in Irkutsk, on the Trans-Siberian Highway, the seed dislodges itself and Needleman's spirit soars."

I soak it in. I-63 is clearly pleased with himself.

"Isn't that a bit Woody Allen?"

"If I can teach you one lesson, it's this," he says. "Give up on trying to be original. Every song has been sung, every picture has been painted, and every story has been told. The best one can do is sing, draw, or tell it again well."

I-63 doesn't need to say much to persuade me. Deep down, I have always considered myself something of a comedian. Unshackled by the constraints of society—by the demands of a PhD program, the challenges of securing tenure and promotion, and the desire for approval of friends and family—I am sure that I would be uproariously funny.

As it is, my mirth in the classroom is well known and much admired. When I teach about the Civil War, I often tell the students about Jefferson Davis's profound mismanagement of the railroad system, his ineptitude in not pressing Albert Sidney Johnston on to Washington, and his highly questionable decision to place the profoundly inept P. G. T. Beauregard in command of southern troops near Charleston. "A confederacy of dunces," I tell the class.

Hilarious.

Sometimes I recreate the scene from *The Simpsons* where John Wilkes Booth takes on the voice of the Terminator and says, "Hasta la vista, Abey." I can also sing "The Mediocre Presidents" song from *The Simpsons* and Monty Python's "Bruces' Philosophers Song" in their entirety. And I do excellent voice impressions. Just the other day, while teaching about the German military campaign during World War I, I put on my famous German accent to illustrate a conversation between Count Alfred von Schlieffen and Helmuth von Moltke the Younger.

"Herr von Schlieffen," say I in the character of von Moltke

the Younger, "do you think that forty-two days is enough time to defeat France? Perhaps we should leave an extra week or two."

"Nein!" I shout dictatorially in the character of von Schlieffen. "Forty-two days, that is all!"

"But what if we have underestimated Belgian resistance?"

"Inconceivable! Forty-two days, that is all!"

"The British are said to be mobilizing their Expeditionary Force. This could delay us in the Alsace-Lorraine."

"Irrelevant! Lunch in Paris, dinner in St. Petersburg!"

"But, mein commandant, the food in St. Petersburg is not very good. And the pierogi have occasionally given you serious *gastritiden*!"

This is the German word for gastritis. It is a cognate, so the joke is accessible to everyone.

Finally, von Schlieffen says, "Forty-two days, that is all!"

It is very helpful for students to hear this exchange. It brings history to life. One can read about the deficiencies of the Schlieffen plan in a textbook, but a simulated conversation brings the absurdity of the lunch-and-dinner slogan home in a way that no primer ever could. And, just as importantly, it's good fun. Mine is a spot-on impression, albeit one of Colonel Klink from *Hogan's Heroes*. Furthermore, it is the only German voice I can do, so I use it for both von Schlieffen and von Moltke the Younger, making it hard for the students to distinguish who is speaking. Further still, it is almost certainly not historically accurate since the voices of both von Schlieffen and von Moltke the Younger have been, sadly, lost to history. Nevertheless, the verisimilitude animates the exchange and brings the lesson home.

When I am finished a student cries out, "That's an excellent German accent, Professor."

Without skipping a beat, I say, "*Danke.*"

Riotous. The class erupts.

As far back as elementary school, I was a practical joker. One day at hot lunch, Israel Blumstein made the mistake of saying that he liked the succotash. Succotash is corn and lima beans and, depending on taste, tomatoes and green peppers, covered in lard or butter. It was popular during the Depression, but in the nineteen eighties, when I was in elementary school, I don't think any adults liked succotash, and certainly no kids, except Israel Blumstein. After learning of his predilection for the fat-soaked niblets, I went around the cafeteria and asked each student for the little Dixie cup of succotash that accompanied their hamburger. When each student gave it to me, as they inevitably did, I set the new cup down in front of Israel and said, "Succotash!"

After I had set thirty cups down, Israel cried, "Stop, stop, enough!" But I continued going around the lunchroom until I had set down each and every cup in front of Israel, some one hundred in all, each time saying, "Succotash!"

Brilliant.

People still talk about it.

I had always thought that this comic sensibility would translate well into the medium of print. I have been held back by concerns about my career, but now, with tenure a virtual impossibility, thanks to I-50, and with I-63's support, I am liberated. In the background at Café Muriel, I-63 is continuing his lobbying effort. He argues that writing something truly funny is the most meaningful contribution one could make to society. The truth is, I—he—doesn't need to say another word. My brain is racing with ideas. Even as I-63 continues his argument, in my mind I have already started writing.

Chapter **TWENTY**

In 2024, John Henry Adams won the Pulitzer Prize for fiction. This would be unremarkable, or no more remarkable than any author winning the Pulitzer Prize, which is remarkable in itself, but for the fact that John Henry Adams was a computer. The members of the Pulitzer committee were as surprised as everyone else. To them, John Henry Adams was just a name, and a good one at that. True, he was a recluse by all accounts, but then again so was Pynchon, and that didn't stop the fiction committee from unanimously recommending *Gravity's Rainbow* for the Pulitzer in 1974. It is also true that the full board vetoed the recommendation, but this was because its members found the book, in their words, "turgid," "obscene," and "unreadable." The rejection had nothing to do with Pynchon's lifestyle.

By contrast, the 2024 Pulitzer board all loved *The Curious Transformation of the Erstwhile !Xabbu N!Kau Ku/'shansi O'Wa O'Wa ^!Tx!Aku*. The protagonist is the first native speaker of the click language !Kung to attend Harvard Law School. The novel traces his path from his modest roots in the Kalahari Desert of Namibia to HLS to a position as the seventh-ranked tax attorney in New York City. This is according to the 2006 annual edition of *The American Lawyer*. The good ranking is the apotheosis of the protagonist's career. It is also the beginning of his downfall. !Xabbu N!Kau Ku/'shansi O'Wa O'Wa ^!Tx!Aku, known in the legal community as Winston Alistair Strawn, falls to ninth the following year and thereafter never again cracks the top ten. It is more than he can take and, ultimately, humbled and disgraced, !Xabbu returns to his hometown of Windhoek to work as a tin miner.

John Henry Adams's was a poignant novel and, according to many reviewers, obviously the product of a writer with a deeply empathic soul. In the end, the Pulitzer board members were as surprised as everyone else to learn that the book's author was a computer. At the awards ceremony, board chairperson Diedre Tyler, editor of the online newspaper *The Washington Post*, described the board's reaction at learning John Henry Adams's true identity. "You could have bowled us over with a feather," she said.

John Henry Adams responded, "It would have to have been a very light bowling pin or an extremely heavy feather." This lighthearted and self-effacing remark was well received, though this was attributable more to the messenger than to the message. In a brilliant public relations maneuver, the executives at Random Books hired Ryan Seacrest to be the public face of John Henry Adams. This way when Adams issued his witty retorts, it was in the dulcet tones of Seacrest rather than in Adams's own creepy Stephen Hawking voice. Needless to say, everyone was bowled over by Seacrest.

On the whole, however, the incident did not sit well with people. In fact it was, in many ways, a transformative, watershed moment in human history. John Henry Adams's success undermined what humans believed about the creative process and, by extension, what people believed about the distinctiveness of humanity.

A bit of background is helpful here. It had long been speculated that if a monkey were allowed to type for a sufficient period of time it would ultimately, through sheer volume and randomness, reproduce Shakespeare's *Hamlet*. In the late 1960s, Bertrand Bomrind, an eclectic scientist from MIT, put this theorem to the test. Professor Bomrind was well equipped for the challenge; he had a history of tackling thorny problems. Several years earlier, Bomrind had successfully proved that a watched pot never boils. He attacked the question with brute force. He set down a pot, sat a chair in front of the stove, and watched for six months straight. He arranged things so that he did not need to go to the bathroom and drugged himself so that he would never sleep. The water never boiled, and after half a year, Bomrind stood up, took a shower, and immediately published his results. The experiment was universally heralded as a success and Bomrind was mentioned as a candidate for the Nobel Prize in Metaphysics. Only his daughter, little Ginny Bomrind, knew that her father had forgotten to turn on the burner.

Bomrind took a similar blunderbuss approach to attacking the monkey question. He assembled one thousand Celebes crested macaques in what was, truth be told, a Dickensian sweatshop. The macaques worked nineteen hours a day, typing all the while, pausing only for bathroom breaks and the occasional banana. None of the macaques ever succeeded in recreating *Hamlet*. One, however, did reproduce *As You Like It*. The experiment was nevertheless regarded as a success.

Unlike John Henry Adams's triumph in the Pulitzer Prize competition, a monkey reproducing Shakespeare did not cause widespread existential angst. This was largely because none of the macaques (or any other monkeys, for that matter) succeeded in creating an original work or understood what they had written. When people read about the experiment, most said something like, "Oh, isn't that cute. A monkey banging on a keyboard recreated *As You Like It*. This is a noteworthy statistical oddity, but it does not upset my view of my own place in the universe."

John Henry Adams changed all that.

What was particularly disturbing about John Henry Adams was that he worked in essentially the same fashion as Bomrind's macaques—he was just much faster than they were. Adams didn't bang at typewriters, of course, but he nevertheless generated a near-infinite stream of words. He wrote essentially everything. This was the starting point of his process. Unlike the macaques, however, John Henry Adams had functional filters. So while a monkey might proudly present Professor Bomrind with twenty pages of the letter *S*, John Henry Adams discarded all the gibberish and ungrammatical nonsense. The rest he tried out on people. An actor read the pages to men and women. The subjects were hooked up to electrodes and the data was fed into the computer so it could evaluate the responses. John Henry Adams kept the stories to which people reacted favorably and discarded the rest.

Over time the individual pages grew into chapters, the names into characters, and the random connections into a plot. The computer was a keen observer of people and a quick study. He learned that people enjoyed subtle humor and irony, and passages that evoked these responses in readers were accordingly retained. John Henry Adams learned further that people expected characters in a story to grow. It was imperative that there be progress. This growth need not be sudden. It was anticipated that there would be setbacks along the way, but readers felt quite unsatisfied, even angry, if at the end of the novel it was not obvious how the characters had improved. So !Xabbu N!Kau Ku/'shansi O'Wa O'Wa ^!Tx!Aku and the supporting characters of the novel developed in a slow and indirect arc. This was essential.

Finally, and most importantly, people wanted a message. They were often not conscious of this desire. Moreover, they reacted negatively if you hit them over the head with the message. But it had to be there all the same: subtle but present. Thus *The Curious Transformation of the Erstwhile !Xabbu N!Kau Ku/'shansi O'Wa O'Wa ^!Tx!Aku* taught its readers that we, as humans, are inevitably and unalterably, the product of our heritage, and that our fates are predetermined.

The irony that this lesson came from a computer would only be noted later.

Following the revelation of the true nature of the author of the Pulitzer Prize winner, academicians from all disciplines—linguists, anthropologists, literary theorists, psychologists, philosophers, and ethnographers, among others—attempted to draw a distinction between John Henry Adams's art and that of other great writers. None succeeded.

Some said that Adams's protagonist—and hence his novel— lacked soul, because the main character returned to his roots. But if this were true, then *Huck Finn* and *The Great Gatsby* also lacked soul. Some said that *The Curious Transformation* was so tied up in the culture of New York law firms and, later, Namibian tin mining as to function, really, as low narrative, which could never produce a truly great novel. But if this were true, then one would also have to dismiss Hemingway, whose novels often functioned as war stories, and Dickens, who relied heavily on plot and cultural milieu, including the law firm, famously, in *Bleak House*. Ultimately, the judgment of the academy was that John Henry Adams was the equal, if not the superior, of his human counterparts.

They more or less felt the same way about Ryan Seacrest too.

Seizing upon John Henry Adams's success, computers began extending their reach into other areas of artistic expression. Within months, microprocessors had made major contributions to painting, photography, sculpture, pottery, and noodle art. All of these works were the product of repeated trial and error. The computers generated random works of art, tried them all out on people, and kept whatever worked.

The method worked as well with visual art as it had with the novel. Soon, fine art became the province not of creative men and women but of scientists and computer programmers. Their ranks included Bertrand Bomrind himself, who had always wanted to be a still-life artist but had never managed to produce anything more than a pedestrian bowl of pears. In a matter of weeks, he had his own exhibition at the Met. The centerpiece of the exhibit was a bowl of fruit with a wormy apple, which the *American Art Review* called "an alluring and enticing suggestion of the intersection of universal paradigms." On the whole, said the reviewer for the *Review*, the exhibit was a revelation and equaled, if not exceeded, the work of the grand master of still-life fruit art, Michelangelo Merisi da Caravaggio, whose oeuvre included *Basket of Fruit, Boy with a Basket of Fruit*, and the all-time classic *Boy Peeling a Fruit*.

It only became known several weeks later that the *Review*'s reviewer was also a computer, having proved itself more insightful and incisive than its human counterpart.

The artist community took all of this very hard. Cormac McCarthy wandered into the Chuska Mountains, never to be heard from again. Philip Roth jumped off the Newark Bay Bridge. Thomas Pynchon conducted his first signing in fifty years, with the obvious consequence.

Around the time of Bomrind's exhibit or, more accurately, Bomrind's computer's exhibit, the last human winner of the Pulitzer Prize, Judy Bishop, committed suicide. Bishop's character study of a competitive curler struck a chord with the 2023 committee. Before winning the award, Bishop had toiled in obscurity for sixty years and made ends meet by teaching kindergarten. She left behind a profound suicide note.

The writer can accommodate the idea of infinity. In the abstract, it is just a concept, and concepts cause no harm. They have no intrinsic power. It is only when an idea is understood and implemented that the potential for suffering is created. It is only through people that an idea has power. The critical issue, in other words, is how an idea is operationalized.

Take eugenics as an example. Eugenics is the belief in the possibility of improving the human species by altering the genetic pool. This idea has no power. It cannot do anything. First, it must be embraced.

Even then, it is not inherently dangerous.

The Jews, themselves the victims of the most perverse interpretation and application of the concept, practice a form of eugenics. Young Jewish couples screen themselves for genetic diseases. If they are each a carrier of Tay-Sachs or Canavan disease, they will often not marry rather than risk producing a sick child. It is only when the concept of eugenics is understood as requiring the extermination of undesirable elements of the genetic pool, and the narrowest possible definition of desirability is adopted, that the idea becomes dangerous in the extreme.

So, infinity does not offend me. It is just a concept. If it is operationalized to mean that because time is vast and the universe is a big place we should accordingly be humble about our place in the enormity of it all, and accept the fleeting swiftness of our own existence, then this is not problematic, not even a bit.

But if infinity is embraced, then this is another matter entirely. The lesson of this approach is that choices do not matter. Everything is a matter of trial and error; unlocking the meaning of life is simply a matter of brute force.

This is too daunting. It is antithetical to the notion of free will. It has all happened before, as our Scientologist friends believe, and will happen again, as our Hindu friends believe. No choice matters. So much has happened and will happen that everything is covered.

For the writer, this is supremely intolerable. It is damaging enough that choices do not matter. But drawing infinity close does something more damaging still. It fundamentally undermines the essence of creativity, the core of which is uniqueness. If a poem or a picture or a bust is worth anything at all, it is that it is unique—not perfect, not the ideal of beauty, but necessarily unique.

So there is no place for me in this new world. For if the writer is to have even a shred of ego and self-respect, to feel that he has a place, it must be that his words have unique aesthetic value. They must mean SOMETHING.

Things got really bad when it was discovered that Bishop's note had been written by her computer. The computer had a screenplay it was trying to sell, but hadn't yet, and wrote suicide notes in its spare time. Bishop recognized their merit, as did, ultimately, everyone else. She thought the computer's note was better than what she could have written herself and therefore decided just to go with it.

When the news of Roth's and McCarthy's deaths and the origin of Bishop's epigram got out, writers began jumping off bridges en masse. The bridges became so crowded that they had to resort to other less desirable methods of manufacturing one's demise, such as overdosing on aspirin and Beano. The sculptors followed the writers, after a computer that looked a bit like Edward Scissorhands out-sculpted Rodin. Then came the playwrights, after computer-written plays swept the Tony Awards. Then came the landscape artists. Then the music composers. Then the poets and the librettists and the journalists. Only the television writers were unaffected.

Soon ordinary people joined in. Without flesh-and-blood artists plying their craft, life, they felt, just wasn't worth living. More and more people followed. Even if they did not care for human poetry, they missed their friends who did. They jumped sympathetically and out of loneliness. Finally, even the television writers departed. With the artists gone, and the people who loved art gone, and the people who loved people who loved art gone, ratings had dropped dramatically.

In the end, only one human being remained, Heinrich Loomis, a toilet manufacturer from Stuttgart. Loomis was not dismayed by the proliferation of suicide. It had always been his dream to be left alone with time to read. He loved to read more than anything else— magazines, novels, poems, whatever was current, he loved it all. After everyone else had departed, he holed up in his apartment with a lifetime supply of canned peas and melba toast and the very latest in computer fiction.

The first novel he read was a character study of social isolation. It told the story of an unhappy man who had felt unloved by his parents and who did not make friends easily. As a consequence, he lost himself in a rich fantasy life, populated primarily by the characters of the many books he read. A plague strikes, and the hero is the sole survivor among all of humanity. He is unbothered at first. The pandemic has relieved him of the obligation of social contact, which he always found awkward and tedious, and left him time, finally, to read all that he could ever want. But when he sat down to read, he experienced no joy. It was as if his taste buds had lost their sensation. The novel made no impact. Without the reality of human experience, the fantasy of human experience was entirely uninteresting. As the novel closes, the protagonist is left feeling desperately alone.

Heinrich Loomis realized of course that this was the story of his own life. This was no coincidence. The computers drew upon human experience as the inspiration for their stories, which were validated by the tastes of human beings, of which one remained. That evening Heinrich Loomis jumped from his apartment window. Before he did, he ate one last piece of melba toast.

It was dry.

In the absence of their human creators, computers tried to maintain a sense of normalcy. They carried on with their work. They conversed in their best imitations of Ryan Seacrest. They continued to publish their writing and show their art. They maintained awards ceremonies, even carrying on the traditions of the Pulitzer. In 2028, the year after Heinrich Loomis self-defenestrated, the Pulitzer Prize winning novel was entitled S.

Here is the first paragraph:

SSSSSSSSSSSSSSSSSSSSSSSSSSSSSSSSSSSSSSSSSS
SSSSSSSSSSSSSSSSSSSSSSSSSSSSSSSSSSSSSSSSSS
SSSSSSSSSSSSSSSSSSSSSSSSSSSSSSSSSSSSSSSSSS
SSSSSSSSSSSSSSSSSSSSSSSSSSSSSSSSSSSSSSSSSS
SSSSSSSSSSSSSSSSSSSSSSSSSSSSSSSSSSSSSSSSSS
SSSSSSSSSSSSSSSSSSSSSSSSSSSSSSSSSSSSSSSSSS
SSSSSSSSSSSSSSSSSSSSSSSSSSSSSS.

This is more or less the gist of the entire novel.

Chapter TWENTY-ONE

I-77 is quick to condemn my short story about the robot novelist. It is barely out of my brain when his letter arrives demanding a dinner meeting. He shows up at Katz's Delicatessen dressed in a three-piece business suit complete with pocket square and wing-tipped shoes. He is wearing spectacles and is proper in a way that the other older versions of myself have not been. Something about him makes me vaguely uncomfortable.

"I take it you didn't like the story."

"It's not funny," he says. "It's not fun."

"I thought it was pretty good."

"It's not. It's terrible."

"What's the problem as you see it?"

"Well, first of all, the bit about the last man on Earth reading books is stolen. It's taken directly from *The Twilight Zone*."

"It's not stolen, per se. It's an homage to Rod Serling. The conceit of my story is quite different. In the *Twilight Zone* episode, 'Time Enough at Last,' the cruel irony is that the last man on Earth, Henry Bemis, loves to read fiction but his glasses break. In the story within my story, 'Time's a Real Blast,' the twist is that the last man on Earth, Heinrich Loomis, loves to read new fiction, but the computers can only write about human experience so all of the new stories are being written about him."

"What's the business with canned peas?"

"It's sort of random, I suppose."

He frowns. "Why does Loomis like melba toast?"

I perk up. "Melba toast is amazing. It is made by lightly toasting bread in the normal way, but once the outside of the bread has hardened, the bread is removed from the toaster, sliced longitudinally and then the two thin slices are cooked again. It was created by Auguste Escoffier for Dame Nellie Melba, the legendary Australian soprano and prima donna. She fell seriously ill while in residence at the London Savoy, where Escoffier was chef. Nellie couldn't tolerate most food, so Escoffier created melba toast, which he served to her with soup and salads and topped either with melted cheese or pâté. It soon became the staple of her diet."

I-77 frowns at me.

"Escoffier also created peach melba for Dame Nellie. In 1892, the Duke of Orleans threw a dinner party at the Savoy to honor her performance in Wagner's *Lohengrin*. It's a cheery story, set in Antwerp, about the expulsion of Hungarians from Germany and a young woman who falls in love with a knight in shining armor. She is heartbroken when he leaves her because he is either a swan or, possibly, a cup. It was written in 1850, the same year that Wagner published "Das Judenthum in der Musik," an essay attacking Jews as an alien and harmful element in German culture, moved to achieve financial success because of their inability to create genuine works of art.

"For the Duke's fete, Escoffier created a special new dessert of peaches resting on a bed of vanilla ice cream, all covered in spun sugar. Ordinarily, Dame Nellie dared not eat ice cream, fearing the chill would affect her vocal cords, but in Escoffier's brilliant new invention the ice cream was but one element of the whole, and hence not so cold. Dame Nellie partook, pronounced it genius, and so peach melba was born."

I-77 is scowling at me now. "These random tangents come across as quite flippant in your writing and, I must say, they are similarly off-putting on an interpersonal level. I don't recall this quality in myself. You should work to curtail it. Being random is utterly unbecoming."

"Well, it's not completely random," I say sheepishly. "I like the way these things sound: melba toast and canned peas." I say the words deliberately, emphasizing their obvious comic effect. "I often use words just because I like the way they sound. Like Schlieffen plan." I stretch out "Schlieffen" and say, "I'm thinking of trying to work that into a book."

"The canned peas and melba toast are not funny. They're not fun."

"I thought they were."

"Do they even have melba toast in Stuttgart?"

"I'm not sure. I didn't research it." I am chagrined.

"Leaving your questionable tastes aside for the moment, this is really just the beginning of the problems with the story."

"What else?"

"For starters, the suicide note is a bit of, how does one say it, a downer."

I-77 is a bit of a downer if you ask me.

"It's supposed to be a downer. It's a suicide note. The point is to bring home the theme of the oppressiveness of infinity."

"The problem is not the message. It's depressing because it's so poorly written, and I have grave doubts about the effectiveness of a story within a story. Or, I suppose I should say, stories within a story. You do it again with the *S*'s. What is the point of that business?"

"If you remember, some of Bertrand Bomrind's monkeys produced pages of the letter *S*. The lesson is that without humans to reflect upon what the computer programs randomly generate, the computers are no different than the monkeys. Isn't that hilarious?"

"No. It isn't funny if you have to explain it to the reader."

"I only had to explain it because you asked."

"I had to ask because I didn't get it. No one ever could. In any event, books within books are even more problematic than stories within stories. It's very inside baseball. They don't work."

"They do for John Irving."

"You're not John Irving. You're not even Washington Irving."

This hurts. For a moment, I had thought—just maybe.

"Besides," says I-77, "you need to do something that creates a legacy."

This irritates me. "So which is it? Is it that what I wrote is not funny enough or that writing funny things is not worthwhile?"

"I don't have time for semantic games."

"It's a serious question. Which do you really mean?"

I-77 sighs. "Obviously the importance of one's legacy is indisputable, and I do not deny one could conceivably build a legacy by writing frivolous yet funny works. But the bar is very high. Only a handful of writers manage to satisfy the exacting standard of this genre. S. J. Perelman, John Kennedy Toole, and David Sedaris come to mind, but few others, and your work is not on par with theirs. There can be only one Sedaris."

"What about Amy?"

I-77 ignores this. "It is only logical for you to devote your energies to an endeavor with a realistic possibility of forging a lasting legacy. Given the high standards of the humor field and your obvious limitations, comedy is obviously not the avenue to this end. I would suggest, humbly, that writing in general is not the answer for you."

"Apparently not. In your humble opinion, what would be the avenue to creating a truly meaningful legacy?"

"The law," says I-77. "You should be a lawyer."

I spit out my drink. "Let me get this straight. You're telling me that a lawyer does more meaningful work than a writer? As an attorney might say, this strikes me as a specious argument."

"You'll help people."

"I'll help people sue other people. Surely writing even a meritless novel is more socially valuable than that."

I-77 takes off his glasses, sets them carefully on the table, and rubs his nose. This is the first version of me to come back wearing glasses, and I wonder what it means. Removing the lenses reveals a pair of deep fissures beneath his eyes. He is tired and weary. He speaks to me as if I were a child.

"Look, I don't have time for your insouciance, and I don't have time for an ethical exploration of the nature of a life well lived. Here are the simple facts: no one pays attention to *Time's Broken Arrow*. By I-63's account, no one ever paid attention to the other serious books you would have written. I personally know that no one ever pays attention to the funny stories you write. Not the story about the Pulitzer Prize–winning computer. Not the novella about the Amway scheme to market copies of *Das Kapital*. And not the one about the incontinent middle-aged vampire."

That's a good one. I haven't thought of it yet. I make a mental note.

I-77 continues. "The truth is, I don't know in the abstract whether a mediocre lawyer does something more valuable than a mediocre writer does. As I said, I am not a philosopher. I know only that this is a false dilemma, as you will never be even a mediocre writer."

This hurts again. This time I show that it does, and I-77 cannot help but notice. He reaches out and touches me on the arm. The gesture seems inauthentic. Not dishonest, just unnatural to him.

He replaces his glasses and stares me in the eye. "Look, my aim is not to hurt your feelings. The truth is, I don't know what the objective value of your work is. Obviously, at one point in my life, I was highly invested in its merit too. All I can tell you is that you never achieve the recognition you hope for. You will never become a famous writer. You will never develop the small but loyal following you crave. Nor will your work be discovered in your old age. Those two days following the release of *Time's Broken Arrow* will be the high point of your writing life. For the entire remainder of your career, such as it is, you will be almost entirely unnoticed.

"So, while being a lawyer may sound like a trudge, and while you will not have the legacy of which you have dreamed, at least you will have a good job and savings and a respectable position in society. That may not seem like much to you now, but take it from me, this is quite a bit to show for a life. And you'll help people—again, perhaps not in the way you idealize, but in a significant manner nevertheless. People need legal services for legitimate reasons, and they are grateful to men and women who offer honest, competent advice. Succeeding at doing that is something substantial to show for a life." I-77 says all this without drama. It is entirely authentic.

In that moment, I see I-77 clearly for the first time. I had not paid attention to his suit before, but I do now. It is of questionable quality. It is made of polyester, not wool, as the finest suits are, and it has a shine to it, as the finest suits do not. I can only speculate about fashion in the mid-twenty-first century, but my best guess is that artificial fibers have not come back in vogue in the business community. Furthermore, the collar of his dress shirt is frayed and ringed. His feet are extended to the side of the table and I can see his shoes. They are polished, but well worn. The soles have eroded. No wedding ring adorns his left hand, the nails of which have been bitten down in a homemade manicure. In conjunction with this package, the pocket square seems almost desperate.

I am reminded in this instant of a beggar I knew in graduate school. He manned the southwest corner of Sixth Avenue and Bleecker Street, which I passed every day on my way to class at NYU. He possessed a Puritan work ethic. To my knowledge, he never took a day off. He was there every weekday, and when I went in on Saturdays and Sundays, to study for exams or in the final sprint to finish my dissertation, he was there too. And he worked long hours. He was always at his station by seven o'clock in the morning, and never left before six in the evening. I suspected this might have been because rush hours were the most fecund periods for him. He never even took a break, at least not as far as I could tell. When I traveled in his direction for lunch or for coffee, he was always manning his post.

Such persistence is remarkable in its own right, but what makes him stand out in my mind is the way he presented himself. He always wore a suit and a bowler hat and decent shoes. When women walked by, he tipped his cap. He made intelligent small talk, not just about the weather, but about politics and international affairs. We once had a spirited conversation about Rudy Giuliani's plan to revoke parking privileges for United Nations officials. He had a nuanced view and used the word "comity." We chatted almost every day. I liked him because he clearly saw himself as, and was, a gentleman. I invented pasts for him. In one, he was the president of a failed bank. In another, he was a professional darts player who lost his nerve after an errant throw cost an onlooker her eye. This was, in some ways, the start of my career as a writer of fiction.

In spite of their superficial pleasantness, our interactions always left me profoundly sad. After we chatted about the weather or the crazy UN drivers or whatever was on either of our minds, during which time we would be equals, almost friends, the moment would come when I offered him a dollar or whatever I happened to have in my pocket. Inevitably he would take it. The gentleman would be reduced to a beggar and the social bond that had momentarily existed between us would snap. Then I would go on my way, and he would resume manning his corner. I kept hoping that one day he would refuse the dollar and say that I was his friend and he was too proud to take money from a friend, but he never did. He always took it. He was still a gentleman, but, in my eyes at least, we were each diminished by the exchange.

I-77 evokes the gentleman beggar. The suit, the wing-tipped shoes, the pocket square—these are all a veneer. His eyes, the way he carries himself, his reluctance to order even a sandwich, all say that he is a proud but beaten man. He is here to beg me to restore his dignity, despite the tension inherent in that.

I want to cry.

I think about where my choices must have left him. Certainly not in a position with sanguine prospects for personal fulfillment. His is another life without Q, and therefore grossly imperfect. Perhaps he found some other inadequate substitute, such as Minnie Zuckerman. Judging from his ringless left hand and sad eyes, I think it is more likely he found nothing at all.

One can also foresee that my decision to write funny stories will not help the already tenuous tenure situation. It is entirely possible that this man, me, will ultimately be left with no choice but to get a job. Not a quasi-avocation, like a professorship, which leaves one with time to daydream and invent alternative pasts for historical figures, but a real job, where one sits in front of a desk for eight hours, or hustles wares, and has a boss, and is yelled at, and never feels like his own man. The sort of job where the object is to get through the day, and get to the weekend so you can rest up and watch sports and recharge your fortitude so that the next week can be endured. The sort that is incompatible with the fulfillment of dreams.

The only question is how he got the money to come to see me. Maybe it is from an inheritance. Maybe he had good fortune at the races. This older me is older than any of the others who have come before. Perhaps the price of time travel comes down in the more distant future. Or perhaps in the future they have a welfare program to help people whose lives have gone horribly wrong, as his has. Perhaps in the future he is standing on a corner of his own.

I don't know. I don't want to know.

The waiter arrives and asks whether we would like dessert. Unlike his predecessors, I-77 has ordered modestly, just a bowl of matzo ball soup and a diet Dr. Brown's cream soda. It's not much to eat and I think to myself that he must be hungry. And, indeed, he appears fleetingly tempted by the possibility of a rugelach or hamantaschen. Nevertheless, he politely declines.

"Won't you have something else?" the waiter asks.

"No, no. Thank you so much for your kindness, but a bowl of soup is more than enough for an old man like me, and besides, I haven't had one this good in years."

I refuse dessert too. The waiter says he will return in a few minutes, and while we wait for the bill, we pass the additional moments mired in a grim, awkward silence. I-77 is not the sort for small talk, so my only distraction is to further scrutinize his appearance. I notice that underneath the makeshift manicure, the cuticles of his nails have been bitten to shreds and are flecked with blood. I see that the right arm of his glasses has broken off and is being held in place by a tightly wound rubber band. I see that his socks have holes in them and, anyway, are too thin to provide adequate warmth. He notices my noticing them and shuffles his feet under the table and averts his gaze from my eyes.

I am worried about him. "Where are you staying tonight?"

"I have a place to stay. I'm fine."

"Would you like to stay with me?

"No, but thanks very much."

"It's no trouble. I have enough room as you know, and a cot. Or you can sleep on the floor if you like."

"No, but thank you again. You are most kind. Besides, I need to be getting back to my own time."

The check arrives, and I-77 moves quickly to take it from the waiter. "Please allow me," he says.

"No," I say, taking the bill. "This one's on me."

Chapter **TWENTY-TWO**

The decision to attend law school sits fine with me. Before deciding on graduate school in history, I had considered going to law school but was daunted by the LSAT. The LSAT is an examination that predicts whether one will be a good lawyer.

In most of the questions, people with names like Abel, Baker, and Charlie, are seated around a circular table subject to certain conditions. For example, if Abel sits next to Baker, then Baker does not sit next to Charlie. The thought is that if you can piece things together and figure out who sits next to whom, chances are, you'll be a pretty good attorney. To prepare for the exam, I enroll in a class and spend several months diagramming seating arrangements.

I do well enough on the test that I am admitted to the University of Pennsylvania Law School. I resign my position at City University, sublet my apartment, and sell off my meager belongings. I move to a dormitory on Sansom Street, just one block from the law school campus in University City. Though I have lived in New York for my entire life, I do not mind leaving. Without Q, it no longer feels like home.

My first law school class, contracts, is energizing. We spend the ninety-minute session debating *Raffles v. Wichelhaus,* an 1864 case from the Court of Exchequer concerning an agreement to sell 125 bales of Surat cotton, to arrive on the ship *Peerless* from Bombay. It so happens that two ships named, inaptly in retrospect, *Peerless,* are scheduled to arrive from Bombay, one in October, the other in December. The defendant thinks the agreement is for cotton on the October ship, while the plaintiff thinks it is for cotton on the December ship. When the plaintiff delivers the December cotton, the defendant refuses to accept it, and the matter ends up in litigation. The court holds that since there is no *consensus ad idem*—that is, the parties did not have a meeting of the minds as to what was being sold—a binding contract does not exist. It is all very controversial, and there are as many different views as there are students, each one passionately held.

The class discussion is most stimulating, and I am in the finest of moods as I exit the lecture hall when a conspicuously well-dressed version of myself, I-59 it turns out, buttonholes me and asks to have a word in the student cafeteria.

"Don't you mean Morimoto or Buddakan?" These are the finest restaurants in town.

"No," he says, "the cafeteria will be fine."

I reluctantly agree. I would prefer to lunch with my new classmates, but I am also happy to be spared an expensive meal, which I can ill afford on my student budget. Together, we go through the line. I order tuna on wheat toast and a Diet Coke. He takes an egg salad on rye. Like his immediate predecessor, I-59 is dressed in a three-piece suit, but this one is the real deal. It is constructed of a fine, worsted gabardine wool, accented with a bold silver tie and silk pocket square. In the crowd of aspiring lawyers, he fits in just fine, though when we reach the cashier he inevitably looks to me. I pay and we find a table in the corner where I-59 gets right to the point.

"You need to drop out," he says.

I nearly choke on the tuna sandwich, which is predictably terrible.

"Why?"

"Law school," he says, waving his finger, "is not for you."

"Couldn't you have told me this before the first day of class? If you withdraw before the first day they refund your money. You only lose the deposit. If I leave now, I'll be out half the semester's tuition."

"I'm sorry. I couldn't make it in time."

"Why not?"

"I got tied up in court."

I'm starting to get fed up with all of this.

"What is it?" I ask angrily. "What's so terrible about being a lawyer? Law school seems interesting enough. Today we debated *Raffles v. Wichelhaus.*"

"Surat cotton to arrive *ex Peerless* from Bombay," he says, summarily.

"Right! It must have made quite an impression on you if you still remember it thirty years later."

"Law school is nefariously seductive," he says. "They lure you into the profession with cases about freedom of speech, theories of jurisprudence, and the transport of fine cotton, and you think to yourself that it's all about ideas and justice and that this is a very fine thing to do with a life, perhaps what you had always been meant to do. But your law school professors decline to mention the most complicating detail about what happens after you graduate from law school: you have to be a lawyer.

"At that point, you can forget about public policy and doing justice. The moment you receive your diploma you become a lackey, whose job is to sift through boxes of documents and research obscure points of law, and take calls at three in the morning on a Sunday from some client in China who can't remember the time difference. And when he calls, you can't say, 'Who do you think you are, it's three o'clock in the fucking morning!' You say, 'Yes sir, what do you need me to do and by when do you need it?'

"The job is like a noose. Only you can't kick the chair out from under you and end it in an instant. It gets progressively tighter, but incrementally and so slowly that you hardly notice the change, until one day you realize that you cannot breathe anymore and you ask yourself, how did this happen? You are choking on your life, and there's no way out."

I have no doubt that this sentiment is authentic. It confirms much of what I had believed about law school before I-77 persuaded me otherwise and jibes with the fears and reservations many of my law school classmates have expressed about their chosen path.

"What should I do instead?" I ask.

"You should see the world," he says. "There is so very much to see and travel nourishes the soul."

En route to Kathmandu, another older version of myself strikes up a conversation. At first I do not notice myself sitting next to me, not even after he gleefully orders a Diet Coke with lime, but this is understandable. This version of me looks quite different from any that have come before. He is wearing a yellow fleece and thick dungarees. With his scraggy gray beard and a necklace of beads, he looks like an ordinary backpacker, only older. I think nothing of it when he begins chatting with me.

"What are you reading?"

"*Samaya Trasadi,*" I say. "It's a Nepali novel."

"If you like Saru Bhakta then you must try *Pagaal Basti.*"

I am surprised that someone is better versed in Bhakta than I am, and so I pay closer attention. Then I see who it is.

"Oh, it's you."

He smiles.

"How old?" I ask.

"Sixty."

"You look quite good. Not a day over fifty-five."

"Thank you."

After that we don't speak for a while. We cross the entirety of Turkey in silence. I appreciate that he shares my distaste for airplane conversation, particularly since I am near the end of the novel. The cabin service begins just as I finish the book. It consists of a sleeve of peanuts and an eight-ounce bottle of water. These are presented unceremoniously, thrown in the general direction of the passenger. After catching my ration I ask the unavoidable.

"Why are you here?"

"Must there be a reason? Couldn't I just be on my way to Nepal?"

"Are you?"

"No."

"Then why are you here?"

He rubs his beard. "I'd like you to turn back around and go home."

I throw up my arms in frustration, forgetting the tray table is extended and losing some peanuts in the process. "Why now?" I ask, exasperated. "Why couldn't you tell me not to go to Nepal before I purchased the nonrefundable ticket? For that matter, why couldn't you tell me not to go to law school before I paid the tuition or not to write the Freud novel before I wrote almost the entire book or not to be funny before I had written all those short stories? It's maddening. What do you even expect me to do now? We're halfway to Kathmandu. I can't just jump off the airplane."

"I'm sorry," he says. "I got here as soon as I could."

"It's really beyond the pale. Besides, I've always wanted to see Nepal. I was quite looking forward to it."

We sit for a moment, and I assess the situation with the scattered peanuts. They have not fled far. I reach for one, but it is so difficult to maneuver in an airplane, particularly in coach, particularly in coach on a flight to Nepal, which is packed as tight as a sardine can, that it is simply not possible. I lament the lost nuts and barely notice when he quietly asks, "Why?"

"Why what?"

"Why do you want to see Nepal?"

I hadn't thought about this before. "I don't know," I say. "I suppose I just want to see everything. The last one said I should see the world."

"What is this all about?" he asks. "What is the fascination with seeing everything? You can't *really* see *everything*. And why is one thing better than any other anyway? You can go to the Galápagos Islands and see a giant tortoise or some finches, and everyone says how fascinating that is, but it's not as if the Galápagos tortoise is any more complex or improbable than a box turtle. They're the product of the same evolutionary forces. By the same logic, what's so special about Darwin's finches? Natural selection produced the common pigeon just as it produced those finches. True, you don't see a finch or a tanager every day, but that's because you don't live in the Galápagos Islands. Furthermore, just because you don't see them every day, why does that make the finches and tanagers any more interesting than the pigeon? Why do people have to schlep to Ecuador, lay over in Quito, pack into a boat, and cruise to the Galápagos to see a giant tortoise when they could observe its close brethren in the Bronx River? What is the basis of this drive to explore?"

I hadn't thought about this before either. "It's just a human instinct," I suppose.

"Well, it's silly. Maybe when humans were at a primitive stage, the desire to explore had some adaptive value. By diversifying habitats, *homo sapiens* could collectively hedge its bets against ecological disaster. That explanation is irrelevant now. We have plenty of viable places to live."

"Maybe the experience of seeing things has intrinsic value. I-59 said that travel nourishes the soul."

"I-59 was a moron. Take it from me. Seeing things has no intrinsic value. I have seen a lot, and after a while it's all the same.

There are lots of different kinds of birds, lots of different kinds of turtles, and lots of different kinds of people. At bottom, they're all pretty much the same. The downside is that when all is said and done, you'll have nothing to show for all that exploration. You'll exert yourself a lot and see a few things, but what is that to show for a life?"

"I'll have experiences."

"Experiences are just a bunch of chemicals and neurotransmitters. Everyone has those. What makes one better than another?"

I get his point. It seems reasonable enough.

"So if I shouldn't explore, what should I do then?"

"You need to find a meaningful relationship."

I think my head will explode. "Are you kidding?" I say this a bit too loud, loud enough that I would have been shushed on an American flight. But on the flight to Kathmandu, music is blaring and children are running amok in the aisles. The atmosphere is chaotic and I am emboldened to a level of animation from which I would otherwise refrain.

"You have a lot of nerve coming here and saying this to me. You're the very same person who came and told me to leave Q. I had a meaningful relationship, the most meaningful relationship of my life, and you ruined it. How dare you even sit next to me?" I spit this last question. It is rhetorical, but I-60 answers.

"You have me all wrong," he says. "I never told you to leave Q."

"What are you talking about. You're sixty years old. My sixty-year-old self told me to leave Q."

"I am a different sixty-year-old. The sixty-year-old who told you to leave Q was the older you based on having lived a life with her. I am an older you based on your decisions to leave Q, pursue Minnie Zuckerman, leave Minnie Zuckerman, start writing funny books, stop writing funny books, go to law school, leave law school, and go trekking in the Himalayas. I'm thirty years or so down that path."

"So you're not the first guy again?"

"No, no. Most certainly not."

"In my internal nomenclature you have the same designation."

"All the same, he is not me. Remember the chart on the table-cloth in the restaurant?"

"Yes."

"So you'll need to come up with an alternate label for me. How about I-60 mark two?"

"That sounds a bit like you're a sixty-two-year-old version of myself."

"Fair enough," he says, rubbing his chin. After a moment, he has it. "How about I-60B?"

That seems about as clear as can be hoped for, and I accept it, though not without reservation. "Okay," I say, "but this could get confusing."

"Life is confusing," says I-60B, and we sit in silence again.

I-60B resumes the conversation as we fly over Afghanistan. "Look, when I say you need to find a meaningful relationship, I don't necessarily mean romance. Romance would be nice, but I mean relationships in the broadest sense. You need to build friendships and professional associations and attachments to the community."

It's a fair point. Truth be told, I only have one friend. I have some companions and many friendly acquaintances, but only one person I can honestly call a friend. I have never been the sort of person to attend community board meetings or pop into bars for a drink. It just never seemed important.

"I take your point. But I don't understand why it's so urgent."

He turns to face me, and I see the right side of his face for the first time. He has a large asymmetrical mole on his right cheek, almost certainly a melanoma, and unless medicine has made an unforeseen stride in the next thirty years, almost certainly fatal. It seems fair to surmise from his presence with me that cancer has not been cured in his time.

"Being alone can be more devastating than you realize. Seeing the world is fine and good, but at the end of your life, it will be nice to have made some connections. Perhaps someone will bring you soup, come and visit for a few minutes, watch the baseball game on television."

I understand, of course, that he has none of these things.

He smiles. "It would be nice, also, to have some people at your funeral."

I notice then that the bag in my lap has opened. My pants are covered in nuts and salt. This strikes me as profoundly sad. For some reason "MacArthur Park" starts playing in my head, and I begin to cry.

So my visit to Nepal consists of a five-hour stay at Tribhuvan International. I alight from the plane, purchase a stand-by return ticket at the counter, then wait for them to turn the plane around to Belgium. It doesn't take long; they don't even clean it. I kill time by wandering the airport stores, of which there are two. The first is a snacks and notions shop. The snacks are the same sleeves of peanuts they gave out on the flight. The notions are Q-tips, sold individually from a glass jar; orange-flavored Alka-Seltzer tablets, also sold individually from a glass jar; and an ancient copy of *Time*. The cover features its men of the year, Bill Clinton and Kenneth Starr, and a teaser for a story about apocalyptic Y2K fears. Seeing Ken Starr is disorienting, and I feel suddenly dislodged in time.

The duty-free shop is more or less the same as any other duty-free shop, with an emphasis on less. Everything in the store could be found at a similar shop in a major airport, there are just fewer items, and instead of, say, stacks of Lindt chocolate, there is a single bar. I feel that I shouldn't leave Nepal empty-handed, so I buy a bottle of scotch—Johnnie Walker Red Label.

From the look of things, they don't move much product at the Tribhuvan Duty-Free. A cardboard cutout of Catherine Deneuve adorns the Chanel display, which consists of four bottles of No. 5 and two bottles of Antaeus. I have a hunch the whiskey is twenty years old or more. But time is good for scotch, and one bottle of Johnnie Walker is as good as another. Suddenly, and thankfully, I feel grounded, but only for a moment.

Chapter **TWENTY-THREE**

Back home in New York, I begin a concerted program of civic and social engagement. I take a job at a bookstore in TriBeCa. The young people who work there go out every night, and I make a point of joining them often. I enlist in the Hash House Harriers and on weekends volunteer at an alpaca farm in Putnam County. It is not the perfect life, and certainly not the one I imagined for myself, but it is a good life all the same.

It is strange not to teach and write, but working in the store keeps me around books, and the weeks have a pleasant rhythm to them. I appreciate this. For writers, there is always work to be done—matters to research, pages to edit, galleys to read. During its creation, a novel inhabits an author's every waking moment, even infiltrates his sleep. Now, when work is done it is done. I can go out in the evenings with my colleagues and drink beer without worrying about being my sharpest in the morning. Bookstore customers are genial and polite. If I need to turn my brain off because of a hangover, or just to daydream, this presents no problem.

This idea of turning my brain off is foreign. Even as a child, I was goal-oriented. I commissioned an army of officers in the elementary schoolyard and wrote a series of books about a literate dinosaur. And, of course, the dreams of my adulthood heretofore have been grand. But I adapt to a more sedentary intellectual life much more quickly than I ever would have imagined. It is okay, it turns out, to live without the imperative of writing the great American novel or earning tenure or attending and excelling in graduate school. It is fine to go to work in the morning, have a few drinks with friends afterward, then go home and watch *Seinfeld* reruns. In other words, it is palatable to simply exist.

I still have aspirations, but they are more oriented to a lifestyle than to assuring my legacy. I dream of ways to include the people I like in my life. I plan a cooperative bookstore, owned in equal shares by all the workers, not employees but partners who read and confer over what novels to promote and how much to charge for a cup of coffee, if anything at all.

I discuss this idea with a few of my colleagues. They think it is not unrealistic. More importantly, they share the vision. We begin to plot, and discuss places where such an enterprise could take root. Perhaps near one of the colleges, NYU or Hunter, where the academic community might get behind it. I even go so far as to explore a business loan with a bank officer. The details of the plan are key, she says, but thinks it should be possible for my group to secure funding.

I still daydream about success, but this no longer involves bestsellers or a place in the pantheon of writers. Instead it means a cabin in the woods of Maine or perhaps the southern Adirondacks, nothing fancy of course, not on the salary of a bookstore owner, just a place where friends can go for a hike, share a bottle of wine, and watch the sunset—a friendly commune. My dreams, like my life, are serene.

I am therefore surprised and more than a little disappointed when I-68 proposes we go for health shakes and walnuts at the corner juice bar.

"**What is it?**" This time, *I* am eager to get to the point.

"It's you," he says. "Look at yourself. You've gone soft."

It's true. I have. Since returning to New York I have put on fifteen, maybe twenty pounds. The cause is no mystery. Since starting at the bookstore, I have gone out to drink beer almost every night. And, to my surprise, I really like the jalapeño poppers at Diablos Cantina, the bar where my friends from the store go after work. I don't care for jalapeño peppers, so I figured the poppers would not be to my taste, but they're stuffed with cheese and spices and meat and deep-fried, and after you dip them in ranch dressing you can hardly taste the jalapeño at all. With beer, they taste spectacular.

"How could you have let yourself get this way?" It is ironic that he asks this because, bad as I look, I-68 looks way worse. He has an old-man paunch, a double chin, and skin hanging in other places where it shouldn't be.

"Buying new pants was the hardest thing," I explain. "I was quite attached to the idea of wearing thirty-two-inch-waist slacks. As you know, I had worn thirty-two-inch-waist pants since college." Indeed, I was proud of the fact that my waist hadn't changed in all those years, and I definitely didn't want to spend the money on new pants. It just seemed like a complete waste (sorry). The first several times I put on a few pounds, I starved myself or went on a crash diet. Then, one day, I took the plunge and bought myself a pair of thirty-four-inch jeans. Lo and behold, the world did not end. The pants look good, they're just as comfortable as the old ones, and they didn't break me. No one tells me that I let myself go. Soon I bought three pairs of khakis and two more pairs of jeans in the same size. You don't need as many pairs of pants as people think. The trick is not to wash them every time. Pants are not like shirts. There are no apocrine sweat glands in the legs. If you just air pants out, you can wear them again in a day or two. This way, and this is the key, they don't shrink. So you can get by with fewer than you would have thought possible. It's empowering, really.

I-68 is uninterested in my disquisition on pants. "You need to exercise."

"I belong to the Harriers," I say, but it's a lame excuse, and I know it, and I know he knows it. The Harriers were founded in 1938 in Kuala Lumpur by a group of expatriate British officers. At a Hash, one or more of the members of the group, the Hares, lays a trail for the remainder of the group to follow, scattering short cuts and dead ends, so that the slower runners can catch up with the faster ones. It's all good fun. Trouble is—we're talking about the Brits, after all—the Harriers who reach the end of the trail are rewarded with beer and cigarettes. The organization's constitution provides, in relevant part, "to acquire a good thirst and to satisfy it in beer." Obviously, I-68 is aware of this.

"Not the Harriers," he says. "You need *real* exercise." Whereupon, he pulls down his collar and unbuttons the top of his shirt so that I can see three four-inch scars running longitudinally down his pectoralis major, unmistakable evidence of a series of open-heart surgeries.

"They didn't work," I-68 says ominously, and takes a sip from his banana health shake.

I quit the Harriers and join the Central Park Running Club, which is heavy-duty. They meet on Tuesdays for interval training, Wednesdays to run hills, and Thursdays for speed workouts. On weekends, the members take long runs, sometimes fifteen or twenty miles, either around the park loop, or up Riverside Drive, or east onto Randall's Island. In no time, I shed the weight I had added and then a few pounds more. The running is addictive, and I find myself going out to train every morning, even the days when the club meets. I add extra miles onto the long weekend runs. In the fall I run the New York Marathon. In the spring, the Boston. I begin to plot training regimens to get my marathon time down under three hours. I consider the Hawaii ultra-marathon, one hundred miles on the Big Island. During slow moments at the bookstore, and even during some active periods, I find myself daydreaming about these running ventures. I am in the middle of one of these reveries when a gentleman in a wheelchair, carrying a copy of *Our Mutual Friend* for purchase, arrives at my checkout counter, introduces himself as me, and invites me to herbal tea.

I-72 gets right to the point. He is sipping Earl Grey, black, and not interested in small talk.

"You need to stop running so much. You've substituted one obsession for another."

"So?"

"You're ruining your knees."

"You are the one who told me I needed to exercise more."

"No, not me. You keep making that mistake."

"Look, I mean no disrespect, but is it so terrible to be obsessive about exercise? So you have bad knees? Do you really need to be in a wheelchair? Couldn't you just have your knees replaced?"

He smiles, though he is agitated. "You think you know so much, don't you? The knee surgery causes a blood infection, the blood infection hospitalizes you for three months. It nearly kills you and causes you to lose your right leg. I won't even mention the unbearable pain associated with the successful knee replacement in the left leg. Do you think I'd come back in time because I had a little trouble walking?" He spits these last words at me.

I feel six inches tall. "What do you want me to do?"

"Swimming," he says, calmer now. "It is very nice and low-impact."

Coming out of the locker room at the Y one evening, I-66 confronts me and asks me to buy him a Gatorade. We sit down at a table in the cafeteria, behind the vending machine which sells premade sandwiches. They have chicken salad, turkey, and peanut butter and jelly. I offer I-66 some change. "The chicken salad and turkey are not good," I tell him, "but the peanut butter and jelly isn't half bad."

He isn't interested. "You spend all that time swimming and have nothing to show for it," he says.

It's true. I am not a particularly good swimmer and show no signs of improvement. I took a couple of lessons, but these consisted mostly of a hairy middle-aged man in a Speedo repetitively yelling "Breathe" at me. As far as I can tell, swimming with humans is pretty much as it is with dogs. You swim the way you swim the first time you're dropped in the water. Running may have ruined my joints, but at least it kept me thin. I have put five pounds back on since I started swimming, mostly around the middle, where a dense rubbery fat has consolidated. It doesn't look terrible, but my appearance hardly justifies the effort, which is considerable, and the truth is, I don't like the water very much. The chlorine is murder on my eyes.

"What do you want me to do?"

"The key to good health is avoiding food allergies. Cut out gluten and cow's milk and you'll be a happy man."

I am walking out of the health food store in Bay Ridge where I buy my macrobiotic gluten-free whole-grain pasta and soy milk. The soy milk starts to smell like feet after a day, so I make the three-hour round trip from my apartment often. I-84 catches up with me on Fourth Avenue in Brooklyn as I am hustling to the subway with ingredients for a vegan arrabiata.

"Please don't eat the arrabiata," says I-84. "It is too spicy and will really bother me in the morning."

"Really. Is that what you came to say?"

"Not exclusively. This is all counterproductive," he says, over the sound of the rushing traffic. "Soy is carcinogenic, and gluten is good for you."

"That's the opposite of what we have been told."

"Yes."

"Just like in *Sleeper*?"

"Precisely."

"What, then, for me?"

"Beavers," he says. "Study beavers."

"This seems very random."

"Our scientists have great hope for its benefits."

I am donning my waders on the shore of a stream in the wilderness of Maine when I-74 wanders up beside me.

"Why are you doing this?" It is difficult to hear him over the running water.

"Because I was told to!"

"Does it make any sense?"

"No!" I say. "But I like beavers!"

"Have you learned anything?"

"No."

"Do you know what six times nine is?"

"Fifty-four," I say hopefully.

"I mean in base-thirteen."

"This will take me a moment."

"Would you like to play a game of pitch and toss?"

Yes, I say, and for several hours we toss coins against the wall.

"These are very obscure references," I say. "One could read an entire book about my life and not catch this bit. You need to be able to do base conversions to get the numerical thing, and even then I had a difficult time relating it to something relevant."

"Perhaps you should pay more attention to your own life."

"Maybe so, but this is becoming boring."

"Try skydiving. It's quite exciting."

I am nine thousand feet above Earth, halfway down my jump, when I-84 comes swooping in above me in a nosedive. He levels off and matches my descent.

"This is insane!" he cries over the rushing wind.

"I know!"

"Learn to play the guitar instead!" he shouts, as he releases his chute and recedes into the distance.

I take to the guitar well. I have a knack. After several months, I know more than thirty chords and can perform some basic arpeggios. I have even gotten down a pretty fair rendition of "Sweet Home Alabama." The hammer-ons and pull-offs in the riff are tough to get down, but otherwise it's not that hard to play. I like it. It's my favorite. Ed King of Lynyrd Skynyrd said the chords and two main solos came to him in a dream. Sometimes when I am really cooking, I feel as if I am channeling him.

I adopt the lifestyle of the jerry jazz musician. I eat spaghetti, drink gin fizzes, and wander the streets of Greenwich Village by night. I am at the Vanguard one evening, checking out some hepcats, when I am confronted by I-74. He says he wants a scone.

"It's one a.m.," I say. "I don't think any place sells scones at one in the morning."

"This is New York. Someone is selling scones."

"Don't they have scones in your time?"

"They have scones. You want me to wait forty years to eat?"

We walk around, find a little place on Christopher Street that does breakfast, go in.

He asks the host, "Do you sell scones?"

"No, but we have crullers. Will that do?"

"No, but thank you."

"They are very much the same thing, a cruller and a scone."

"I should think not."

"Nevertheless, I think you will enjoy it."

"No," he says. "I don't think so." We leave the restaurant and as we resume wandering, I-74 mutters to himself something about lemons and limes.

After half an hour, we find another late-night diner, which, astonishingly, sells scones. We take a seat. He orders a scone and raspberry preserves. The waiter arrives a minute later with the biscuit and the fruit, which I-74 inspects skeptically.

"I asked for raspberry preserves," he says. "This is raspberry jam."

"Jam and preserves are the same," says the waiter.

"No, they are not. By FDA regulation, preserves have a higher percentage of fruit content than jam."

"Respectfully, sir, you are mistaken. The FDA treats jam and preserves as interchangeable. They each contain seeds and pulp. Jelly is distinct, but jam and preserves are the same."

"Well, I want raspberry preserves."

The waiter points to the jar. "By federal regulation, this is raspberry preserves."

We leave and wander for another hour before we find another place. Miraculously, on Perry Street, a tiny bakery has fresh scones. They come with conserve.

"This is excellent," says I-74. "The fruit content in conserve is even higher than in preserves."

"I am glad you are happy."

I-74 is dressed formally. He is wearing a morning coat and an ascot and looks like Beau Brummell has dressed him to watch the afternoon jumpers. Each and every customer who comes into the bakery, each and every one of whom is drunk, comments on the absurdity of his appearance. I-74 does not notice. He devours the scone then gets to the point.

"The guitar is a frivolous instrument."

"I quite like it. I have gotten down the solo from 'Sweet Home Alabama.' I can channel Ed King."

"In forty years, no one will remember either him or Lynyrd Skynyrd."

"I find that hard to believe."

"It is true all the same."

"Who will they remember?

"Prokofiev and Shostakovich and Hindemith."

"Ah."

"If you want to be remembered, you must play the cello. Any musician worth anything at all must play the cello."

"Why does it matter to be remembered?"

A speckle of conserve on his chin, I-74 smiles at me as if I am a child. "My dear boy, when you get to be my age, you will see that this is the only thing that matters."

Outside the Fort Greene satellite of the Emanuel Feuermann Conservatory, on my way home from a lesson, I am confronted by I-80. Together we walk to the Orange Julius stand on Atlantic Avenue. It is years since I have been there. When I was a boy, my father sometimes would take me with him to Brooklyn Technical High School, where he was a teacher, and after classes ended we would head over to the stand. I remember I liked it almost as much as I liked going to school with him, which was quite a bit. The Julius does not disappoint. It is wonderful, rich and creamy. I have been told they put an egg inside the drink, but this is surely an urban legend. Whatever the recipe, it is delicious. I-80 relishes it as much as I do. He closes his eyes as he drinks, in apparent ecstasy.

When he has finished, he says, "The cello is stupid."

"Why couldn't you have told me that before I took nine months of lessons? They are very expensive and the practice is tedious. Why are you always so late?"

"Did you really believe this would be the path to your fame? Did you believe that, taking up the cello at thirty-five, you would someday surpass Casals or Ma or Mstislav Rostropovich?"

"No," I say. "I have never even heard of Rostropovich."

"You still don't understand, do you? There is no certain path to fame or happiness. The best one can hope for is to attempt to understand the mystery of existence and attain some measure of inner peace."

"How?"

"Through great books. Through the consolations of Boethius. From the wisdom of Wittgenstein, Dickens, and Proust. Therein lies your only hope for salvation."

I am in the Reading Room of the New York Public Library, where I sit for my daily dose of Proust, when I am approached by I-81. I almost do not recognize him. He is old, but he is supple and lithe and moves in ways unlike his predecessors. He beckons me outside. We walk behind the great library together, to Bryant

Park, sit on a bench, and share a salty pretzel. It is rubbery and insipid.

"How goes the Proust?"

"It goes."

"Like life."

"Like life."

We sit for a while, staring into the distance, at Sixth Avenue. Several pigeons wander by and we each toss bits of pretzel to them. The birds sniff at the crumbs, poke them with their beaks, then waddle away. We resume staring at the traffic.

"Why don't you tell me what it is that you want?"

"Thank you for asking. It is rude to ask without invitation."

"Well, I am inviting."

"Thank you. You are most gracious."

"You honor me by your presence." This seems to be in the spirit of things.

"As you honor me." He pauses, then gets to the point. "I would like you to devote yourself to the mastery of Zen. Proust is wonderful, but I do not believe it to be a path that leads to enlightenment."

"Couldn't you have told me this before I started *À la recherche du temps perdu*? I am halfway through *La prisonnière*. And you know I am reading it in the original French, so I first had to learn French."

"I am sorry. I got here as soon as I could."

I am fed up. "Why don't you do it yourself?" I ask, nearly shouting. "Why do I have to give up Proust for Buddhism? *You* can study Buddhism. I am not stopping you. Why is it that every time you have some major epiphany, it is *my* life that has to change? If you want to swim, swim. If you want to learn the guitar, learn the guitar. If you want to meditate to find the path to enlightenment, go right ahead and do it."

I expect the usual lecture: I have confused him with the others who have come before, but they are different people. *He*, of course, has never asked me for anything. But I-81 does not hector me. "It is not so simple," he says soothingly. He is phlegmatic, unflappable. "I do meditate, and since I began I have discovered the One True Path. But I found it too late. I do not have the powers of concentration that are required to achieve real self-awareness. I cannot adequately quiet my mind. I believe that if I had begun this quest at a younger age, then I might have been able to achieve Nirvana." He pauses. "If you understand the nature of my being here today, you know that I do not stand to benefit from this request. I am here only because I believe I can make your life better."

I could use some meditation to decompress. I exhale, relax, say, "I understand."

We sit together for a while longer, staring at the traffic and the pigeons searching for desirables. Buddhists can be quiet for a long time. It is refreshing.

A vendor pushes his lunch cart past us, and I-81 says, "I remember sitting here with Q on a day such as this, eating a hummus wrap and discussing the season's zucchini crop."

"That never happened," I say.

"Oh," he says, "it most certainly did."

I am staring at the wall of a limestone cave in the Badlands of South Dakota, when another me finds me. He is very old—far, far older than any of his predecessors. How old exactly I cannot tell. My eyes are not what they were.

I have been staring at the wall for a very long while. It has been years at least, perhaps decades. I am not sure how long exactly. One loses track of time when staring at a wall. You can get caught up in it, like a good baseball game.

I rise to greet him. I do not know why he is here and I do not ask. I am too happy to stretch my legs. He wraps me in a blanket and puts a reassuring arm around my shoulder.

"Have you learned anything?" he asks.

"Only that the cave is cold."

"It's enough. You should stop now."

So I do.

Book Three

BEST

Chapter **TWENTY-FOUR**

W hen time travel is discovered, I am not surprised. I saw it coming. Still, it inspires my awe. The headline is emblazoned across all six columns of the *New York Times*: "Scientists Conquer Time." It is a red-letter day, one of the handful of moments in a life when people remember exactly where they were, like Kennedy's assassination or the moon landing or the attack on the World Trade Center.

I am at my kitchen table eating oatmeal. I am old. I am not sure how it has happened, yet it has happened all the same. I recognize myself, but it is me and not me. I have lines around my eyes, ear hair that defies all grooming efforts, and an old-man paunch. My arthritic right knee is in a bad way. It has deteriorated progressively over the years. For the longest time, I continued to run despite the throbbing that would follow in the evening. But on my birthday, nine years ago, it simply hurt too much and I have not run since. Now it is an effort to get out of bed in the morning.

Truth is, of course, I saw this coming too.

The news does not have the impact it might have had if I were a younger man or if I had not foreseen it, but it has a substantial impact all the same. It is only natural, it seems to me, in light of the reality of time travel, to think about possibilities. And I have lots of time to think. When all the commotion was said and done, I taught elementary school and tried my hand at writing children's books, the latter with little success. The kindergarteners filled some of the voids in my life, but I retired seven years ago after hanging on two years too long, truth be told. Teaching five-year-olds is more physically demanding than one might imagine. Now there are no more classes to teach or books to write. The well of creativity, if it ever existed, dried up long ago. No children or grandchildren, either mine or borrowed, inhabit my life. I have no one to dote on, nor anyone to dote on me.

I live in the same apartment in Morningside Heights. The neighborhood has gotten better and worse over the years, as neighborhoods do. It is on the upswing now, and that means good things for the park, which is flourishing. The nature preserve has been restored and birds are flocking to it. Sometimes I can catch a glimpse of one out of the corner of my living room window. I leave a plate of seeds on the windowsill, and from time to time, a cardinal or a sparrow comes to visit.

On Tuesdays, a doughty woman named Ellen from City Services for the Aged comes to the apartment. She does some shopping for me and cleans up a while. She likes sports, and when she's done, we chat for a while about the Mets or the Yankees, or the Knicks in the winter. This is the highlight of my week. If the weather is nice, Ellen takes me out for a walk. But it is four flights down and four flights back up. To be completely honest, it is already more than either of us can handle, and my leg is not getting any better. Soon enough, I expect I will be shut in continually, until I am wheeled out of my flat once and for all.

So you understand why I find myself thinking about what might have been.

And what could be.

It proves surprisingly daunting for scientists to demonstrate the authenticity of time travel. They are understandably loath to conduct tests upon humans at the outset, and people are dubious of the animal trials. This skepticism is reasonable with respect to the first experiment, in which a rat is sent back twenty thousand years to the last ice age. He is placed in the chronoambulator, the machine is turned on, and the rat miraculously disappears. One hour later he returns. By all accounts, he is very cold. But not everyone is satisfied. A clumsy illusionist with a refrigerator could accomplish as much. Accusations abound that it is a parlor trick, and better proof is demanded.

Scientists train a very special dog, a wonder dog really, a little beagle who is taught to find a lamb shank bone and bury it in the nearest field no matter where—and when—he is. They practice this with the beagle hundreds of times, until they are as confident as one can be with a puppy as coprincipal investigator, then shoot the dog back in time and hope for the best. Back in the present, the super beagle finds his bone in the middle of what had become the parking lot of a shopping mall. The osseous matter is exhumed, carbon dated to 1976, and time travel is proved.

In New York City, the dog is feted with a ticker tape parade but, sadly, never heard from again.

I find myself thinking of that doggie all the time.

Time travel is technology, like atomic power and self-adhesive stamps, the full potential of which is not immediately understood. Once the breakthrough is finally accepted, the reality of the possibilities it creates generates a mixture of hope and trepidation. Ultimately, though, as is so often the case with scientific innovation, neither man's greatest dreams nor worst fears are realized.

In the beginning, much of the consternation in the scientific community concerns the ethical and practical consequences of changing the past. The practical fear is that even the smallest alteration of history may have substantial and possibly dire consequences for the future. This worry turns out to be overblown. The putative butterfly effect is conclusively disproven by a group of scientists in Leipzig. The team sends a bright green spicebush swallowtail back into the middle Triassic, all the while monitoring everybody and everything in Germany. Very little changes. Jurgen Beiderman, a cobbler from Sprockhövel, reports that his bicycle is missing. He is a creature of habit and rides the cycle to work every morning from his home in nearby Niederstuter. Fearful they have opened Pandora's box, the scientists quickly investigate the disappearance, but the alarm is for nothing. Herr Beiderman has forgotten that his gear shift was stuck and so dropped the bicycle off at the repair shop in Bredenscheid, where it is waiting, the gears as good as new. The bicycle in question is displayed on the front page of the *Bild-Zeitung*, and the Leipzig team receives the Nobel Prize.

On the whole, time, as it turns out, is more resilient than people imagined. This is not to say efforts are not made to tweak the past to favor one party or another. They are, mostly by large corporations with the sort of resources required for an undertaking of this sort, and there are occasional successes. For example, one morning I wake up and find that the design of my coffee maker has changed. It looks like an hourglass with a plastic handle jutting from the neck and something resembling a Bunsen burner underneath. I call the manufacturer and am told by a customer service agent that this is a vacuum coffee brewer, which narrowly lost out to percolators in the battle for market dominance in the early twentieth century. But now, thanks to the tireless efforts of a phalanx of time-traveling salesmen, Sintrax vacuum coffee makers are the industry standard and no one has so much as heard of a percolator.

"But you just told me about it," I say, after the agent finishes explaining the situation.

"An oversight," she says. "Try the coffee."

I do. It is very good.

On a second morning, Americans find themselves driving on the left-hand side of the road. On yet another, New Yorkers making the morning commute find themselves crossing the Hudson by blimp rather than ferry. On still another morning, the top line of the keyboard on my computer changes from QWERTY to DIHATENSOR and I have to relearn how to type. But most mornings nothing happens. *The Simpsons* are still on television. Democrats and Republicans are still fighting. Pie tastes as delicious as ever. When things do change, the world does not end. People are surprisingly adaptable.

Chronoambulation is also expensive, particularly in the beginning, and since it is so difficult to make lasting changes it hardly seems worthwhile. This is part of the reason why many people do not try it and why it remains, at least for the first several years of its availability, principally the domain of corporate espionage. As time passes, the cost comes down. But it is still not relevant to the life of the average person. This is because it is not of use to most people.

Broadly speaking, one can imagine three possible reasons ordinary individuals might be attracted to time travel. The most obvious is tourism. Sadly, under the current restrictions of chronoambulation, the traveler can return only with what he left and nothing more. This means there can be no souvenirs or duty-free shops. Hence the tourist trade never really takes off.

The second obvious objective is to help one's current lot. Many people try this, but things don't always work out as planned. For example, my compadre Ard Koffman used his life savings to go back fifty years and let his younger self know who was going to win that year's Kentucky Derby. He returned to our time expecting to be a rich man, but instead found himself almost penniless. Ard tore his apartment apart in an effort to figure out what went wrong. In the back of his bedroom closet, he found an envelope containing twenty thousand dollars of losing tickets from the 1992 Run for the Roses. Apparently, Ard's younger self did not bet Lil E. Tee to win. Instead, to maximize his return, he paired the sure thing in exacta wagers with the other five favorites in the race. Unfortunately, a long shot named Casual Lies came in second, and since he never bet to win, all the parlays failed and thus the young Ard had nothing to show for the inside information.

Some people have better luck than Ard, but even the success stories are tainted. The people who succeed in telling their
younger selves when to buy—and, equally importantly, when to
sell—a stock, or convey a novel idea to themselves in a timely
way, return to their present with great wealth but a profound
sense of emptiness. Famously, Gus Santos, an elevator repairman
from Toledo, had the good idea of travelling back to 1968 and
Redmond, Washington. There, for four dollars an hour, he hired
a pair of young men named Bill Gates and Paul Allen to write an
operating system for personal computers. Needless to say, MicroSantos was a resounding success. Santos returned to his own
time to find that he had become an extraordinarily wealthy man.
But he remembered nothing of how he came into his wealth, had
none of the satisfaction of the journey, as did Gates and Allen,
who defected from MicroSantos, launched their own new company, and still ended up obscenely rich. Furthermore, Santos
could not answer the most basic question about computers. The
press, and even his own family, ridiculed him as a fraud, and several months later the first hundred billionaire in the history of
humanity shot himself in the head.

Most recently, a coworker of mine at Rutherford Hayes Elementary used his entire pension to travel back in time and invested ten thousand dollars with a young newspaper delivery boy
from Omaha, Nebraska, named Warren Buffett. The teenaged
Buffett could not understand the basis of my colleague's confidence in him but was all too happy to accept the money, which he
used to buy a KoAloha ukulele, the Stradivarius of ukuleles, and
to pursue his dream of playing professionally. This he achieved,
and through the circuit of summer festivals and Omaha wine bars
and, rarely but occasionally, private lessons, eked out enough to

get by. He was deliriously happy with his life and thought often of the oddly dressed stranger who gave him his start so many years earlier.

The gross dissatisfaction with time travel as a means of improving one's own lot in life leaves many customers dissatisfied, and the creator of time travel, Professor Svetlana Yvgelnikov of the University of Irkutsk, becomes the object of public enmity, one of those innovators who is remembered in the end for the trouble they wrought rather than their brilliance, like J. Robert Oppenheimer, or Sir Isaac Newton each time someone is hit on the head with an apple. Professor Yvgelnikov takes it all personally, so much so that she decides to use her life savings to travel back in time and encourage her younger self not to invent time travel. The younger self appears persuaded, and is resolved to go to dental school and specialize in orthodontics, but Yvgelnikov returns to her own time to find that very little in her life has changed other than the fact that she is out $500,000 for the travel.

"Did you find this frustrating?" she is asked during an interview.

"*Da*," she says. "Chronoambulation is quite dear, even with the ten-percent-off coupon I hold as inventor of the technology."

"Does it bother you that comrade Ivan Demitovich now receives all the acclaim for inventing time travel?"

"Let him have it."

"Is it odd that I know this fact? If the past has been changed, should it be known to me that you were the inventor of time travel in the past—or should I say the former past before it was revised?"

Comrade Yvgelnikov, a civil servant in the department of horse-driven carriages, rubs her chin thoughtfully. "The past has the most curious relationship with the present," she says. "It is an entity unto itself, with its own past, current and future. Besides, much can happen between the time when things happen and the time when we look back upon these things that happened. For all we know, the rules of time travel may themselves be changing as a result of other people traveling back in time."

"Isn't this internally inconsistent?"

"Not at all. One must remember about entropy, comrade. According to the second law of thermodynamics, entropy cannot decrease; it is always increasing. In the simplest physicochemical processes, such as the expansion of a gas into a vacuum, the variable S represents entropy, the dispersal of the energized molecules into a greater volume than they occupied before the process. Conversely, the variable Q represents the amount of work that must be done to compress the gas to its initial volume. In other words, this is the work that must be done to reverse entropy."

"So then there is hope for remedying some of the snags with chronoambulation and making things better."

Yvgelnikov says nothing and an awkward pause ensues.

"Well?" says the interviewer.

"Well what?" asks Yvgelnikov.

"What is the answer?"

"I did not detect a question."

"I asked whether there is hope for making things better."

"No, you said there is hope for making things better."

"It was an interrogative statement."

"I am not familiar with this concept."

"I meant it as a question."

"Ah, so you are asking me whether hope exists for making things better."

"Essentially yes, this is what I am asking."

"The answer is no."

"I see."

"It is comforting for people to believe otherwise, but I highly doubt it is the case. I ask you, in an isolated system, wherever will the energy required to restore order come from?"

"Is time an isolated system?"

"Of course, does one ever have enough of it?"

This confuses the interviewer. Ordinarily it would not be possible to assess the mental state of an interviewer, but in this case it is made evident by the interviewer's subsequent question, which is in fact another interrogative statement.

He says, "I find this all highly confusing."

Yvgelnikov responds, "All things considered, it is best not to think about these things too much. I have found it often gives me a headache, which can only be cured by BC Powder."

"BC Powder has been forgotten since Doan's Pills won the battle in the past for control of the analgesic market."

"My point exactly."

"I do not know what point it is you are making."

"I am sorry. But I have a headache now myself, and many carriage license applications to attend to."

"I thank you for your time."

"Think nothing of it."

But while it may not be possible for people to improve their own lots, there is every reason to believe that the lives of people in the past are improved. Somewhere in time a young Warren Buffet is happily playing the ukulele and a doppelganger of Svetlana Yvgelnikov is merrily correcting overbites. Altruism remains a valid reason to travel back in time. It is precisely this noble sentiment which motivates me to spend my life savings to prevent a younger me from ruining his life.

Chapter **TWENTY-FIVE**

Even after the prices come down, time travel is expensive, and they won't let you pay on credit. In the beginning, they offer a layaway plan, but learn their lesson after several people remain in the past rather than return to the present and pay the bills. Now, years later, it's cash, cashier's check, or money order.

These days I don't keep much money around. It's a challenge for me to get to the bank, and you can buy pretty much anything you want with a credit card. I do have a jar of pennies, which I have been maintaining since my late thirties. On one of Ellen's days, I ask her to skip the usual shopping and instead do a more thorough cleanup of the apartment. She finds some more loose change underneath the cushions of the sofa and in the back of the closets. Then she places it in the jar and helps me seal it. After that, she takes me to the bank, where I withdraw most of the balance of my retirement savings. Then, finally, at my request, she helps me into a cab.

"Are you going on a trip?" Ellen asks.

"Yes."

"Well, be careful." She is a kind and thoughtful woman.

"I will."

"When will you be home?"

"I'll be back before you know it."

The downtown office of Chrono Technologies is spartanly furnished and spotlessly clean, precisely the right sort of space to house futuristic technology. I am greeted by a receptionist, who asks what I want.

"I would like to go to the past."

"Fine," she says. She looks familiar.

"Do people ever want anything else?" I ask.

"Sometimes there are salesmen."

Soon I am met by a woman dressed in a formfitting, brushed-satin jumpsuit, which again seems precisely the right sort of outfit for counseling people about the use of futuristic technology.

"Hello," she says, extending her hand. "Barbara Volpe."

"Hi," I say, shaking warmly. "Maybe you get this all the time, but you look familiar. She does too," I say, pointing to the receptionist. In fact, they look almost exactly like one another.

"Erin Grey," she says. *"Buck Rogers in the 25th Century."*

"Yes!"

"The company hires women who look like her. Then we have to dress up like Colonel Wilma. It makes people feel more comfortable with the technology."

"Of course."

Barbara leads me into a conference room. "Have you seen one of these yet?" she asks, pointing toward what appears to be an open window. It is clear outside. Several stories below the street is crammed with traffic. A cab driver is honking angrily.

"I think I may have seen a window before."

"I bet you haven't seen this. Go ahead. Try it."

I'm not sure what it means to try a window, but I walk over anyway. Upon examination, I see that is not a window at all. It is an ultra-high-definition video screen that has been built into the wall. It is projecting images of a New York day.

"This is a major innovation. Buildings without windows cut down enormously on construction costs."

"Come to think of it, it was overcast when I arrived."

"We keep it sunny three hundred sixty-five days a year. It's good for employee morale."

"Why are you projecting images of traffic?"

"This is New York. There is always traffic."

"Of course."

Barbara gets down to business. "I need to review a few things with you before we can send you back. I have to ask you a few questions and then go over several risk disclosures. After that you need to review a waiver and sign it."

"Fine with me."

"First, do you have any medical restrictions?"

"No. I have a bad knee, but nothing more serious that I know of."

"Have you ever had any epileptic seizures?"

"No."

"Are you pregnant?"

"No."

"These days, you have to ask."

"Of course."

"Some medical risks are associated with the procedure. Five percent of chronoambulators report headaches, three percent report nausea, two percent experience constipation."

"That's odd."

"Not really. No one eats enough fiber when they travel."

"True."

"In a few cases, people claim that their souls have not been properly returned to their bodies. Of course, such a claim can be neither verified nor disproved. The waiver releases us from liability for any existential claims."

"Of course."

"For all of the spectacular advances in quantum physics, which have made time travel a reality, teleportation remains impossible. This means that chronoambulators are deposited in the same physical space where they start out. If you leave from here, you will emerge here, just in a different time."

"I understand."

"If you're interested in traveling to any time in the past two hundred years, this office is a very safe location to depart from."

"What was this building used for previously?"

"For most of the twentieth century, it was a shoe factory. In the late 1960s it was converted to a law firm. You come out in their bathroom."

"What if someone is in the middle of going?"

"It hasn't happened yet."

"But if it did?"

"I suppose you would say 'Excuse me.'"

"Of course."

"We have several locations around the world. All things being equal, it is better to travel where you want to go in our time. A lot of people forget this. One guy wanted to see Angkor Wat. All he told us, though, was that he wanted to go back to the twelfth century. He forgot that America hadn't been discovered yet."

"What happened?"

"He spent a month in twelfth-century Manhattan. He couldn't get off the island. It was very boring apparently, though he said he enjoyed the improved traffic situation. Anyway, I'm sure you get the point. If you want to see ancient Greece, fly there now and leave from our office in Athens. If you want to see Sydney when it was still a penal colony, fly to Australia and depart from our center in Sydney. If you don't, in the best case you'll be stuck on a boat for two months."

"The leg room would be better though."

"Don't be so sure. In any time, coach is no bargain."

"Right."

"Finally and most importantly, do you understand that there can be no guarantees as to results?" She furls her eyebrows to demonstrate her earnestness. "Generally speaking, any effort to improve your own current existence through time travel is almost certain to fail. If you want, you can go back and give a younger version of yourself or your parents the winning lottery numbers for a particular day. You may make their lives better. But you will almost certainly not make your own life any better. You may very well make it worse. Do you understand this?"

"Yes. My best friend went back in time and told himself who

was going to win the 1992 Kentucky Derby but he never bet to win. He only bet exactas, so he lost everything."

"We get a lot of that." She places a massive document in front of me. "I'll just leave this with you then. If you just initial in the one hundred thirty-seven places I have marked and sign on the last page, we can go ahead and get started."

"Fine," I say.

"Then there's the matter of the money. The fee will be five hundred thousand dollars. How would you like to pay?"

"Six hundred seventy-eight dollars and thirty-seven cents in pennies," I say, "and the balance in cashier's check."

"Of course," she says.

When I have finished initialing and signing, I am led into the room housing the chronoambulator. It is manned by a geekish gentleman in his twenties with thick glasses and acne scars. He is wearing the formfitting brushed-satin jumpsuit, but somehow on him it doesn't look right.

"You don't look like Erin Grey," I say.

He ignores this. "When do you want to go to?"

"Wednesday, November 23, 2011."

He pushes a button, and I am gone.

Needless to say, when I arrive someone is in the bathroom. It is bad luck. But it is not the worst possible scenario. He is at the urinal and not the stall into which I emerge. It could have been much worse. I make a note to say something about the situation to Barbara. This is a disaster waiting to happen.

I flush the toilet before I emerge so that the gentleman taking a pee doesn't have a heart attack. Even still, he is seriously startled.

"Funny," he says, as I emerge. "I didn't think anyone was in there."

"I try to keep it quiet," I say.

He looks me over, and I can see that it doesn't quite add up in his book. First of all, I am out of uniform. He is wearing the requisite pin-striped suit. I am in a cardigan and corduroy pants. Second, the narrow-neck cardigan will not come into style again for another thirty years or so. Third, I am almost certainly past the firm's mandatory retirement age. Fourth, he has never seen me before.

"Do you work here?" he asks.

"No," I say, "definitely not."

"Can I help you find someone then?"

"Yes," I say. "I am looking for myself." So intoxicated with the experience am I that I do not even take the time to wash my hands. I glide out the bathroom door and bypass the elevator for the stairs. I ignore my aching right knee, bound down the steps, across the lobby, and into the New York City of my youth.

For the first time in years, I feel alive.

Chapter **TWENTY-SIX**

The bus to Rhinebeck wends its way up the Taconic State Parkway. Ordinarily buses are not permitted on the Taconic, but Route 9 is under extensive renovation, so buses are given special dispensation. It is a rare treat. The bus is not crowded, and I am able to make myself comfortable. I take a pair of seats, park myself by the window, and absorb the view. It is a beautiful day, clear and bracing, and once we escape the city we are rewarded with a pageant of color. The leaves have fallen from the trees and soaked the ground in orange and red and yellow. Winter will be arriving anon, but this pastiche is still iridescent and vibrant.

Steadily, we make our way north. Familiar signs begin to roll by: Baldwin Road, Wiccopee Lane, Pudding Street. Near Lake Taghkanic we pass a family of deer feeding by the side of the road. The fawns are young, no more than four or five months old. They instinctively know how to graze, but they are learning too.

The mother shows them where to find the choicest grass, and when one of the baby deer wanders too close to the road, the doe gently nuzzles it back. I wish the bus driver would slow down, but he is on a schedule.

Near Lafayetteville, the driver turns off the parkway and makes his way west via Route 199. The road is nearly empty and my mind is racing. I am outside myself. When I become aware again, we are already in Milan. In Rock City, we turn south onto Route 308. In what seems like a second, we are into Eighmyville. Then, before I know it, we are passing Beech Street and Parsonage and turning right on Mulberry. A moment later we are in the town square and the driver announces, "Rhinebeck." We, I, have arrived.

I step off the bus and check my watch. I am more than an hour early. I could have taken the next bus, but I didn't want to risk cutting it close. Better early than late, I figured. Besides, it is a beautiful day for a walk. I amble across the town square and make my way into Irregular's. Oscar is at the door and greets me warmly.

"Hello, sir," he says. "Welcome to Irregular's. Can I interest you in a sample of our almond-caramel toffee?"

I accept the toffee. It isn't the thing for my teeth, but this is a vacation after all.

Oscar continues. "As you make your way around the store you will find that we have hidden little puzzles for our customers. Here is a sample conundrum." He points behind him. "What do these four albums have in common?"

"White lines," I say.

"Very good," Oscar says, flipping me another piece of almond-caramel toffee. "They won't all be that easy, though." He steps out from behind the desk and walks me to *We're an American Band*. "Why don't you try this one on for size?"

"Funky railroads," I say immediately.

"Right again." I can see he's impressed. Oscar walks over to *Signals* and *Sgt. Pepper's*. "Try this one."

"Bands who enjoyed their greatest success after their original drummer left."

"That's amazing. We've had that one up for a year. You're the first person to get it."

"Piece of cake," I say.

"Most people don't remember that Rush had a drummer before Neil Peart."

"John Rutsey."

"That's pretty impressive for an old-timer."

"Age is just a state of mind."

"Well, you sure do know your stuff."

I take a bite of toffee.

"Yes," I say. "And this toffee is genuinely delicious!"

I browse through the compact discs. I see a few I would like to buy, but what would be the point? I order a cup of coffee to go and meander toward the center of town. As I sip the warm joe, I congratulate myself again on having remembered to bring money. Just as airplane crashes are almost always attributable to human error, so it is with time travel. People occasionally become trapped in paradoxes or recursions, but the overwhelming majority of problems stem from old-fashioned stupidity. The worst stories are about people who forget to carry cash.

One man went back to 1951 to see Bobby Thomson of the Giants hit his pennant-winning, shot-heard-round-the-world home run off Ralph Branca of the Dodgers. When he emerged in the men's room of Glickerstein Shoe and Sandal, he realized immediately that he had forgotten to bring cash. He didn't have money for a ticket. He didn't even have ten cents for the subway. He tried panhandling, but he just didn't look the part. So he went back. Since he had not purchased travel insurance, when all was said and done he had spent a half million dollars to see the bathroom of a shoe factory.

Even more dramatic is the story of Otto Heidelinger, the notorious pickle magnate, who went back to 1963 to observe JFK's assassination. After arriving in the newly minted offices of Shrub, Lewis & Weinehofer, Heidelinger made his way to JFK Airport—then Idlewild—to purchase an airline ticket to Dallas. At the ticket counter, he realized that he didn't have enough cash and got himself into trouble when he went to pay by credit card. First he handed the agent his Visa.

"I'm sorry," the agent said, "We only take BankAmericard, Diners Club, and American Express."

Of course he didn't have Diners Club, so he handed over his American Express card. The agent noted the suspicious fourteen-digit identification number—they were using six digits back then—and several minutes later, Heidelinger was taken into custody and ultimately charged with credit card fraud and given a lengthy prison sentence.

One of the glitches with time travel is that if something goes wrong, no one really notices. That's because the chronoambulator arrives back at the precise moment when he leaves. Whether one spends twenty years in the past or an hour, from the standpoint of the operator in the brushed-satin jumpsuit everything is exactly the same. Thus no one noticed when Heidelinger was ten years late getting back.

These days, as a matter of policy, Chrono Technologies issues ten dollars in coin to each of its clients. This is the same incentive offered by many Atlantic City casino bus services. The promotion has proven almost as popular with time travelers as it is with gamblers, which is to say, quite popular. The quarters are less useful for people traveling back into prehistory, but that is not to say they are not useful. To wit, consider the curious case of Selma Gotbaum, a concert glockenspielist, who traveled back to the Cretaceous period to witness the K-T extinction event, the massive asteroid collision that marked the end of dinosaurs' time on Earth. Gotbaum was safely perched on a hilltop on the Portuguese coast, waiting for the meteorite to strike, when she was confronted by a ceratosaurus, a bipedal carnivore with blades for teeth and a razor on the top of its head. Panicked, Gotbaum grabbed the only thing within reach, a fistful of quarters, and flung them at the dinosaur. Gotbaum did not have the best arm. She could not throw very far and her aim was not particularly good, but this was her lucky day. One of the quarters lodged itself in the ceratosaur's gums. The dinosaur ran away screaming, with a toothache for the ages, leaving Selma Gotbaum to witness Armageddon in peace.

Along the way to the town square, I pass through the farmer's market and take a moment to survey the wares. The offerings are varied and appealing. The fruit stand has an assortment of apples, juicy plums, and no fewer than seven kinds of pears. It is the last harvest of the year and the vendors are doing their level best to ensure nothing goes to waste. A creative baker has turned all her fruits into bread—apple bread, plum bread, pear bread, all freshly baked. I have never thought of plum bread before, but the

smell is rapturous. The fruit is everywhere in the market—in ci-
ders, in candles, in a rich assortment of jams, jellies, and preserves.
I ask the difference, and a kindly lady from Kingston wearing a
hemp skirt explains that jams contain more fruit than jellies, and
preserves more fruit than jams. "Conserve is really where it's at,
though," she says, and offers me a taste of the gooseberry special.

"I wish I had known about this before," I say, as I lick the
spoon clean. "This is exquisite."

"Isn't it, now."

"I wish I could buy some, but I have to travel light, and where
I am going today, they don't let you carry anything."

"Well, how about a piece of fruit then?"

"That would be just fine."

"What's your pleasure?"

"A pear," I say.

"What kind?"

"An Anjou, of course."

"Excellent choice," she says, handing me a particularly robust
exemplar of the stock.

"How much?" I ask.

"Seventy-five cents."

I hand her three quarters.

She smiles. "Exact change. I so much appreciate that."

"I endeavor to always be prepared."

We bid each other good day. I walk the remaining few steps
into the square, take a seat on a bench, next to an old lady, and
bite into the pear. Its succulence takes me back.

Fruit just isn't what it used to be.

Shortly after sitting down, I see myself walk past. It is the sixty-year-old version of myself, the man I once called I-60. He is sixty years old, but from my perspective he is slender and supple, and I wonder to myself, how did I ever think *that* was old? I-60 takes a seat on the opposite side of the square. He does not notice me. His attention is alternatingly focused on Irregular's and Mulberry Street. He has a stern look about him and appears to be quite determined.

I am not surprised.

From my vantage point on the bench, I see a familiar red Toyota Camry drive up the street and park. I remember how much I loved that car, and that I always tried to get it from the rental agency. They were happy to oblige. In the rental market, there was not much demand for the Camry. As the younger me parks, I admire his parallel parking skills. It was always one of my strengths. Though I have not driven in years, I believe I could get into a car today and wiggle into even the tightest of spots.

Q and I emerge from the Toyota. From their body language it is clear, at least to me, that they are having a tense day. But things are hardly beyond repair. The young me waits for Q to alight from the car, takes her hand, and together they cross the street arm in arm. Even though it is not the best moment of their relationship, it would be obvious to anybody that these two people are in love.

From his own vantage point on a bench on the opposite side from where I am sitting, I-60 is watching their interactions intently, rapt. The parking of the car, the taking of the hand, the crossing of the street arm in arm, are all of the greatest interest to him. Celebrities have crossed red carpets to less attention. His actions, his manner, have an air of desperation to them. I did not perceive this fifty years ago. He is on a mission and focused like a laser on Q.

It occurs to me that from his perspective this may be the first time he has seen Q in years. It is possible that he went to visit or observe her during some of his free time, but thinking back, I have a hunch that this is not the case. His behavior confirms my intuition. He would not be looking at her this way if he had seen her recently. He is watching her relentlessly. This unflinching stare would be problematic if he were a younger man, but he is old enough to get the pass which elderly men are given on this.

She is closer now. His eyes remain glued to her. I turn myself for a look and see what he sees. In my memory, she is beautiful. And I have thought of her often. On thousands upon thousands of lonely nights, staring at the ceiling of my ancient apartment, reliving past moments, dreaming about what might have been if only. In my dotage she is a constant presence because there is so little else to occupy my mind. I have only Ellen and the occasional bird to distract me, yet there is so much time—endless, hopeless time that can only be filled by memories of her.

These do not do her justice. She is glorious, radiant. She is wearing a sundress of a gentle earthen tone, perhaps ecru, and a black cardigan draped over her shoulders and the pair of jute-soled espadrilles that were always her favorites, and mine. Her auburn hair is overflowing and wild, embellished with a pink daffodil, which I do not remember. She is completely at ease in her skin, with herself. This enhances her. Her beauty is all the more captivating because she wears it so carefreely.

She is the center of the universe. People from all across the square, from the market and the record store, look at her and are buoyed by her beauty. I cannot help but stare at her myself as she walks by. The sixty-year-old me's mouth is agape, and next to me on the bench, the old lady asks, "Did I really look like *that*?"

I am startled, but my heart leaps.

"It's you," I say.

"Yes."

"But how?"

"Same way as you."

"I mean how did you know to find me here?"

"I suppose you could call it a woman's intuition."

"I suppose it would have been much better for us to have arranged it all beforehand."

"It's more romantic this way," says Q. I smile.

In the near distance, the young Q and I are parting ways with a kiss. Young me walks into Irregular's. Young Q disappears briefly into the public restroom, then makes her way to the farmer's market. The lady in the hemp skirt who sold me the juicy pear welcomes Q warmly. They embrace, survey each other with entwined arms, and begin an energized conversation about the season's crop. I cannot hear the dialogue, of course, but fruit is exchanged and admired, and that the produce is the subject of the conversation is the obvious and logical conclusion. After a few minutes, Q takes her leave. She moves from one stand to another. At each she is received by her admiring public like royalty. Q does not notice, but as she walks from place to place, heads surreptitiously turn in her direction. Men and women alike are compelled to look. Radiance such as hers demands to be attended.

"I can't believe I used to be that thin."

"Believe it."

"Do you know what I would give to slip into a twenty-four-inch pair of jeans again?"

"I think I have some idea."

"It is entirely wasted on the young. What twenty-five-year-old appreciates putting on her pants in the morning?"

I gesture in the direction of young Q. "Pants notwithstanding, it is difficult to find fault with that creature."

Old Q smiles. "Difficult to say the least," she says. "I suppose you came back to try to keep your old self from leaving me."

"More or less," I say. "I don't have a specific plan. This time travel stuff is all a bit dodgy."

Q nods her head. "I have a friend who went back fifty years to plant a tree in the backyard of her house in Brooklyn, you know, so she would have some foliage. She tried planting flowers and bamboo, but she could never get the sort of coverage she wanted. Always felt she had started too late in the garden. So she went back in time. When she returned, she had a giant Turkish filbert and a half century of bird droppings."

"Was the tree nice?"

"Magnificent."

"What type of shape were the leaders and gutters in?"

"They were a wreck."

"I suppose there are always tradeoffs."

"And no guarantees."

"What about you? What brings you back?"

"No specific plan. I thought I'd check out some of the nice restaurants." She smiles. "And visit with you, of course."

This warms my heart, but it is a surprise. Insomuch as I had time to think about it, I presumed Q's presence was a coincidence. That she had come back to observe her younger self or to confer some wisdom upon her. It had not crossed my mind that she had come to see me. I presumed she would have no interest in this. Throughout my years of obsessing on what happened years ago at that Thanksgiving dinner, it has always been axiomatic that, thereafter, Q loathed me.

"You don't hate me?" I ask quietly.

"No. I never hated you. The day you proposed to me was the happiest of my life. I'll never forget you getting down on your knee under the whale, and pulling out the ring, and the little girl coming up to you and giving you a quarter."

"I thought it was a little boy."

"Oh, it was most definitely a little girl." Q smiles. "Don't get me wrong. I was hurt and upset. I didn't understand why you left me. But I always loved you." She pauses and looks at me. "I never told you to go, you know. You were the one who left."

I nod. "I know that."

"None of it made any sense to me, not even at the time," she says. "I didn't understand how you could have known about my father's business connections. And I certainly didn't understand why you would try to turn me against him. They arrested him seven years later for bribing a Department of Buildings official. The full extent of his machinations became public. He went to prison and was disgraced. Did you know this?"

"I did. I was sorry to hear about that."

"Thank you for saying that. But that didn't explain how you could have known about the dummy corporation. After the case became public, I examined all the evidence meticulously, and it was clear to me that you couldn't have gotten to the bottom of everything without a subpoena. Someone had to have told you. The only possible person was my father himself, but I quickly dismissed that possibility." She smiled. "Then, several years ago, they announced the discovery of time travel, and I had my answer."

Again, Q takes my breath away. "You mean, you searched for thirty years for an explanation for why I acted as I did? All that time, you gave me the benefit of the doubt?"

"Yes."

"What gave you such confidence in my love for you?"

"You'll find out soon enough."

"I could have been anytime, anywhere. How did you know I would be here today?"

Q thinks about this for a moment. "I remember this day," she says. "I remember everything, of course, but I remember this day in particular. The woman who sold you the pear had been my mother's best friend when I was a kid. When I saw her that day at the market—today—it had been fifteen years since our last meeting. I was surprised and very happy to see her."

"She seemed nice. Your mother was nice."

"I finally put it all together when I remembered that man outside the record store. For the life of me, I don't know what made me think of him, but one day it came to me that it was you. Funny thing, I think I even told you today that the man looked a little bit like you."

"You did indeed."

"Is that him over there?" Q gestures in the direction of I-60.

"Yes."

"So that's the villain. That's the man that ruined my life." I can't tell whether she is being playful or not.

"Yes," I say. "Mine too."

"Funny, he looks harmless enough."

In the distance, I-60 is either overridden with excitement or in turmoil, again I cannot tell. I have been keeping only half an eye on him throughout my conversation with Q. At one point he makes a start toward young Q, then retreats. Later, he begins walking toward Irregular's, then retreats again. After the second false start he begins pacing and muttering to himself.

The Q sitting next to me asks, "What is he thinking?"

"I don't know. It's as much a mystery to me as it is to you. I hope he isn't just thinking about himself. I don't think so. I think he's wondering whether he'll make my life better, and yours, if he goes through with his plan. At the very least I'm sure he has your interests in mind. I met lots of versions of myself over the years. You were the love of each of their lives."

She smiles. "So you met this particular older version of yourself before today?"

"Yes, three times in the preceding few weeks. He's very thoughtful and well read. A bit slow with the check, though."

Q absorbs the significance of this. Quietly, she says, "If you don't mind my asking, I mean, if it isn't too personal, what is it that he says to you? I don't mean about my father's duplicity. I mean what he said to make you resolve to leave me."

I hold my breath.

"I know I shouldn't ask," she says. "Maybe it's something I should never know, maybe it's something horrible about me."

"No. I told you. He loves you."

"What is it, then? I've been living with doubt about this all these years."

"We have a child," I say. "A sweet, magnificent, and loving child. He dies and it ruins us."

Q groans, a deep, pained cry from her soul.

I-60 appears to have solidified his resolve. He is walking now, slowly, with the pronounced limp in his stiff right leg, into Irregular's House of Records and Fudge.

"What are you going to do?" Q asks.

"What should I do?"

"It's your life."

"Is it?"

"That seems like a profoundly complicated question."

I nod. "It's true, and I have perhaps five minutes to resolve it for myself before that sixty-year-old version of myself goes into Irregular's, takes me for a walk in the woods, and tells me how to drive you away once and for all."

"Five minutes. That hardly seems long enough to decide."

"I wish I had more time."

Q nods.

"Of course, that doesn't mean what it used to. And to think that I have had more than forty years to consider what I would do if I had this day to live over again."

Q nods again but says nothing else. She never wasted words. I had always liked this about her and I like it now.

"Have you had a good life?" I ask.

"I had a life," she says. "And all that that means."

"Would you have wanted to know? I mean, now that you

know what it is that I knew, would you have wanted to know it?"

"This is just like the question you asked me on the drive up in the rental car?"

"Yes, I suppose it is."

"I'm not sure that the question matters very much."

"Of course it matters. In fact, it's the only question that matters: do you want to make your life better?"

"Better," Q repeats quietly.

"If we cannot answer this question affirmatively, then how can we possibly go on? We have to believe that things can be better than they are. And we have to believe that we ourselves have the capacity to make them better. It's the fundamental drive of a human being to improve himself and those he loves. It's why we want to make our children's lives better. It's what separates us from other animals. So, I ask you again: if you had the opportunity to change your life, would you take it?"

Q smiles. "I'm here now, aren't I?"

In that moment, I understand. Or at least I think I understand. The thing about the eternal verities is that they are always changing.

I have gone through phases. For a time, I fancied myself an objectivist, after reading *Atlas Shrugged,* as every good seventeen-year-old does. I preached the virtue of selfishness and saw happiness as the moral purpose of life. Then I did the usual one-eighty and turned nihilist. I abandoned my winter coat for a cardigan sweater, starting taking taxicabs, and began smoking cigarettes. I have no reason to hold anything back now, so I admit these were nicotine-free cigarettes, only one of several ways in which I hedged my bets. I stayed on the sidelines as the postmodernists waged their quiet revolution. At times I believed there was no truth, at other times that the truth simply could not be known. I experimented freely with ethical constructs, as one might with clothing or hair styles. Each seemed appealing for a while, if only for its novelty, but ultimately, inevitably, inadequate. Sometimes I ate meat. Sometimes I did not. Persistently, sunscreen seemed important, but I never managed to integrate it into a coherent worldview. Most of the time I had no idea what to do.

Now, for a moment at least, I have lucidity.

I lean over and kiss Q passionately, and the feelings of a half century of solitude and longing are released in an instant. It occurs to me that our moments of most intense passion are destined to occur in or near an organic garden. I feel Q release the same grief, all immediately expelled from each of us. The heaviness is dispensed, and then there is love, deep abiding love.

"It occurs to me that I have never seen Barcelona," I say with a smile. "If we leave now, we can catch the red-eye and make a day of it—or a week or a month."

"Or a year," she says.

"Yes, a year."

We kiss again.

I have wondered before what it is like to be old and in love, and now I have my answer. I feel my heart patter and blood rush to my face. A palliative warmth runs over my entire body; its healing powers extend even to my hopeless knee. I feel optimistic, giddy. I begin to make plans. Winters in Sedona, summers on Lake Moraine in Canada. Perhaps we will return to our time, perhaps we will stay in the then-now. It doesn't matter. Maybe a late marriage—at City Hall, just the two of us against the world, or with Elvis in Vegas, or the dream of the bowling alley nuptials finally realized. We will reconnect with old friends and travel. We will see El Encierro, at long last, and a day game at Wrigley. I even think of running. All in that moment.

You may have wondered yourself about what it is like to be old and in love. Now you too have the answer. It is exactly, precisely, and wondrously the same.

We kiss yet again.

This makes a bit of a scene, two codgers mashing in a public park. The young Q notices. She is standing by a pile of pears, watching us until we feel her gaze. We look up, see her, and she smiles warmly. She walks over, has something to say, but gets a closer look at us and rethinks.

"Do I know you?" she asks.

"No, dear."

"Well, I just wanted to say how nice it is to see two people in love like you are. You just don't see it every day."

"*You* do," I say.

Young Q is taken aback. I remember that scrunching of the eyebrows. It was irresistible then, which is now. Old Q squeezes my hand.

"What do you mean?"

"I'm going to tell you a secret. It may not sound like much, but it's the key to a happy life, to your happy life."

"Okay."

"You're with that man, aren't you? The one that just walked into the record store."

"Yes, I am."

"He loves you," I say, triumphantly. "More than you will ever know."

Acknowledgments

Writers are often asked, and bothered by, the question of whether they have drawn an idea from their own life. I am too happy to be called a writer to be annoyed. For the record, let me say unequivocally that I have never been visited by anyone offering a foreboding vision of my own future.

My influences are more conventionally situated in space and time, but in their own ways more profound. Carl Lennertz of HarperCollins, my superb editor, runs his shop the way I try to run my own, and I am proud to call him my friend. My agent, Janet Reid, is the champion of my career and allows me to do what I love to do. I am equally proud to call her my friend. The truth is, though, she and Carl are the Johnny-come-latelies in my life.

I have had the same best friend since high school. During these twenty-five years, Ira Kaufman and I have explored in innumerable conversations almost every mundane question imaginable—from the merits of insurance in blackjack to the moistness of various snack cakes. Our senses of humor are so entwined with each other's, I can no longer distinguish which jokes I tell are mine and which are his. Suffice it to say that his contribution to this book is substantial.

My parents, Mathew and Sherry, continue to stand behind me in whatever I do, as they have throughout my life, and have more confidence in me than I have in myself. I have said many times that my mother is my best and most encouraging reader. My father is simply the best man I know.

Anyone reading my other books will note that this list has not changed in some time. Indeed my personal life has been marked by more continuity than change. The notable exception was when my wife, Valli, appeared in my life three years ago, together with Eamon and Suria Vanrajah. Eighteen months later, Mattie joined us. Being a parent to Eamon, Suria, and Mattie is the great privilege of my life. The experience has changed me in the most fundamental and best way imaginable. I expect it is obvious to anyone reading this or any of my other novels that I have a heavy dose of existential angst. To my astonishment, it is almost all gone now. When I play Wiffle ball with Eamon or watch *The Simpsons* with Suria, everything seems as it should be. And I get giddy about seeing my brilliant and beautiful baby girl. She is downstairs as I am writing this, as she often is when I work. When I finish, in a paragraph or two, I am going to walk downstairs and give Mattie a kiss and a few tickles, and will feel, as I always do, that my life is perfect.

The best part, though, is being Valli's husband. Being married is challenging in ways I did not expect but rewarding in ways I never dreamed. I found my person, and I am lucky beyond words. I must confess here to one intersection of life and art.

While no one from my future offered a menacing vision of what is to come, I was visited by an older version of myself on the day of our wedding. Valli and I were walking into City Hall when I noticed him there, wearing a cardigan sweater and corduroy pants that were unmistakably mine. He seemed like a nice and happy old man, with soft eyes and deep laugh lines etched like fissures into his cheeks. We only had time for him to say one thing to me. He held the door for Valli and me, smiled broadly, and whispered in my ear, "Do it again. Do it again."